Wild Blue Yonder

A NOVEL

For Dave —

With grateful thanks for all you do,
and I'm glad to call you a friend as well.
With best regards,

J A C K   B .   R O C H E S T E R

The author gives thanks and appreciation to the artists and copyright owners for permission to use the following material, which has so enriched this story:

"*Eve of Destruction.*" Words and Music by P.F. Sloan and Steve Barri. Copyright © 1965 UNIVERSAL MUSIC CORP. Copyright Renewed. All Rights Reserved. Used by Permission. Reprinted by permission of Hal Leonard Corporation.

Excerpt from "Little Gidding" from FOUR QUARTETS copyright 1942 by T.S. Eliot and renewed 1970 by Esme Valerie Eliot, reprinted by permission of Houghton Mifflin Harcourt Publishing Company.

"Light My Fire." Words and Music by The Doors. Copyright © 1967 Doors Music Co. Copyright Renewed. All Rights Reserved. Used by Permission. Reprinted by permission of Hal Leonard Corporation.

"To Fuck With Love, Phase III" from *The Love Book* by Lenore Kandel. © 1966 Stolen Paper Review Editions, San Francisco.

"White Rabbit" by Jefferson Airplane. Words and Music by Grace Slick. Copyright © 1966 IRVING MUSIC, INC. Copyright Renewed. All Rights Reserved. Used by Permission. Reprinted by permission of Hal Leonard Corporation.

"The Marriage of Heaven and Hell, Plate 14" from *The Marriage of Heaven and Hell* by William Blake, © 1975, by permission of Oxford University Press.

"Visions of Johanna." Copyright © 1966 by Dwarf Music; renewed 1994 by Dwarf Music.

"Stuck Inside Of Mobile With The Memphis Blues Again." Copyright © 1966 by Dwarf Music; renewed 1994 by Dwarf Music.

"Bob Dylan's Dream." Copyright © 1963, 1964 by Warner Bros. Inc.; renewed 1991, 1992 by Special Rider Music.

"Howl," from *Collected Poems* 1947-1980 by Allen Ginsberg, Copyright © 1955 by Allen Ginsberg. Reprinted by permission of Harper Collins Publishers.

"Yü: Enthusiasm" and "Sung: Conflict" from the *I Ching* or Book of Changes, Richard Wilhelm and Cary F. Baynes, tr. © 1966 The Bollingen Foundation, by permission of Princeton University Press.

"Principles and Purpose of Vedanta" pamphlet. The Vedanta Centre, Cohasset, MA. © 1937 Swami Paramananda. Used by permission.

Lessons 2, 44, and 48 from Tao Teh Ching, translated by John C.H. Wu, © 1961 St. John's University Press, New York. Reprinted by arrangement with Shambhala Publications, Inc., Boston, MA. www.shambhala.com.

A Joshua Tree Press Book

Acknowledgements

I've been fortunate to receive support and encouragement from many wonderful and inspirational colleagues and friends while writing *Wild Blue Yonder*. I would like to extend my grateful appreciation to

Lee K. Abbott, author and professor of English and creative writing at Ohio State University, my workshop leader at the Gettysburg Conference for Writers

Joni Cole, my mentor, editor, and writing coach, director of the Writer's Center of White River Junction, Vermont

David Gardner, my friend and fellow novelist from the Minuteman Fiction Writers Group

Diane O'Connell, editorial director at writetosellyourbook.com

Jerry D. Simmons, a sales and marketing veteran at several New York publishing houses

Casie Vogel, my copyrights editor, for her assiduous efforts in obtaining permissions

Audrey Beth Stein and the other six aspiring novelists in my Advanced Novel Development course at the Cambridge Center for Adult Education

I would also like to acknowledge and thank Joshua Rivers, my son, ever a wise and insightful counsel; Oliver Chu, who might as well be my son; my brother Gregg Rochester; Hao Yuan Kueh, his wife Munyi Shea, and Lea Geontoro, who were there from the start; Daniel J. Finn; John Gantz, my long-time writing partner and brother from another mother; and Roger S. Peterson, my partner in Business Book Ghostwriters and staunch supporter of my efforts in fiction-writing.

My mother, Jacqueline Rochester, taught me to be independent, inspired my creativity, and showed me how to be an entrepreneurial artist. After a long and successful career as a painter, she passed away at age 85 in February, 2010. It saddens me that she did not have the opportunity to read *Wild Blue Yonder*.

Dedication

I began writing this novel after a long career as an editor and writer in nonfiction. I could not have kept going, nor could I have completed it, without the constant support and endearing love of my wife, Shiou Lung Lai Chu. In the face of distractions, paying work and life's many complications, she told me again and again that *Wild Blue Yonder* was Job Number One. Moreover, she gave me the inner sense of safety and confidence when I was unsure about my efforts or whether it was all worthwhile. She has never flagged in telling me this is the most important book I've ever written. I hope these insufficient words will in some small way serve to thank her for all she has given me, in my work and my life. *Xiexie*, 謝謝, Darling.

Table of Contents

The United States Air Force Fight Song. ix

PART I: AIR FORCE BLUES

Chapter 1: Me or Them 3
Chapter 2: Fall In 15
Chapter 3: Hurricane! 29

PART II: GOIN' TO CALIFORNIA

Chapter 4: Goin' to California 45
Chapter 5: Haight-Ashbury 59
Chapter 6: Memphis Blues Again 75
Chapter 7: The Summer of Love 93

PART III: DEUTSCHLAND ÜBER ALLES

Chapter 8: First Sergeant Buford 107
Chapter 9: Stars and Stripes Forever 119
Chapter 10: Der Alten Scheune 133
Chapter 11: Sedition. 143
Chapter 12: Zeitgeist. 155
Chapter 13: The Pieces Fit 167
Chapter 14: A Writer's Life. 181
Chapter 15: Change of Command. 191
Chapter 16: Liederhalle. 203
Chapter 17: Children of the Future 215
Chapter 18: Socrates Island 227

Chapter 19: Time Has Come Today. 243
Chapter 20: Oktoberfest. 253
Chapter 21: Touch and Go 261
Chapter 22: FIGMO. 267

PART IV: HOME

Chapter 23: The December of My Dreams. 277
Chapter 24: No Place Like Home 285

Bob Dylan's Dream. 295

The Official United States Air Force Song

Off we go into the wild blue yonder,

Climbing high into the sun;

Here they come zooming to meet our thunder,

At 'em boys, Give 'er the gun! (Give 'er the gun now!)

Down we dive, spouting our flame from under,

Off with one helluva roar!

We live in fame or go down in flame. Hey!

Nothing'll stop the U.S. Air Force!

Part I
Air Force Blues

Chapter 1

Me or Them
January 19, 1965, 5:45AM

I stood outside the Chicago Loop bus terminal with my mother. Huge, sopping wet snowflakes struck the umbrella I held above us like mallet blows on a kettle drum. Icy water cascaded over its edge, soaking my shoes. I hated getting wet feet. I hated the cold. I hated everything about being here, waiting for a bus that would take me to San Antonio, Texas, to begin my four-year prison sentence in the United States Air Force.

Dozens of strangers my age stood around in a tableau that reminded me of nothing so much as a dark, bleak, miserable, chiaroscuro version of my favorite painting at the Chicago Art Institute, Seurat's "Sunday Afternoon on Le Grandes Jatte." I looked at a tall fellow in a tan private-eye overcoat, darkened across the shoulders by the wet snow, who glared back at me. Near the terminal doors, a guy jabbered loudly into the pay phone, his free arm swinging in wild arcs; he was loudly sobbing "Lauren, Lauren." Embarrassed, I shifted my gaze to those who paced incessantly in and out of the ice-cold rain without benefit of umbrellas. A sleazy hood in a black leather motorcycle jacket, his hair carved into fins on each side of his head and a cigarette dangling from surly lips, sneered at everyone who walked near him. I caught a look of utter dejection on a long-haired, pimply-faced kid who stood next to a stocky older man, their hands and wrists covered by a thick neck scarf.

I sighed, loudly, in an unsuccessful attempt to get my mother's sympathy. I couldn't stand this, waiting in the cold, grey darkness. I just didn't want to think about where my life was headed once I embarked upon the impending bus ride.

A powerful gust of bitterly cold, damp wind blew off Lake Michigan through the bus tunnel. My mother, Adele, although bundled up inside her thick wool car coat, shook, shivered, and shuddered. *What a jerk I was,* causing her this anguish — more anguish, anguish upon anguish, just when she was beginning to get over the loss of my dad and now me, flunked out of the University of Chicago. Fired from a construction job as a mere manual laborer. A draft notice from the Army. Then that little talk at the kitchen table.

"Nathaniel," she'd said, "I think it's time you go in the service."

The military. The service. Serve my country. So that was it. No discussion, no alternatives. The service. That was the only option left for someone like me.

A big silver Greyhound bus pulled up, splashed slush at us, and stopped with an ear-splitting wheeze. The door slapped open and the driver emerged wearing a natty uniform, his captain's hat tipped back on his head. Everyone watched him trot into the terminal without a glance, a smile, even a grimace. I looked back at the bus. Beside the door was a small oval window that displayed the bus's destination. It read:

CHARTER SAN ANTONIO

It might just as well have displayed Dante's exhortation, "Abandon hope all ye who enter here." This bus would take us to Lackland Air Force Base for induction and basic training. Something thumped in the pit of my stomach. I glanced around; others were lining up, toting gym bags like my own with those things the recruiter told us we could bring. Mine held a toothbrush and powder, my Norelco electric shaver, a change of clothes, and a few books: Faulkner's *The Sound and the Fury*, Mark Van Doren's biography of my namesake, Nathaniel Hawthorne, Joyce's *Ulysses*, and a recent paperback, *The Catcher in the Rye*, by someone named Salinger of whom I had heard praise.

We stood around for another fifteen minutes or so, but it felt like an hour. Nobody was making a move to board the idling bus, its stinking exhaust blowing right at us. The driver emerged from the terminal and ran lightly up the steps as he shouted "Board!" over his shoulder. He jumped into the driver's seat and hit the gas a few times, spewing clouds of fumes.

My mother intuitively grasped that, at this moment, her parental responsibilities were at an end. A librarianship graduate from a small women's college in

Minnesota (the name escapes me) she'd spent her entire adult life as a wife and mother to me and my two little brothers, Ernest and Francis Scott, six and seven years my junior. With my father's sudden death a year and a half earlier – he was only 43, and my mom 39 – she was forced into retail commerce, selling ladies' undergarments to women of means far greater than her own. I wondered whose ignominy was greater, hers or mine. But what made me saddest was my poor little brothers. The lost look on their faces. I don't think they were able to understand what happened to our dad.

Arms crossed tightly against the cold, she turned to me and said, "Nate, our dear departed President John F. Kennedy said that a young man who lacks the fortitude to perform military service is...oh, I can't remember the rest. Your father was proud to serve his country. Make yourself proud to serve too."

I looked her right in the face, but the words I wanted to say wouldn't come. She must have seen something in my eyes, though, because in an uncommon act for her, she hugged me and gave me a peck on the cheek.

• • •

My father, John Flowers, served in the Navy during World War II. He died August 10, 1963, less than a month before I was to commence my college career. His heart failed while on his usual early morning run in Washington Park; he was gone before the ambulance arrived.

He taught English (he called it Rhetoric) and American literature at Emily Dickenson High School in Waukegan. He left me two gifts, if that's you want to call them. One was my name, Nathaniel Hawthorne Flowers, after the man he regarded as the greatest writer in American literature. He named my two little brothers after his second and third favorites, Ernest Hemingway and Francis Scott Fitzgerald. Dad invariably called me as Nathaniel, never Nate as my mom usually did. The second gift was a love of the world's great literature. Our house was a veritable library, filled with thousands of books residing on clumsily-made bookshelves my father built himself. I never wanted for something to read, whether it was a classic by Henry James or Charles Dickens, a modern novel by Robert Roark or John Steinbeck, or even one of the lasciviously sexy and violent mysteries of Mickey Spillane. Once or twice a week, dad would tell Ernest and Frankie and me the story of one of the great novels in our library. He didn't just tell the story, either; he acted it out, changed his voice for different characters, then at the end told us what it meant. Afterwards, I'd often grab the book from his hands and race off to my room to read it. Sometimes I'd read it to my brothers, but their tastes mostly ran to comic books about The Lone Ranger or Sergeant Preston of the Yukon. I came to believe that everything good, even great, about understanding life was in these stories. My father frequently announced to anyone nearby that I would surely follow in my namesake's footsteps and become a great writer.

I wrote my first short story in my Big Chief tablet when I was 14 years old. It was entitled "I Am A Rock," about a large talking boulder in city park. When I read it to my brothers, Ernest said, "Rocks don't talk, Nate."

• • •

I looked toward the bus, which my anonymous brothers-in-arms were stoically boarding. I turned back to my mother, but still found myself unable to utter a word. She gave me a deep, long, possibly sad gaze and said, "Write me." A sudden panic, such as Raskolnikov might have experienced, flashed through my mind: No turning back. I had to leave now. A desire to tell my mother of my attempted suicide rose up inside, but just as quickly I realized that making such an admission was (a) unlikely to engender any sympathy, since I was clearly still alive, and (b) would do nothing to keep me off this bus. In the case of (a), it was far more likely she would think I, the writer, was fabricating another my wild fictions. In the case of (b), I had already signed the enlistment agreement, and not even a mother's love could give me reprieve from that. Like it or not, this was a bus ride to my destiny.

"Thanks, Mom," I said, "for everything," almost as if I meant it. "'Bye." I took a step toward the bus.

"Nathaniel!" my mother cried.

I stopped. I was still holding the umbrella and it had tipped, drenching her in melted snow. She snatched it, glared at me, turned on her heel and headed for the terminal.

"Take good care of my car," I called after her. For safekeeping, I had signed the title to my 1958 Plymouth Golden Fury over to her, a special-edition two-door hardtop with gold trim. It was the most beautiful car ever made; I had earned all the money to buy it from my construction job, before I was fired. My Fury mattered more to me than anything in my whole life. She glanced quickly, unsmilingly, over her shoulder. "And don't let my little toad brothers get into my stuff!" This time she didn't look back.

Outside the bus door stood the fat man and the pimply kid, seemingly in a wrestling match until I saw the handcuffs that joined them. He set the boy loose and gave him a shove up the stairs. A little taken aback, I clambered aboard, spied an empty row, shoved my gym bag into the overhead rack, pulled off my coat, rolled it into a ball, stuffed it next to my bag, and flopped into the window seat. Moments later the driver swooshed the door shut, crammed the bus into gear with a great gnashing, and jerked away from the terminal, calling over his shoulder, "Sit back and relax, boys, it's a long, looong ride to San Antone." *You can say that again.* I looked out the window, hoping to see my mother one last time, but she was gone.

I leaned back and squirmed around, trying to get comfortable enough to fall asleep. I pulled my damp coat down and stuck it against the window for a pillow. I squeezed my eyes shut as tight as I could, but even at this ungodly hour of six in the morning, to which I was a complete stranger, sleep would not come.

The seat creaked. I glanced to my left. Beside me was a rather chubby boy with reddish-blonde hair and a flagrant cowlick, a broken front tooth, and a large, friendly smile. He stuck a hand toward me and said, "Howdy. Ah'm Dennis Marshfield. From Looville, Kentucky. How y'all doin'?"

"Nathaniel," I said shaking his hand. "Nathaniel Hawthorne Flowers, of Waukegan. Just north of Chicago."

"Nice to meetcha, Ah'm sure. Y'all look like ya could use some comp'ny."

Oh, sure, just what I wanted.

"Mah middle name is Athabaska, on account a mah granddaddy on mah mother's side. Dennis Athabaska Marshfield, now that's a mouful, ain't it?" He laughed. I smiled. "He ran a lathe, made hickory baseball bats, mah granddaddy. Louisville Sluggers. So did mah daddy. 'Spose ah woulda too, 'cept for the draft." We were both silent for a while, then he said, "Flowers. Now that's a unusual last name."

I told Dennis Marshfield about my father's occupation and his passing in the fewest words possible.

"Ah'm right sorry to hear that," he replied. "Didya go off to college anyways?"

I nodded. Even though I'd been on the honor roll the last six semesters at Waukegan High, even though I'd received a full academic scholarship, the University of Chicago intimidated the hell out of me. I got off to a bad start, and that's pretty much where I stayed all year. Try as I might, I just didn't feel like I fit in at Chicago. Everyone seemed smarter and more sophisticated than me. I had trouble making friends, but that wasn't anything new. For some reason I lacked the enthusiasm or energy to do much of anything. Inside I just felt bad, bad, bad and didn't know why. I spent most of my time sleeping, drinking, or playing cards. Were I a football player, it would have been said that I hit the record for fumbles. In my case, the fumbles were scholastic. I slogged through my first quarter, got two Bs, a D and an F, and was put on academic probation. Winter quarter was a struggle, but I got my grades up to a C average. Then spring quarter, I eclipsed my fall quarter grades with all Ds, Fs, and an incomplete.

"And you? Did you go to college?" I asked, hoping to avoid any further discussion of my dismal self.

"Nah," he shook his head and grinned, that broken-off tooth catching on his lower lip. A red scar told me this happened frequently. "Nah, Ah ain't college materal. 'Sides, Ah ain't but eighteen years old! Ah got outa high school last spring and right away the Army was a-bitin' at my heels, Ah tell ya!" He laughed lightly, without a trace of irony.

I laughed with him. "Yeah, me as well. You found it preferable to spend four years in the Air Force to two years in the Army?"

"What Ah found pref'rable was not totin' a rifle in the swamps of Vee-yet Nam, killin' folk."

"Indeed, I agree. I say, Marshfield, what career field did you sign up for?"

"Aw, fixin' somefun, Ah do not rightly recall what it was, but it sounded innerestin' and like somefun Ah could do." He twisted his neck and looked up at the luggage racks across the aisle, then whipped his face back toward mine. "Simmilators? That sound like somefun'?"

"Flight simulators?" I queried.

"That's it!" he cried, slapping his hands together. "How about yerself, Nate?" Already he had lapsed into the familiar truncation of my name, which nettled me.

"Jet pilot," I replied.

"Well now, Ah'll be hanged," Marshfield said. "Dang, don't that beat all! Y'all gone be flyin' a jet airplane, shootin' off machine guns, droppin' bombs, gettin' in them dawgfights with them bad ole Vee-yet Nam-ese and all. Hot damn, Nate, don't that beat all!"

I fell silent. Truth be told, I hadn't much thought about this aspect of piloting high-speed fighter aircraft, my imagination not having taken me much beyond the romantic vision of the dashing Air Force officer and his sleek, glimmering jet plane. Nor had I considered I would be sent to Vietnam, the avoidance of which was the reason for joining the Air Force instead of the Army. I thought back to how I'd arrived at this choice. After receiving the summons from the Army, and at my mother's — shall I say encouragement — I stopped by the Waukegan Post Office to visit with the Navy and Air Force recruiters. They were appallingly like car salesmen and tried with all their might to get me to enlist on the spot. At first I was inclined toward the Navy because it was my father's choice, but when I learned I'd be on a nuclear sub at the bottom of one ocean or another for six years, I lost all interest. The Air Force recruiter said that since I'd been to college, I could become a fighter pilot. My imagination was rife with the opportunities for success I so passionately craved. The recruiter said he'd put it in writing, but it was guaranteed only for 24 hours, so I accepted his offer. I asked for, and got, sixty days before I had to report, which would mean I'd be home for Christmas and New Year's — my 20th birthday — then it would be off into the wild blue yonder.

. . .

We spent thirty-one hours on the bus to Lackland. Groggy upon arrival, we were met by two crass soldiers wearing crisp tan uniforms and flat-brimmed hats like the Illinois State Police. They said they were our training instructors, or TIs, and immediately began belittling us. One was a huge Negro named Lowery, clearly in top physical condition, who introduced himself as a technical sergeant. The other was a staff sergeant named Johannssen, an overweight, belligerent monster with steely blue eyes and dirty blonde hair, obviously a Lutheran from Minnesota. They said they were in charge of us for the next six weeks of Basic Military Training, or BMT, the purpose of which was to destroy our civilian personalities and crush our wills, thereby transforming each and every one of us into an obedient soldier. This would occur through a rigorous regimen of physical conditioning and classroom training. It sounded absolutely dreadful, and I wondered again how I'd gotten myself into this.

Lowery and Johannssen both immediately began yelling at us, calling us "rainbows," talking over one another and contradicting each other's orders. Try as we might, we didn't seem to be able to do anything right for them. They screamed us into two rows and marched us to the In-processing Center where we had our heads shaved, our buttholes examined, and our arms shot up with who-knows-what-all vaccinations. We were ordered to empty our duffel bags and relieved of all our possessions except our "civvies." I protested having to relinquish my treasured

9

books, which the TIs found quite humorous for some reason. "You ain't gonna have no time for readin'," Johannssen said, and viciously threw my treasures into a large steel waste bin. We were issued dog tags and fatigues and marched to a vast mess hall where we were fed some kind of salty muck on burned toast. Serendipitously, Marshfield and I were reunited and, along with other rainbows, marched to a building referred to as a barracks. We were told that the forty of us were officially Flight 09 of the 3711th Squadron.

The process of destroying our individuality began.

Right from the start, I was certain Lowery and Johannssen despised me. Although I tried awfully hard to be responsible, to learn, to get things right, it seemed they went out of their way to find fault with me. I was convinced they were harder on me than any of the other rainbows. I can't say I particularly liked either of them, but I came to look up to TSgt. Lowery. He was consistent in his orders, and even when doling out punishment, for example giving a rainbow 50 pushups for improperly presenting arms or wearing scuffed brogans, he was fair and just. I respected his military bearing, and I found myself trying to emulate him. Johannssen, on the other hand, would be viciously strict one day and conciliatory the next, seemingly without rhyme nor reason.

After spending the first few days of BMT in what I can only describe as a state of near continual shock and fear, one night the TIs took me into their little office in our barracks. I immediately assumed I was in trouble for something. "At ease, Flowers," TSgt. Lowery said. SSgt. Johannssen pointed to a chair and I sat. They were both rather cordial and we chatted about how it was all going.

"What career field did you sign up for?" Lowery asked.

"Pilot. Jet airplane pilot," I replied.

The TIs burst into laughter. I looked quizzically at them. Lowery rocked back and forth on his chair, while Johannssen glared at me with his watery blue eyes as if I were an idiot. "Flowers," he said, "you're an enlisted *airman*. Enlisted troops don't fly aircraft. *Officers* fly aircraft. Do you have a college degree?"

Dumbfounded, I shook my head.

"Only college graduates can become officers, Flowers," said Lowery somewhat more kindly – perhaps pitiably.

"Who told you you'd be a pilot?" Johannssen snapped.

"My recruiter," I replied. They burst into laughter again. I felt so stupid that my faced burned. If I wasn't going to become a pilot, then what? Had I screwed up again?

"Well, Flowers, seems your recruiter recognized your leadership potential," said Lowery, then proceeded to tell me they were making me the Dorm Chief. I had no idea what this meant, so they explained I was in charge of the flight whenever they were not present. They gave me a braided rope to wear on my shoulder, representing my new authority.

BMT taught us how to march, salute, shoot a rifle, straighten the gig line, eat fast, wait, wait, and wait some more, spit-shine brogans, make a bed so snugly a quarter bounced on it. We memorized officer and enlisted ranks and insignia, the military code of conduct, and an absolute plethora of other military conventions. The experience was so mindless and absurd that I had absolutely no idea how I was faring, but my appointment as Dorm Chief inspired the belief that I was capable of excelling. I began giving my flight pep talks, for example on the importance of *esprit de corps*. I was particularly keen on asserting how we were a team and must defer our individual selves to the good of the group. My assumption was that the other troops could easily grasp this fundamental instruction and see its practicality. However, this was not the case. I quickly came to realize these troops had no interest in the honor of serving the military of our country, a notion I had now come to embrace. Moreover, I was no longer one of them: I was now the kiss-ass of the TIs, whom everyone hated, and now they hated me as well. It was profoundly distressing. What I had thought would bind me more closely in the brotherhood of the uniform had instead rent the fabric we had supposedly been creating with such perseverance. Even as I recited to them the affirmation of Dumas' famed three musketeers, "Unus pro omnibus, omnes pro uno," I knew it was nothing but a cruel fiction. In reality we were not "one for all and all for one," but were and would forever remain, "me for me."

As the weeks passed, my disappointment and regret turned to abject bitterness and my demeanor, I'm sure, became more officious and authoritarian. My outlook was further despoiled when it became evident the military was just like the town without pity in Gene Pitney's song, ruthlessly "washing out" those who weren't up to snuff. For example, the TIs started picking on a fat kid named Dillman, threatening him if he didn't lose weight. Once the TIs began, the troops joined in on him. I recalled how Piggy was ostracized in *Lord of the Flies*, except with Dillman we went out to drill one day and when we came back he was gone. Then there was Nichols, a tall, quiet troop from West Virginia. He rarely spoke, kept to himself, and never caused anyone a moment's trouble. Well, at noon chow he poured an entire bottle of French's Prepared Mustard all over his food —meat, potatoes, ice cream, cake, everything. Then he ate every bite on his plate while we sat there staring at him. By the end of the day he'd disappeared, too.

One day on smoke break, Marshfield took me aside. "Nate, they's some boys who's got shivs." Handmade knives were referred to as shivs, and possessing any kind of weapon was, of course, forbidden by regulation. After discreetly questioning a few other troops, the rumor seemed confirmed: it was three Mexicans from Southern California who had enlisted in the so-called buddy system. I knew my duty was to inform the TIs, but part of me argued that to do so was to dishonor the musketeer's credo in which I so passionately believed. Thus torn asunder, I stalled and did nothing.

Our six weeks had whittled down to two days remaining until graduation, and everybody was jazzed. Our flight photograph was taken. Soon we would be on our way to our various training assignments. Lowery and Johannssen, finally satisfied with our marching and dress-right salutes, had been lightening up on us, promising we'd get a pass to go off-base into San Antonio. As I did every night, I performed last inspection and bed check, then called lights out at 2130 hours.

I don't know how long I'd been asleep – not long – when the instructors came banging through the doors, running up and down between our bunk beds screaming at the top of their lungs, "Get up! Get out! Get the fuck out of here!" We were terrified. What was going on? We scrambled into our fatigues and raced out into the night. An awaiting bus took us to an aircraft hangar. We fell in and two Air Police, armed with rifles, escorted us double-file into the hangar. No one spoke or even looked at one another. It felt even colder inside than outside.

Johannssen came in and ordered us to attention, then parade rest. We stood there for what seemed like an hour, then he came back in with the APs and said we could fall out for a smoke break. We lit up and milled around, asking each other what was going on. A truck pulled up and we watched two troops unload our foot-lockers outside. I looked at my watch: 0230 hours. Johannssen began screaming at us, extremely angry. "Stay away from those footlockers! And field-strip those butts! I don't want to see even one single fuckin' ash on this fuckin' concrete," he said, "or the whole squad will be scrubbing this deck down for the ENTIRE FUCKING NIGHT! Now, Ten-HUT!" We snapped to attention, then after half an hour or so Lowery yelled, "At ease."

The TIs came in and out screaming ten-hut, at ease, parade rest, fall out, fall in, ten-hut, over and over. The APs, in dress blues, polished boots, white helmets and gloves, guarded us like we were prisoners of war. I had no idea what was happening and was desperately afraid. Fear drove me to approach TSgt. Lowery. I said, "Sir, as Dorm Chief, maybe I could talk to the troops, sir. Tell them what we're doing here. You know, put their minds at ease, sir."

He gave me a cruel look and said, "Take that rope off, Flowers. You're not no Dorm Chief no more." I was crushed by his brutality. This man, whom I had come to respect, was now treating me with abject cruelty. Why? Had I not served him well? I unbuttoned the rope, handed it to him, and walked back to the ranks in humiliation.

As dawn began to break, half a dozen buses pulled up outside. The TIs came in and Johannssen barked, "Listen up! We're going to give you your training base assignments. Try to follow instructions for once, all right?" Lowery called a troop's name; he stepped forward, Lowery handed him his orders, then he fell out into his group. I received mine; I was to report to Keesler Air Force Base, Biloxi, Mississippi. Each group marched to their own bus. Six of us, including Dennis Marshfield and myself, were the last. I looked back into the hangar. The three Mexicans were still inside.

We boarded the transport aircraft and strapped into the long bench seat that ran along the hull. Soon we were in the air. Dennis Marshfield had taken the seat beside me. He leaned over and said, "Ah tole the TIs."

"Huh?" I said, still reeling from the night's experience.

'Bout the Mexicans. Plannin' to kill y'all. T'weren't right," he said, shaking his big head back and forth.

"Kill me?" I asked, incredulous. "What? The Mexicans? Wanted to *kill* me?" I broke out in a cold sweat.

"Yep. Morales an' Gutierrez an' Pacheco. Ah heard 'em talkin' 'bout it. Them boys, they's in a street gang back home. Got inna lotta trouble. Judge tole 'em join the military or go to jail." He paused. "Gonna shiv y'all. 'Cuz ya was the Dorm Chief," he said.

I was jolted by the memory of the pimply-faced kid in handcuffs. "So, you knew they were going to – stab me – last night?"

"Naw, Ah din't know when. Mebby tonight. Maybe tomorry night in San Antone."

They were quiet, those three, and always kept to themselves. What I didn't know was that they hated me, or apparently hated the authority I represented, so much.

"So ah tole 'em, ya know," said Marshfield, shaking his head. "The TIs. T'weren't right."

"Well, thanks, Marshfield," I replied. "Denny. Buddy. Thanks a lot." I put out my hand to shake, but he didn't seem to notice.

"Ah dint like ya's bein' Dorm Chief none neither, ya know, actin' like ya was a big shot with your high-falutin' talk and all, but killin' ya fer it, that's not right t'all."

So this was how I was perceived by my fellow troops. It wasn't the way I thought of myself, nor how I wished to be thought of by others. No, not at all.

The plane bucked, bouncing Denny and me up and down in our harnesses. I looked at him and smiled. He smiled back, his chipped buck tooth scraping his lip. The propellers roared with an awful din as the plane began gaining altitude. I leaned back and closed my eyes. Within moments I was sound asleep.

Chapter 2
Fall In
March, 1965

The plane's landing jolted me into wakefulness as it slammed onto the runway, bounced, and banged down again with a wild shriek from the tires, followed by a violent roar from the engines. Tethered in my harness, I was thrust up, down, and sideways as the plane struggled to slow down. Denny Marshfield was nearly hanging across my chest. We looked at each other and then began laughing, probably to allay the fear. The plane stopped and the noxious smell of burnt oil filled my nostrils.

"Well, now, weren't *that* somethin'," Denny said, a grin on his face. "Mah first airplane ride."

"Mine as well," I replied. I thought of how the trip from Chicago to Lackland was my first bus ride. I looked out a porthole at the bright light of day. Glancing at my watch, I saw it was 1020 hours. "I wonder if all airplane rides are this odious."

"What's a 'odious'?"

"Uh, unpleasant. Something unpleasant."

"Well, dang, Nate, then why don'cha just say unpleasant? Ah know that word just fine."

He was right, of course. By dint of my extemporaneous speaking to the troops in BMT, I had become increasingly aware that much of what I said went over their heads. "You're right, Denny." I continued to stare out the window, watching the landscape move by. "I think I need to work on – not standing out from the

15

crowd, so to speak. I…." Something caught in my throat. "I would really like to be thought of as just one of the troops."

Denny clapped me on the shoulder. "Just get off yer high hoss, Nate, and ya'll be fine, just fine." We grinned at each other.

A small blue bus took the six of us to temporary quarters. To a man, we threw ourselves on our bunks and fell into deep sleep, and that's pretty much how we spent Saturday.

• • •

We reported for duty the next morning and two minutes later were dismissed until 0800 hours Monday. The others would transfer to their student squadrons to begin training, while I would remain and undergo aptitude tests to determine my career field.

That afternoon, Denny and I decided to tour the base. It was quite warm; the air smelled like trash cans behind a restaurant. We traversed untrafficked streets past rows of identical three-story, U-shaped buildings, blindingly white in the bright sunlight. Outside each was a large metal sign proclaiming it to be a student squadron. At one such sign Denny stopped and said, "Nate, this here's gonna be mine!" My thoughts flashed back to the dorms at the U of Chicago and my brief time there, not without some wistfulness. As I gazed upon these uniformly ugly cinder-block monstrosities, I wondered which would become my new home.

We crossed a runway, apparently unused by aircraft, as a metal grandstand stood alongside it. Large aircraft hangars loomed in the distance, but I saw no airplanes. Just ahead was a tree-shaded park with an American flag waving atop a tall flagpole, surrounded by offices with neatly lettered signs in front of each proclaiming "Base Ops," "ATC HQ," "Officer's Club" and the like. Nearby, inside a wide swath of lawn were four white wooden bungalows with blue doors and shutters. A sign read

341 Ith WAF Squadron
OFF LIMITS TO MALE PERSONNEL
By Order of Base Commander

Giving the area a wide berth, we eventually reached a tall chain-link fence that ran alongside a two-lane divided highway. Cars passed between us and a large body of pale blue-green water, waves crashing against a sandy beach littered with driftwood, piles of smelly, decaying green plant life, rusty cans, bottles and trash. Two scraggly palm trees dipped toward the water. A few hundred yards away stood a gate and guard house, an Air Policeman standing outside. I shuddered a little at seeing another AP so soon after our incarceration in the hangar at Lackland, but as we approached we received a friendly greeting. He wore summer khakis, a white helmet, white gloves, a blue plastic name badge that read KRASNEWICZ, and two stripes on his sleeve.

"What's that water?" I asked.

"That's the Gulf of Mexico, troop," he replied. "You boys must be new here." We nodded.

"The Guf a Mehico, huh? Well, Ah'll be danged," said Denny. "We anywhere near Biloxi?"

"It ain't said *By*-locksy," the AP replied. "It's Beh-*luxy*. Yer in it, boy. You go half a mile down this here road, yer in bee-yoo-ti-ful downtown Biloxi," he said, with derision. "You go ninety miles the other direction, yer in N'awleens."

"Well, Ah'll be danged," Denny said again. "Nate, what say we walk on down and see the town?"

"Can't do that," said the AP. He stiffened and brought his heels together.

"How come?" I asked.

"Troops ain't allowed off base in fatigues."

I looked down at my baggy, wrinkled greens. My leather name tag holder was partially bent from sleeping on it.

"You gotta wear civvies or a dress uniform to go off base," Krasnewicz continued.

"Well, hey, then, let's go change," said Denny, looking at me.

"Gotta have a pass, too," Krasnewicz said.

"And just how we go about doin' that?" Denny asked.

"Squadron's first sergeant issues passes. You troops are students, right?"

We nodded together. "We've just arrived," I said. "We're still in temporary quarters."

"Well then, you ain't gonna get no passes," Krasnewicz said. "Yer confined to base until you get assigned. I know, 'cause that's what happened to me, too, my first three days here." He abruptly snapped to attention and saluted a car approaching the gate. "And besides, you ain't gonna get no pass on Sunday, 'cause the first shirts don't work on weekends."

We stood in silence and contemplated what Krasnewicz had said. "Soooo," I began, "You need to obtain a pass from your student squadron first sergeant, on a weekday, and wear civilian clothing to leave the base…."

"Or khakis or dress blues." Krasnewicz inserted. "*And* you can't go off-base during duty hours."

"What?" cried Denny. "And so what are duty hours?"

"Oh-six hundred to midnight, Monday to Friday," Krasnewicz replied. "Curfew is midnight to 0600 hours every day," he added.

"Well, jee-hosaphat!" Denny snapped, shaking his head.

"So you can only go into Biloxi weekends?" I asked.

"Nope. Biloxi is off-limits."

"*Off limits? Completely?*" said an incredulous Denny.

"Well, you can go to the bus station to catch a bus somewheres else, like Mobile or Pensacola. Saturday or Sunday. But if you get caught by the APs in a bar, or on the streets at night, you'll get tossed in the brig and get a Article 15. And you can't go to N'awleens when it's Mardi Gras neither." He leaned toward us and said in an exaggerated whisper, "Unless you don' get caught, that is." Another car approached the gate and Krasnewicz waved it through. Apparently not an officer, like the first.

Denny and I stood looking past the chain-link fence at the world outside. Cars whizzed by, people inside laughing, talking, enjoying a Sunday afternoon drive, probably unaware of their perfect freedom to do whatever they pleased. A thought leaped into my mind: Was Krasnewicz here to keep people off the base, or to keep us in? Apparently the outside world was, by and large, off limits to us. Like the lettering on the blue bus, we were for official use only. I recalled two thoughts simultaneously. One was from my philosophy course at Chicago, some ancient philosopher – I didn't remember his name – who wrote about the idea of freedom of choice. The other was the Code of Conduct we'd had to memorize in Basic, our pledge to defend our country with our lives. It seemed to me that by willingly enlisting in the military and swearing allegiance to my country, I gave up my freedom of choice. I wasn't so sure I wanted to do that.

We trudged slowly back to our temporary barracks, stopping at the Base Exchange where I bought a tube of toothpaste and Denny a deck of cards. Beside the BX was a laundry with a curious sign in the window: WE TAILOR FATIGUES. Neither Denny nor I understood its meaning. After chow, the six of us passed the evening sitting on the floor playing five-card stud. I lost three dollars and sixty-five cents. I also lost my only friend; the next day Denny slung his big blue duffle bag over his shoulder and headed for his training squadron.

• • •

Keesler AFB, Biloxi, Mississippi
March 4, 1965

Dear Mom, Ernest and Frankie,

Well, here I am at Camp Granada. Ha Ha! Remember that funny song about the kid at summer camp who's having a miserable time? Yep, that's me. Why? The recruiter lied about becoming a pilot. That's for officers and I am enlisted, so I don't have a career field. I've been here for nearly a week in the transient barracks. The other five guys I came here with from Lackland have already started their training programs, while I've been getting tested for my military and technical aptitude. The good news is I've scored in the 97th percentile, which means I will qualify for a technical program, probably in electronics. I'm not unhappy about this turn of events, but I'd sure like to get my hands around that recruiter's neck.

I'm sorry I haven't written much, and I know my letters from Basic Training weren't very interesting. You know they made us sit on our footlockers and write those letters, then mailed them for us. They were probably read and censored. I must say that I don't believe I'm suited to military life, but on the other hand I don't think it will hurt me to have this experience. I've come to realize my life so far has been rather sheltered, so to speak, and I'm learning quite a lot about fraternization and how different those around me are. For example, I became quite good friends with a boy from Louisville, Kentucky, who barely graduated high school but has fine character and is wise in ways I am not. As the fellow – I can't remember his name – sings in that Hello Fadda, Hello Mudda, song, life is *very* entertaining.

March 5. *Good news* – I've just gotten my orders! I'll be joining the 3382nd Student Squadron and begin training for radio intercept and cryptography on Monday. I'll learn how to use equipment that monitors Communist communications from the U.S.S.R. Kind of like James Bond, huh? The bad news is, I'll be in school here for nearly a year. I understand the training is quite thorough, and I won't be able to tell you much about what I do, since upon graduation I'll have a Top Secret clearance!

Love,
Nathaniel

• • •

"All right, you meatheads, FALL IN!" It was 0530 hours Monday morning and an Airman Second Class wearing a gold rope, like the red one I'd worn as Dorm Chief, was ordering us into formation for the march to school. Overhead, the sky was an oily grey streaked with thin, long clouds whose underbellies were catching orange light from the yet-unrisen sun. It was chilly, and a damp breeze made my fatigues flap. I glanced around; unlike me, most of the troops looked sharp in snug-fitting fatigues. *Tailored*. I resolved to get mine tailored, too. "Ten-HUT!" the rope barked. We shuffled to attention. "Fuh-waad, HUH!" Brogans scuffed across the concrete in a groggy staccato, so the rope began chanting, "Yer left, yer left, yer left right left," until we got in step. I recalled the good feeling of marching in step from Basic, and it felt good again now. I began clunking my heels down with spirit.

We marched off the launch pad next to the 3382nd and turned onto the street, falling in with a multitude of flights from other squadrons. We soon reached the runway where Denny and I had trod a week earlier; ahead were the bleachers, where an officer stood. As we approached, our rope sang out, "Eyes RIGHT! Present ARMS!" We snapped our heads and a salute at a second lieutenant who stood like a statue, wearing an unhappy face and holding his salute as flight after flight passed in review.

We reached one of the hangars Denny and I had seen. Big trailers painted blue, army green, and red-and-white checks were parked outside. Our leader called, "Flight, HALT!" and then dropped his voice. "All right, troops, fall out for class." Everybody started shuffling toward the building. I followed them into a hallway lined with doors numbered 30001-007, 20501-012, 30301-010. I had no idea where to go, so I stuck my head into the first classroom and asked the tech sergeant for directions.

"Where's your orders?" he snapped. I fumbled them out of my shirt pocket. "See this number?" He stabbed at the paper. "That's your AFSC. And this? That's your class number. Now go find the door with those numbers, son. You're late for school!" Snickers arose. I smarted from his dressing me down in front of the troops. And he'd called me son. *Nobody but my dad can ever call me son,* I said to myself.

I bid him quick thanks, ducked back into the deserted hallway, and ran to my classroom. The desks, just like in high school, had filled from the back. On each was a thick blue binder with the Keesler AFB Technical Training Command crest emblazoned on it. A staff sergeant stood in front of the blackboard, knuckles resting on his desk. His blond flattop was impeccably flat and his blue eyes glared at me above a thin-lipped grimace. I slid into the only empty seat in the front row.

He read roll call, pausing to glare at me again when he came to my name. "My name is Whitmarsh. I am your Instructor for Basic Electronics Training. I will tell you what you will learn, then I will explain it to you, then I will tell you what you've learnt. And you *will* learn it. That is my solemn promise to you, because for the next 26 weeks I *will* own your hearts, your minds, and your asses." Eyeing me again, he added, "And you *will* be at your desk at 0600 hours *sharp.*"

So began my 26 weeks of Basic Electronics Training. I was on the first shift, 0600 to noon; two more six-hour shifts followed. We studied all six hours, with two smoke breaks. My dad always claimed a kid was either good at math and science or in English and the humanities, but not both. Surprisingly, I quickly grasped Boolean algebra and electronics theory. Even so, I hated the military regimen. I ground my teeth whenever Whitmarsh said "you *will.*" I grimaced with ever-increasing malevolence whenever I saw a "you *will*" order posted on the squadron bulletin board. Uncle Sam had my ass and the undeveloped part of my brain, but he did not and would never have my will. I even began to bridle when I heard the order to fall in. It made me think a lot about freedom and that philosopher, whose name came back: Erasmus. He had said, "In the land of the blind, the one-eyed man is king." I made a promise to myself to always be a king, and I started by getting top grades in class.

Whitmarsh stopped glaring at me.

• • •

The inside of our barracks was painted the color of barf. The floors were black linoleum, which we waxed and buffed to a high shine every Saturday. I shared a four-man room with two other troops. One was a great, tall, very shy lunk named Richard who wore thick glasses. The other was a fat, really dumb kid named Kenny who was constantly pulling Saturday detail for not making his bed, messy fatigues, unshined brogans, being late for formation.

Our entire barracks was BET. Everybody had dumb nicknames like Pinky, Moonshine, Flathead, Goofy, Loverboy, Chickenman, as if it was too militaristic to use last names and too personal to use first. Richard was christened Dunce, because he was so smart; Kenny was Porky, who washed out halfway through. Mine was Thorny, from my middle name, and I have to say it made me feel accepted. Unlike college we had no homework, so troops tended to go in and out of each other's rooms looking for conversation or a card game. Troops never tired of telling how great things had been in the Real World, which I learned was the name for the life we'd left behind. They'd all had sex a multitude of times with beautiful girlfriends, worked at great jobs where they earned oodles of money, and drove cool, fast, customized cars, yet here they were in the same boat as me, who had never experienced any of these things. In its interesting way, the military had taken away our freedom and individuality, to be sure, but replaced it with a commonality we all shared. Nearly everybody had pictures of Playboy bunny centerfolds and favorite cars taped inside their locker doors, and a calendar where they X'ed off days. Everybody knew exactly how many days they had left. I had 69 down, 1,391 to go. I wrote home for a photo of my Plymouth Fury to tack up next to my calendar.

Quiet Richard spent most of his time lying in his upper bunk reading books or comics. I liked him, and sometimes he'd open up and talk to me. He lent me an interesting science fiction novel by Robert Heinlein called *Stranger in a Strange Land* which we discussed often because some of its ideas seemed pertinent to our military life. Sex was something troops thought about. A lot. One night as I was reading I asked Richard, "Why do you suppose Jubal is celibate?"

"He lives to be an example to Mike," he said, rolling over on his stomach. "And the others. He realizes how difficult it is for the others to change their point of view, or their beliefs. He knows he can, but he can't preach it to others because Mike proves how difficult that is. Impossible, really. So he only imposes his existential beliefs on himself, and if anybody else wants to follow them, they can. So his celibacy is only an aspect of his existentialism. Of course, all great science fiction acknowledges that man is truly alone."

The discussion reminded me of my dad and his literature lectures. I listened, nodded, then turned back to the book.

A few troops had record players in their lockers, so we'd often just sit around smoking cigarettes, talking about the music or just listening to it. Bob Dylan and the blues were popular. So was a 45 called "Eve of Destruction," an anti-war song by Barry McGuire. When he sang:

> *You're old enough to kill, but not for votin'*
> *You don't believe in war, but what's that gun you're totin'*

we'd loudly chime in on the chorus together:

> *But you tell me*
> *Over and over and over again, my friend*
> *Ah, you don't believe*
> *We're on the eve*
> *of destruction.*

Dinky, a little guy from Alabama, had an old Jimmy Reed album everybody loved. We'd gather in his room to listen to woozy, sexy songs like "You Got Me Dizzy" or "Baby What You Want Me To Do." Dinky knew all the words to all the songs, and got us all pronouncing his name "JimmaReed." He was always saying things like, "Hey, he's from Miz'sippi, you know," or "Wow, man, listen to him! He's so juiced on horse he can barely remember the words," or "Jeez, that is *some* blues gee-tar."

But it was Dylan we listened to the most, and I learned all the words to "Masters of War" and "Blowin' in the Wind" and "The Ballad of Hollis Brown" and "The Lonesome Death of Hattie Carroll." My mother had educated me in classical music, and my dad in bebop and cool jazz. For the first time, I began to feel there was a musician whose music spoke to me about important things.

• • •

Summer arrived, with its searing heat and unbearable humidity and a typewritten letter from my mother.

June 4, 1965

Dear Nathaniel,

Thank you for taking the time to write us. When was that, back in March? We talk about you at the dinner table and wonder how you like the Air Force, military life, Mississippi, school and such, and if you miss us.

23

I have enclosed a photograph of your car, as you requested. It's dirty, because it's been sitting in the carport for the past five or six months. I tried to start it so I could move it into the sunlight, but the battery is dead.

We are struggling, Nathaniel, to make ends meet. Would you be able to send us a portion of your pay? I spoke with your recruiter, who sends his condolences for your not making it into flight school, by the way, and he said many airmen send money to their families back home. You can request an automatic deduction from your paycheck and the Government will send a check directly to me. That way you'll never miss it. We thank you for this, Nathaniel.

She went on and on with claptrap about the neighbors and how Ernest and Frankie couldn't wait for summer vacation and selling a dress to some famous socialite, but I stopped reading. There were two photos. One was my little brothers, their big sad eyes and faint smiles. *Poor little buggers, now they didn't even have me around.* The other was my Fury, covered with encrusted dirt and leaves. Streaks from melted snow and rain ran down its fenders. I crumpled the letter into a ball and threw it in the trash. I tore the picture of my car to shreds. I stuck the photo of Ernest and Frankie in my back pocket and went to the first shirt's office to find out how to send money home.

• • •

The heat and humidity made waiting in formation to march back from school increasingly difficult to endure. Sweat poured off us, turning our crisp fatigues to mush. Troops often got kind of stupid during fall-in time, loudly proclaiming how much they hated the Air Force and shoving each other around. One especially hot day two troops, Martinelli and O'Hanlon, launched into an insult contest. It started with "Your mother wears combat boots," a fairly common and harmless euphemism among troops. The other countered with "Your sister's so ugly she breaks mirrors when she walks by one," and it escalated from there until Martinelli said, "You're red on the head like the dick on a dog." The redheaded troop, O'Hanlon, punched Martinelli right in the face. Martinelli tore into him, and it took five troops to break it up.

Mostly, though, troops boasted about what their life had been like back in the Real World. I believed it all at first, and sometimes joined in the banter, just to be one of the troops. Sometimes I talked about my Fury or Sasha, the first and only girl I ever loved.

. . .

The leaves had turned and it was getting cold when we met. Sasha was practicing piano on the stage in the UC Mergenthaler Auditorium. I immediately fell in love with her. She was beautiful, long, thick brown hair cascading over a thick yellow turtleneck sweater, a woolen plaid kilt skirt that met her knee-high argyle socks. I stood in the back, watching her play Chopin's Piano Sonata Number I, and applauded as it ended, startling her. "Bravo," I said. "My name is Nate. Freshman. English."

She was a music major, a freshman from the North Shore. We went to a nearby coffee shop, where we sipped hot chocolate and stared into each other's eyes. Hers were an extraordinary emerald green, and they flashed every time our conversation hit a lively topic: Beethoven, Mozart, Chopin, Liszt. I couldn't take my eyes off of her. I asked if I could walk her back to her dorm, and as we crossed campus I took her mittened hand in mine and she let me hold it. When we reached the door, I asked if I could see her again. She nodded and smiled. "What's your last name? Y'know, so I can ask for you at the front desk?"

"Sonnenschein," she said.

"Sonnenschein? That sounds like sunshine."

"It's German for sunshine. What's your last name, Nate?" I told her the whole Nathaniel Hawthorne story and how my dad had died two months earlier. "Then I shall always call you Nathaniel," she said, and looked deep into my eyes. "I'm *so* sorry to hear about your father. *Please*, take good care. That's a blessing."

Sasha believed her blessing had great power. I realized I had been living sort of randomly or carelessly, and I wanted her to see that because of her I was taking better care of myself. I often wondered how Sasha, just eighteen years old, could have so much more wisdom than me.

My roommate, Ronnie, was a rich kid whose father owned a publishing company in Burr Ridge. He'd bought his son a brand-new, black Chrysler convertible for high school graduation. Ronnie's girlfriend, Martha, was a cheerleader and had the looks to go with it. One night, Sasha and I were in the dining hall eating their crap food when she blurted out, "Do you have a thing for Martha?"

I looked up at her, startled. "No, of course not," I said, scooping more mashed potatoes into my mouth. "She's Ronnie's girlfriend."

"I see the way you look at her sometimes," Sasha said, shaking her head almost sadly. "I *know* you have a *thing* for her."

"No, Sasha, I have a *thing* for *you*."

"You're a man," she retorted. "You can have a thing for two women. Three! Maybe more!"

I reached across the table and took her hand. "Sasha, I only have eyes for you," I sort-of sang the song by the Flamingos. She softened a little, squeezed my hand and smiled, but I knew she didn't believe me. She was right. I did have a thing for Martha. She was Ronnie's girl, but still I thought about having sex with her.

"You know this will never work out, don't you?" Sasha said, startling me again. Our fingers were still entwined.

"What? Why? What won't work out?"

"Us. You and me. Being together."

"Why?"

"Nathaniel, I'm Jewish."

"Yeah, I know, and I'm Methodist. So what?"

"My family would *never* forgive me if I married outside my faith."

"Sasha, we've only been seeing each other for, what? five or six weeks. Let's cross that bridge when we come to it."

Big tears welled up in her lovely emerald eyes; one rolled down her cheek, followed promptly by others. All thought of mashed potatoes forgotten, I stood, went around the dining table and sat down beside her, taking her in my arms as she continued to sob. I comforted her, dabbed her tears away, murmured sweet sounds, until she composed herself. Sasha wrapped her arms around me, tight; it felt wonderful.

Friday, Ronnie asked me if we wanted to double-date to the football game with him and Martha. Sure, I said. We could drive to the game and park right behind the stadium so we'd have a place to make out.

It was a very cold night as the Maroons played against Carnegie Institute of Technology, who we were sure to beat. The four of us sat in the bleachers wrapped in Ronnie's car blanket, nipping at a flask of vodka, laughing and cheering, but soon Ronnie and Martha were snapping at each other. I saw Martha take a swing at him, but he caught her fist. By the half, Sasha and I had drunk just enough to feel a romantic buzz. We climbed into the back seat and were quickly tangled up in each other's arms and legs. I was about ready to slip my hand inside her blouse when the passenger door opened. It was Martha, sobbing.

"Oh Natey, Natey, Natey, please help me," she blubbered, climbing into the back seat as if Sasha wasn't even there.

"What's wrong?" I asked, startled. Sasha and I were trying to sit up and pull our clothes back in place.

"That Ronnie, that bastard, oh shit! *I hate him!* I just broke up with him for the *last time!*"

And with that she threw herself on top of me and let go with another crying jag. I took Martha in my arms and held her close. Sasha sat there looking at me — us — with total bewilderment on her face, then pushed the front seat forward, reached over and opened the door, and was gone. Martha might have been drunk, but she understood what had happened and pressed her body closer to mine, reaching up to pull my face to hers. Martha! It was a dream come true. We were kissing madly and my hands were roving all over her body. We slid down on the back seat, belly to belly, nose to nose, and began pulling at each other's clothes....

I awoke to a great commotion. I was on top of Martha, who was screaming at me to get off her. Somebody was pounding me on the back: Ronnie. Martha and I still had our clothes on, but just barely. I had obviously passed out before we'd had a chance to go all the way.

Next day, Ronnie and Martha made up. Ronnie moved into another guy's room. I saw Martha walking to class; she winked at me. Of course, I'd totally blown it with Sasha. She refused to see me or even speak to me. I understood why. This was our destiny, not to be. She was the perfect woman, and I, an incredibly imperfect man, wasn't worthy of her. Probably unworthy of any woman. Ever.

• • •

"All right, heads up, troops!" I snapped back to the present; it was our squadron rope speaking. "Time for all good little boys to go to school.

"FALL IN!"

Chapter 3

Hurricane!
September, 1965

9 September 1965. Local radio stations had been announcing all morning that Hurricane Betsy was heading in the general direction of the Mississippi Gulf Coast. The thought was somewhat exciting to the 16,500 electronics students and personnel of Keesler Technical School, Keesler Air Force Base, Biloxi, Mississippi. The advent of something unprecedented, unique, an event that would break the monotony of our daily routine, was an event not to go unnoticed.

It was Saturday morning and I was pounding on the typewriter in the empty squadron admin office. It had been an eventful week. I'd graduated from Basic Electronics Training a week ago yesterday. The Air Force generously gave me the entire weekend off before beginning Radio Intercept and Cryptography training on Monday, 6 September. That gave me plenty of time to sew my new stripes on my uniforms; I was now officially an Airman Second Class, with a raise to boot. My mother would be thrilled. Three days later, as I sat in class, Hurricane Betsy ripped through the Gulf Coast. Maybe it was my academic upbringing, but I took notes on everything that was happening to us.

At 1420 hours the Instructor Supervisor was back; "School is dismissed. Return to the barracks. You're restricted to base until further notice. Well – what are you waiting for?" He grinned and left, and so did we.

I can't really say why, except it was just about the most exciting thing that had ever happened to me, but I felt compelled to write about it, like for a college course I was no longer taking.

At 2100 hours we moved our mattresses out into the hall, all twenty of us, and closed up the rooms. No one would leave the hall for the duration of the night. At one end of the bay a card game was in progress; elsewhere troops read, listened to a portable phonograph, or played guitars, but everyone kept one ear open to hear developments on the radio.

We tried to visualize what was happening outside; we could hear the wind, as it was banging the louvers of the ceiling fan on the roof, viciously. Yet to imagine the trees involuntarily leaving the earth, salty water washing across the beautiful white sand of the beach in walls 10 to 12 feet high, cars floating, people fleeing their homes – all this was somewhat incomprehensible. Here were we, safe and sound in a cement-block fortress, with electricity, food, lights, dry beds, listening to Red Cross directors telling people to bring blankets, flashlights, and food to evacuation centers, and that children must be accompanied by parents. The greatest and most glaring contradiction, it seemed, was that we were safe, content, happy, while citizens of Biloxi, Gulfport, Bay St. Louis, Pass Christian, New Orleans and the rest of the area were in such immediate, mortal danger.

Not that we had a peaceful night – the wind raced up and down the hallway, tearing our blankets from us, waking us up with its banging the fan vents, in addition to the fact that we were cramped between the narrow walls. Shortly after 0500 hours the student shift leader woke us up and said we could return to our rooms. Blissfully, we re-retired to our bunks. There would be no school today.

As I wrote, I relived everything that happened two nights before. I struggled for a way to conclude my paper, wishing I could write in mighty and compelling words just how intense and terrifying it was, but I could not find those words. Instead I wrote:

The relative calmness and faith was the mark of note as far as the base and the 3382nd Student Squadron personnel were concerned. We had been told that the situation was in good hands and not to worry, so we didn't. Precautions were taken before absolutely necessary. Strictly obeying orders was imperative, and they were carried out to the letter. People of every conceivable background, from every part of the country, all worked in unison and no emergency situation was encountered. The student leaders were on an all-night vigil to safeguard our safety. This, then, was the beauty of the moment.

The hurricane ran its course, did its damage, and gave us all something to write home about. Yet we were protected from it, by the common sense and experience of our leaders and by our own military discipline. In more ways than one, we have learned much, have much to be thankful for.

Yuk! What tripe! I dug in my shirt pocket for my Luckies, shook one out and lit up, staring at the words "much to be thankful for." I blew out a cloud of disgusted smoke. I rolled the sheet out of the typewriter, reading, smoking and pondering what to do with the story. My first thought was to send it home, but then I had an idea: *What if I could send it home as a published article, maybe in the newspaper?* Stubbing out my cigarette, I went over to the casual room and pulled the *Gulfport Citizen* off the newspaper rack. I flipped through the pages, then went back to the orderly room, inserted fresh paper and carbons in the typewriter, carefully retyped the whole thing, and mailed it to the editor.

• • •

A runner came to my room and said Master Sergeant Reynolds, the first shirt, wanted to see me. "Take a look at this, Flowers," he said, tossing a newspaper across his desk at me.

"Sarge! They printed my story!" I grinned like a lunatic.

"I can see that, Flowers." Reynolds leaned forward, not smiling, eyes locked on mine. "Thing is, you didn't have permission to do this. You gotta go through the base Public Affairs office you want to do something like this. Get a PA officer to OK it."

"Oh."

"You only get a reprimand this time," Sgt. Reynolds continued, picking up a baseball from his desk, "especially 'cause there's no classified information in it and you showed us in a favorable way. But see that you get clearance you want to

31

do something like this again, else you'll get an Article 15." He tossed the baseball up and down a few times. "And I will personally give you a beaner. Understand?"

I grinned, nodded. Then I said, "Can I have it?"

"Can you have what?" Reynolds looked at his baseball.

"The newspaper. My story."

"Oh. Yeah, get it the hell out of here," he said. As I turned to leave, Reynolds said, "By the way, the PAO told me to tell you that you write a good story."

I took the paper back to my room and read my story carefully, noticing the editors had changed a few words and phrases. I guess "obeyance" wasn't a proper word, because they had rewritten it "strictly obeying orders." I had wanted to use obeisance, but thought better of it.

• • •

Tech school was a lot harder than Basic Electronics. Most nights I found myself doing homework. Our big three-ring binders were filled with daily encryption lessons we had to turn in, and I found myself sitting on my bunk muttering Russian words and phrases we were expected to memorize and translate. I felt pretty good that I'd graduated BMT at the top of my class, but my miserable college career lingered in my mind and I worried about mastering how to search for radio frequencies and de-encryption stuff. A smart kid named Hubbard from South Dakota was in my class, and sometimes I'd go down to his room on the second floor and practice with him. One night, as we sat translating, I burst out laughing and he asked me why.

"Look at what I just translated. In English it says, "Something is rotten in Denmark and it isn't the cheese."

"Hmmm," said Hubbard, studying the Cyrillic characters. "Sounds like code words, all right."

"It's from *Hamlet*," I said. Hubbard raised his eyebrows. "Except it's a misquotation. In the play, the guy says 'Something is rotten in the state of Denmark,' but he doesn't say anything about cheese."

"Okay…," said Hubbard, "So…."

"Well, I just figured if this was some kind of coded message they'd want the quote accurate, so, you know, if they had to look up the quote in the play…. I mean, *anybody* would know it *is* Shakespeare."

"Never read 'im," Hubbard replied.

Hurricane!

After six straight hours of training, five days a week — not to mention the daily march to school and back to the Triangle — when the weekend came we were ready to relax, but such was not our fate. Saturday morning was a mandatory GI party to get ready for Monday morning inspection. If a troop had earned too many demerits, he got Saturday detail on top of it. O'Hanlon, the kid who'd gotten in the fistfight because of his red hair, pulled a lot of Saturday detail. He was on my floor and I saw him Saturday after Saturday scrubbing urinals, scraping the old wax off the hallway floors with a razor blade, washing windows — all the worst grunt jobs. Once I asked him about it, and he said the floor rope had it in for him.

"I've been on this stinking base 47 weeks and I've been on Saturday detail 39 of them," he said. "I hold the record, and I don't deserve it." His face scrunched up into a contorted scowl. He was a funny looking kid, his big red hair cowlick, freckles, big nose and a warbly kind of mouth. "*Nobody deserves to pull grunt detail this much.*" He was probably right. I began to notice that if some troops were screwing around, he'd be the one who always got singled out. He didn't have buddies. Nobody seemed to want to be around O'Hanlon. Maybe troops were afraid they'd get in trouble along with him. O'Hanlon, I concluded, was a demerit magnet.

On the other hand, I was pretty good friends with my roommate Dunce, Dinky, the kid from Selma who knew all the great blues music, and Hubbard (who we called Hubba-Hubba), a Mexican kid from San Diego named Teja but who we called Taco, and Jon David, or JD. They were all in radio/cryptography with me. Sometimes we'd go to the base theater for a movie on Saturday night, or just cross the highway and sit on the beach and drink beer and bitch about the military.

Somebody said there was an all-girl's college full of nymphomaniacs in Gulfport, about half an hour from Biloxi. Hubba, Dinky, JD and I got weekend passes. We hopped the base shuttle bus to Biloxi to catch another bus to Gulfport and when we walked into the Biloxi bus station, I couldn't believe my eyes. There was a "Whites Only" sign above the water fountain. Then I saw another one outside the bathrooms. I glanced around and saw yet another over the door to the seating area. That left the Negroes nowhere to sit at all while they waited for a bus.

"Segregation, it's called," said JD, noticing my dumbfounded look. "It's pretty much like this in Baltimore, too. It's the South. If there's any Negroes on our bus, they'll have to sit in the back." I looked toward the doors leading out to the parking area. A Confederate flag was tacked to the wall, the words NEVER FORGET painted below. It kind of soured my mood.

"That stuff you learned in your history books is a bunch a propyganda," Dinky said. "Civil War ain't over. Never will be. My folks and most of my people figure the South will rise again, and we better have slaves on hand when it does. That's just the way we is, Thorny."

Gulfport was clean, bright, happy, unlike dingy, run-down Biloxi. We walked along palm tree-lined 25th Street, ate ice cream cones, sat on the sandy white beach pointing out yachts and ships to each other. For the first time in a long time, it felt like we were just people, not GIs.

We never did see any nympho college girls. When we got back, Dunce said it probably didn't matter, what with all the saltpeter they put in our mashed potatoes. "Oh, Dunce, you gonna start in on that again?" said Dinky.

• • •

October 25, 1965

Dear Nathaniel,

October is ending and so is the nice weather. It's starting to get cold here, and I'm getting out the boys' winter clothes. I watched the weather map on television and apparently it doesn't get very wintry on the Gulf Coast, which must be nice for you.

Thank you for sending the article you wrote about the hurricane. Of course we had heard all about "Billion-Dollar Betsy" – it was on the nightly television news, although Mr. Cronkite mostly spoke of the damage to New Orleans. I was, of course, thrilled to read your first published work, Nathaniel.

Frankie and Ernest and I also thank you for the extra money you're sending us. Congratulations on your promotion. I'm sure you're very proud to be wearing two stripes. Your father would be smiling from ear to ear if he could see you now. We are wondering if you plan to come home for Thanksgiving, and I hope you will. It would be wonderful to have us all together again like last year. I've invited your Uncle Ned, Aunt Millie, Aunt Bertie from St. Louis, and your Grandpa and Grandma Whitaker, of course, and your Grandma Flowers. I'm especially glad she is coming, since she didn't feel up to it last year. I called the sergeant at the recruiting office and he said that many boys apply for leave and come home for Thanksgiving and other holidays.

Huh, there she goes, checking up on me through the recruiter again. The mere mention of Thanksgiving tied my stomach in a knot. *Your* uncle. *Your* aunt. I mentally raced back through the past two Thanksgivings since my dad died, trying to think of something to be thankful for, a reason to want to spend one of the most insipid events in history with the most boring and dull people in my life. With the possible exception of my Uncle Ned. After all, he'd taken the time to come visit me right after I started at Chicago.

• • •

My uncle Ned, Dr. Edmund Leander Simmons, is a Professor of Philosophy at the University of Wisconsin in Madison. I didn't know him really well, except that he was my mom's brother and a bachelor and I usually only saw him at Thanksgiving or Christmas. When he arrived at my dorm lounge, he was wearing a three-piece suit and paisley bow tie; come to think of it, I never saw him when he wasn't wearing a suit and bow tie. He even wore a bow tie with his black suit to my dad's funeral. He looked like Fred Astaire.

We went to lunch in the cafeteria. I got a slice of pizza and he had a bowl of soup. He showed the cashier his UW faculty ID card and asked if she would give him a discount. "Five percent," she said. Uncle Ned didn't thank her.

"How is college life treating you, Nathaniel?" he said over his soup spoon. I said I guessed it was going OK. "Well," he said, "Socrates said the unexamined life is not worth living," and ate some more soup. He held the spoon at a right angle to his mouth and slurped the soup from its side. He looked kind of silly, glasses perched on his nose, his pale skin, the bright bow tie bobbing below his Adam's apple as his lips quivered. I noticed it was hand-tied. "And of course Plato, Socrates' student, started the Academy, which we think of as the first institution of learning and from whence our notion of acquiring knowledge from those wiser than ourselves began."

Obviously my uncle was, for all intents and purposes, still in his classroom, delivering a lecture. I listened quietly while munching my pizza, wondering what this visit was really about. He prattled on and my thoughts drifted until I heard him say "limbo of the fathers." I raised my eyebrows quizzically.

Uncle Ned paused, pressing a paper napkin to his lips, then said, "You see, any relationship in which a young man learns from an older man could be called a father-son relationship. Aquinas – St. Thomas Aquinas, you know – saw many levels of symbolic meaning in the relationship between Jesus Christ and God, needless to say," he giggled. "One can never forgot that Jesus felt his father had forsaken him. But you know," he said between slurping more soup, "it was that brilliant Spanish philosopher, Miguel de Unamuno, who said that a man grows deeper as his capacity for anguish increases. What he meant, I believe, was that we attain more, well, spirituality in direct proportion to our ability to thrive – nay, *triumph* – in this tragic life we're forced to live. Of course, de Unamuno was, like Aquinas, a Catholic...."

A stillness settled on me. I realized Uncle Ned was trying to say something to me about my father – perhaps something meaningful, or heartfelt, or important – but for the life of me I didn't know what it was. Yet what stuck with me was the comment that life was tragic. I'd never thought that, but now I realized it was exactly how life felt to me. Life was really strange and sad and difficult and confusing. A lot of the time I just went day to day without much purpose in mind. Now it dawned on me that I missed my dad, sometimes a lot, but I hadn't let myself feel it. Maybe Uncle Ned was trying to step in as a substitute for my dad. As he talked and I half-listened, I wondered if my mother was behind his little visit.

There was no way Uncle Ned could fill my dad's shoes, but he did whet my interest in philosophy. Winter quarter I took a junior-level course called Philosophical Constructs. Professor Cohen was an elderly lady who wore her long braid of gray hair wrapped around her head. She had a mighty intellect, one that matched her build, which resembled that of a German opera singer. Her lectures often went over my head, but one idea stuck with me: existentialism. I prodded her to explain the links between de Unamuno and Nietzsche and Sartre, and wrote my term paper on existentialism in modern life. I got an A, and the prof wrote "great paper" on it. As I left class, she stopped me and asked if I thought I was an existentialist. I said no. But then I said, "Well, maybe." Then I thought about something else de Unamuno had written: "Only in solitude do we find ourselves; and in finding ourselves, we find in ourselves all our brothers in solitude." So I said, "Yeah, I guess so."

So that was it. I was no longer a Methodist. Now I was an existentialist.

• • •

A big troop named Rasmussen was on the mess line, slopping mashed potatoes, turkey and cranberry sauce on our plates. As usual, he wore his white chef's hat at a jaunty angle and said "Merry Christmas," to each of us as we passed down the line, his big gold front tooth gleaming.

I smirked at him and said, "Hey, Rasmussen, this is the same slop you served us for Thanksgiving."

"Thanks for remembering, Flowers," he replied. "Just for that you don't get seconds."

"Aw, gee, you're breakin' his heart," said Hubba-Hubba, right behind me.

"God bless us troops," said Rasmussen, pointing his finger at each of us standing in line, "and God bless the United States of America!"

"Yeah, God bless us, every one," said Dunce, our very own Tiny Tim.

"Hey, give Dunce an extra dose of saltpeter on his mash pahtatahs, will ya?" said Dinky, then launched into a shrill, off-key version of "We Wish You A Merry Christmas."

And that was pretty much our Christmas. I lay in my bunk, glad to have my buddies, and wondered what my family was doing with their Christmas on this Saturday afternoon. I thought about the round blue tin of Danish cookies, supposedly from my brothers, long ago gobbled up by my brother troops. I thought about the two books my mother sent, *In His Own Write* by John Lennon of the Beatles band, and *The Winter of Our Discontent* by John Steinbeck. Both bore the stamp of the Waukegan Public Library and another, in bold black type, that read DISCARD. In her brief letter, my mother apologized for sending secondhand books. I picked up her letter and read it again:

I know you won't like hearing this, but we are moving. I simply cannot make ends meet, even with the promotion to commissioned sales at Friedman's Fashions. I listed the house with a real estate agent back in August and he has sold it. We'll be moving into an apartment in Hinsdale over Christmas vacation. And I've found a wonderful job as a librarian there. Ernest and Frankie are *very* upset to be leaving their home and their school, but I simply have no choice.

I've also sold your car. Bill Brekkus at the Dodge-Plymouth dealership appraised it and said it would be hard to sell because it was, in his words "a hot rod," but he gave me a fair price for it nevertheless. I had to do it. We needed the money for the move. I'm sorry, Nathaniel, because I know the car meant a lot to you, but there will be others. I hope you will understand and forgive me. Here is a better photo Mr. Brekkus took especially for you.

That sleazeball Brekkus! He really conned her. He, who sold me the car in the first place, telling me it was a "collector's item" that would appreciate over time, now telling my mom it was a worthless hot rod. Was that the way the world worked? You could just change the truth to fit the situation?

I slowly wadded the letter into a tight ball and lobbed it across the room. It bounced off the trash can rim. I got up and pinned the photo inside my locker door, along with:

- a magazine photograph of Richard Burton, my favorite actor
- my ticket stub from the premier of the Beatles movie, *A Hard Day's Night*
- my countdown calendar
- a photo my mother sent of my brothers and me standing in front of Mt. Rushmore on a family vacation, the three of us wearing identical striped T-shirts with our names printed on them: NATE, ERNIE, FRANK.
- A hand-lettered quotation, "In the land of the blind the one-eyed man is king," inspired by my experiences with Sgt. Whitmarsh in BET
- A photo of Rebecca, my second cousin, who is a high school senior and pretty cute, which is why I put it up. Her parents and mine conspired for years to get us together, but I couldn't stand her. She sent the picture with the most Godawful gushy letter, on perfumed paper no less, which was promptly basketballed into the trash can
- The letter Trevor Finch, editor of the *Gulfport Citizen*, wrote thanking me for my op-ed on Hurricane Betsy and telling me he'd like to see anything I wrote
- Lines from T.S. Eliot's poem, "Little Gidding":

With the drawing of this Love and the voice of this
Calling...

We shall not cease from exploration
And the end of all our exploring
Will be to arrive where we started
And know the place for the first time.
Through the unknown, unremembered gate
When the last of earth left to discover
Is that which was the beginning;

Hurricane!

• • •

I had read Eliot in college and liked his poetry – "The Waste Land," "The Love Song of J. Alfred Prufrock," and "Four Quartets." The famous lines came up with Richard one night. Dunce was no dunce – this I already knew – but I was in awe of his interpretation of "Little Gidding," explaining how Eliot was trying to find peace in the World War II world without faith or hope.

"He saw that we are all just on a rotating cycle, a wheel, going round and round," Richard said. "The wheel of life. Just like the seasons, we grow in the spring and die in the winter. As a metaphor, you know."

"We begin. We end. We begin again." I said.

"Just so."

I was silent for a while, then said, "I wonder where my end place is. You know, the one I'll know as the place where I started."

Richard laid back on his bunk and tucked his hands behind his head. "I wonder that a lot. Sometimes I think there may be more than one."

"Hmmm," I said. "You may be right."

• • •

Even though I hadn't mentioned it, Richard figured out when my birthday was and got the troops together to celebrate my 21st. January 1, 1966, was on a Saturday and we had no trouble getting passes to go out to dinner on the big riverboat at the Broadwater Beach Resort and Marina. This was considered a respectable place, unlike the dives and bars in downtown Biloxi. In fact, we had to wear our uniforms or a button-up shirt and tie to get admitted. I was also celebrating my "graduation" from Keesler; soon I'd be shipping out to my first duty station, San Ramon Air Force Base, just north of San Francisco, California.

A waitress about my mom's age served me, Dinky, JD, Hubba-Hubba, Richard, and O'Hanlon steak dinners. We had many, many glasses of Seagram's VO and Cokes before, during, and after, with O'Hanlon leading drunken toasts to my birthday and imminent departure. A live band played; a pretty blonde lady wearing a polka-dot dress and white gloves belted out songs like "Shrimp Boats Are A-Coming" and "I've Got You Under My Skin" and "Old Cape Cod." They played "Happy Birthday" for me, my buddies howling the lyrics, and the waitress brought me a cupcake with a teensy candle stuck in it. I ended up getting totally smashed, something new for me. My fellow troops dragged me on their shoulders down the gangplank to a taxicab.

The next morning, thankfully a Sunday, I awoke with a vicious hangover and a stupid thought that went round and round in my head: I had now reached the age of majority. I was now allowed to vote, take out a loan, get married, legally buy liquor. I could even join the military without my mother's consent. The words from "Eve of Destruction" came back to me. "Whoop-de-doo!" I cried aloud, fell back on my pillow, and slept until three in the afternoon.

• • •

On Sunday, 6 Feb, 1966, I arrived back at the Chicago Loop bus station from whence I'd departed a year earlier. So much for Mr. Thomas Stearns Eliot. My mother was there to drive me home. Instead of heading north, we drove south through new housing developments my mom called the suburbs. She kept saying how good I looked in my uniform and asking me how it felt to be 21 and telling me how much Ernest and Frankie were looking forward to seeing their big brother.

Her apartment was in a new complex. Every building looked exactly the same except painted a slightly different shade of off-white. I pulled my duffel bag off my shoulder and looked around. The walls were bare. "Where are dad's books?" I asked.

"Boys! Nathaniel's home!" my mother called down the hall. She turned to me and said, "You'll be sleeping on the hide-a-bed. But just temporarily," pointing at the davenport. *Temporarily until what happens?*

My little brothers came rushing out and threw their arms around a leg. I quickly learned the reason for their warm welcome: In their bedroom I found my KLH portable stereo, records, games, tennis racquet — in short, nearly everything I'd left locked in my steamer trunk, which now sat in a corner, the broken padlock still hanging from the hasp. Without a word, I turned and walked out so I wouldn't beat the crap out of them.

My mother and I argued over something every single day:

Are you still going to send us the monthly allotment from your pay?

When will you get a raise? Will you be able to send us more?

Have you stayed out of trouble with the officers?

What were your grades in technical school?

Have you learned a skill that will get you a job when you get out of the service?

What about college? You need to finish college.

Well, if you don't want to discuss it with me, then I want you to talk to your Uncle Ned about your college problems again.

You should write a letter to that dean at the University of Chicago and apologize.

What do you care about that old guitar? Let the boys have it.

Why can't you write more often?

Do you remember your Aunt Bertie? No? Well, she....

On and on it went, questions I never seemed to have the right answers for, which drove her to nag on me all the more. The only thing that made life bearable was they were gone all day, but I had nothing to do but rattle around the apartment. It was half a mile to the nearest bus stop, as if I had anywhere to go, and besides, it was cold as hell outside. One day I stomped into my brothers' room and took the things that mattered the most to me, including my stereo, slung my duffel bag on my shoulder and called for a taxi. I left a note on the dinette table:

Thanks for everything, Mom. Nate.

I had wasted exactly nine days of my 30-day leave. That evening at Union Station, I boarded a sleek silver westbound train, climbed the stairs of the dome car, stowed my gear and plunked down next to the window. Suddenly, silently, we were moving and began gathering speed. The bright lights of Chicago zipped past me, but were soon gone as we became lost in darkness.

I leaned back against the seat and closed my eyes. I was going to California.

Part II
Goin' to California

Chapter 4
Goin' to California
February, 1966

Daybreak. The train clattered down the track with a staccato beat worthy of a jazz drummer. I peered through sleep-filled eyes at the impossibly bleak landscape of the Midwest winter rushing by outside. My head was cold where it had rested near the ice-rimed window. Biloxi was ugly, to be sure, but this was a different kind of ugly: stark, dead, barren. Iowa, Nebraska, I wasn't sure where I was, but all I could see was infinite row upon row of crops that had been chopped down, leaving little black stubs sticking up out of the snow. I stared at them until my vision blurred. They became little GIs standing at attention in formation waiting for orders from God, country, or the weather to improve.

I got up, stretched, looked around the car. There was a murmuring whispering sound in the air, but it looked like the other passengers were still asleep. Restless and bored, I walked to the diner car but it wasn't open yet. I couldn't read, couldn't sleep, and found myself longing to see the Rockies, the Great Salt Lake, something, anything but this feeling of being trapped on this train for two more days and not knowing a thing about where I was going or why. Strange, but that's exactly how I'd felt right after I flunked out of Chicago and decided to commit suicide.

• • •

I didn't actually *decide* to kill myself. I'd been home from college maybe two weeks when the letter from the dean at the University of Chicago arrived, advising me

> …to give thoughtful consideration to your academic objectives and, in light of your performance during the 1963-64 academic year, consider other educational institutions for pursuit of those selfsame objectives. Perhaps, at some future date, and with an academic transcript of merit, the University may be in a position to consider your readmittance. However, I regret to add that since the terms of your scholarship have not been satisfactorily met, it has been revoked so as to favor other students whom may be in need.

I couldn't believe this was happening to me. Me, who had graduated with honors from Waukegan High, who had never been in any kind of trouble ever in my whole life. Thinking back on everything that had happened in the past year totally drowned me in an immense tidal wave of existential ennui and remorse. I was beginning to have an inkling that blowing things with Ronnie, losing Sasha, my drinking, behaving stupidly, missing classes, all of this was in some way because I'd lost my dad. Now, here I was back home again, my mother nagging me to find a job, babysitting my brothers, nowhere to go and nothing to do and a great big case of Eddie Cochran's incurable "Summertime Blues." It felt like all I had left was my beloved Fury, so I got behind the wheel and took off.

I got on Route 20, no real destination in mind, just wandering and wondering what was going to happen to me now. A job? Easy: My granddad Simmons would give me a job painting houses. Continue living at home? Right, keep on giving all my money to my mom. Go to a community college, as the dean recommended in his letter, to get my grades up? Uh-huh, take the courses I flunked all over again with a bunch of stupid flunkies at a flunky two-year school. Yeah, sure.

No answers were coming. I began seeing signs for the Mississippi Palisades State Park; had I really driven all the way to the Mississippi River? I turned into the park and drove north on Route 84, alongside the river. The road climbed the limestone bluffs, and I could see the river hundreds of feet below. In an instant I decided to drive my Fury off those cliffs and into oblivion, to put an end of this absurd, existential existence of mine. I was alone in the mess I'd made of my life. I didn't matter to anybody, so why not just off myself? Yes, die in the romantic way of Goethe's Young Werther. That'd show them!

Finding a way out to the edge of the bluffs proved difficult. I drove hither and yon until I couldn't even remember where I was trying to go. I turned onto a steep rutted little dirt road, stepped on the gas and scraped the mufflers right off the bottom of my car. I sat there, stunned that I'd damaged my beautiful Fury. After a while I backed down and took off with a huge roar of the exhaust. It was kind of cool at first, like having lakes plugs, but after a while it just sounded awful. How I got home without getting pulled over by a cop I will never know.

• • •

I stepped off the train at the Oakland station on a bright, sunny morning. California. It felt happy, sunny, not sad and bleak and old and cold like the Midwest. I felt happy. This was my new life.

I found a bus to San Rafael, then an Air Force shuttle took me to San Ramon Air Force Base. I was dazzled by the white stucco buildings with red tile roofs, palm trees and green lawns everywhere, B-52s landing and taking off, and crashing waves on the other side of the runway that had to be the Pacific Ocean.

I reported to the duty NCO at the 1876th Air Force Communications Service and was given a room assignment. The barracks was a hotel compared to Keesler. I would be bunking in a two-man room with a guy named Lee Moreau. I didn't have to report for duty until my leave time was up. Wow! I had two weeks to explore Frisco and the Bay Area. I left my stuff in the room and spent the afternoon walking around the base and out to the Pacific, where I promptly took off my shoes and socks and splashed into the waves.

When I returned, Lee was in the room. He was a kind of funny looking guy, short with beady black eyes and black straight hair, a fat nose and fat lips that smiled almost all the time. He was an Airman First Class, radar maintenance, with about a year more time in service than me. Three stripes to my two. On his fatigue shirt pocket he wore the Air Force Communications Service patch, a fist holding lightning bolts against a backdrop of the universe. Above it his last name, MOREAU, was embroidered on a blue cloth strip. Lee told me he came from the Northeast Kingdom of Vermont, a self-proclaimed Canuck whose French-Canadian grandfather had married an Abnaki Indian princess.

"You're gonna like it here," he said. "San Ramon is laid back."

"What's that mean?"

"I mean it's not real strict military rules and regs," he said. "You know how tight-assed everything was in Basic and Keesler, by the book, y'know? Well, here everybody lets everybody get by. Just keep your nose clean."

He went on to tell me that our outfit, The 1876ᵗʰ AFCS, had its own barracks. We were not subject to the same crack-of-dawn wakeup calls and routines of the rest of base personnel because we had to maintain our electronic equipment and support the mission twenty-four hours a day, seven days a week.

"See, the NCOs only work the day shift," Lee said. "They don't care what hours we work so long as all the shifts are covered. We change it around a lot. Sometimes we work a rotating shift with a day off in between. Sometimes we pull three days of alternating twelve-hour shifts, and then get three days off. Most of us don't hang around the base any more than we have to."

"Great!" I told him I had two weeks' leave time before I had to report for duty, and how great it had been to splash around in the Pacific.

"Pacific? As in Pacific Ocean?"

"Yeah, right over there. Across the runway."

"That's not the ocean! That's San Pablo Bay! The ocean's about twenty, thirty miles west. You were going east."

"Oh," I replied. We were quiet for a minute, then I said, "You been to 'Frisco?"

Lee gave me a friendly frown. "You don't say 'Frisco.' It's 'San Francisco.' Or 'The City.' Yeah, sometimes, but there's lots to do around Marin too. Hey, you legal?"

"Yeah." I felt a sudden surge of pride, which felt strange.

"Well, let's go get a pizza and a beer. Oh yeah, we also get separate rats because of our schedule."

"Separate rats?"

"Yeah, separate rations. It means we don't *have* to eat in the mess hall. We get $77.20 a month to buy our own food."

"No kidding," I said. Money I would not have to send home to my mother each month. "No kidding."

• • •

We blasted down Highway 101 at a high rate of speed in Lee's 1962 Austin-Healey 3000, top down. "I'm restoring it," he shouted above the wind. "Beautiful though, ain't it? Six-cylinder. Fast, huh? New paint job. They call this 'arrest-me red.' Ha-ha-ha-ha-ha!"

We pulled into a parking lot in front of a building that looked like a ramshackle shed. Fragrant smoke poured from a metal smokestack; an old surfboard hung above the doorway with "Woody's Place" and "Eat Here" crudely painted on it. It was dark inside; a few people sat at tables and benches carved from thick planks of wood; the floor was littered with peanut shells. A fat man in a dirty green T-shirt with the word ORYGUN across his back stood at a grill, flipping hamburgers.

"Goddammit, Woody!" Lee yelled. I looked at him, startled.

"God*dammit*, Leon," Woody growled back, a big grin creasing his unshaven face. "Where'n hell you been, boy? And who inna goddam hell's this scrawny kid with ya?"

"This's Nate. Nathaniel Hawthorne Flowers. Just arrived on base."

"God*dammit*, Nathaniel Hawthorne Flowers!" Woody yelled at me.

"Goddammit? Woody?" I stuttered. A few churlish-looking drinkers, watching, clapped their hands.

"You want the usual, Leon, Goddammit?"

"Yeah, a big one, and two drafts." He turned to me. "You like pepperoni, right?" I nodded.

Woody checked my ID and poured two huge beers for us. "You ain't too good tah drink Olympia beer from Warshington, are ya, Mr. Flowers?" he roared, leaned across the counter and whispered, "I read Hawthorne. Oh yeah, I read ole Nathaniel Hawthorne. House of the naked gables. Goddammit!" He half-growled with a big laugh.

Lee gulped down about half his beer, then picked up a slice of pizza, rolled it up, and shoved half of it into his mouth. "You're an '03 now," he said and chomped another mouthful of pizza. "What's your AFSC?"

"My? – oh, Air Force Specialty Code. It's 51203. Crypto Radio Intercept."

"OK," he said, "so you'll get assigned to an NCO for your training to become an '05. OJT. On-the-job training. I don't know how long yours is; mine was almost a year. If you pass, your AFSC will be 51205 and you'll get another stripe and a raise. You'll pass. Don't worry. It ain't hard. Your boss will make sure you pass, unless you're a total moron. Then you're done. No more training. You planning to stay in?" He downed the rest of his beer and signaled Woody for another.

I looked down at my beer glass, still three-quarters full. "I don't think so. Probably not. So far, I don't care much for military life."

"You might change your mind. After you're finished with your training and get used to it, it ain't so bad. Like the guy says, you put in four years, then re-up

49

for four more. That's eight. Add two years and you're halfway to retirement and a lifelong pension. Ha-ha-ha-ha-ha!"

"You planning to stay in?"

"Aw, maybe. Can't say for sure at this point. I'd like to travel, you know, see the world. Not 'Nam particularly, just get out of the States. I'll see. I got time before I gotta make a decision."

• • •

I reported for duty wearing crisply tailored fatigues, shiny with starch, bearing my new blue FLOWERS name strip and AFCS patch. My OJT supervisor was Staff Sergeant Maurice Selaterre, an old veteran everybody called Mo. We spent most of the first day filling out paperwork and reviewing the training manuals. It was like Keesler training, only it was hands-on and mostly self-study. I had daily forms with lists of tasks and skills to check off as I was taught how to do them. I was bored by the end of the day, in part because the Performance Maintenance tasks were mind-numbingly trivial, like "Identify the volume control knob. It is black with a pointer that increases sound volume as it is rotated clockwise." Mo, having trained just about everyone who had ever been assigned to San Ramon, was equally bored and boring.

Lee mostly wanted to go to Woody's and drink beer, but I got restless to see and do more. "You need a car," he said, which prompted my telling him what had happened to my Fury, the loss of which I still mourned. "Yep, you need a new car. Cars, they're like girlfriends. You love the one you got but when you lose her, ya just go get another one, then you're fine." Lee grinned. He had no girlfriend, but he did have a car and he drove me to the used car dealer in San Rafael where he'd bought his. Big banners hung over the lot: "Welcome Airmen!" and "We Finance ANYBODY" and "Buy Here, Pay Here." An hour later, I drove a 1959 MGA roadster, British racing green, "once belonged to Sterling Moss," the salesman told me, off the lot.

My two-striper paycheck, even with separate rats, wasn't enough to support a car. "Don't worry, troop," Lee said, "I'll take care of ya." To earn extra money, he worked in his free time for an old Dutchman named Swede — don't ask me why — who painted light airplanes at the nearby local airfield and had painted Lee's Healey. He got me a job with Swede, too. We worked together cleaning old paint off planes. It was grueling work that involved using paint stripper, scrapers and wire brushes. Swede demanded absolutely bare metal, and if he found even one speck of old paint he'd erupt into endless oaths about our incompetence. Yet he paid well, and I worked for him whenever I was off-duty. As the end of summer came around my MG was paid off, I'd installed an AM-FM radio, and even had a little saved.

• • •

"Expand Your Horizons" read the poster for San Rafael Community College on our squadron bulletin board. After all the Air Force training, I was ready to put aside my snobby attitude toward two-year colleges and get back to a real classroom. I enrolled in an evening Creative Writing class that started in September.

San Rafael CC was perched on a knoll with a great view. It was the first night and break time; the sun was slowly sinking into the Pacific as I stood smoking and taking it all in. It felt good to be off the base, out of uniform, here in California, around other students. Two girls about my age walked up to me.

"Got a light?" asked the one dressed all in black. I flicked my Zippo and fired up her cigarette. She was small, really pretty although a bit chubby, with dark, shimmering, soulful eyes and coal-black hair that fell like a waterfall down her back.

"My name is Nate," I said.

"Yeah, we know, "Nathaniel Hawthorne Flowers, like the novelist," she said, blowing smoke, a bored look on her face.

"Yep, that's me," I replied, grinning, "but I don't remember your names."

"I'm Jane, Jane Chandler," said the other girl with a sweet smile. She was a pretty blue-eyed blonde, kind of tall with a sleek, petite, tanned California-girl look. She wore a T-shirt, shorts and sneakers; I figured her for the athletic type. "And this is my best friend, Kathleen O'Donovan."

I took her hand and said, "Pleased to meet you. Do you prefer Kathy? Kate?"

"I prefer *Kathleen*," she replied, blowing another puff of smoke. *Boy, she smokes like an exhaust pipe.* I stuck a fresh Lucky between my lips.

"So, what do you girls write?" I asked.

Jane said she wrote short stories. Kathleen said, "I'm a poet." I immediately fell in love with her strange and mysterious and diffident ways. A breeze caught her long hair. She flipped me an exasperated look and said, "And what do you write? *Gothic* novels?"

"A little of everything," I said, feeling uncomfortable in a way I didn't under-stand. "I'm in the Air Force. San Ramon. But before I got sent here, I was sta-tioned in Biloxi, Mississippi, when Hurricane Betsy ripped the Gulf Coast up pretty bad. I wrote a story about it for the local newspaper and they printed it."

They both stared at me. "You're *published*?" said Jane. "Oh, God, that is *so cool!* You're a published writer!"

Kathleen gave me a wry grimace. I could tell she was impressed even though she was trying hard not to show it.

"So," I said, feeling a need to shift attention from myself, "this is quite a view from up here. What's the building down there with the blue roof?"

"The Marin County Civic Center, *of course*," said Kathleen.

"Designed by Frank Lloyd Wright," Jane said.

"Wow, how about that. I didn't know he did stuff out here. He's from Wis-consin, you know, just north of Illinois. Where I grew up. Illinois, I mean."

"Chicago?" Jane asked.

"Waukegan," I said, "a little north of Chicago." Kathleen had turned toward the Civic Center and was still looking away, smoking. "I went to college in Chi-cago. For a year."

"What college?" Kathleen asked over her shoulder.

"The University of Chicago," I said, and almost said I'd gotten kicked out, then thought better of it.

"Ohhhh," said Jane. Kathleen turned to me and asked for another light.

• • •

Smoke-break conversations became a regular thing for us, even though Jane didn't smoke. I desperately wanted to ask Kathleen for a date, but I thought if I did it in front of Jane she might feel bad, so I connived to think of other ways to get Kathleen alone. One night I suggested we go out for coffee after class. Kathleen said yes, if I promised to give her a ride home in my MG. Jane used her family's car to drive them both to class, but said she had to get up early for work the next day and bowed out. Things couldn't have worked out better.

"What do you think of Mrs. Harrison?" I asked Kathleen. We weren't in a coffee shop but a cocktail lounge, and I had just bought a Manhattan for her and a beer for myself. I hoped she didn't want another one, because I didn't have enough money to pay for it.

52

"Oh, I don't know," Kathleen said. "I mean, she's not a writer or anything. She hasn't published anything. You know, she's just another English teacher on the faculty. She and Mr. Faber take turns teaching Creative Writing. But Harrison *is* the faculty advisor for the literary magazine."

We fell to talking about writers we admired. I was sure I had met the love of my life when we began discussing existentialism and learned she'd read de Unamuno and T.S. Eliot. "My god is Baudelaire," she said. I said I didn't know who that was. "Hmm, I would have thought you'd studied him at Chicago," Kathleen sniffed.

By the time I'd dropped her off at her parents' home in San Rafael, I'd talked Kathleen into going out to the movies that weekend. However, when I arrived to pick her up, her mother said she wasn't home. She stood me up two more times until I asked her if she'd like to go to San Francisco for a poetry reading at City Lights Bookstore.

She wore all black, as usual, a beret, cape and long scarf that trailed in the wind as we drove across the Golden Gate Bridge to North Beach. We walked up and down Broadway past the Condor Club where Carol Doda danced topless, Big Al's, an outdoor café called Finnochio's where interesting people sat at tables drinking espresso coffee, Basin Street West where the sounds of Wes Montgomery's guitar wafted into the street. When we got to City Lights Bookstore the place was packed and we ended up sitting on the floor. The poets were Gary Snyder, Diane DiPrima, and Lawrence Ferlinghetti, the owner of the bookstore who also published poetry books. The last to read was a tall Englishman named Alan Watts, who gave a kind of lecture about Zen Buddhism. He was fascinating. Several times he recited parts of Diane DiPrima's poems on Buddhism, from memory. Afterwards, coffee was served in tiny paper cups and people milled around the poets.

"C'mon," said Kathleen, and we found a quiet corner where we began reading out loud to each other from several books until Ferlinghetti, rather exasperated, asked us if we were going to buy something. We bought a copy of his *Coney Island of the Mind*, then Kathleen led the way next door to Vesuvio, where we drank more cognacs than I could afford and talked about Jack Kerouac, Allen Ginsberg, Henry Miller, Anaïs Nin, Samuel Beckett, and of course Sartre.

The conversation deepened. Our voices fell to whispers and our faces moved closer and closer. I could smell her perfume, the cognac and cigarettes on her breath. Our lips were practically touching and for a moment I thought my chance to spend the night with her had finally come, but without even a farewell she slid off the barstool and walked out the swinging doors. I followed. Kathleen turned left and wobbled down the brick-paved alley in her high heels on black-stockinged legs, her black cape swaying, the black beret perched sideways on her head, the diffused light from streetlamps falling on her and reflecting in puddles of water. Then she disappeared into the darkness of the night, and in so doing became a perfect romantic vision in my mind. Late that night, alone in my bunk, I wrote this poem.

September Love Song
by
Nathaniel Hawthorne Flowers

The second hand of my watch is counting
as the minutes since our parting pass by;
Pale violet light from streetlamps illuminates the fog
and my feet scuff the pavement.

Minutes turned hours mark the passing of my recollections
of our words, our touching:
Dim now, elusive, like the scent of perfume behind your ear
lost to the cold kiss of the wind.

Few cars pass by as I walk away from you,
you, now asleep under covers in your quiet room;
My senses tingle at the thought and my jacket
clings to me, as if to remind…

The silence screams my separateness:
fog clutters, obfuscates my mind;
All I have of you I clutch to me, hold fast,
our bond in the worldly, lonely night.

I hold the passing of time immobile with you;
your image walks with me into the night.
The light will ever be in front of me,
the fog lifted, in your three-syllable good bye.

I couldn't wait to show Kathleen, but she didn't show up for class. I asked Jane about her at the break. She just shrugged and said Kathleen had lost interest and dropped. "That's Kathleen."

After class, I asked Jane if she wanted to go out for coffee, and she gave me a big smile and nodded her head. We had fun talking about writing. Jane worked part-time at the Ouroboros Book Store in San Rafael and told me stories about the weird customers who came in for books on mysticism, alchemy, the Tarot, yoga, spiritual detoxification diets. We laughed a lot. When we walked to our cars, she asked me to come over to her house Saturday afternoon.

The Chandlers lived in a nice house in Corte Madera. Jane's dad, who owned a lumber yard, built it. Her mom commented that Jane and I were both the oldest and we both had two younger brothers. Her father started a charcoal fire and grilled hamburgers for the family. As we sat at the picnic table, it dawned on me that this was the only family I'd ever been around, except for my own. Later, as dusk was falling, Jane and I sat on the big porch swing and talked. I told her stuff I hadn't told anybody before, about my failures and my dad dying and my mother forcing me into the service, even about my little creep brothers breaking into my trunk and taking all my stuff. She just listened, all the while looking earnestly at me. Once in a while she nodded or rubbed my shoulder. Slowly, the bad old feelings began draining out of my system.

• • •

One night on break, Jane asked me if I'd like to go for a hike.

"Sure!" I said, as if hiking mountains were something I'd done every weekend growing up in Illinois, which of course couldn't be farther from the truth. "Where?"

"Oh, Mt. Tam, of course. It's the best!"

We chose a weekday afternoon when neither of us was working. "Ah," I said, "What's Mt. Tam?"

It was a beautiful day in early October when we parked my MG in the Muir Woods parking lot. We began our trek. I let Jane lead the way, ostensibly because she'd done the hike before, but in truth because she was wearing a pair of snug Levi's that showed off her cute tail end.

"Mount Tamalpais is the highest point in Marin County," Jane said over her shoulder. "A very popular place, so it's good we're not hiking on the weekend."

55

When we got to the summit, the view was incredible. Jane pointed out the Farallon Islands to the west and Mt. Whitney and the Sierra Nevada range to the east. We found a nice spot to eat the sandwiches she'd made.

"This is great," I said. "I'm having a great time with you. Thank you." Her face lit up. She was such a pretty girl, her deep blue eyes sparkling, the glow of freckles on her cheeks, the smile that never stopped. Being with her filled my heart with a contented kind of happiness, and I gave her a hug. "You know who you remind me of?" I asked. She shook her head. "Well, it's not a face but a song. 'Lady Jane' by the Stones. You know it, don't you?" Jane nodded. I clasped my hand to my heart and sang, 'I pledge my soul to Lady Jane,' and we both laughed. Jane was becoming my best friend, but deep down – probably foolishly – Kathleen was my unrequited love.

It was still early afternoon when we got back to the car and Jane suggested we drive up Highway 1. We drove the twisty road up and down, down and up, putting the MG through its sports car paces, and stopped at Muir Beach Overlook. "Hey, take a look at this," I said to Jane, who was gazing out to sea. "This sign says soldiers were stationed in this emplacement during World War II, to watch for the enemy." Jane wiggled her eyebrows and turned back to the view.

We got back on the highway and drove through dense forests. "What are these big trees along the road?" I asked. They were tall, smooth, pale-colored things. Huge branches and chunks of shredded bark lay in piles underneath them.

"Eucalyptus. You see them everywhere in the area."

"Well, I will now that I know what they are."

After a long, winding drive we arrived at Stinson Beach, a beautiful stretch of sand behind a quaint village of tiny shops and restaurants. We were both ready to head back inland, but at the service station we learned there was no road going east; we could only return the way we came or continue to Olema, some miles ahead. I looked at Jane. Jane looked at me. We wiggled eyebrows and continued. The road flattened out and we drove alongside a large body of water for quite a while, then passed through a place called Dogtown where we saw several low-flying birds. I pointed them out to Jane, who said, "Those are red-tailed hawks searching for field mice." Then it was up into the eucalyptus forests again. I kept trying to play the radio, but there was no reception here. Eventually we reached Olema, which appeared to be little more than an intersection. A right turn would take us back to San Rafael, while a few yards further a left turn would take us to Point Reyes.

"Oh, Nate, what do you say? Shall we drive out? I haven't been here since I was a kid! There's a lighthouse, and some beautiful beaches. Let's go, OK?"

I agreed and we started off. The scenery kept changing, and when I said I wished I could see more of it, Jane offered to drive. "Can you drive straight stick?" I asked.

"Of course I can drive straight stick!"

We stopped in Inverness and switched seats. Jane was a good driver, and I soon began enjoying the constantly changing environment — forests, watery lowlands, cattle farms where milk cows roamed vast fields, even an oyster farm. Soon we were climbing a steep grade with signs warning against hiking the cliffs, then we were at the end of the road: the lighthouse.

We parked and walked a ways down a rather steep path to the very end of land, where the red-and-white lighthouse stood. Monstrous waves crashed all around us, deafening even though we were hundreds of feet above the raging ocean.

"Wild and crazy beautiful, isn't it?" Jane cried above the sounds of surf. I nodded. I'd never seen scenery like this in my entire life. "Want to see a whale?" I turned to look at her. I opened my mouth but nothing came out. "C'mon!" Jane started running back up the path. At the top we turned toward a small viewing point. She scrambled down the steep face in front of it a few feet and tucked herself into the rocks. I followed and did the same. Even though the sun was warm, the wind blowing off the ocean made it kind of chilly, so I put my arm around Jane and tucked her in close. She nestled right in. We sat like that for a few minutes, then she looked up at me and said, "Want to smoke some pot?"

Pot? Marijuana? Jane, Sweet Jane, was asking me if I wanted to use drugs? I had a sudden recollection: Marijuana was sometimes known by the nickname Mary Jane. I had to smile at the coincidence, which Jane took as a yes. She opened her purse and removed a crude little cigarette. She held it up for me to see, laughed with her eyes, and lit it with a stick match from a box. She took a drag, then passed it to me.

"Take a small toke, first time. Hold it as long as you can."

I took a puff like I would from a cigarette and immediately began coughing. Jane laughed. "I told you, silly. Don't worry, this happens to everyone at least once. Just take small puffs." She took a few tokes to show me how to do it and I tried again, successfully. I held the smoke a long, long time, and as I did I could feel time getting longer and longer and my head growing lighter and lighter. What a strange sensation this was, not unpleasant at all, nothing like what I'd heard. What had I heard? Now that I thought about it, I really couldn't recall anyone describing how it actually felt to smoke pot.

"Jane," I asked between tokes, "what do you call this euphoria that comes from smoking pot?"

"Getting high," she said. "Sometimes you just say 'want to get high' instead of 'want to smoke some pot.'"

I exhaled; hardly any smoke came out. "Yes, it does make you feel high, doesn't it?" I smiled at her and she smiled back, and we sat like that, just smiling and smiling at one another. It was a wonderful smile. Then we turned back to the sea, the Pacific crashing into the rocks below us, making white-crested waves all the way up the coast to our right as far as we could see. It was a beautiful sight, a sound that was full of majesty and power, and it gave me a feeling of how vast was the natural world and what a small aspect of it I was. Jane reached up and took my hand, as if she understood what I was thinking. Her hand was soft in mine but her grip was firm, as if we were bound as one in our adventure. That was a comforting feeling; I wasn't sure I wanted to have a solitary experience while being high. I stretched out my other hand to support myself on the rock ledge, and at once felt connected to nature. Then I thought: we are all in a continuum, people and nature. We aren't separate entities or forces. We came from this water and we return to this earth. We are elemental, no matter how much we think we aren't. Yes, thinking, that's what gets humans in trouble, getting all those big ideas when the very best ideas, and indeed the truth, they're simple and elemental. Not existential. *Elemental*. Right here to know with the basic five senses. It's what we have. It's what we use. And right now I am using my senses at a very high – ha! – level of perception, and it is very good indeed.

Jane tugged at my hand. I realized I had been off and away, and looked at her. She smiled. "You know what I was just thinking?" she asked.

I smiled back and shook my head.

"I was thinking about our names. Mine is Jane. Yours is Nate. Four letters. Two consonants, two vowels. Rearrange Nate and you get Tane. That's almost Jane. Tane and Jane." She giggled. "Isn't that funny?" then she stretched up toward me. Our faces grew close and I bent to touch my cheek to hers, but she stopped me with her lips. A kiss. A short kiss, but nonetheless one that filled my senses and stimulated my – ah, loins. I pulled back a bit and said, "Jane, where are the whales? I haven't seen any."

She laughed and said, "And you won't, silly. They've migrated south to warmer waters. No whales until spring."

Chapter 5

Haight-Ashbury
October, 1966

We cuddled and talked and watched the huge golden red ball of fire slowly extinguish as it fell into the ocean. When it started getting cold we headed back to the MG, put the top up, smoked a few more puffs of pot, and I slowly, stonily, drove the long and winding road to civilization. We turned onto Sir Francis Drake Boulevard at Olema and soon topped a mountain, passing a sign that said Fremont was just ahead. Jane flicked the radio on; we had reception again. It was KMPX, a San Francisco station that played rock and roll. We listened to "Shapes of Things" by the Yardbirds, "Good Vibrations" by the Beach Boys. "Wild Thing" by the Troggs came on and we sang, "You make everything groooovy," which cracked us up. The deejay cut in and said, "My name is Tom Donahue and you're listening to KMPX, 106.9." Then the powerful organ chords of "Light My Fire" by the Doors pulsed out of the speaker. "Oh, cool!" I said. Jane leaned into me. Jim Morrison sang:

> *You know that it would be untrue*
> *You know that I would be a liar*
> *If I was to say to you*
> *Girl we couldn't get much higher...*

We looked at each other. It felt like Tom was playing it just for us. We sang the chorus together:

Come on baby, light my fire
Come on baby, light my fire
Try to set the night on fire

Ray Manzarek let loose with his organ solo and Jane cried, "Oh, Nate, it's the *long* version!" We'd heard there was a long version, but no radio stations had ever played it. I grinned a totally stoned grin at her. She threw her arm around my shoulder and leaned over and gave me a peck on the cheek.

I had to force myself to pull away and pay attention to my driving. Robby Krieger's sitar-like guitar solo began. Cool night air blew in through the MG's plastic side curtains. An aluminum slice of moon topped the trees in the sparkling night sky. We held hands on the gearshift knob. I was one with my car, the night, the music, and Jane, feeling the sweet high from smoking pot for the first time in my life, and in perfect harmony with the universe. It was so cool, how Tom had made those songs all flow into one great cosmic idea. I had a flash recollection of my conversation with Professor Cohen about the tragic sense of life, but a flash later I couldn't remember it. No matter; philosophy couldn't dream up anything as good as this. Jim cried,

Try to set the night on fy-ure.

· · ·

As I spent my days in service to my country, it felt like all I lived for was the time I spent not serving my country. My creative writing course, the high point of my week, ended just before Christmas. "September Love Song" was published in the SRCC literary magazine. I wondered if Kathleen ever read it.

Jane and her mother invited me for Christmas dinner. Jane gave me a silver Cross ballpoint pen with *Nathaniel* inscribed on it, "to inspire your writing," she said. I gave her an ankle bracelet with a peace sign. On New Year's Eve I went with the family to the annual Holiday Tree Burning outside the Presbyterian Church. Afterwards, Jane and I celebrated my birthday smoking a joint and drinking champagne from the bottle as we sat at Vista Point, watching the infinite streaming flow of glowing headlights and blinking red taillights crossing to and fro on the Golden Gate Bridge.

At midnight, fireworks lit the San Francisco skyline. It was 1967. I was 22.

• • •

I was in my bunk reading a new novel, *The Crying of Lot 49*, by Thomas Pynchon, when Lee came in. He often spent his evenings at the Airman's Club drinking beer, shooting pool or watching TV, but tonight he had a funny look on his face. But he wasn't drunk.

I looked up from my book and said, "Lee."

"Nate," he said. "How you doin', man." "What're ya reading?" he said, easing himself into the big purple velour overstuffed chair we'd bought at a second-hand furniture store for seven dollars. I held it up. "Huh. Good?"

"Yeah, I guess so. A little too early to tell."

"You ever read *Stranger in a Strange Land*?" he asked.

I sat up on one elbow. Lee, reading a book? "Yeah, I have. Why? Have you?"

"Naw, not yet. But I'm thinkin' about it. Some other guys I was — we were talking about it."

"Yeah, I read it at Keesler." That made me remember Richard; I wondered where he was now. "It's pretty far out."

"I think I could grok it," Lee said, and barked "Ha!"

Wow, Lee using the word grok? "Ah, sure, man, you could probably *grok* it," I said.

He flung a leg over the arm of the chair and lit a cigarette.

"Yeah, you know, like *dig* it? Get into it? Me and these other troops, you know, we're talking about how, ah, sometimes we feel like strangers in a strange land."

Oh, jeez, has Lee stumbled into existentialism? "Yeah, lots of stuff to think about in that book."

"Yeah. Huxley, too."

"Huxley? As in Aldus Huxley? The guy who wrote *Brave New World*?" I asked.

"No, not that book, the other one, I can't remember..." Lee replied.

"Umm...oh, you mean *Animal Farm*?" I asked.

"No, no, I don't think so," said Lee. "It's about doors, doors of experience or something like that. Jim Morrison named his band The Doors because he read this book."

"Huh. Not remembering this, Lee."

"Nate!" Lee sat up in the chair and looked at me hard. "Jeez! You get high?"

"What?" I said, shocked.

"Man, you're so thick I can't believe it! Nate, I can tell you're a head! I'm trying to tell you, man! Now I'm one too!"

I relaxed, dropped my feet over the edge of my bunk. "Well, cool, man, that's really cool," I said.

"So, let's take a ride," he said, kind of winking.

"Yeah, cool," I said, kind of grinning.

We jumped in his beautiful red Healey and took off, top down, the exhausts roaring as we sped down 101. Lee pulled off at Sausalito, drove through town and parked alongside the water. We lit up the joint he'd brought; it was very strong and we were high in no time. We sat there, the radio on low, looking out across the bay at Alcatraz and the twinkling lights of the Bay Bridge beyond. "There's a lot of troops turning on, Nate," Lee said. "It's not as big of a big secret as you think it is."

We walked back to a waterfront bar called the Trident. Lee said another troop had said some musicians from San Francisco bands liked to hang out here, but the place was pretty much filled with people with long hair and hippie clothes, so who was to know. We downed an expensive beer then drove back to the base, still pretty stoned. Once in our room again, we sat cross-legged on the rug and lit cigarettes, which seemed to help keep the high going. Lee put a record on. "I want you to hear this," he said.

It sounded pretty funky. He liked the blues, the old Negro soul and folk stuff like Muddy Waters and John Lee Hooker and my old friend from Keesler, JimmaReed.

"John Mayall and the Bluesbreakers," Lee replied. "English blues guys." Halfway through, he reached over and moved the needle to a new song. "Listen to this guitar player. His name is Eric Clapton. He's really good. This is called 'Hideaway.'"

We listened. "Yeah, you said it," I replied, "he's *really* good." Lee lifted the needle again and said, "Listen to this! 'Parchman Farm.'" Then moments later, "This is 'It Ain't Right.' Ain't it great?" and he laughed a good old stoned laugh, then changed the record. "Here's another really far out band that Clapton was in before, the Yardbirds."

"Yeah, I like the Yardbirds," I said. I didn't know the names of the individual musicians like Lee. I would have preferred hearing the songs in their entirety, but we were rocking to the music and digging being together. "Y'know," I said, "we should go into The City and catch some music. I heard some really good local bands like the Grateful Dead and the Charlatans and Country Joe and the Fish play at places like the Avalon and the Fillmore for pretty cheap. Sometimes they play for free."

"Yeah, for sure," said Lee, "and we should go to the Haight." Haight-Ashbury was a neighborhood in San Francisco where hippies and beatniks lived. Jane and I had talked about going there.

"Yeah, there's a place on the corner of Haight and Ashbury called The Drugstore that's supposed to be very far out," I said. That's what Jane said; it was *far out*. I wondered if it was off-limits to GIs.

"Don't think so. I know a few other troops who've been down there."

"Huh? I was just thinking that."

"You said it out loud, dude," Lee said.

"Oh. Don't we kind of, you know, stand out? With our short hair and clothes and stuff?"

"They say nobody pays no attention to that," Lee said. "If you're cool, they're cool. This one troop I know, he puts on a leather cowboy hat and his old fatigue jacket, you know, with all the stripes and patches ripped off, and wears a big peace sign on a leather thong around his neck. He's just another hippie to them people. Hey, listen up. This is 'Over, Under, Sideways, Down.' Ultracool tune!"

I closed my eyes and got down with the Eric and the Yardbirds and thought about Haight-Ashbury, just a half-hour drive south. I was glad we'd talked about it. Lee's stories calmed me. I could do it.

• • •

Saturday, 14 January. Lee and I drove my MG into the parking lot at the Polo Grounds in Golden Gate Park. Somebody had stuck a flyer announcing a free hippie gathering on his windshield, a perfect excuse to go to the Haight. Across a huge grassy area we could hear drums and flutes and tambourines. People – *lots* of people – were singing, dancing, dressed in all kinds of colorful clothes. I popped the trunk and we took out our hippie disguises: vests, huarache sandals, a hat for him and a headband and string of beads for me. Sunglasses. To look more hippie-ish, we'd both let our hair grow a long as regs would allow and were growing mustaches.

We walked into the huge crowd and were instantly greeted with smiles, hippie handshakes from the guys, full-body hugs from the chicks, and pot. Lots of pot.

I would no sooner take a toke and pass it on than somebody would hand me another joint or pipe. At first it made me paranoid to be smoking, because for sure a GI could not afford to get caught, but after toking up a few times and getting pretty high, I mellowed out and just accepted what was happening around me. After all, I thought, no way could the cops single us out among these thousands of people, and we weren't causing any trouble. Plus, I hadn't seen a single cop anywhere.

We wandered through the throngs. Many congregated in small groups, sometimes just sitting in a circle or dancing and chanting to music or hugging and kissing. We came across some kids who had taken off most of their clothes and were inviting everybody to hug and kiss. A girl threw her arms around my shoulders and pressed her naked breasts against me. She gave me a really deep, passionate kiss, and I felt myself getting a boner. She pressed her hips tighter to me and whispered, "Far out. Hey, let's find Owsley and trip together." I wasn't sure what she meant. A super-skinny guy wearing a leather loincloth grabbed her and off they went. Lee was standing to one side, watching, a look of chagrin on his face.

Eventually we came upon a small stage where an older guy was sitting lotus-style, speaking softly into a microphone. Many gathered around listening to him. "Hey, man, is that Owsley?" I asked the guy standing next to me.

"Naw, man, that's Leary. Timothy Leary, you dig? That's Owsley, over there." He pointed to a little guy with long dark hair wearing a headband, aviator sunglasses and a cape, standing at the side of the stage. Hippies were lined up in front of him. "He's giving away tabs. Just say, 'Hey Bear, can I have a trip?' and he'll give you one."

I wasn't quite sure what he meant and I didn't want to ask. I looked at Lee, then my attention shifted back to the old guy on the stage. He was talking very slowly, almost chanting, about a psychedelic revolution and that we were its revolutionaries, except we were princes and princesses, stardust, golden children, the beautiful people. He went on and on like that and it all seemed to make sense. "If you take the game of life seriously," he said, raising his voice a bit, "if you take your nervous system seriously, if you take your sense organs seriously, if you take the energy process seriously, you must turn on, tune in, and drop out."

I confess I was mesmerized as he explained turning on was using LSD to get in touch with your senses. Yeah, that sounded interesting. Tuning in was learning to see the world through a psychedelic understanding. I didn't quite get this, but I hadn't used LSD yet. Dropping out was rejecting life in the world of squares and digging a new way of life, which everyone was free to make up for themselves. That sounded incredibly exciting, like something I wanted to do, but it would have to wait: I still had 745 days to go in the military.

Leary ended his speech by putting his hands together and chanting "Om," and everyone joined in. "Om" completely filled the air until I couldn't hear anything else. I opened my mouth and "Ommmmmm" floated out. It felt wonderful to chant together. I smiled at the girl beside me, and she smiled back and handed me a joint. I took a big hit and passed it back. We said "Om" together.

Leary was speaking again. He introduced a woman named Lenore Kandel as "my favorite poet in the galaxy." She spoke very softly, telling us she'd written four poems that were published in a little book, *The Love Book*, which she held up. "I'm going to read two poems," she said. "The first is 'To Fuck With Love, Phase III.'" Then she began reading this incredibly erotic poem:

to fuck with love
to love with all the heat and wild of fuck...

It was beautiful, truly, and I heard myself say, "Wow, that's so beautiful." Lenore's voice rose and fell intensely as she read. I glanced at Lee, but he was rather stoically — stonily? — staring at Lenore. I looked at the girl and she returned my gaze and held it, so we kissed just as Lenore raised her voice to say "We touched!" The girl took my fingers and entwined them in hers. We stood like that listening to the poem. I kind of wished Kathleen was here with me. Or Jane. The poem ended, gently and tenderly:

At night...sometimes...I see our bodies glow....

The crowd was totally silent. I whispered, "Wow, that's so beautiful," again, and the girl squeezed my hand and we gazed into each other's eyes for a long, stoned time. She was kind of pretty, nice brown eyes, long light brown hair, large complicated silver earrings dangling from her ears, chains beads and necklaces falling between plump breasts which were having trouble staying inside a tiny leather vest held together with two big silver buttons. Her paisley granny skirt fell all the way to the ground. She leaned up close to my ear and, pointing at Owsley, said, "Wanna go drop some acid together?" I froze up. I'd never even thought about LSD, much less consuming it, and now I'd had two invitations in a single afternoon. The idea still freaked me out. It felt like I'd been asked me to jump off the lighthouse cliff at Point Reyes or something. I frowned a little, nodding toward Lee, and shook my head; she understood.

I looked back at the stage to see Lenore introducing another poet, Gary Snyder. "Lee," I said, "Kathleen and I heard Gary Snyder read. That time when we went to North Beach." He began reading. I looked the other way. The girl was gone. I looked back at Lee. He gave me a cockeyed look and said, "How do you do it, man?"

"How do I do what?"

"The girls, man. Kathleen. Jane. Now these hippie chicks. How come you always get the girls?"

• • •

The afternoon sun fell warmly upon the Polo Fields and I fell into a dream as Lee and I found ourselves packed shoulder to shoulder with hippies to hear a band called Jefferson Airplane. I had never heard music like theirs before: the guitars blending and then spinning off from each other into folk-rock-jazz-like riffs as the intricate harmonies, driven by the incredible voice of the chick lead singer, lit me with fiery thrills. And the wild imagistic poetry in the lyrics! Like "your mind's been cheated, it's all you ever needed," and "you're my plastic fantastic lover" and "do away with people laughing at my hair, do away with people frowning on my precious prayers" then I heard somebody say "psychedelic rock" and realized that's what it was, that their music was touching me deep in my stoned place inside. I was completely lost in the music.

The chick singer was so beautiful, so cool, her brown hair in bangs and falling down her shoulders. I completely fell in love with her. She introduced the last song, "How Do You Feel," and said they would have a new album out next month called "Surrealistic Pillow." It was a gentle, loving song with a sweet chorus repeating "How do you feel, how do you feel," over and over for who knows how long and as the girl sang I kept falling in love with her over and over. The audience joined in and chanted along, swaying, singing, everybody getting higher and higher until the Jefferson Airplane gently touched down and left the stage.

It dawned on me that the Airplane was singing about their tripping. That made me want to go deeper into the music, deeper into myself, maybe even drop acid to see what this music felt like when I was on a trip, like them. As the afternoon concert continued, more bands played but it was Country Joe and the Fish that told mind-blowing tripping stories with their music, driving me into this wild enchanted world all the more.

Lee and I crashed in our sleeping bags beside my car. The next morning the radio told us we'd been part of the first Human Be-In, maybe twenty or thirty thousand of us. It was big news, but the important thing for Lee and me was our initiation into the Haight. I wasn't scared any more. I was on fire for new experiences and people and music and, and, just all the experiences I could possibly have.

We started going down whenever we could until the Haight felt like it was our neighborhood. We'd hang around The Drugstore or outside Amoeba Music or the Jeffrey-Haight Café. We bought papers and roach clips and beads and buttons that said "Smile" and "Flower Power" and "Peace" at head shops. Sometimes we'd just walk the streets, taking in the scenes like watching a movie. Hippies were everywhere, talking, playing music, panhandling, selling copies of the local underground newspapers. And getting high. We'd walk up to them, smile, and they'd pass the joint. We were family, and that was an incredible feeling. It was what I'd expected in the military but never found. I mean, here we were, troops, brothers in arms as they said, and I thought that meant we were all the same but we weren't. Now here I was in the Haight with a bunch of strangers who would say "I love you, man," or give me spontaneous smiles and hugs and kisses and a toke. Where did I belong? Believe me, I knew.

What made me really happy was when Jane could come with me. She liked to wear her paisley-patched Levi's, a tie-dye T-shirt or a peasant blouse, hippie sandals, and an Indian princess beaded headband with flowers or feathers stuck in it. We'd walk through the crowds, stopping to talk to people or listen to a street band, holding hands, loving being together and loving being with everyone around us. Sometimes hippies hanging out windows invited us up for a smoke, even though they'd never seen us before in their whole lives. We bought a copy of "The Doors" album at Amoeba. We ate ice cream cones at The Drugstore. We admired the wildly artistic psychedelic clothing in Mnasidika. We watched mimes performing on the street. We got high and recited made-up poems. We laughed. We had fun. Lee was my best buddy, and Jane was my best girl friend.

On a May Sunday night, Jane and I went to hear the Grateful Dead at the Fillmore Auditorium, our first time at one of the big music halls. Lee and I had heard the Dead, as they were called, at the Human Be-In. Being into the blues thing, he really liked them a lot and I wished he could have come, but he was on shift. We got our hands stamped and walked inside. The air was clouded with the smell of marijuana.

The show started with some beautiful hippie chicks putting on a psychedelic fashion show. Tables surrounded the ballroom floor, people selling homemade jewelry, pipes and roach clips, scarves, headbands, sandals, buttons and patches. We had our Tarot cards read. Once the Dead started playing, everybody just sort of formed one big dance group, so we joined in. It felt good to be stoned and to groove to the music, every body and note and smile and touch flowing together in long sensuous coils and continuums that, like the songs, never seemed to end.

After the concert we walked outside and just stood around, breathing the fresh night air and kind of coming down. A guy walked up to us and stuck his hand at me in the hippie handshake. "Man, What a concert! The Dead are too far out, huh?"

I looked him and nodded. He was tall, kind of stocky, had on a tie-dyed T shirt, bell-bottom jeans, a Beatles hat and purple granny glasses shaped like hearts.

"Hey, man, you going back to the base tonight?" he asked.

"Huh? Base? Huh?" I replied.

"C'mon, man. I'm a GI too. Name's Tony Rizzo. A2C. SAC air transport scheduling. Hitched a ride down here tonight, but I don't want to risk hitching back. You know...."

"Aw, sorry, man, I didn't know...." I said. Hitchhiking was against Air Force regs, and the Air Police always seemed to know if you had, probably because you had to hike half a mile down the base access road from the highway.

"No, man, it's cool. I came on too fast, too strong. But I really could use a ride."

"Well," I said, glancing at Jane, "I'd like to help you out, but we're in a two-seater."

Without a pause, Jane said, "I can sit on his lap. You have to drop me off first anyway."

"You cool with that, man? Your old lady sitting on another guy's knee?" Tony asked, a big grin on his face.

"Yeah, sure, if Jane's cool with it, then I'm cool with it." After all, Jane wasn't my old lady. And I'd just learned a new hippie term.

"Far out. But listen, before we go back, how'd you like to meet The Dead?"

Jane's face lit up. "You're kidding."

"Aw, that would be too much, man," I said. "How we gonna do that?"

"It's easy. I know a hippie, name is Errol. Saw him at the concert. He knows the band, told me where they live. It's 710 Ashbury. Says we just knock and tell 'em Errol sent us. Get high with the Dead? Probably get to watch them jammin'!"

I looked at Jane. She was silently jumping up and down on the sidewalk. "Yeah, that would be *very* cool," I said. "It's worth a shot, I guess."

We parked on Haight and walked a few blocks to Ashbury. We turned up the hill and there was the house with big "710" numbers beside the door. The Dead's music poured out the windows and into the street. We knocked the big brass lion's head door knocker. A guy opened the door wide enough for us to see one of his eyes. Tony told him that Errol sent us. He said "Wait," and closed the door. When he came back he shook his head. "Too many of you," he whispered.

Tony said, "Three? Three's too many? Errol invited us...."

"Sorry. Don't know no Errol, dude," the guy said and closed the door.

The Dead's music kept riffing through my head as we left The City. I glanced over at Jane, her hair flying in the wind, all smiles. "Great concert tonight," I yelled.

"Totally great *everything* tonight," Jane replied, balanced sideways on Tony's knees and holding the top of the windshield.

"No lie," Tony cried and laughed a wild, hysterically funny Ha! Ha! Ha! Ha! Ha!.

Jane looked down at Tony. "You're pretty cool."

"Well, you both are *damned* cool!" Tony replied.

We cruised over the beautiful red GGB, up through the tunnel and down the fast steep mountain highway into Sausalito and on to Corte Madera, where we dropped Jane off at her house, then reluctantly drove on to our cruel fate, the military.

• • •

I worked in a locked-down classified area in the Base Operations building, opposite the Air Traffic Control center. Two of us were always on duty, one doing intercept, one listening and translating, with a NCOIC present. One was SSgt. Trank, a young guy from Oklahoma who'd just re-enlisted and gotten his fourth stripe. Married, with a toddler kid, clearly going to be a lifer. The other was Mo, my training NCO, a lifer who was getting short for retirement. When I came to work on Monday, 30 January, he was sitting at the desk with his usual cup of black coffee. He stuck out his hand and said, "Congratulations, Flowers," somewhat wryly. "I filed your '05 competency cert this morning," he continued. "You should be an E-4 by 1 March."

"Hey, great, Sarge," I said, really happy about this. It meant that I'd success-fully completed my training and would be promoted to Airman First Class, earn-ing a third stripe and a pay raise. "Thanks!"

• • •

The first of March came and went without my new orders. All my fellow troops were celebrating their promotions, but not me. I asked Mo, but he knew nothing and told me I should ask our First Sergeant, Master Sergeant Masters. All he could tell me was my paperwork had gone in, approved by him, our Mainte-nance Officer, First Lieutenant Cretin, and the unit commander, Major Macadam. He even showed me a carbon copy of the completed and signed form.

"Well, what should I do?" I asked MSgt. Masters.

"Apparently, for some reason, you didn't get approved. Maybe you missed the PECD. Or maybe there was a discrepancy on your DVR so the AFPC didn't grant the EPR. Did Mo include your PFE and SKT? No promotion without them, Flowers. Or maybe there was a quota issue with your AFSC. You'll just have to have Mo resubmit your paperwork again and wait until the next promo-tion cycle."

"Which is...."

"That would be...1 October."

Six months! While every last one of every last one of the troops in my shop got a new stripe and a pay raise. Except me. I was still an Airman Second Class and poor as a church mouse. This was so unfair!

"Can't you find out what happened to my paperwork?" I asked. MSgt. Masters took pity on me and told me he'd look into it.

"Seems your paperwork got lost, Flowers," he told me the next day. Some air-man clerk stuck it in the wrong basket on his desk and it wasn't submitted.

"Can't they just resubmit it, Sarge? I mean, it's only been a month —"

He shook his head. "Nope, your DVR would need to be done all over again and submitted to the SRB, but that's no guarantee it would be approved. Might even upset the Board. Better just to wait, Flowers."

I felt dread and disappointment, just like when I flunked out of college. I asked to see Lt. Cretin, who said, "Well, Flowers, that's just life in this man's Air

Force now, isn't it? Perhaps you could get your T.S. card punched by the chaplain?" I saluted, turned on my heel and left in disgust.

I asked MSgt. Masters if I could talk to the commander and he arranged it. Major Macadam mouthed Lt. Cretin's words about taking it like a man and how others endured greater disappointments than mine. His platitudes went in one ear and out the other. Here was my CO, my leader, who was supposed to take care of me. Now he let me down, too, and I was on my own again, just like when my dad died.

Other troops taunted me. I can't remember how many times I heard someone say I needed to see the chaplain to get my Tough Shit card punched. I told Lee, thinking he might have some insight. He said, "Figures. Nobody really cares what happens to us, dude. We're just little cogs in the military machine, that's all."

"Sure, I know, but still it's not right, man."

"Right? Wrong? You're talking about church, not the military. Hey, why don't you write your Congressman? Ha, ha." At first I shrugged off his comment. It was something every troop said when something went wrong, but nobody ever did it. But the more I thought about it, I figured what did I have to lose? That night, I sat in front of the typewriter in our shop and began to write. I knew I'd have to make this good — *really* good.

> A2C Nathaniel H. Flowers
> AF17707615
> Air Force Communications Service
> Box 387
> San Ramon Air Force Base, California
> 94949
> March 16, 1967

The Honorable Congressman E. J. Deschutes
118 Schotts Court
Washington, D.C. 20002

Dear Congressman Deschutes, Sir,

I was born and raised in Waukegan, which I believe is also your home town in Illinois. I am presently an Airman Second Class in the United States Air Force, and am having a problem which I hope you can help me with. Sir,

I have completed all the training and testing required for my promotion to Airman First Class, but am being denied my promotion due to a clerical error....

...So those are the facts, sir. Because of a person or persons not performing a routine clerical job that is what they are supposed to do every day, and because Western Command denied my request to reconsider my delayed paperwork, I must wait another six months before I am eligible for promotion. I feel I have completed my part of the bargain and have done everything that was expected of me. I am sure you understand the importance of a promotion and pay raise to a young man in his country's service. It recognizes his hard work and the reward of advancement in his career field. Yet I am being denied all of this because my paperwork was put in the wrong basket on somebody's desk. If you could help me rectify this injustice, Congressman Deschutes, I would be most indebted to you. Thank you for taking the time to hear my plea for justice.

Sincerely,

Nathaniel Hawthorne Flowers

• • •

A few days later, Tony and Lee and I headed down to the Haight, me curled up in the jump seat of Lee's Healey, to pick up the Grateful Dead's first album at Amoeba. "Listen to Garcia's guitar opening," said Tony as we listened to "Viola Lee Blues" in his dorm room that night.

"Wow, just like they played at the Fillmore!" I said.

"This is *so psychedelic!*" said Tony. "I love that opening guitar riff! Boinnnng!"

"Psychedelic blues, man, far out," said Lee.

"So," Tony said, pulling out a joint, "Let's light one up and see if we can get kinda psychedelic, too."

• • •

The next day, Mo came banging into the radio ops center, his eyes wild. "CO wants to see you, Flowers. NOW!"

I ran up the Base Ops steps to his office and reported. Major Macadam sat very still behind his desk, holding a piece of paper. He looked up, returned my salute, then said, "Airman Flowers…what…HAVE…YOU…DONE?" He shoved the letter at me. It had the Air Force seal and DEPARTMENT OF THE AIR FORCE in blue at the top. I reached out to read it, but the Major snatched it back. I opened my mouth, but he said, "Shut up, Flowers. SHUT UP! Christ, what have you done to my career? DISMISSED! GET OUT OF HERE!"

I snapped off a salute and retreated. I was scared as hell. For days afterwards, Lt. Cretin ignored me. MSgt Masters ignored me. Mo gave me shit-eating grins. Then on 25 April he handed me an envelope. I ripped it open. Inside were my orders for promotion to Airman First Class, effective 1 May 1967.

> A2C Nathaniel H. Flowers
> AF17707615
> Air Force Communications Service
> Box 387
> San Ramon Air Force Base, California
> 94949
> 26 April 1967

Dear Congressman Deschutes:

Please allow me to send you a heartfelt thanks for your excellent assistance in obtaining my reconsideration for promotion. Shortly after I wrote you, my Commanding Officer shared a letter from a Colonel at the Pentagon who had received your letter inquiring into my situation. My CO was quite emphatic about having the issue resolved, and I was granted my promotion….

…Thank you again so much, sir, for your efforts on my behalf. I now have recovered my faith in the military institution of the United States Air Force and the Democratic Way of Life that we have come to know and hold dear as United States of America citizens. I once again trust that the my superiors can be counted on to do the right thing, and that truly, one voice can be heard above the crowd.

Also, please rest assured I will vote for you in the next election.

> Sincerely yours,
> Nathaniel H. Flowers, A1C (almost)

Chapter 6

Memphis Blues Again
July, 1967

"You get it on with Lucy yet?" Tony asked, his voice almost a whisper. We were at Monterey Pop, camped out on the football field in our sleeping bags with hundreds of other kids. Lee was sound asleep in his bag, snoring to beat the band. It was Saturday night – Sunday morning, really. We'd heard so much great music: Moby Grape, the Byrds, Quicksilver, Big Brother, Canned Heat, Electric Flag, Steve Miller, the Airplane. Country Joe's refrain, "Whoopee! We're all going to die!" from his anti-Vietnam song, "I-Feel-Like-I'm-Fixin'-To-Die Rag," played on in my head. Now, in the deep of night, the wee small hours, musicians from several bands were jamming, soft and quiet, giving us a free nightlong concert.

"You know, Lucy? In the sky with diamonds? Or you a virgin?" Tony grinned his big old goofy grin, barely visible in the darkness.

I tucked my hands behind my head and gazed at the Milky Way above us. "Lucy in the Sky with Diamonds." Third song, side A of the Beatles' *Sgt. Pepper's Lonely Hearts Club Band*. Of course I knew what Tony meant. He and I went to the Haight to buy the record at Amoeba the day it came out. I was so excited I could hardly stand it. As we walked down Haight Street, a guy called out from a second-floor window. "Hey, man! Izzat Sgt. Pepper's under your arm there? C'mon up!" We joined a bunch of hippies around a spool table, passed the pipe, put the record on and had our minds totally blown. Totally.

"So, you haven't dropped acid yet."

I blinked, rolled my head back and forth a little.

"Hey, it's cool, really, not putting ya down," Tony said. "You want to, right? Lots of folk on acid here, I'll betcha. You and me, we're gonna do it together. I am gonna be your psychedelic guide and guru. Make sure your first acid trip is a good one. When you're ready."

Since the night I drove Tony back to the base, we'd really hit it off. We started hanging out together, a lot. He and Lee didn't really take to each other, but Jane liked him and he was probably the most interesting person I'd ever met, next to my dad. His brown eyes danced with mischief and he was constantly skipping weekly haircuts and getting ordered to the barber shop. He'd gone to UC Berkeley for two years but dropped out: "When Mario Savio said we had to put our bodies on the gears, that was all I needed to hear. I was all done with Establishment indoctrination. Done. Finis. Out. Of. There." He'd read *The Crying of Lot 49* and soon we were saying, "You got the potsage?" as a secret code for getting high. Tony also knew all the lyrics to all the music and had an uncanny knack for dropping the needle on a song that reflected what we were doing or talking about.

And now here we were a few weeks after Monterey Pop, motoring up Highway 37 in my MG toward Napa, where Tony's family had their vineyards, on a two-day pass to celebrate Independence Day by dropping acid. If there was anybody I wanted to do my first acid trip with, it was Tony.

The top was down, the radio was up and the country air blew through our hair as we passed a joint back and forth. To our right was the north side of San Pablo Bay; to the left were old farmlands strewn with dilapidated buildings and rusting farm equipment. We drove north into the rolling hills and vineyards. Just before Napa, we turned onto Old Sonoma Road. Huge ancient eucalyptus trees stood on either side; I recognized their dead fronds lying all over the place. "Here! Turn left," said Tony. I never would have seen the totally nondescript dirt road between two old wooden fence posts, barbed wire dangling. We drove half a mile or so, vineyards on either side. Up ahead I saw a long, low, pale yellow adobe house with a red tile roof and wide windows sunk deep in the walls. Barns and outbuildings clustered around the house.

"Whoa up, man," Tony said, "I'll be right back." He hopped out and ran over to a heavy wooden door and pushed his way in. He was back in no time, jumped over the door into the bucket seat, and said, "Keep going straight."

"That's your house? Everything OK? With your parents?" I asked.

"Yeah, everything's cool," he said. "They aren't even home. They're in Argentina. I just let Maria, the housekeeper, know that I'd be up at my place. That's where we're headed. Ha! Headed, get it?"

I laughed back. "I didn't know you had your *own* place." I hadn't even thought about that; what were we going to do, drop acid in his bedroom while his family watched TV? Geez, sometimes I was so dense.

The road wound through the vineyards and eventually up the side of a low hill. The bottom of the MG scraped a rock and I slowed down. "More of a Jeep road," Tony said, laughing. I remembered the last time I'd scraped bottom. Lee was right; I no longer missed my Fury.

Then we were there. The road ended in front of an enormous round wooden drum that stood on a frame of thick wooden beams about twelve feet off the ground. A wooden staircase with handrails made of gnarled tree branches led to a door cut in the side. "Wow, man, what is this?" I asked.

"A wine vat. Oak, fifteen feet in diameter, twenty feet tall, walls two inches thick."

Tony led the way and unlocked the massive padlock, then I found myself in a most incredible space. There were two leather easy chairs with footstools, a rug covered with Indian symbols on the floor. Lamps and candles and Mexican pottery stood on small spool tables. A small kitchen and bathroom off to one side. Half a dozen porthole windows cut into the dark-stained walls poured diffused sunlight inside. A circular staircase curled up to a hole through to the second floor, probably Tony's bedroom.

"Wow, this place is far out," I said.

"All mine, I made it all," he replied, a huge smile on his face. "I got the vat from a winery we sell grapes to. They were ready to turn it into firewood. Dad's farmhands helped me move it and set it. I scraped a lot of the charcoal and grape mash off the inside, but you can still smell it. Funky, but it's all mine!"

"You're what one of my profs at Chicago would call a Renaissance man," I said.

"I kinda vaguely remember that from UCB," Tony said, "but refresh my mind." He lit a joint, took a hit and passed it to me.

"It just means you have many talents. And you're smart as hell," I tried to say while holding the smoke in. "Leonardo da Vinci was a Renaissance man."

"Yeah," Tony said, letting his breath out, "that's me, Leonardo da freakin' Vinci!"

We both started laughing again, standing there passing the joint back and forth. Tony and I laughed a lot, like Jane and I laughed a lot. It was mid-afternoon and the sun was starting to sink, so Tony lit two huge three-foot high candles in wrought iron stands and some incense in a little Buddha statue. "You thirsty?" he asked.

"Yeah. Got a beer?"

"Naw, let's not drink alcohol today," he said and got me a Coke instead. We sat on the rug at a spool table. "I poured a thick resin on the top," Tony said. There were Mexican coins, pieces of silver jewelry, scraps of paper with writing embedded in it. One read, "to be or not to be..." and another "the road less traveled."

"Very cool, Renaissance man," I said.

Tony picked up a small wooden box from a table, opened it, and handed me a little piece of purple cardboard. "Owsley's Monterey Purple," chortled Tony. "Made just for Monterey Pop. I scored two tabs when we were there, just for this day!" We put the tabs on our tongues and let them dissolve. Tony pulled *Surrealistic Pillow* out and played the last cut on side two, "White Rabbit":

> *One pill makes you larger*
> *And one pill makes you small...*

He looked at me and grinned. "You know The White Rabbit's another name Owsley goes by, right?" As the tune wound down, he and I howled together:

> *Remember what the dormouse said*
> *Feed your head, feed your head, feed your head!*

Tony got up and slipped *Rubber Soul* out of its cardboard sleeve.

"Good choice. Everybody loves this album."

"Sets a good mood for tripping," he said. "Mellow. Calm. Peaceful. You want to be really laid back, especially at the start. You learn how to do it from this trip, then afterwards you can always have good trips."

The Beatles played "Norwegian Wood." It sounded good; it felt like good wood, that Norwegian wood, like the wine vat wood that surrounded us. It was also good that we were in a round room. It felt like it could be the room John was singing about, "Isn't it good, Norwegian wood." It ended; Tony moved the needle and I fell deep into "The Word," the word is love, the word is love, the word is love. "Michelle" followed. I rocked gently as I sat in the lotus position on the rug, the sweet sounds pouring in and out and over and through me. Yes, the mood was perfect as I felt the acid begin to fill my cells.

Tony played "In My Life." "This..." I paused, trying to get the thought right, "this is what I think about a lot." Tony looked up. "But I don't have those kinds of friends," I continued. "I mean, that's what I want, to have friends like that, that I remember like that, but I don't." Tony nodded.

I kept blabbing: "I didn't have close friends in high school. Not even a girl-friend. Just my family. Well, just my dad, really, but you know he died. And I studied all the time. I almost had a girl in college, but I blew that. Blew it with my roommate, too. We could have been friends. Well, I don't know; maybe not, I guess. I mean, college was just too...."

"High school was a masquerade," Tony interrupted. "Nobody was real. Strawberry Fields! All posing. College, at least at Berkeley, was about finding a cause to believe in. Or to rebel against!" He laughed.

"No, man, not at Chicago. At Chicago it was about *style*. Your clothes, your car if you had one, the frat you pledged, where you bought your Ivy League clothes. That was how other people knew who you were."

"Sheesh," said Tony, "Forgot you're from the Midwest. But you're not like that."

"I don't know what I'm like," I said. "'No one I think is in my tree.' Maybe that's why I didn't feel like I fit in at Chicago. So I thought I'd find a way to, you know, identify in the Air Force...."

"Oh, you can do that all right. Wear tailored fatigues. Get your hair cut every week. That's what lets them know you want to be a lifer."

"Yeah, but I *like* wearing tailored fatigues!" I said.

That made us both start laughing our heads off. Tony skipped to "Run for Your Life" and for some reason I got up and started prancing around, waving my arms and singing my own lyrics: "Run for your lifers, man, hide your head in the sand, man, rather see you dead than be a lifer, man," over and over. Tony turned up the volume and clapped to the rhythm. It felt weird to be singing made-up lyrics. It felt strange to be moving, like everything was in very slow motion, but at the same time I knew I was dancing in time to the music. I wondered how I knew that. I thought about it, and the more I thought about it, I thought things were actually going faster, not slower. I wondered how I knew *that*.

Tony changed the record. The needle found its way into the strange sounds of the sitar winding through cloud-filled horizons and the marching fierce staccato drumbeats that wild Indians sang to within the twisting entangling keyboard avenues of "Tomorrow Never Knows" and as John sang his words turned to electric colors that came from a place just at the edge of the sky sweeping in and out like contrails of sound. I saw the music in my mind's eye played to the whooping and screeching vocals John sang pouring like water into the deep, light-blue universe and listening to the color of my dreams playing the game of existence to the end of the beginning, yes, and I was dancing and swirling and singing "of the beginning" over and over with John, and each time he sang the words they pulsed like bright new comets flashing through the universe I saw inside my head. Stars blinked like snowflakes of different sizes, shapes, colors, pulsing in and out of the universal multicolored flow.

I realized the acid had truly kicked in, ever so gently. It felt so absolutely cool to know that John had dropped acid too, that his song was teaching me what he had learned. I was sharing the same consciousness as him and the other Beatles. "Tomorrow Never Knows" was totally hammering my consciousness with perceptions I knew I was supposed to understand but were so new and kept coming so fast I couldn't grok them. I wanted to slow the song down, make the ideas, the concepts, more compact so I could understand them, but they were swept up in such a powerful flow of stars and light from comet tails and the Milky Way energy flow all pouring out of the cosmos into my head. My head, my head, what was happening inside my head? Now it seemed like it was all cosmic gibberish sensory information pouring out – or was it pouring in? – I couldn't tell, I felt connected to a cosmic interstellar TV channel broadcasting in sight, sound, tone, feeling, physical pulsations. My teeth chattered as if I were cold, except I wasn't. I became aware of my breathing; each breath I took sounded like I was breathing through a scuba mouthpiece, and when I breathed out it sounded like the whoosh of a jet airplane exhaust. Too loud, too loud. I shifted my perceptions, somehow, and the sound of my breathing receded; now I could hear my heartbeat thumping in my chest like a pile driver, then moving up into my head so that my temples pulsed with a funny squishing echo.

"Tony," I said, "I can feel my blood flowing. I'm playing a pinball machine. I *am* a pinball machine. My thoughts are getting glued to chord changes. I can't find the rhythm of the music anymore."

Tony looked up and smiled. "Nate. You're not in control any more," he said, "which makes it very important for you to take control. You know when George sings, 'Life goes on within you and without you'? The acid's coming on, you're sensitized to the minutest sensations. But you can move your consciousness in any direction you want, man. You've never been able to do this before in your whole life, but now you can. You're master of your five senses. Sixth sense, too. You decide which senses to turn on, which to turn off. Your choice, man. Focus. Point. Select. Go where you want to go, explore. It's all in your mind."

I went. I made myself really thin by sucking in my belly and turning my head sideways, then slipped through the crack my mind made in the wall that my mind had made into another mindspace. All the sounds inside my body went away. "I am very stoned," I said.

"You'll get more stoned," Tony said. "We've only just taken off. Off we go, man, into the wild blue yonder!" he cried.

I hadn't thought about tripping in terms of time. "How long?" I asked.

"Four hours, maybe six. Does it matter?"

No. I wasn't afraid to be tripping that long. I did as Tony advised — I took "control" of my trip, although I could hardly think of it as control. I felt like a train barreling down a wildly warped track, and even though I had no idea where I was going or how I'd stay on the track, I could choose the speed, the scenery, the things I wanted to concentrate on. I looked out a window and saw the sunlight catching something that refracted like in a prism. That sent me on an incredibly interesting trip up the beam and into the cosmos. I saw it but I also *was* it: my fundamental essence, a speck of intelligent life able to move with the speed of light anywhere in space. I was like the fastest jet airplane in the world, flying through the universe. It should have been scary, but it was too amazing. At first I just flew, like a leaf on the wind, but after a while I figured out that I could guide myself. I zipped around in deep space for a long, long time, I guess, whatever time was. When I came out of it into my present existence in Tony's wine vat, I felt like I was in charge of my trip.

Tony was looking at me. "Been to a good place?" he asked.

"I think I just experienced my eternal spirit," I answered, "and what happens to me after death. That there is no death. I exist forever as a tiny blue blip in space."

"Yeah," said Tony, "Cool, huh? I've done that one too."

I raised my eyebrows.

"The Great Truth? We're just energy. LSD opens the doors of perception. Psychedelics help you understand things…."

"Did you say doors? Of perception? Lee said Jim Morrison named the Doors after- "

"Huxley's book, *The Doors of Perception*? The book he wrote about dropping mescaline for the first time."

Ah, so Aldous Huxley tripped on mescaline? Wasn't that something similar to acid?

Tony stepped to his bookcase and selected a book. "The poet William Blake wrote,

> If the doors of perception were cleansed every thing would appear to man as it is, infinite.

> For man has closed himself up, till he sees all things thro' narrow chinks of his cavern.

It was like what I just did, turning sideways! Did Blake get high? I wondered. Then Plato flashed into my mind. "Tony, that's what Plato said, too. The cave allegory? You know?"

"Yeahhhh," Tony said. He was going deep, too. "Everything is definitely connected...."

Everything Tony said seemed to have multiple meanings. I felt like we were leaping from one great insight to another, like skipping from rock to rock across a river. Each rock was an idea that turned into a planet; the stream was the Milky Way. The ideas, planets, poured by me too fast, melding into the galactic river. We *were* all connected. Everything *was* connected. Wasn't it?

I flashed on how pot made me feel closer to others I was getting stoned with, and how we always seemed to share the music. Now I was flashing with Tony, but at a much deeper level than just the music. At least I thought I was. Somehow, I felt I was moving deeper into initiation, but at the same time I felt I was being denied access to deeper levels of the trip because I didn't yet understand what was going on. If that were the case, then what else was going on that I couldn't perceive? I felt like Tony and I were having a simultaneous experience. Was he guiding me, or was he challenging me and denying access because I wasn't going deep enough? Maybe both. Should I ask him? Part of me said, If you have to ask then you're not there. Another part said, Your psychedelic guide *wants* you to ask so that he can part the curtains and admit you to the next deeper level. I felt like either way would betray that I wasn't in control. Or that I was in control because I knew I wasn't. Yet being able to understand the whole control thing seemed to say I *was* in control. So why was it so hard to ask Tony what was going on? I just couldn't do it.

Meanwhile, I was plummeting deeper and deeper into the acid trip. I was truly, deeply, utterly tripping and it was incredible. I heard Tony stir and opened my eyes. A large candle's flame flickered and danced slowly in the deepening twilight. I reached out toward the flame and felt my arm growing toward it. It felt like my arm could stretch infinitely. My thumb and fingertip touched the flame, although I felt no heat. Then Tony laughed lightly and my arm was completely normal again, sticking into the air. I twisted my wrist, extended my fingers and watched them ripple with goldenorangered colors; I poked with my index finger and electricblue shot into the air. I watched as the hairs on the back of my hand began waving and dancing, all the way up my arm to my biceps, which also pulsed in multiple colors as I flexed. The sleeve of my T-shirt moved with my arm, turned into black bats flying in the wind.

I watched all this, aware that it was the acid. It was weird, fun to watch. I actually began wishing things would get more weird, more intense, more exaggerated, and that's exactly what began happening. I closed my eyes and started seeing bizarre movies playing on the insides of my eyelids: a pack of hundreds of green bears running across an Arctic glacier, three cowboys on horseback wearing chaps and kerchiefs and big cowboy hats crossing a deep river, a naked old couple having grotesque sex in time to sped-up Mozart, a rain forest where plants grew faster than the eye could see, only to be eaten by enormous schools of flying shark, Cossacks prancing to the banging of kettle drums and cymbals. I wondered if these scenes were coming from memory or imagination, but I immediately knew the answer: a memory was like a tape recording of a real experience, but these films were totally new and unfamiliar. Not even imagination. More like dreams. Acid-weird dreams.

I closed my eyes. Seven red monkeys danced in a circle around a purple tree with yellow leaves and as they danced they made the leaves move and turn into propellers that spun into the green sky making a vortex that drew me up up up while the monkeys, now blue, chattered with glee, then I was looking down as the earth receded extremely fast. I passed through red and gold and pink clouds; I extended my arms and began to fly toward a group of people hovering over a snow-capped mountain, Mount Whitney or maybe Everest, while the monkeys, now pink, were throwing orange peels toward its peak, the peels turning into flaming spears that sizzled in the snow as they struck. Someone handed me a spear but I really didn't want to throw it, I just looked at it in my hand and saw its tip glowing. In its reflection my face, but I was really, really old.

I opened my eyes. Tony had handed me a stick of incense. I sniffed it like a flower. He said, "Let's go outside. Night's falling."

We got up and I was amazed to find I walked as normally as if I weren't tripping. My senses refocused on my surroundings and we went out, down the stairs, into the cooling evening air. I noticed for the first time that fruit trees grew all around the wine vat house: orange, lemon, grapefruit, something a deep dark orange. I reached out to touch it. "Blood orange," said Tony. "Planted these trees after I finished reading Xanadu. I was seventeen."

"Xanadu?" I asked.

"That's what I call my house. Coleridge's poem?

> *'In Xanadu did Kubla Khan*
> *a stately pleasure-dome decree...'*

"The story goes he was smoking opium and fell into a dream and had a vision of the poem. He started to write it, but someone came to the door and he forgot the whole thing." Tony laughed gently.

"Oh, yeah, we read "Kubla Khan" in high school, but the teacher never said anything about the opium dream." I began to wonder how many things our teachers never told us. Or our parents. Or the military. I could be denied promotion, but in a moment the regulation could be overturned. I realized I should doubt the lessons and rules society made up for its good citizens to follow.

We stood looking at the colorful fruit hanging from the branches, the mountains turning misty purple against the setting sun. It was so peaceful, so quiet I could hear the warm and cold air molecules rubbing together, making a whirring sound like crickets but so soft you could barely hear it. I wondered if the whole universe made sounds like that, like ships make when they move through the ocean waters, but we're too busy with our own sounds to hear it. A faint breeze teased the leaves, not enough to make the fruit swing, then moved on. I looked down at my huaraches in the reddish-brown dirt and saw little wisps of dust move over my toes. Then the dirt began moving by itself, creating patterns on the ground that reminded me of Indian designs, like the weaving in an Indian rug, like the one we sat on inside, yet each time the pattern came clear it would begin to change again. *God, being on this acid trip is fantastic.*

"Yeah, it's totally far out, isn't it?" Tony said. I looked over at him, staring into the distance with a faint smile on his face.

"How did you know I was thinking that?" I said, awestruck.

"Ha!" You said it out loud, Nate! Ha!"

I laughed too. Laughing felt like breathing. We walked around in the fruit tree orchard, then Tony led me up the side of the hill in back of his house. I started hearing sounds from inside my body again as it had to work harder to climb the hill. My heart pounded in my chest and temples. I could feel the blood as it pulsed through my heart and into my veins. It was very intense, so I tried shifting my focus to hearing my steps, touching trees, looking at bark and leaves and the dust motes in the air. As soon as I concentrated on them, they began turning into psychedelic patterns again. I shook them out of my head.

As we approached a huge old tree, Tony grabbed a large limb and swung himself up into a wooden structure. I followed him into a tree house. "Wow, this is cool," I said.

"This oak is older than my great-grandfather," Tony said. "My dad and I built this tree house for me when I was six. I was so little I had to climb a knotted rope to get up!" he chortled. "I've always loved this view across the valley."

Almost as far as I could see were green vineyards. Beyond them were rolling tan-colored hills, outlined against the darkening blue sky. As I gazed at their soft rolling contours they began to move, like incredibly huge slumbering lions awakening.

Nature on acid. Amazing. I turned around. Behind us, the sun was falling behind another ridge and the shadows were almost gone. With the evening cooling came a purple haze over the vineyards, like a mist against which the dark vines stood in relief. I was seized with the desire to paint this scene, even though I had never in my entire life thought of taking up a paintbrush.

Tony lit a joint and passed it to me. I looked at him quizzically. "It'll feel good," he said, "takes a bit of the edge off the acid." We passed it back and forth and it was as he said. "I never get tired of this place," Tony said. "Maybe because I haven't really been anyplace else. Sometimes I think about this poem we read in American lit. Can't remember the poet, but he's from somewhere around here, Northern California. Oh, Robinson Jeffers. His poetry makes me remember how this country feels. I really *really* love it here."

I nodded but didn't say anything, just tried to absorb the feeling Tony was trying to share. I thought about Chicago, the upper Midwest, the few trips our family took to Wisconsin. There was nothing this beautiful. We sat there long after we'd finished smoking the joint, watching night descend in the valley, smelling a multitude of indescribable scents filling the air until it started to get a little cool.

"Want to go back inside?" Tony asked, and I nodded. We climbed out of the tree. Tony picked some blood oranges. As we entered the wine vat, the smell of the burnt, wine-soaked wood filled my nostrils, powerful and rich – you might say *intoxicating*. As I looked around the room, I could see molecules in the candlelight moving slightly, dancing in and up and out of the candle's flame, exploding and disappearing like tiny fireworks.

Tony put on "Tomorrow Never Knows" again, went into the kitchen and came back with a plate of sliced oranges. I wasn't exactly hungry, but the taste was beyond delicious. Cool, sweet juicestreams ran around in my mouth like little creatures and dripped off my chin. My senses were totally wide open, like some-body – maybe named Lucy – had turned on a fire hose of sensations. We finished the oranges and were sitting cross-legged on the Indian rug again when Tony said, "Remember the Butterfield Blues Band?"

"Yeah, Monterey Pop," I replied.

"Here's something they didn't play. It's from their *East-West* album."

"What piece?" I asked.

"'East-West.'" Tony moved to the stereo.

"Yeah, you said that. What's the name of the song?"

"'East-West.'" He laughed again. "The name of the song is the same as the album name! But it's more than just a song. It's a trip. In a way it's like classical music because it's completely instrumental, but it's – really different. Listen."

It was an electric blues composition, and it wasted no time getting into a groove. The bass and drums thumped a steady rhythm and my pulse fell into synchroniza-tion. Notes flashed off the electric guitar, soaring as my thoughts tried to keep up, then the harmonica came in, the two in duet in the stereo speakers like two different channels in my brain and I felt my whole self merge into the musical menagerie. The guitars, driven by the bass, built M.C. Escher castle staircases that climbed larger higher building and building into a crescendo that exploded and I exploded with it, like a bubble struggling and then bursting free into a beautiful peaceful meadow with tall green grass and utterly blue skies and little butterflies in the warm air, the cool breeze in my face as I ran through the grass, me and the music running, run-ning, and everything easy now, the struggle over and I'm free, the music says so, we are loping swiftly along on horseback and it feels perfect, free, soft plings of the guitar in front of the soft pat-a-pat of the tabla drums, the horse a unicorn now Pegasus and we are on wing the strings of the guitar higher higher the bass steady steady as we merry-go-round with others riding unicorns I know them! I know them! they're circling round round like a tornado like the rings around Saturn now all one spinning together laughing the spinning ride becoming a flying saucer spinning spinning the sunlight sparking off it grows brighter brighter just shrieks once and is gone into outer space then a huge musical thump and I am left in its silence.

I sat for a long time, I don't know how long because time had ceased to exist for me, my eyes closed and the remnants of "East-West" still replaying in my head. It had assaulted my ears, a force of nature driving my external perceptions into retreat, but I was glad for it. I'd never heard anything so intense, or so long, before. Like Tony said, it *was* kind of like classical music, maybe even jazz, which made me think of my father, but his jazz was Dave Brubeck and Shelly Manne and Maynard Ferguson, nothing like this.

"It's like jazz, riffing but with the long solos," I said.

I opened my eyes and pinwheels of color coiled out into the room, spiraling larger and larger until they were consumed by the dense pattern of moving molecules. "And like the Beatles, 'Within You Without You'...."

We both said "Within You Without You" at the same time. That started us laughing again. My perceptions were open so wide: smell, taste, hearing, even my thoughts and speech. There was absolutely no difference between the thought and the act. I remembered how I stretched my arm toward the candle, seeing the molecules in the air and everything. Wow, I thought, there's so much reality I've been unaware of!

"That's how I felt too, after the first time I tripped," said Tony. "Still do, actually."

"There I go again, huh?" I said.

"There you go again!" he replied, and again we laughed. It was so easy to laugh!

We fell silent. My thoughts and feelings and perceptions were weaving around like cars changing lanes on the freeway. Then, more or less without my bidding, I said, "You know so much...so much. I mean, wow, man, you are just...so... wise...?"

Tony shifted his large, tall body a bit, squirming around in slow motion. "Naw, not wise." He put his forefinger on the Indian rug and drew the infinity symbol. "Just paying attention. At least I try. To see everything. My mind reacts to everything and I pay attention. Not because I actually *want* to. Don't have a choice, it's just the way I was built or born or something. For some reason, I just seem to be able to get inside of everything."

"Wow, man, what's wrong with that?" I asked.

"Sometimes it's a curse. The curse of consciousness. Huxley described how mescaline opened his doors of perception. How our brain understands it can't process all the sensory information out there. It'd probably drive most people nuts if they got the full load all the time. So our brain narrows the incoming channel so that we can deal with reality, or whatever this space is. Like a funnel."

"That's what the LSD did for me. Is doing," I said. "I mean, my doors of perception are wide open, maybe wider open than I've ever known. No, not even maybe. But I'm OK with it, it's cool, really cool. I'm not having a problem. I like it. But maybe I need to think about if I'd like it to be like this all the time." So I did think about it and immediately it seemed like I would never not be tripping.

"Huxley says we just can't," Tony replied. "But for me, it left a kind of residual consciousness. I became aware of new – ways of seeing. Now I can't go back. Can't *not* see those things in life and society and myself any more. Buddha called it enlightenment. You know, what happened under the tree. You're OK with all this so far, but I don't think we've peaked yet. So now it's what you *do* with it. You're at the controls. You want to stay comfortable? Or you want to push the edge?"

I thought about that and then I wasn't tripping forever any more. "Well, I'd like to see what else is out there, I guess. I'm not sure how to do that. Most of what's happened seems to come to me without my asking for it to happen."

"Right. We use our senses to push the limits. I told you a long time ago it's best when you get high where you feel comfortable and safe. You can stay in that place for your whole trip if you want to. Right now, everything that's happened has pretty much been because that's what you want to happen. Limits you set for your imagination and senses, even if you don't actually realize it. So, I introduce another experience unfamiliar to you, makes a change in your perceptions, and that could change your experiences. Get it?"

"Yeah, I get it," I answered. "If I'm straight, the way I handle experience is based on a non-changing basis for reality. If I'm on psychedelics, the reactions I have to different sensory experiences or perceptions I may or may not have ever had in the past could be completely and totally unpredictable. Does that sum it up?"

"Does indeed," Tony replied. "I'm your guru, I take responsibility for initiating your trip, but you assume all responsibility for how you perceive and react then on. Going to a good place or on a bummer." He stood up and began fanning through his albums.

"What is this, some kind of legal contract?" I asked, almost chortling.

"OK, OK, I'm going overboard," said Tony, chortling as well. "It's just that I had to take somebody to the emergency ward once. Really bad trip. Made me take my responsibilities a lot more seriously."

"He pull out of it OK? The dude on the bummer?"

"Yeah. Never want to go through that again. Freaky. I was tripping too, so I was going through what she was going through. We kind of mind-merged, you know? Nearly freaked out myself."

Oh. A she, not a he. I was starting to feel a freakout just by listening to Tony describe it, so I was glad he got up and moved to the record player. I blinked my eyes a couple of times to change perceptions. It was like rotating the knob on a TV set to change channels. It worked. I went back to a comfortable place in my head.

"You need to hear some Dylan," Tony said.

"I've heard Dylan," I replied. "We listened to *The Freewheelin' Bob Dylan* all the time at Keesler."

"Cool," said Tony. "You know he went electric at Newport?"

"Sure," I replied. "Who hasn't heard 'Rainy Day Woman'?"

"But have you heard anything else from *Blonde on Blonde*?"

"I'm not sure. That's the double album?"

"Right. Even if you've heard it, I want you to hear some of the songs now. While you're tripping. This is 'Visions of Johanna.'" Tony smiled as he got up and put on the album. It took him two tries to drop the needle into the lead groove. Then, as he sat down, I heard Dylan's guitar strum, followed by a few toots on the harmonica then his band came in with the snare drums, bass, keyboard and he sang

Ain't it just like the night
To play tricks when you're trying to be so quiet
We sit here stranded
Though we're all doing our best to deny it

I was hooked, no longer in the comfortable place. I knew this song but as I listened to the story Dylan told I knew I didn't know it at all. The poetic couplets were just that in non-stoned reality; under Lucy's influence were totally cohering into a play, a musical novel in verse and just what were these visions of Johanna? Was the song about Dylan's visions of her, or were they Johanna's visions that she is telling to him and he's retelling? *Ghosts of electricity.* The acid makes me feel like that. *Mona Lisa with the highway blues.* I can see her, long curly tangled black hair, pink cheeks, button mouth, in jeans and cowboy boots standing by the side of the road with her thumb outstretched. *In museums, infinity goes up on trial.* Is he trying to say something about us being told by the museums what is art and what's not? No, there's nothing to turn off: *Jeez I can't find my knees.* Dylan, his poetic allusions high as kites, never telling us to turn on to these visions, like that guy Leary, not to reject but not to take anything at face value, for granted, for being what it is because it never is, yes, that's what he's saying, never tells us to do or be anything because it doesn't matter it's all visions, just that, visions, they'll keep you up half the dawn and they'll drive you crazy but in the end they're all you have. But this one is Johanna's, not yours. Go get your own.

It ended; Tony was up again, changing the record. Again he hunted for the groove he wanted. I saw him move through the curtain of molecules, which swooshed like a beaded curtain in his wake. Recrossing my legs. *Movement: is that part of time?* Looking out the windows; energy vibrates in the air; totally dark outside now. Waiting for the song to start.

Dylan does a folk fake, opening with the harmonica and strumming guitar, then explodes into the snare drum and electric guitar as he begins singing.

> *Aw, the ragman draws circles*
> *Up and down the block*
> *I'd ask him what the matter was*
> *But I know that he don't talk*

And I already know that this song is a dark song, a song of infinitely more intricate meanings than anything I've heard from him before. By the time he gets to the refrain,

> *Oh, Mama, can this really be the end,*
> *To be stuck inside of Mobile*
> *With the Memphis blues again*

I know I'm in for it. I'm a goner, lost to this song and it's going to take my trip on a trip and there's nothing I can do but flow with it. This is heavy. For the first time, I feel some dread and concern because I'm not in my comfortable place. I know I'm somebody who looks on the good side of things, and even in my times of loss and screwing up I still think things will turn out for the best. Dr. Cohen said I was an existentialist, but then again I wrote my Congressman. I need things to work out by the rules. But what is Dylan saying, about being stuck in Mobile with the Memphis blues? Is Mobile being a straight? Is Memphis blues the curse of consciousness? You can't let yourself get stuck in Mobile after you've been to Memphis, maybe. But was consciousness existential? Why did I keep thinking everything cool was about existentialism? There was no existentialism! It was a joke, a big phony joke! Here was Dylan, no existentialist at all, revealing hidden and deeper meanings to life than a stupid mean nasty little philosophy. Here was Dylan, singing in profound layers of symbolic meaning that once you've turned on with psychedelics – once you've got the big-town Memphis blues, there's no way you can go home again to Mobile and your mama and be content there. I knew that. I did that, left mama. Suddenly I was very proud of myself for knowing that, except it was unconscious at the time.

With each verse, I found myself moving further away from anything I'd ever known or had in my life and coming to terms with a new understanding of the many relationships between ideas and things and people and what they stand for symbolically. The image of the ragman, in the first stanza, leapt into my mind as a fully formed being, even though I had never met or known a ragman or even knew what one was. Sometimes I felt like Dylan was teasing me with his lyrics, but even when I questioned his images I never doubted his authority as my guide. Yes, that honky-tonk keyboard and his sing-song lyrics and quixotic refrain were absolutes in my tripped-out acid universe. So when he sang

> *Now the rainman gave me two cures,*
> *Then he said, "Jump right in."*
> *The one was Texas medicine,*
> *The other was just railroad gin.*
> *An' like a fool I mixed them*
> *An' it strangled up my mind,*
> *An' now people just get uglier*
> *An' I have no sense of time.*

My God! Tony had not wanted us to consume alcohol when we dropped the acid, and here was Dylan giving that advice! Texas medicine: that wasn't acid, but it was probably peyote. Don't mix alcohol and psychedelics. Dylan, our guru, tells us so and then he sings

> *An' here I sit so patiently*
> *Waiting to find out what price*
> *You have to pay to get out of*
> *Going through all these things twice*

I knew on an intrinsic level that there was a deep message in these lyrics, even though I couldn't think of an instance they applied to. Yet it was way too abstract to grok. I had to be content knowing I should remember this.

As the song, which by this time I had figured out was entitled something like "Stuck Inside of Mobile with the Memphis Blues Again," moved into the final acoustico-electric chords, sending intense vibrations down my spinal cord, its powerful conclusion — each instrument, each note — was a distinct message to me that resonated from my spine up into my brain and deep into my soul. I wanted to assimilate every word, every note, every image and symbol and phrase while at the same time realizing it was impossible to do so. Five guitar strums emanated from the speakers and went straight through my forehead into my mind like dazzling thunderbolts bolting right on out my medulla oblongata like comet contrails plummeting into deepest space at an incredible speed, five pinpoints of brilliant light flashing and then disappearing and causing an obliterating hallucinogenic reaction, literally knocking me backwards on the floor. The contrails swirled around me, before and behind my eyes and I stared up and into space trying to follow the points of light but my eyelids were compelled to close. When I opened them again, morning sunlight was pouring through the windows.

Chapter 7
The Summer of Love
July-August, 1967

There was nothing normal about returning to normal after my acid trip with Tony. I knew I still had acid running around inside me, that my doors of perception were still open, altering the way I saw everything around me. Sometimes I'd see the world in sepia tones, like watching an old silent movie. In fact, sometimes the so-called Real World was like watching a movie. One time it was like looking through a piece of glass smeared with Vaseline. Another, people and buildings and cars and trees were cardboard cutouts. I'd walk along and hear sounds that seemed to come from a huge speaker behind the movie screen. Clouds pulsed as I inhaled and exhaled. Sometimes it felt like my feet didn't touch the pavement. Sometimes all this was kind of fun. Sometimes it got uncomfortable and I wished it would stop. Mostly it was, well, trippy and I wondered if, indeed, it would ever stop.

After a few days it did. Like in Dylan's song, I was in back in Mobile and as soon as that happened, I wished I was in Memphis. Dylan says he's waiting patiently to find out the price he has to pay for going through things twice. Well, I wondered what I still had to learn from 562 more days in the military. I became increasingly aware that I was mostly surrounded by troops who were barely educated, sometimes vulgar, utterly lacking in creative thought or imagination. I knew Tony was different. His talk about the curse of consciousness went round and round in my thoughts. I wondered if I was going to catch it. I could see it happening.

The more time Lee and I spent smoking the ganja, the more I wondered about his reasons for getting high. He didn't guzzle multiple beers any more, but he had no interest in getting into Pynchon's symbolism with Tony and me, or books at all for that matter, and never joined in when we talked about the meanings of songs. He was still mostly into his blues music, driving his Healey fast and trying to get girls. Was he just looking for the cheap thrill from getting high? As a matter of fact, wondering about Lee made me wonder about my own motives for getting high. I felt sure there was something more to it than cheap thrills, but it was all too new. I just didn't know what it was yet, but I wanted to find out.

. . .

"I'm, well, just seeing the world different," I said. "The military. And the Real World. You know?"

"No, can't say that I do," Jane replied in her usual point-blank way. The sun was setting and we were sitting in the big swing on her front porch, eating cookies and drinking iced tea she'd made. She took a bite and made sky-blue goo-goo eyes at me, as if daring me to explain it to her.

I wasn't sure how much I wanted to tell her. "Well, OK, I used to think of the military in one way and the Real World in another. I mean, I'm enlisted in the military and I have to follow the rules and regs. I have to do what they want. Follow orders, OK? But the Real World, that's what we call the outside. Where you live. The place we can only visit. We count the days until we can go back to live in the Real World. You with me so far?"

"Yep, perfectly. Not too hard to follow." She grinned.

"OK, but listen up, Jane, this is important stuff I'm trying to figure out. So now I'm kind of starting to see that there really isn't a lot of difference between the military world and the Real World." I slugged down some iced tea. "The military's totally uptight and you have to wear a uniform. Well, the Real World is pretty uptight too. Squares, they like being square and want everybody else to be square, just like them. It's about conformity and men in suits and women in hats and gloves and trying to be like the Joneses next door." She stuck a cookie in my mouth. "I mean, is this what I have to look forward to? When I get out? Marching off to work with a briefcase? Maybe that's why a lot of troops just decide to stay in, rack up their twenty years, retire and get a pension. I mean, what's the difference?"

Jane took my hand and gently rubbed her thumb in my palm. "Nate, the real world is what you make of it. You know, like George sings? 'Life goes on within you and without you.' If you only see what's out there, if you let the outside tell your inside what's real, then you'll probably have a negative view of the world. But if you get into your inner self, really into it, where your spirit lives, well, that's how you'll see your world."

I nodded. She was right. Tony said it, too. I remembered the glimpse of my inner spirit, the tiny blue spark I turned into on my acid trip. Suddenly I realized why Tony saw the same thing: in spirit we were all one, together in the singleness of the universe.

"I sure don't see you wearing a gray flannel suit and working at some desk job," said Jane. "I think you're a nonconformist." She took my hand in both of hers. "I think you're going to be a great writer whose books will change people's lives."

"How come?" I was pleased and flattered and a little surprised to hear her say this.

"Well, I loved 'September Love Song,' even though you wrote it about Kathleen," she said, cocking her head a little. I felt a wave of shame or embarrassment like I'd felt when Sasha said I was into Martha.

"Well, see, the reason I wrote that...."

Jane raised her hand to silence me. "No, that's not the point. The point is, you've written a lot of really good stuff. Remember 'San Francisco Story'? The last assignment in Creative Writing?" I nodded. "I loved that story!" She jumped up and ran into the house, the screen door banging behind her. "Jane!" her mother yelled. A minute later it banged again as she came back with my manuscript. Her father yelled "Jane! Stop banging the damned door!" She wiggled her eyebrows and grinned. Flipping pages, she began to read.

...Market Street and its constipated traffic, belligerent buses, incessant trolley tracks, people, people everywhere and not a soul in sight! A wild, fantastic Mingus composition, set to life; flutes weaving in between cars from curb to curb, a myriad of tonalities constantly changing tempo all over the sidewalks, blending, losing pitch and barfing in the gutter, floating over theater marquees, sibilant in overtones of business suits; drums and top hats and pounding, thumping bass of Negro fingers saying sailors and sots and streetwalkers, beware! Anxiety is all around, thump, thump, thump, stealing your interlude with life, taking your shuffling walk, your cares not caring. And all around you swirls the Concerto of Frustration, and you don't care!

95

The Great Flood of Envy will coming rushing down and pound you into a bloody pulp of limpid laughter. Back, back to your boats, beds, bottles; we have no time for those who are satisfied. Look, but don't touch? No, don't even look.

"Wow, you know that just blows me away! You are so observant and a very, *very* talented writer!"

"You see so much, more than even I can see," I said, looking into her clear bright smiling blue eyes.

"Well, I see a lot of things in *you*." She looked down. "I think it's because I've kinda been getting into reading books at the Ouroboros."

"Yeah? Like what?"

"Oh, like the soul, or the spirit, never dies, it just changes its material form. We're just energy and we change from one lifetime to another. I learned that from *Vedanta*."

I shook my head in disbelief. She was describing the blue spark!

"Here, I want to show you something." Jane took my hand and we got up. Dusk had fallen. She crossed the porch until we were away from the light cast from inside and sat down cross-legged facing each other. She put her hands on her knees, touching her first finger and thumb together in a circle. I did the same. "This is from yoga. Now, close your eyes and listen to your breathing. Slow it down, and keep slowing it down. Concentrate on nothing except your finger and thumb touching and your breathing."

I did. Pretty soon, I stopped thinking about things and my senses began to open up. I heard the ocean breaking on the beach and the caw of the gulls, felt the salt spray in the air, the warmth of the sun.

"Where are you?" she asked. "I'm at the beach." I couldn't believe it. I was tripping – no, *we* were tripping on the beach together, without LSD, without even smoking a joint. I settled into a serene place inside. After what seemed like a long time I opened my eyes. Jane was looking at me. She smiled. I smiled. We smiled and smiled.

"That was really – serene," I said. She nodded. "Far out." After a long, peaceful moment I said, "Jane, I need to tell you something."

She leaned forward and said, "Yes?"

"A few weeks ago – when Tony and I went to his place in Napa for the Fourth – we did some LSD."

She straightened up. She didn't act upset exactly but, I don't know, it just seemed like it wasn't what she expected to hear. "Wow," she said. "How was it?"

"It's hard to describe. Like pot, but different. Deeper. It was good; I saw things differently, not just slowed down like pot. I mean, all my senses were *really* intensified. The music…the music. And I thought about things in new ways, I thought about brand new things I never thought of before. Saw things in a new light, you know? You — you've never done acid?"

"No, no," she answered quickly. "I would, but it would have to be with the right person…you know…."

"Exactly. That's why it was good to do it with Tony, 'cuz I trust him." Then another wave of embarrassment or guilt passed through me. "Of course I trust you too," I hastened to add. "I'm sure we'd have a good trip together. Tony only got two tabs when we went to Monterey Pop…."

"Oh, sure, that's cool, I mean, I didn't mean to imply anything, I was just saying…."

"Yeah, me too, all I was saying was it was Tony's tabs, so…."

"…only two…"

"Right…but you know, just now, doing the yoga thing, it reminded me of the acid trip, you know, moving into a quiet spiritual place."

"Yeah, I know," Jane said and scooted forward until our knees touched. She put her hands back on her knees so I did too, then she looped our thumbs and forefingers together like links in a chain. "Remember that. We do this to find our spiritual place. Our path." She gazed deep into my eyes. I nodded solemnly. "At least that's what I read. What comes up over and over is that there are many paths to enlightenment. But everyone I read — Crowley and Gurdjieff and the *Vedanta* say we're supposed to strive for higher states of consciousness."

"If you're ready," I said, "If you are ready to — willing to — accept the — consequences." Tony's comments about the curse of consciousness were flashing through my thoughts. "Because you can't go back. Like Dylan says, you don't want to get stuck inside of Mobile with the Memphis Blues again."

Jane raised her eyebrows and said, "OK, whatever that means. Speaking of music, want to listen to *Sgt. Pepper's* again? All the way through?" I nodded and she went inside, banging the door, causing her father to yell again. She moved the stereo to the living room window, like always. We started dancing and singing along.

"Jane!" her dad yelled, "Turn that damned thing down! We're trying to watch television!"

. . .

The Summer of Love. That's what the *Oracle* said was happening. It was the Human Be-In, but bigger. Longer. Uglier.

Kids from all across the country were coming to The City, thousands and thousands of them, and the streets were chaos. The *Oracle* urged people to have their own Summer of Love somewhere else. It seemed like San Francisco had become an overgrown Hashbury with hippies and runaway teenagers and drugs and motorcycle gangs. We were curious to see for ourselves, so one afternoon we headed south, Lee and Tony in the Healey and Jane and me in the MGA, the Byrds, a new song by The Jimi Hendrix Experience, all of whom I'd seen at Monterey Pop, and Moby Grape, blasting away on KMPX.

We parked on Arguello, blocks away from Golden Gate Park. Panhandlers, bums, and alkies begged us for money all the way back. Inside the park were multitudes of tents and wild encampments. Masses of people in hippie clothes and various stages of undress, trees decorated with peace flags and flowing scarves, as far as the eye could see. Music blared from loudspeakers. Tents with Red Cross markings. I turned to Lee and said, "This is *not* the Human Be-In." He shook his head sadly. It was really hard seeing this. So we left.

. . .

"We're lucky we even made it to Monterey Pop," said Tony, "before they lowered the boom." Tony, Lee and I were drinking coffee and chain-smoking cigarettes at the Base Ops cafeteria a few days later, trying to make our coffee break last as long as possible. The base commander had just issued an order declaring San Francisco off limits. It stated that any troop found on the other side of the GGB, no matter where or for what reason, would be court-martialed.

"No shit," said Lee.

"At least we know we're not missing anything," he continued. "Snot-nosed blueblood college kids from back East trying to act like hippies. Shitting on the lawn in Golden Gate Park. Shooting heroin in The Haight. Singing 'If you're going to San Francisco, be sure to wear some flowers in your hair.'

Sheesh, what a stupid piece of shit that song is. Andy Williams meets the Mamas and Papas."

"That Scott what's-his-name-McKinsey ought to be court-martialed for ruining San Francisco," I said.

"No shit, but I'm sure glad me and Nate got to go to the Human Be-In," Lee chimed in. "That was a truly fine day, you know?" I nodded. Lee turned to Tony: "But sheesh, man, I still can't get over how this guy gets girls. Every time he bumps into a chick she wants to screw him."

"Hey, you troops hear about my new TDY?" I said to change the subject.

"Whaddaya mean, temporary duty?" Lee asked. "You ain't gone anywhere."

"This is true, but I've been relieved of my radio ops duties," I replied.

"Huh?" said Tony.

"Yup. I'm now the Maintenance Chief, which means I check off all the PMs every day and enter them on punched cards for the computer every Thursday."

"Yeah, I know what you do. Easy duty," said Lee.

"You still have your secret security clearance?" Tony asked, eyebrows knitted.

"Ah, yeah, I think so," I said. "Nobody said I didn't."

"They don't *have* to tell you if they downgrade you," said Tony.

"Why would they?"

"You wrote your Congressman, dummy. Now you can't be trusted."

My heart sank into my stomach. "You really think that's why they moved me out of radio?" I asked.

"Aw, I don't know," said Tony. "Who was Maintenance Chief before you?"

"Trank. Staff sergeant. Just re-upped and got promoted."

"OK, well maybe it was just attrition, you know, promoting him out of it. Forget me. I'm always looking for the deeper meaning. You know, curse of consciousness and all that shit."

I knew. Now I was getting it.

"Besides, I'm kinda paranoid. Been getting into a bit of trouble myself," Tony added.

"Haircuts?" I asked.

"Well, that, but I've been late for duty. Oversleeping. Not sure why, except I'm really bored. Loading stuff on aircraft isn't the most exciting work, you know. If I'm late once more I get an Article 15."

"Yeah, well come on downstairs and do PMs on radar screens and see if you like that," said Lee.

"CYA," I added.

Tony grinned.

A week later, he got orders for England.

"It's just normal rotation," he told me as we sat on Jane's porch. She came out with iced teas for us and plunked down.

"What's that mean?" she asked.

"I've been stationed here eighteen months, Jane. I'm due for rotation. If they didn't assign me a new duty station, I'd be stuck here another twenty-seven months."

"My, wouldn't that be terrible!" she said, grinning.

Tony took a huge slug of iced tea. "Of course not. But this way, they can only rotate me to a new assignment for eighteen months. I'll get out early. Maybe seven months early!"

"Can't beat that deal. England and an early out," I said.

"When do you leave?" Jane asked.

"Ten August. Two and a half weeks. Kind of sudden."

"Something's up," I said.

Tony nodded.

• • •

Something was up indeed, for when 1 August rolled around every single troop in my squadron got orders for Southeast Asia, effective 1 September. Everyone but me. Lee was going to Thailand, Trank and Mo to the Philippines, and pretty much everyone else in radar and radio to Tan Son Nhut Air Base, Vietnam.

"I'd rather go to Vietnam and be with the rest of our buddies," said Lee.

"Count your lucky stars," MSgt. Masters told him. "I've been to the Philippines. They *like* us there. You will surely get laid, you may not get the clap, and you will probably come home alive."

I got orders, too, not for Southeast Asia but for another TDY at the base newspaper. Why me? I wondered, so I went to see the first shirt. "No idea, Flowers. I just do what I'm told and so do you. Well, *sometimes* you do," he said, frowning at me over his glasses. "In any event, you're going to be editor of the *San Ramon Flyer* for a month while the *real* editor is on leave. Do not ask me why they chose you."

"Maybe because I took a creative writing class at SRCC?" I asked.

"Of course, that's it! Somebody likes your poetry. Flowers, you do crack me up sometimes. No, more likely it's your name. It'll look good on the masthead:

Nathaniel Hawthorne Flowers, Editor-in-Chief. Har! Har! Har!"

Afterwards, I remembered the article about the hurricane at Keesler. Maybe that was why.

• • •

Being Dorm Chief in BMT was bad enough, but the hostility in the newsroom of the *Flyer* was so thick you could cut it with a knife. I tried to be humble and called upon the reporters and editors to carry on doing what they did, and promised to stay out of their way. They did, and I did. I had to. I wrote exactly one story, just to show I was one of the troops. I showed it to the editors. They said it was great and published it on the front page.

San Ramon to Lose Entire AFCS Squadron to Southeast Asia

By

A1C Nathaniel H. Flowers

Acting Editor-in-Chief

San Ramon Air Force Base, like the Spanish missions it resembles, is a peaceful place nestled near San Rafael. To the east lies San Pablo Bay and to the west the Pacific. From the Base Ops tower, the Marin Civic Center, designed by the famous architect Frank Lloyd Wright, can be seen. Yet underneath this calm exterior lies a beehive of military activities focused on supporting the Strategic Air Command and its attack B-52s as well as the vast fleet of tankers and transport that provide services spanning the globe.

But a shock wave rocked this small base when, on 1 August, virtually all personnel of the 1876th Air Force Communications Service squadron were issued orders to Southeast Asia. Vietnam, Thailand, and the Philippines. Some crypto and radio intercept personnel are being sent to Laos and Cambodia, but not publicly because U.S. troops are not legally permitted in those countries. The intent behind these covert operations....

...Members of the United States Military are not permitted to speak out in public against actions or decisions made by leaders, but in off-the-record interviews with this reporter, most troops said they were fundamentally opposed to the U.S. presence in Southeast Asia.

One surprising note was the speed at which the 1876th AFCS, as well as a number of Strategic Air Command (SAC) personnel, will be shipped out: less than 30 days, while most orders state 60 to 90 days. Although it is unknown why the departure is with such haste, it is presumed that there is a major build-up under-way in anticipation of violence when Vietnamese elections are held in September.

The *Flyer* came out on Monday, 7 August. Tuesday morning, MSgt. Masters personally relieved me of duty and handed me orders to report to the 6069th AFCS, Kleinelachen Army Air Base, Stuttgart Germany, effective 1 September. I was FIGMO, and would be shipping out the same date as Lee and the other squadron troops. I just had time to tell Tony what had happened before his C-130 took off for England. He grabbed me by the shoulders and shook me, almost like he wanted to give me a hug.

"Keep up the good work, man. I'll write ya," he said.

"Don't forget the potsage," I replied. We grinned and grabbed each other's hand in a hippie handshake.

• • •

That night Jane and I sat together in the swing on her front porch. I showed her a copy of the *Flyer* and chortled, explaining why it got me in trouble. "I sup-pose it was all confidential, but all I did was speculate. But obviously it was enough to get me shipped out."

"You're…leaving?" she said haltingly.

"Yeah. Germany! Everybody else got orders for the combat zone, but I get to go to Germany!"

"You're *leaving?*" she asked again. "But we were going to take another class together this fall…."

"I know. But I ship in three weeks. They can't wait to get rid of me! I wonder how much this has to do with my writing my Congressman – "

"Nate, I can't believe you're leaving," Jane said, shaking her head slowly. "For how long?"

"Well, it *is* the end of my tour of duty, after all. Germany! Three years in Europe! I couldn't have asked for a better assignment."

She looked up at me. Tears began streaming down her cheeks. A sob escaped her lips. She looked down and covered her face. I was stunned. "Jane, aren't you happy for me? I mean, don't you think — "

She threw herself across my chest and let out a loud wail. "Oh, Nate, how can I be happy about your leaving me? I love you so much! I don't want you to leave! Oh, oh, oh, oh, oh…" she gurgled. I put my arms around her, beyond words, feeling my shirt getting wet. She raised her face up and kissed me, a kiss from the depths of her heart. I could do nothing but respond in kind.

"Jane, Jane, I didn't know," I said, coming up for air, then she pressed her lips to mine again. Over her shoulder I could see her mother looking at us through the screen door. I closed my eyes to make her disappear.

Jane. Jane. How could I know.

Part III
Deutschland über Alles

Chapter 8

First Sergeant Buford
September, 1967

Friday, 1 September, 1930 hours. Pale, diluted sunlight cast my shadow, long and weak, across the oval patch of grass and weeds upon which I stood. A rutted gravel drive encircled the flagpole that stood in the center of the green. To the east were six buildings the color of dark gray-brown mud. North was Base Ops, a two-story building and tower. I stood before a lone cinder-block block painted seafoam green. A crude, hand-painted wooden sign read

6069th AFCS HQ
Wipe Your Feat

The blue Air Force van, having dropped me here, putted away. I knocked on the door. Knocked again. Hearing nothing, I gave it a push. It squealed profoundly. Inside to my left hung a naked light bulb from a single strand of electrical cord above a desk. It cast a pale circle of light on a large, lumpy man tilted back in the desk chair, boots resting on the desk next to an upright typewriter. His snores rippled like the staccato beat of a lawn mower with a bad spark plug. The smell of cheap whiskey and cigar smoke was heavy in the stuffy atmosphere of the windowless building. The wooden name plaque on his desk read

Wilford H. Buford
First Sergeant

The inscription was flanked by a Staff Sergeant insignia and the Air Force Communications Service crest.

"Sergeant Buford?" I said, not too loudly. The snoring continued.

"Sergeant BUFORD?"

He awoke with extreme prejudice, babbling "Hrabbarabbahubbamubbayaoh!" swinging his feet off the desk, knocking the typewriter to the floor, snapping to attention and raising his right hand in salute. Instinctively, I saluted back.

The man standing in front of me was about five foot six, weighed something over 250 pounds if I guessed right, wore rumpled fatigues, and combed a gob of hair up one side of his head and over a prodigious bald spot. Fat lips barely hid buck teeth below a big squashed nose and two beady eyes. His ears were not what I would call oversized, but they seemed to flap slightly when his head moved. Given my lack of sleep and food, maybe I was just seeing things. I'd met NCOs like Buford before, dim-witted, nearly illiterate lifers who couldn't cut it in the Real World.

"Airman First Class Nathaniel Flowers, AF17707615, reporting for duty, Sergeant." I slipped my hand into my blue USAF wool blouse and pulled out a three-page document, neatly folded lengthwise but seriously damp with perspiration, and handed it to him. I went to parade rest and glanced around: more seafoam green. Behind Buford was a row of four-drawer filing cabinets. Above, a rusty corrugated roof. My stomach groaned. It was unlikely the Kleinelachen mess hall would still be serving, if there even was one.

Buford glanced at my orders, threw them back across the desk at me, and bent to pick up the typewriter. "Nathaniel Hawthorne Flowers, eh?" he said. "Purty fancy name. That yer real name or one yer picked up out there in Fairyland Cally-forny?" Before I could answer, he said, "Weren't 'specting yeh 'til Monday."

"Sarge, I took off from San Ramon yesterday morning at 0700 hours. I've been traveling for 38 hours. I had no idea how long it would take to get here. I just got here when I got here. I'm tired. I'm hungry. All I've had to eat today was a bowl of oatmeal in England."

"You *will* call me *Sergeant* Buford, *sir*," he replied.

I shook my head. "With all due respect, you're a staff sergeant, E-5, four stripes. I am an Airman First Class, E-4, three stripes. We're both enlisted and I am not required to call you 'sir.' That ended in basic training. With all *due respect*, Sergeant Buford."

"Oh, so we got us one of those eddy-cated enlisted types, that so? An' on top a' that, from Cally-forny, full up a all that peace and love shit, that so?"

• • •

My thoughts drifted back to my last days in California. Bittersweet days they were. It was hard to see Lee, my hippie roomie buddy for a year and a half, leave for Vietnam because I had a feeling I'd never see him again. Tony, my acid guru, gone. Jane left behind in sadness and shame. Some of the very best times of my life, now just memories.

I wrote home to tell my mom and brothers the news and said I was sorry I wouldn't be able to see them before I left. I had less than 30 days to muster out; there was no way I could squeeze in a leave. My mother's reply came just before I left:

> ...Nathaniel, I cannot under any circumstances understand why you have chosen to go to Germany for three years without first taking a leave to spend time with your family. You've been in California for a year and half and I've had exactly three letters from you. Of course we thank you for continuing to send us the allotment, but you have deeper responsibilities to this family, if not to me then to your brothers. You apparently have chosen to completely neglect us. I cannot say I'm proud of your behavior.

Laying in my top bunk, I wadded the letter up and made a perfect overhand hook shot into the wastecan.

As for Jane, well, she came around. We were still best friends. She gave me a string of tiny beads I could wear secretly under my T-shirt, along with my dog tags. I left her the MG so she'd have something to drive to work and college.

"No, Natey," she said, "I can ride my bike or use mom's car," but honestly I didn't have time to sell it and couldn't think of anyone else to leave it with. I gave her my stereo and records so she could listen to music in her own room, but I took my favorite books.

• • •

"Well, let me tell y'un one more somfun', Airman *First Class* Flowers," Buford was still carrying on as I returned to the present. His fat belly pulled at his fatigue shirt buttons as he pointed at me. "Iz 'bout that l'il stripe a shit on yez upper lip."

I touched my mustache, purely by instinct, then wished I hadn't.

"We ain't got but one kinda *boy* wears that shit on they face, and they ain't the same color as you, and iff'n you want my advice," Buford said, rubbing the four stripes on his sleeve with one of his big sausage fingers, "you'll shave it off 'fore you come on duty official-like."

I stood in shocked silence, not believing what I had just heard come out of the mouth of the squadron's first shirt. Perhaps it was because I was so tired and hungry, or maybe because this man offended me at the deepest level, but without any common-sense deliberation I replied, "Well, thanks for the advice, *Sarge*, but I've got three stripes," sliding my fingers up and down *my* sleeve, "and I don't think I'll be getting another one. And I *like* my mustache. It stays."

I stared first shirt Buford down and tried not to smirk. I'd made an enemy and without any doubt I would live to regret it. But right then I didn't care. To me, he was nothing more than a racist thug in uniform.

After a long moment staring at me with his rat's eyes, Buford said, "Barracks is across the way. Got Army and Air Force both in there. Find a bunk with yeh's own so's yeh don't have to fall out with the greenies ever morning at oh-four-forty-five. Far's I'm concerned, you ain't here yet. Report at oh-eight-hundred Monday morning. Got that, Mister Smart-Ass Airman First Class Nathaniel Flowers?"

"Far out," I replied, snapping off a left-handed salute.

He almost saluted me back, but caught himself in time.

A smirk leaked out. I couldn't help it. God, I was in for it now.

• • •

I stepped outside into the rapidly descending twilight. Fatigue hit me like a punch in the face. I gazed across two active runways at Stuttgart International Airport, or Flughaven as the Germans called it, where I had landed a few hours earlier. Its bright lights flickered, punctuated by the constant *thump* of landing aircraft, their whistling jet engines, the screech of tires hitting the pavement. I turned away. The last thing I wanted to see right now was another airplane.

So this run-down old German military post was Kleinelachen. Shit. The place was a dump, perhaps worthy only of being leveled by a bulldozer. I slung my duffel bag on my shoulder and trudged across the green, past the flagpole with its flag clips banging psychotically, toward the only barracks building with lights on. I felt like Heinlein's stranger in a strange land and wondered what time it was in California and what Jane was doing. She said she'd take care of my car but wouldn't drive it, but I told her to use it. "It'll stay in better condition if it's driven," I told her. *And besides, I won't feel so guilty about being such a schmuck with you.* I showed her dad how to fill the dampers in the SU carburetors with oil, a weekly PM on an English roadster. He was happy to oblige, but I couldn't help feeling he was looking at me funny. I'm sure he knew how Jane felt about me. She probably told her mother and her mother told her father and now he was thinking, *here's the guy my daughter's in love with and he's jilting her.* Sure, I liked Jane and all; whenever we heard the Airplane play "My Best Friend" we sang the whole song together. We followed our dream. Of course we were best friends. I mean, it *was* Jane who got me stoned the first time.

I yanked the outside door handle. A single overhead globe lit the small entrance; coat hooks lined the walls, but no coats. At the opposite end were two doors with small square panes of glass laced with chicken wire leading into open dormitories. On the left door was a large U.S. Army Corps of Engineers insignia and beyond a spic-and-span room lined with two rows of perfectly made-up beds. Taped to the door on the right was a hand-lettered piece of typewriter paper that read

6069 AFCS <u>ONLY</u>!

I pushed through. At the opposite end was an identical door with an EXIT light over it. Most of the bunks were stripped, the mattresses folded in half. As I walking down the aisle, I heard the faint sound of someone humming or singing. It came from a guy about three bunks away, lying on his back. He raised himself on an elbow and looked up at me. "Who're you?" he said.

He crawled off his bunk and stood. He was taller than me, had sandy hair, blue eyes, a dimpled chin. An easy smile crawled across his face. Without waiting for an answer to the first question, he crossed the short distance between us and stuck out his hand. "I'm Dylan McKreven. Brooklyn. Let's go get a beer." Another three-striper, just like me. "Just call me Irish. Let's go get a beer."

I introduced myself, shook his hand, and threw my duffel on the bed across the aisle from his. "I don't officially report until 0800 hours Monday," I said.

"Let's get a beer," he repeated, his face all smiles. *He must be pretty lonely here all by himself.*

This time I laughed. "Sure, but I need some food, too."

"Then we're off to Ma's," he said.

We walked out and turned up the gravel road. About three hundred feet ahead was a steel gate. On the other side was a small wooden building with warm yellow light pouring out the open door and windows. "Welcome to Ma's," he said. "You're now on German soil, in the village of Zweiflüssehausen." The place was about half-filled with men wearing laborer's clothes, drinking beer from bottles with some kind of wire and white cap contraption on them. A large older woman in a shapeless floral dress leaned on a small counter, smiling broadly at us.

"Guten abend, Frau Kissel. Das ist mein Freund Nate. Zwei bier, bitte," Dylan – Irish – said, but she was already onto him, swinging two bottles around from her substantial backside and plunking them on the bar. I shook her hand and Irish ordered zwei something, which I hoped was food. Irish showed me how to pop open the ceramic cap and I had my first taste of local German beer, served at room temperature.

"She's got a wee stash she keeps chilled," Irish said. "Tell her you want *kalt* next time. Me, I just got used to drinkin' it warm. It's great beer, brewery's just down the *strasse*, who cares?"

I looked at the label: Zweiflüssebrau, then took another swig and looked around again. The floor, walls, ceiling, tables, chairs, all seemed made of the same rough-hewn wood. The sweet smell of coarse tobacco hung heavy in the air. I pulled out a pack of Camels and offered one to Irish, who said "No thanks." As I lit one for myself I noticed two Germans sitting near us eyeing the American cigarettes, so I tossed the pack on their table with a nod. One of the men raised his eyebrows but picked up the pack and shook one out for himself and another for his friend.

"Danke schoen," he said, a bit of a grin creeping across his grizzled face, handing the pack back to me.

"Say 'bitte schoen,'" Irish whispered. "It means 'you're welcome.'"

"Beeter shurn," I said, and the two Germans gave me a hearty laugh in return.

We sat down and soon Frau Kissel – Ma – returned. We ordered fresh beers, mine *kalt* this time. She tossed two cardboard coasters decorated with pictures of beer mugs on the table, pulled a fat pencil from her hair, and made two hash marks on our coasters. "'S'how they keep a tab here in Deutschland," Irish explained.

"This is called a deckle – see, it's basically a beer advertisement – and they make a mark for each round."

Our sandwiches arrived, along with a third round. The sandwich was delicious, a huge slice of breaded fried veal cutlet in a homemade bun with lettuce and a slice of tomato, pickle on the side. While I devoured it, Irish told me he'd been on base for nearly a month and was still waiting to go on duty. "I'm ATC," an air traffic controller. "But no aircraft. All our planes are using Stuttgart. We ain't even got a radar set yet. This base is gettin' built from scratch."

I said I knew nothing about the base or its mission. Irish said we were part of a joint military operation called United States Armed Forces, Europe, or USAFE, that was newly under the command of a four-star Air Force general named Daniel Beauregard. He was stationed at USAFE headquarters at Ramstein Air Base, about an hour north of Stuttgart. When the General traveled, he flew his own T-38 jet and needed a place to land when he was at USAFE HQ.

"How come he doesn't just land his jet at Ramstein?" I asked.

"Ramstein's a TAC base. And NATO. F4s, some recon, some KC-135s for mid-air refueling."

"Yeah, so? I mean, he's the highest ranking general in Europe? He can't land wherever the hell he feels like?"

Irish shrugged his shoulders, wiggled his eyebrows, grinned a wry grin. "Ours is not to reason why..." he began.

"...Ours is but to do or die," we finished in unison.

"So General Beauregard needed a landing facility, and we're it," I said.

"You got it. USAFE re-commissioned this fuckin' derelict World War II German army air base called Kleinelachen and sent the Army Corps of Engineers in to fix it up for us Air Force troops.

"C'mon, let's cut the shop talk and get out of here and go do some serious drinking," Irish said. I looked at my deckle: it had five hash marks on it.

"Sure," I grinned. "It's getting kinda thirsty out."

We walked back across the base to the motor pool, a new quonset hut obviously erected by the Army troops. Irish opened the door and cried out, "Eric! Dammit, man, what're ya doin?" A2C Miranda was reading a German girlie magazine, which he hastily stuffed into a drawer.

"Irish," he said. "What can I do for you, as if I didn't already know?"

"You do indeed know it, lad," Irish replied. "You know Airman First Class Flowers?"

"Sure, we met already," Eric said. "I picked him up at the Flughaven." Eric Miranda started for the blue Ford Econoline van, but Irish stopped him and pointed to the Plymouth sedan instead. Eric shook his head but said nothing and drove us out the main gate, where a lone two-stripe Air Policeman stood outside a tiny hut and waved us through. We turned onto a two-lane paved road and twenty minutes later Eric dropped us off on a busy corner in downtown Stuttgart. "When should I come back for ya?" he asked, looking at his watch. It was getting late, 2240 hours.

"Probably not necessary, me fine friend," Irish replied, stuffing a couple of bills in his hand. "We'll find our way home, thank you just the same."

Stuttgart was quite wide awake, and for some reason so was I. A large ornate stone building across the street bore a sign with the German word BIERSTUBE. Irish and I headed for it. The place was brightly lit, and at the far end of the room three guys wearing waistcoats and ruffled white shirts and little green hats were playing polka music as couples danced and laughed up a storm. The bar was magnificent, maybe thirty feet long, made of dark wood that shone from many years of polishing. A gilded mirror lined the entire wall behind it. Dignified gray-haired old men waited tables wearing white shirts with lace cuffs, red bow ties, green leather shorts with suspenders, knee socks, and handlebar mustaches. We wedged ourselves between some other drinkers at the bar and Irish called out, "Zwei Heineken und zwei *schnaps*, bitte."

My command of the German language grew to eight words.

· · ·

When I awoke, I didn't know where I was. My cheek felt scratchy; I opened my eyes enough to see my face rested upon a brown wool government issue blanket. Rotating my gaze upward, I saw the curved corner of a steel bedpost. There was a profound pain in my hip. I reached down to touch it and pulled an empty Heineken bottle from my pants pocket. *Heineken*. I sat up and gradually realized I was in the barracks. Kleinlachen. Germany. Across the room was Irish, still in the sack.

On my wrist was a watch. A fancy, handsome one called a chronometer. I had no recollection of it. The time read 10:27, Monday, 04 September.

Monday. Not Saturday. Monday.

I was two and a half hours late reporting for duty.

114

• • •

"You're AWOL, Airman Flowers." I was back in the squadron admin building but instead of facing left toward Sgt. Buford, I was now facing right, standing at attention in front of the 6069ᵗʰ commanding officer. A naked bulb hung from a cord overhead, just like Sgt. Buford's, but the CO had a brass desk lamp with a green glass shade that illuminated the litter of handwritten notes, piles of thick reports in brown covers, Air Force regulations in blue binders, half a dozen Air Force-issue ballpoint pens, and dried coffee stains pooling out in ever-widening patches from three mess-hall-issue thick white coffee cups. His name plaque read

Theodore X. White
Commander, 6069 AFCS

and was flanked by the silver maple leaf and AFCS crest. Just like Buford's. Behind his desk stood the American flag beside a framed photograph of our Commander in Chief, President Lyndon Baines Johnson.

Col. White was a thin, sallow man who looked like someone had hooked a tube up to him and sucked out about eighty-five percent of the life. The hair on his head was almost gone; his sparse sidebars were clipped short and combed straight down to his ears. His cheeks hung like a basset hound's jowls on either side of the thin little gash of a mouth under a long, narrow beak of a nose. He wore the summer khaki uniform, and his skinny arms stuck out of the sleeves of his short-sleeved blouse like the shirt was three sizes too big. I stood sweating in the same blues I'd worn the week before.

"Yessir," I said, saluting. "I apologize, sir. I overslept." I saluted again.

"Harumph," said Buford from behind me. His chair squeaked and I imagined him tilting back, enjoying this high amusement.

"This is the military, Flowers. There is *never* an excuse for not reporting for duty on time," the colonel said, casting a dour look at me. His eyes, pale blue, milky and faded, looked directly into mine. The look was intended to convey his authority, but it suddenly dawned on me that he was a boozehound. Contrition and gaining the sympathy of a kindred spirit seemed the high road, so I simply blurted out:

"Sir, I regret to say the reason for my not reporting on time this morning was due to exploring the sights and sounds of Stuttgart over the weekend whilst consuming a not inconsiderable quantity of beer with a fellow airman. This is my first time out of the country, sir, God bless our flag and the United States of America, and I was unprepared for what befell me. Again, sir, please accept my sincere regrets. It won't happen again."

Long pause. "See that it doesn't, Airman Flowers," the colonel replied.

"Harumph," said Buford, clearly unhappy that I hadn't been locked in the brig to await execution as a deserter. I looked over my shoulder and threw him a quick smirk. It was so dark in the place I wasn't sure he caught it. God, this room had bad vibes: concrete floor painted gray, cinder-block walls painted military seafoam green, no windows, stale air, government-issue gray steel desks, file cabinets, book-cases. It reminded me of a prison cell.

"Now," he said, picking up a sheaf of papers, "let's talk about your duty assignment." He looked up at me, his eyes floating a bit, for a few long seconds. "At ease, Airman Flowers."

I spread my feet and cupped my hands behind my back. He began reading from my Airman of Record file, asking me verify my name was Nathaniel Haw-thorne Flowers, my ID was AF17707615, my career field designation, going right down the page, line after line, box after box, querying the obvious and boring me to death. I was still hung over to beat the band and couldn't remember the last time I'd eaten. My mind kept drifting to the raw ache in my gut. Nausea swept through me, vile, malignant waves crashing against rocky cliffs, except it was waves of Heineken still churning in my bloodstream. I could still taste it, probably because I hadn't brushed my teeth or even showered for that matter. Heineken. God, what awful-tasting beer, especially after drinking that fine local brew we'd started out with. I never wanted that swill to pass my lips again. Then I remembered we'd been drinking German boilermakers – Heineken plus some kind of colorless, taste-less alcohol. Schnapps, I think Irish called it. I looked at the large black armchair facing the CO's desk with a crest and St. Olaf College painted in gold letters. I suddenly felt unsteady and sat down on it. The colonel looked at me askance, but said nothing.

"You were transferred here from San Ramon?" Colonel White asked.

"Yessir, that was my first duty station after I got out of training. At Keesler."

"San Ramon," the CO said. "Beautiful area that Marin County, mostly orange trees, olive trees, grapes too, as I recall. Mt. Tam." He leaned back and chuckled.

"Yessir," I chuckled back. My stomach was chucking as I chuckled. The past few days were really starting to catch up with me. Stabs of memory were coming back in no particular order, and it scared me to think it was I who might have done the things I was recalling. I preferred to think they were hallucinations or scenes from an art-house movie. Anything but real events, yet even as I fought against them I knew they were undeniable.

Oh, Irish, I thought, you are a wicked lad.

Sgt. Buford's chair squeaked as he got up, saying "I gots tuh run over tuh base ops, sir, see when that radar set's gonna get here," and he lumbered out the door. He'd probably heard the CO's military history story before, maybe more than once. Like maybe every time a new troop showed up for duty.

"Army Air Corps we were back then," the colonel said, still apparently under the assumption I was interested.

"Of course, we became a separate branch in '47," Col. White continued. *Oh, sure, I remember. I was three at the time.* "U.S. Air Force."

His hands jiggled as he held my paperwork: no wedding ring. Married to the military: another lifer.

"Always loved the military," he said, as if he'd read my thoughts. "Freedom within a predictable structure. Do your duty, act with responsibility, dignity, respect for others, and possibilities for more responsibility are yours. Take as much responsibility as you like, or level off at the altitude you're most comfortable. That's the military way," he said, leaning forward. "I love it. How about you, Airman Flowers? From your file here, seems your tour of duty at San Ramon wasn't a bed of roses? Isn't that a pun?"

I winced a little in the big wooden St. Olaf College chair, whether from his skewering or the wrenching in my upper intestine I couldn't tell. Maybe both.

"Sir, can we keep this between us?" I asked.

"Of course, Airman Flowers." He put on a sincere look, but instantly I surmised that first shirt Buford had already briefed him. I changed tack.

"Colonel, I do my duty to the United States Air Force. I honor my commitment to military servitude — er, I mean service. I would never have done anything to compromise my country or its confidential information. That's nothing to do with losing my security clearance, swear to God."

"Then suppose you tell me what happened, Flowers, so I can believe you're telling me the truth," the CO said, rocking back in his chair again. "Lot of gaps in your AoR that I expect remained confidential with AFCS Command."

I sat there, staring at him for a long time. So I had lost my Secret clearance. He was correct, of course; derogatory information about a GI is often kept confidential for obvious reasons. In my case, I was pretty sure none of the high-ups at San Ramon wanted to admit I'd pulled out the big Congressman gun, or written a defamatory article in the base newspaper. Now I was faced with the decision about how much I should reveal while under the influence of a hangover the size of Alaska.

Heineken. Green beer in a green bottle. Never again. My innards were in total turmoil and I could feel all the blood draining from my skull. I dragged myself to my feet and said, "Sir, I am really not feeling well. Sir, if it's all the same to you I'd like to fall out and resume this discussion later, sir."

"I see you extended your enlistment eighteen months for your tour here at Kleinelachen," Col. White said, as if he hadn't heard a thing I'd said.

Without a reply I stood, whipped off a salute, stumbled out the door and loped across the green to the barracks, where I hooked one hand on the toilet bowl handle and attempted to coordinate the flushing action with my oral discharges. This went on for an extended period of time, then I crawled to my bunk and passed out.

When I awoke, Irish was sitting on my bunk. "How'd it go over at The Dungeon this morning?" He was smiling like a Cheshire cat.

Chapter 9

Stars and Stripes Forever
September, 1967

The day after The First And Worst Hangover Of My Life, I stood again in front of Col. White and heard my orders. "Airman Flowers, you will fall in immediately as the Kleinelachen base correspondent and reporter for the *Stars and Stripes* newspaper. You're still in the AFCS 6069th Squadron, but you will report to Staff Sergeant Theodore Tremblay, an editor of the *Stars and Stripes* up at Ramstein Air Base. Ramstein is USAFE HQ," he added.

I nodded, stunned. The CO continued.

"You will write military-approved news stories and submit them to Sergeant Tremblay on a weekly basis," he continued. "You will obtain prior approval for stories in advance from him, or he will give you assignments. And according to these orders, you'll be taking photos, too."

A writer! Could I believe my good fortune? I'd only written two articles and got in trouble for both of them. My thoughts drifted back to Mr. Diedreich, my high school English teacher and faculty advisor for the Waukegan High literary magazine, cleverly titled *wô-kē'gən*. Two of my stories, "I Am A Rock" and "I Wait for the Red Light" and a poem, "I Am In Love," were published here. Mr. Diedreich was always coming up behind me, wrapping his arm around my shoulders and giving me a kind of awkward squeeze as he breathed, "You're a writer, Nate, down in the blood and bone," into my ear. His cheek rubbed mine; I could smell his Jade East cologne.

The CO was saying something as I returned to the present. "Thank *you*, Colonel," I blurted out at a somewhat higher volume and pitch than I anticipated. "Where will I work? How do I contact Sgt. Tremblay? Where do I get a typewriter? And a camera?"

The Colonel leveled a look at me. "Flowers, have you been listening to me?" he said, exuding the essence of calmness. "You'll work at Base Ops. I'm sorry, but First Sgt. Buford and I simply don't have room for you here."

Oh, gee, what a bummer. Behind me, Buford was banging filing cabinet drawers open and closed. It sounded like exploding cherry bombs.

"Base Supply will issue you a camera. Use the courier or the radio telephone to contact Sgt. Tremblay."

Radio telephone?

"Yes *sir*," I said, coming to attention and snapping off a crisp salute, "Thank *you*, sir!" The CO raised a weary hand to his temple and pushed it at me, then looked down at his desk. Probably wondering if he could squeeze in a little work before falling out for a liquid lunch at the Officer's Mess. I didn't dislike the colonel the way I did Buford; I felt pity for the old soldier more than anything. I did a smart about-face and left The Dungeon.

· · ·

Airman Second Class Milo Gunderson was chief admin clerk for Kleinelachen. He was about my age, slender, a little pale, blonde of hair, blue of eyes. I knew immediately he was sharp as a whip.

"So, the base reporter for the *S&S*," he said. "Not bad, not bad. Still officially a 51205, Confidential security clearance…." *Confidential?* So I had been downgraded. "Your desk is…" he swiveled in his chair and pointed across the room "… there. I'll walk you over. You know, orientation," Milo grinned.

"Where you from?" I asked as we walked down the aisle between the troops wearing identical summer khakis sitting at identical desks, taking pieces of paper from IN baskets, writing, typing or rubber-stamping them, putting them in OUT baskets. They looked like cardboard cutouts.

"Indianapolis," Milo replied.

"You're kidding. Chicago."

"You're kidding," he said.

Just like that we were best buddies.

"Here," said Milo, and we pushed the sole unoccupied desk near the window. "Quieter, and you have a view." I could see the 6069th building's rusty corrugated metal roof and the American flag flapping on its flagpole.

"Far out," I said and sat down. A stack of blank paper rested in the IN basket; the OUT basket was empty. I inserted a sheet in the typewriter, spun the knob and typed

Now is the time for all patriots to come to the aid of the Trystero and buy potsage.

I pulled the paper out and put it in the OUT basket. I was ready to begin my new career as a reporter. "Milo, what's a radio telephone?"

"Aw, that's a lifer word for U.S. military dedicated lines. We don't use the German telephone system so as to keep our comms secure. I'll get you a phone."

No doubt about it, Milo didn't just run Base Ops. He ran Kleinelachen.

Milo and I fell out for lunch at the mess hall, where we had sliced turkey cooked until it was dry as a bone served on Wonder bread and sluiced with brown gravy, a dollop of jellied cranberry, and a piece of semi-wilted lettuce with a wedge of tomato on top. He told me he'd been in the first wave that arrived back in late June, setting up the admin and support functions.

"What's the deal with this place anyway?" I asked between bites.

"Kleinelachen was one of the launch sites for German aircraft attacks on Great Britain during World War II," Milo said. "The airfield was quite visible to the Allies — meaning the English and Americans — so when they flew over on bombing runs the Gerries folded the aircraft's wings up and drove them into underground tunnels and flooded the airfield to look like a farmer's irrigated field. Farmers still grow wheat or hay or something, between our runways and Stuttgart's. Cows graze here, too."

"On *our* military base?" I asked.

"Yeah, we have to let 'em. They were here first. You saw the barn, right?" I shook my head. "There's a great big old barn full of hay a hundred feet behind our barracks."

He went on about how Kleinelachen had sat unoccupied and dilapidated since the end of World War II, until a few years ago when the Army Corps of Engineers decided to bivouac here. That brought the place to the attention of the brass at Ramstein. "The Air Force decided to take it over. Ordered the Army Corps of

Wild Blue Yonder

Engineers to fix the place up for them." Milo leaned forward. "They definitely resent us for that. They're still working here. Try to be nice to them."

"So, why do we want it?" I shoved some cranberry sauce in my mouth.

"General Beauregard — he's commander-in-chief of USAFE — needs a place to land his personal jet."

"Yeah, Irish McKreven told me."

"We provide all the support services — maintenance, hangar, radar, radio, ILS, the works," said Milo, forking a piece of roast beef and waving it at me, "but we also have a daily courier transport that flies from England to Ramstein to here once a day. Just to make it look like we're a legit air base."

"So, the support troops for the General's plane, they're about…."

"…a dozen or so. Your outfit," said Milo. "But it takes over a hundred support troops to support your dozen troops."

"To support one aircraft…"

"…Which will probably land here about once a month," said Milo, scooping some mashed potatoes, "but don't forget the courier. Nothing can stop the U.S. Air Farce," Milo sang in a falsetto voice.

I grinned, shook my head. "Do you know where can I find a copy of the *Stars and Stripes*?"

"Geez, that's a good question," he said. "I'm not sure I've seen it here on base. I'll get the courier to bring some in."

That afternoon I went to Base Supply for a camera. A fat grumpy tech sergeant named Murphy asked me for requisition paperwork, which of course I didn't have, but Milo got me the AF44663-I to fill out. However, there was no camera. "I'll give him a nudge," Milo said, continuing my orientation.

• • •

I decided gathering news meant meeting the new troops when the courier arrived, which led to picking up the mail sack for Sgt. Buford along with the daily batch of the *Stars and Stripes*. Sometimes troops arrived at Stuttgart International on commercial flights, so Eric The Mad Chauffeur Miranda and I drove over to pick them up.

A2C Tim Rosencrantz, an Air Traffic Controller, arrived by courier. He was tall, incredibly skinny, light brown hair, hazel eyes. He had a viciously pocked face and wore a cynical expression to go with it. When I stuck out my hand to welcome

122

him, Rosenkrantz said, "Power to the People. The United States Air Force violates my civil rights."

"Yeah, uh, right on," I replied, but he had already brushed past me. My reporter's instincts told me this troop had a story.

A few days later, A2C Richard Broward, another ATC controller, climbed into the Econoline and said, "Aw, fuuuuckkkkk! Germany?" He had a cigarette tucked behind his right ear, bleached blonde hair, a cowlick hanging over his forehead, a great tan, and clear blue eyes. "Where'n fuck am I gonna surf?"

Ricky was as boisterous as Tim was reserved. Tim had been stationed in Greece; Ricky was straight out of tech school. His hair was always too long and he wore his garrison hat with the brim curled into a near circle, but never got reprimanded for either. He never called anybody by their name, but instead cried "Troooop?" He talked about Southern California all the time. Even though he was good-humored, I wasn't always comfortable around him.

Two troops from my career field arrived on the courier together, Alan Gardner and a kid named Henry Henry. I figured one or both were taking my place. We hit it off right away, maybe because we had crypto and intercept in common. They were in the same class at Biloxi, started about six months after me, and after graduation were sent to a dreary little base in western Texas. Just six months later they were transferred to Kleinelachen. I wondered about that.

• • •

Eric drove me to Ramstein, about an hour away, for my first meeting with Sgt. Tremblay. It was a big, busy place. The *Stars and Stripes,* All Europe Edition, occupied the entire second floor of an admin building. The room was filled with the nearly deafening sound of clacking typewriters. I had written my first piece for the newspaper, inspired by the colonel's words about freedom and responsibility, which had come to mind more than once as I settled into my new job. I had an extraordinary amount of freedom in my daily duties, which I appreciated, as well as a profound sense of responsibility in my new role as a journalist for the world-renowned daily military newspaper.

SSgt. Thomas Tremblay was a ruggedly handsome fellow, probably around 30 or so, with thick, spiky brown hair and brown eyes, heavy features, hairy knuckles, and a cleft chin. He spoke with a crisp, almost curt tone, as if I were a real pain in his butt. "You *will* deliver a news story approximately 500-700 words long, with

123

or without photos, to me every Friday morning by 1000 hours." *Will.* After two and a half years in the service, I still got mad when somebody told me I *will* do something. I began to describe my first piece on the theme of duty and responsibility and handed it to him. I looked at his desk plaque, identical to Col. White's and Buford's, as he read.

WHAT IS MY DUTY?
By
Nathaniel H. Flowers, A1C
Kleinelachen Air Base Correspondent

What is my duty? This is a question every man and woman in the military must answer. We are ordered to perform our assigned duties, which are cast in the stone of military protocol. In time of war, those duties are very clear cut, and intended to protect us from the enemy and preserve our nationalistic freedoms. We know and understand these duties, because we have been trained to perform them. We do so with the utmost responsibility and integrity we are capable of. But there are other, higher duties for which we are responsible, not just to the military but to our fellow man, and to God.

What is that duty? It is to think, speak and act.

I think, said the philosopher Sartre, because I am. It is our human nature to think, but often people play a game of abstractions with themselves and with others. We smile proudly, strike forcefully, react seriously. These ego-games continue *ad nauseam*, until no one cares what we do, only impatiently await their chance to also react. I think we care too much about matters which, in the final analysis, will make little, if any, difference. It is our duty to think about the most important matters so that we forge the new consciousness of the world.

I speak when I have something to say. My words are not always wise, nor always true. I am a finite creature, subject to infinite subtleties and capable of change. To recognize this requires going beyond mere words, mere abstractions, to truths. Truths themselves are subjective and interpretive, mine no more valid than yours. To discuss them is to listen to them, and in that light I will never consider mine more valid than yours. Yet there are universal truths, and it is each person's duty to know them.

When I act it is after I have thought over my action. In situations involving other people, my thoughts have found voice, and my ears have heard the concepts, thoughts, truths of others. My action, when taken, is deliberate and above reproach. In military life, this is essential in order to perform our duty and to be responsible to our fellow troops. In most cases you will agree with my actions, because they are in both yours and my best interests. But you may find them reprehensible at other times, and if so you must respect that I have thought carefully before acting. But upon the point of acting I am fulfilling my deepest duty, and in that I shall not be shaken.

After a while he set the papers down gently on his desk, tapped his fingertips, stared quietly at me. After a long pause he said, "What is this?" I didn't know how to answer him, but no matter: he answered for me. "This is not journalism, Flowers. This is an essay for a tenth-grade Civics class. At best. But it is *not* an article for the *Stars and Stripes*." His eyes stared at me like bullets. "Don't ever give me a piece like this again, Flowers, or I'll have your ass. You will write to my specifications. I seen that piece you wrote when you were at San Ramon. You know the one. Keep your nose clean, boy."

I felt awful, small and stupid and worthless. No one had ever criticized my writing like this, and it felt terrible. Then he lightened up and asked what else I had in mind. I gathered myself together and told him what I'd learned about Kleinelachen, not mentioning that Milo was my sole source. "OK, Flowers, then that's your assignment. Your audience is all the other military people stationed all over Europe. Tell them about your base. Where is it? What's its history or origins? Why is it there? Who mans it? What makes it important to USAFE? Get the reader interested. Start with that and see where the story leads you," Tremblay said, then he leaned back and cracked a thin grin. "I'll expect your copy next Friday."

After my meeting, Eric The Mad Chauffeur drove me to the PX for supplies. There was a record rack, but I was disappointed to see junk my parents would listen to: Perry Como, Rosemary Clooney, Tony Bennett, Ray Conniff, and *The 101 Strings Play the Beatles*. On the way back to base I talked Eric into driving to Stuttgart, where I bought some spiffy corduroy pants, a few shirts, a pack of French Gitanes, and an English recording of Jimi Hendrix's *Are You Experienced*. Ricky had a phonograph. He'd play it and I'd tell the troops about seeing Hendrix at Monterey Pop.

Wild Blue Yonder

. . .

Jane wrote me letters at the rate of about one a week in a loopy, sensuous hand. Although there was a "Dear Diary" aspect to them, I eagerly read each one right out of my mailbox.

…I took the MG out for a drive in the country the other day. I've gotten quite good with shifting the gears, and it was high times!! on the twisty little back roads up to Petaluma. It was warm and sunny so I had the top down and the wind blew through my hair (I'm growing it long for you – don't ask me why! – but I thought you might like it longer) and the radio played songs we both love. I stopped at the A&W for a root beer float and, well, the only thing missing was you, and I do I do I do miss you so much, Nate. I know it's hard for you to understand some of this, but maybe it's because you don't really know your own feelings very well.

I'm not sure I will like this American Literature course I'm taking. The teacher, a Mr. Sutton, is so serious he's almost grim. We're working our way forward in time, and he's told us he is avoiding what he calls "the chestnuts of American Lit," like *Moby Dick* and *The Great Gatsby*. Right now we're reading *Wieland* by Charles Brockden Brown, which he wrote in 1798. Do you realize how old that makes it? 169 years old!

I wrote her back, telling her about the tiny base and my new assignment:

I have to write a 500- to 700-word article each week. I meet the courier each day to meet the new troops. Two guys I like a lot are Alan Gardner from Boston and Tim Rosencrantz from somewhere in Michigan. Alan doesn't say much, but he's paying attention to what's going on and he seems thought-ful. Tim, I think, is what you would call a radical. Oh, you won't believe it but we have practically no music. One guy from Southern California has a portable stereo, but he won't let anybody else play their records and all he listens to is Jan and Dean and the Beach Boys surfer music. Yep, he's a surfer all right!

. . .

Stars and Stripes Forever

Date: 13 September 1967
TO: All Personnel 6069 AFCS
FROM: Lt. Col. T. X. White
SUBJECT: Monthly Squardron Meeting

You will fall out at 1000 hours 14 Septmember 1967 for the meeting in the Base Ops Conference Room.

Signed,
SSgt Wilford H. Buford
First Sergeant

As Buford introduced Colonel White I smirked, thinking about the typos in his bulletin board memo. "Welcome one and all to the AFCS 6069th. Men, I know you'll be happy to hear, as I was, that the radar set is scheduled to be delivered tomorrow." A satisfied murmur circled the room. "It is being flown by MAC on a C-130 from England to Frankfurt and delivered here by truck." Military Airlift Command. England. *Wasn't that where Tony got stationed?* I wondered what the radar looked like; it sounded huge. "We expect it to be operational within 48 hours of delivery," the colonel continued. "Soon we will be actively fulfilling our mission." Everybody murmured again, nodding at each other that they were glad to hear this, because it meant they could finally get to work. Even GIs get tired of not working: besides, there were rumors we'd be put on grounds maintenance or in the mess hall if the radar installation was delayed much longer. *Well, this was my next story.*

The other news was that next Monday, 18 September, was the 20th anniversary of the United States Air Force. "General Beauregard will be officiating," Col. White said. *Whoops, hold the presses.* The troops let out a somewhat more cheerful sound. *Aha, that's why they're so anxious to get the radar up and running.* Then the CO said, "There will be a full-dress inspection and parade and all Air Force personnel will fall in…"

Groans.

"…followed by field ceremonies," the colonel continued, "and after that a celebration with food, beer, wine and music in Hangar 2…."

A great cheer.

"We'll need some personnel to set up the party…"

Hands and cheers went up at once.

Buford barked "Ten-hut!" and everybody quieted down. The colonel turned toward Buford and said, "Sgt. Buford will be in charge of selecting the personnel for Hangar 2 duty."

Groans.

Buford stood up and glared like a lunatic around the room, obviously delighted at his newly bestowed power, then sat down again.

• • •

I was at my typewriter the day after the Air Force birthday party, nursing The Second Worst Hangover Of My Life, when I heard the radar set was finally going to arrive. I'd have just enough time to write and file the story by my Friday morning deadline. I'd hoped to take pictures with my camera, a Hasselblad 500 single-lens reflex with a motor drive. It wasn't new, but it was in perfect condition and just about the coolest thing I'd ever held in my hands. Unfortunately, Murph told me it would be at least another week to get film; so much for photos of the radar installation.

I hopped in a van with Ricky, Tim and Irish and we headed down the runway access road to check out the radar set. We passed the big barn Milo had told me about; a farmer unloaded a wooden wagon of hay bales. Ricky was driving; a small transistor radio on the dash playing a loud, distorted "A Quick One While He's Away" by The Who from Radio Luxembourg, and it was making him drive too fast.

"Great song," said Ricky, "but I wish they'd play some fuckin' Beach Boys once in a while."

"I saw them do this at Monterey Pop," I said.

"What the fuck? Who? *The Who?* What the *fuck?*" Ricky said over his shoulder. "You were at fucking Monterey *Pop?*"

"Yeah, that's right, The Who," I said. "In June, just before I came over here. It was really far out. You could walk anywhere and watch the bands setting up. Lee — my roomie who shipped out to Vietnam — he and I wandered into a tent and there's Peter Townsend sitting at a keyboard playing little riffs. I stood right behind him. He looked up at me and smiled and said, 'Hello, mate!'"

"Oy vey, Peter Townsend, oh wow," said Tim.

"Yeah, we saw lots of musicians that afternoon. Not as close as Peter. David Crosby. Grace Slick. Man, she's so beautiful. A lot we didn't know. Somebody said the Beatles were there." Ricky had slowed the van; everybody listened intently.

"And then that night," I went on, "Saturday night, there's The Who on stage. I'm about twenty, maybe thirty feet away, and they're all dressed in these really cool paisley psychedelic looking mod shirts and jackets, and you know Roger Daltry? He's got on this cool little cape, and they play, you know, really fine, just playing the songs like usual until the last one, 'My Generation,' you know, 'hope I die before I get old,' and Townsend is wailing on his guitar, windmilling his pick hand up into the air like he does, then he just starts smashing his guitar on the stage like a sledgehammer, and it busts up and starts squealing and groaning and still he's like smashing the neck into his amplifiers. Then the roadies rush out and start hauling mikes and stuff out of his way and he and Roger walk off the stage while Keith Moon, man that guy is the world's greatest drummer, I swear to God, he's still thrashing the drums 'til the end when he kicks them over and walks off the stage after Townsend and Daltry and Entwhistle! It was un-be-lievable!"

There was silence, then "You saw all that?" Tim asked. "You were at the *whole* Monterey Pop concert?"

"Well, yeah," I answered, "I pretty much remember it all. But we were, you know, ah..." I squeezed my thumb and forefinger together and pressed them to my lips.

"You smoked pot?" Tim asked. I nodded. "Wow, I would like to do that some time."

"Aw, it's not such a big deal," said Ricky. "We used to get high all the time when we surfed."

"Eh, you can keep the drugs," Irish said. "Gimme a beer any day. But, so why did he do that? Why did he bust up a perfectly good guitar?"

"Well, I think he was trying to drive home the message of 'My Generation,' to let us know he was really serious about turning away from the straight world where you would never expect somebody to do something like that. The straights would think, well, just play the song and we'll clap at the end. Pete was saying Hey, I'm really serious about this message, you know, not digging what we say. It's bullshit, all of it, and I'm going to prove it by destroying my guitar, my own music. Then I'll just walk off the stage. No bows or encores or any of the crap you'd expect from a — a *performer*. You know what I mean?"

"Yeah, I dig what you say," said Irish, a grin and grimace crossing his face. Tim nodded solemnly again and again while Ricky stared straight out the windshield. I wondered what he was thinking; probably not what I was. I turned to look out the window. The Kleinelachen runway was still in pretty bad shape. Weeds were everywhere, big bushes of them growing out of cracks in the concrete, but Army troops were hard at work on them.

"Look at those poor bastards out there," I said.

"What a shit detail," said Irish.

"Yeah," said Ricky, "proof once again that shit does roll downhill."

We slowed down as we approached a flatbed trailer truck with two big Army green boxes tied down on it. They looked like small railroad boxcars and rested on big fat tires.

"Oy vey, not a Gilfillan," Tim said.

"Tim, knock off the fuckin' oy vey, will ya?" barked Ricky.

"What's a Gilfillan?" I asked, the reporter on assignment.

"It's the company that makes this radar set," Tim said. "This is the oldest gear in the Air Force. Built in World War II. I haven't seen one since tech school. They must have dragged this one out of mothballs *especially* for us."

I remembered where I'd seen these big boxy trailers before: Keesler.

"Well, I heard it came from a base in England," Ricky said.

"Probably been sitting up there since World War II," Tim replied.

We pulled up on a large poured concrete pad, clearly new. A couple of sergeants and a bunch of airmen were talking.

"What about lifting them off with the forklift?" one of the three-stripers said.

"Nope," said a tech sergeant. "They're too heavy. Tip the forklift right over."

A pretty stiff wind blew. For the better part of half an hour, they tried to figure out how to get the two radar set trailers off the flatbed truck. There was no story here, at least not yet. Ricky and Tim joined the huddle. Irish walked around smirking.

The next day I was back, watching an Army UH-1 Iroquois helicopter which had flown over from Patch Barracks lift the trailers off the flatbed and set them on the pad. Three Air Force NCOs jumped out of the Huey wearing crisply starched fatigues, bloused and tucked into spit-shined black field boots. They leveled the trailers and installed the radar and radio antennas. Two tall utility poles stuck out of the pad. One was metal with a wind sock on it, showing a pretty steady wind blowing again today. The other was a wooden telephone pole with a thick electrical cable that dropped into a metal box.

Once the engineering NCOs had finished the setup, one came over to the box, opened the panel door and looked inside. "Hey!" he called out to the others, "This is Kraut juice."

"You have *got* to be shitting me," said one of our noncoms, coming to look. "Jesus Mary and Joseph, this is just what I needed. 240 volts, 50 cycles. We can't even run a light bulb on this."

A week later, two more Army Hueys came wop-wop-wopping in, each with a blue diesel generator nearly as big as a radar trailer suspended from its belly. Buford had been scrambling to find two generator operators. He eventually found them at Karlsruhe, and they were none too happy about getting assigned to our dreary little base. It was rotten duty, 12 on and 12 off; the generators roared twenty-four hours a day, seven days a week, to keep the radar set humming away on 120-volt, 60-cycle electricity. One of them said to me, "I'd just as soon the dang thing breaks and hafta fix it as sit on mah arse in here all day."

• • •

My story on the 20th anniversary had shipped to SSgt. Tremblay the week before. There were escapades I couldn't repeat – something about Tim saluting with his middle finger, maybe? — and probably others I simply couldn't remember. This week, my story was about Kleinelachen becoming operational. I gave it the title, "Out of Farmland Fields Rises Kleinelachen, a New American Air Base." Each day I scanned the *S&S*, looking for my story, but none was to be found. I called Tom Tremblay and he said, "Be patient. Rome didn't burn in a day."

Chapter 10
Der Alten Scheune
October, 1967

"OK now, troops, watch this," Antonio Bartolomeo Rizzo said, opening a small paisley bag and withdrawing a funny little thing from inside. He adjusted it; a red belt moved between two rollers. He stuck two fingers back into the bag and withdrew a quantity of marijuana, which he stuffed into the belt. He rolled the rollers, inserted a thin piece of paper from a little packet, and rolled them again. He licked the paper and rolled once more; out popped a joint as perfect as a cigarette. Tony held it up for us to see in the dim light of the lantern. "Pretty groovy, huh?"

We — Tony, Alan, Henry Harold Henry, Tim and I — were sitting in a circle upstairs in the old barn behind our barracks. Tony had surprised me by stepping off the courier that morning. "Hey, man," I said, "What're you doing here?"

"Came to see you," he said.

"But how did you know where — "

"The radar set. It was at my base, Mildenhall. We shipped to down to Ramstein." He leaned close to me and said, "MAC knows all, sees all," and handed me a cardboard box.

"What's this?" I said.

"Film for your Hasselblad," he grinned, and threw an arm over my shoulder.

The sun had set and the world of Kleinelachen had grown quiet. The gentle smells of nature were lost in the sweet scent of marijuana smoke. Tony handed the joint to me; I lit it, taking a long hit. It was the first grass I'd smoked since coming to Germany. As I held the smoke in my lungs I could feel it moving through my head, slowing time down, turning all five senses on. I gazed at the soft yellow light from the lantern and, for the first time, noticed the little bugs flying around in its light. I exhaled toward them; no reason they couldn't get high too.

I took another toke and passed the joint to Tim. He looked at it, looked at me and back at the joint. "It's cool, Tim," I said. "Just take small puffs this first time," I instructed him, just as Jane taught me. He did. He still coughed. The rest of us still laughed. Meanwhile, Tony handed the joint-roller and pot pouch to Alan.

"Ahh, I don't need that thing," Alan said. He pulled two papers out of the package, licked the edge of one paper and glued it to the other. He shook weed into it and hand-rolled a lovely bone. Just like Jane used to. Jane. I thought about our times getting high, singing, dancing, laughing at nothing and everything. Alan lit up, took a toke, and looked at the book of papers. "Riz La. Haven't seen these before."

"They're French. Made of rice paper," said Tony.

"No wonder they smoke so smooth," Alan said, taking a toke and passing the joint on. Now we had two circulating. "So, how did you and Nate meet?"

"San Francisco. Haight-Ashbury. At a Grateful Dead concert, more or less." Tony grinned at me.

"The Haight. Wow, that's far out," said Henry Harold Henry.

"Yeah, he bummed a ride off me back to base," I said, and between us we told our story. I glanced at Tim; his head hung from his shoulders, rolling slightly back and forth. Stoned. Grooving.

"Nate," said Henry, "you didn't tell us you got a girlfriend back home!"

I'm sure I blushed, but nobody could see me in the dark. "No, she's not my girlfriend, we're just friends, she's a good kid — "

"Yeah, right, you're so dense, Nate," Tony said. "That girl is head over heels for you!" He laughed, the way he always did, in staccato bursts, "Ha! Ha! Ha!" The others joined in, except for Tim, who was clearly gone to a higher plane of consciousness.

"How'd you meet her?" Alan asked. I told him. "That reminds me. How come you're named after an old dead author from Boston?"

"My dad. It was my dad's idea. He thought Nathaniel Hawthorne was the best ever American writer."

"You...have...got...to...be...shitting...me," drawled Henry Harold Henry. Then he burst into stoned-out laughter.

134

"Well, some families name kids after aunts and uncles and grandparents... yeah, what about your name, Henry?"

"Yeah, you got me," Henry Harold Henry said. "And I'm the third."

I pointed at Henry and Alan. "How did you guys meet?" I asked, anxious to shift attention from myself.

"Good question," Alan answered. "I think Henry Harold Henry got stuck to the bottom of my brogan."

Laughter.

"Yeah, fuck you too, Alan," Henry Harold Henry chortled. "He needed help with his homework. And him, wid' both his parents college profs." Henry often chortled at the end of a sentence, which I found a likeable trait.

"I believe it was the other way around, triple-H."

"You guys," I said.

"Don't you believe in the Cosmic Giggle, Nate?" Henry said.

On it went like that, everybody chiming in to tell a story or two about themselves.

Alan had a full head of bushy dark brown hair, a matching mustache, and deep brown eyes that always looked like there were interesting and mysterious things going on behind them. He was from Cambridge, Massachusetts, but didn't seem to want to talk about his family or his previous life in the Real World. "The alten Scheune is a pretty far out place to get high, you know it?" he said. We nodded.

Henry Harold Henry grew up in blue-collar South Philly, son of a steelworker and stay-at-home mother taking care of six kids. He was a wiry, short guy with sandy brown hair, quick, bright light brown eyes, a long, sharp nose, and a thin mouth that smiled most of the time.

Tim, returning to the group, said he was an only child whose father was a tailor who ran a dry cleaning shop with his wife. Tony told the story of his multi-generational vintner family, and I told them about his wine vat house and what we'd done there.

"Psychedelics," said Alan with reverence in his voice. "Yeah, man, I really want to do some acid. Do some real tripping."

"I can get you guys anything you want in London," said Tony. "Anything. I can hop it down here on the courier. I'm in transportation so nobody pays me any attention. But you guys gotta come to London Town. It's like no place you've ever been."

135

"That would be totally far out," said Henry, and began rolling another joint from Tony's stash.

"Yeah, far out," said Tim, who took a toke then laid down, slipping back into his stone. We were all getting really stoned and the conversation began to dwindle, each of us drifting in our own thoughts as our high went on, on, far into the night.

• • •

When we finally untangled our legs and climbed down the ladder out of the hayloft, Tony grabbed an empty bunk in our barracks and everybody crashed. The next morning as we ate chow, he told us about a place called Baden-Baden, a Canadian PX where we could buy stereos. "Not stereos like your mom and dad's big piece of furniture, or even like your old record player. You buy a receiver – that's the amplifier and the radio part – and a record player, that's called a turntable – and speakers. You hook them all together and you get really high quality sound reproduction. Some of the troops at Mildenhall have stuff they got at Baden-Baden. They call it 'stereo gear.'"

"You guys want to go?" I asked. Alan and Tim said yes, but Henry had duty. "I'll see if I can get Eric to drive us there." He didn't want to, but to my surprise he checked out the van to us. We headed for the Autobahn and into the headlong traffic. I stuck to the slow lane and the official military vehicle speed posted on the dashboard. We made our way deep into the Schwartzwald and down the road, heading for stereo nirvana.

"Nate," said Tim from the back, "Where does your old man teach?"

"Ah, he doesn't. Anymore. He died of a heart attack. In 1963." Four years ago. Had it really been four years already?

"Oh, I'm sorry," said Tim. "I didn't know."

"Well, it's OK. I don't talk about it much. I still miss him."

"Believe me, he does," said Tony.

"How do you know?" I said.

"'Whom the gods love dies young,'" said Alan. "Herodotus."

"Interesting," I said. We were silent for a while, then I said, "He used to tell us stories at night. Ernest, Frankie, and me. He'd tell us the stories of the great novels, shortened you know, and read passages from them. Like Reader's Digest Condensed Books, I guess. He was a great reader. Performer. Really knew how to tell a story."

"Yeah?" said Alan. "Can you tell us one? Like your dad did?"

"Well, let's see." I thought a bit. Tony, who was sitting in the passenger seat, began rolling a joint and said "Give him a minute." We laughed. The joint went around, then I pulled over and stopped. "Somebody else drive, and I'll tell the story. I don't think I can do both at the same time — stoned." Tony took the wheel.

"OK, this is a story from my namesake. Most everybody's heard of *The House of the Seven Gables* and *The Scarlet Letter*, but Hawthorne wrote hundreds of short stories, too. Let's see, which one should I tell..." and as I paused, one came to mind without my conscious thought. "OK, it's 'Dr. Heidegger's Experiment.'"

"OK, so there's this old doctor named Heidegger, and he calls four friends — three men and a woman — to his house one afternoon and tells them this decanter on the table contains water from the Fountain of Youth. No one believes him, but he entices them into taking a drink and sure enough, they begin to grow younger. It feels so great they all drink again and grow even younger. They drink a third time and feel all their age leaving them — you know, wrinkles and aches and all, and they become immature, like kids again, and begin to squabble and it comes out that all three of the old men had crushes on the woman when they were youth, and now they begin to argue over her all over again. Meanwhile, old Dr. Heidegger is watching this -"

"Hey," said Tony, "drinking the waters from the Fountain of Youth. It's kind of like us getting high, isn't it?"

"Oh, far out," said Alan. "I didn't think of that. Great connection."

"Yeah, yeah," said Tim, "changing your perspective on things. I've never had so many new thoughts and perceptions, ever. From smoking pot, I mean."

"And so back to the story," said Tony.

"Here's the thing. Old Dr. Heidegger, he doesn't partake. He remains the same. He's just watching this all going on, right?"

"Yeah, that's the perspective thing, I guess," said Tim. "Hawthorne wants us to see him as the stable, mature, wise grownup who watches as the others act more and more foolish, like children."

"That's a decanter full of bullshit," said Alan. "Fuck adults and adulthood and being mature and looking down on childhood as childish. I *want* to be a child on a quest for wonder for the rest of my life."

"Perspective," said Tim. "Times change. Values are a lot different now than when Hawthorne wrote."

"I wonder," said Tony. "I truly do. I think our parents and their generation still push their grown-up trip on us. 'Grow up.' 'Be a man.' I mean, hell, what's the military all about after all? Conformity. Maturity. Responsibility."

I nodded. Growing up? What did it get us? I wondered which I preferred to be, the child or the adult.

Ahead of us, a sign said

Baden
Baden-Baden
5 KM

"You guys ever wonder what you're doing here?" Alan asked.

"Ha! Ha!! You mean as in 'Why Are We Here?'" said Tony.

"No, not the big one. You kind of don't count, Tony. You didn't get sent to Kleinelachen. I mean, why did the Air Force send us to this base?"

I had to admit I hadn't given it a thought, except the thing about writing my Congressman and how sending me to Vietnam might be construed as punishment for it. But I didn't say anything. "Hey Alan, I said, looking over my shoulder. "You went to college, right?"

Baden
Baden-Baden
4 KM

"Are you serious? College is a farce," he said. "Another institution for creating a uniform society of conformists. Think about it. Everybody dresses the same, reads the same textbooks, learns the same social rules. There's no way to develop your individuality or creativity, and by the time you graduate you're one of *them*."

He went on raving like that as I wondered if this was why I'd done badly at Chicago. Perhaps I didn't fit the mold, even though I was unaware I was being molded. No, that wasn't it; I think I wanted to fit in. Belong.

"That's the propaganda we get fed by the institutions – family, society, education, business, work, all of them to mold and shape us into docile, responsible, citizens making this supposedly a better world."

I'd never questioned the mold before. "Yeah, I guess you're right."

138

"You damn betcha he's right," said Tony. "But look at us now, in the military. What could be more of a society of conformists than this?"

Baden
Baden-Baden
3 KM

"Did you *choose* to join the service, Tony?" Alan asked. "I sure didn't. Society forced me into a corner. Don't want to go to college? OK, then we're gonna draft you. Don't want to go in the Army and become a trained killer? OK, then you can join the Air Force or Navy, but you have to serve twice as long. So yeah, if that was my choice, yeah, I made it. But at least we don't have to kill Commies."

"That's why I'm here," said Tim, speaking for the first time. "No draft, no Army, no killing Commies for me. Peace, man."

"But those were our choices," said Tony. "No choice. I hate the military. Man, I thought I hated college, but now I *know* I fuckin' hate everything about the military. You know something? In basic training, I had to chow down as fast as I could so I could go behind the mess hall to memorize the insignias for rank. I didn't know an officer from an enlisted man! But this is their establishment, man. Everybody has to have a title and their little rank on their shoulder or their sleeve so everybody knows their place in the pecking order."

"Speaking of which," I said, "What do you think of this new reg changing ranks?" As of 19 October, Air Force Regulation 39-36 (revised) designated us E4s as Sergeants, not Airmen. "I think they're just putting us on. Nothing else changed, not our stripes or our pay grade. It just a sort of trick to entice us into re-enlisting." Even as I said this, another part of me felt sort of proud.

"Not something I think much about," said Tony. "I got busted back to E-3 twice. I don't think I'll get promoted again. I just want to stay out of trouble until I'm out." *Twice.* Tony hadn't learned Dylan's Memphis Blues price for not repeating mistakes.

Baden
Baden-Baden
2 KM

"So," Alan said, "maybe you do qualify after all. I ask again: Why are we here? Why aren't we in Vietnam? Anybody?"

139

"Hmmm. Not sure," I said. "Everybody else in my outfit at San Ramon went west, not east. Well, there was this thing with my promotion to E-4...."

"What do you mean, *thing?*" Alan asked.

"Um, well, I got passed over because an admin lost my paperwork..."

"And so?" said Alan.

"So I wrote my Congressman..."

Tim and Alan burst into uncontrollable laughter which ricocheted off the bare steel walls of the van. Gales of laughter. Whoops of laughter. Knee-slapping, can't-come-up-for-breath laughter.

"YOU WROTE YOUR CONGRESSMAN!" Alan cried out. "GOD! NOBODY WRITES THEIR CONGRESSMAN FOR REAL!"

Tim was wiping tears from his eyes.

"Well, that's what I did, and..."

They started whooping again.

"...and you know what, he called some full bird colonel at the Pentagon."

"Yeah?" Alan asked.

"Well, I got the stripe, of course, and then about a month or so later I got orders for Germany. I was pretty psyched."

"Yeah, psyched, okay," said Alan.

"Well, you know what I mean. First off, I wasn't going to the combat zone. Second, I thought it would be cool to see Europe. Thirdly, I got this new duty assignment, base correspondent for the *Stars and Stripes.* The only thing was, the orders were for a three-year tour. So I had to re-up for an extra eighteen months."

"And you did that?" Tim said. "You actually signed an extension for another year and a half?"

"Well, yeah, I did."

"That totally bites," Alan said.

"No, it's OK," I said, hastily. "I mean, I don't like the military, for sure, but this is pretty light duty. I mean, I have a lot of freedom with my journalism job, you know."

"Yeah, and a dog has a lot of freedom at the end of his leash," Alan shot back.

"I'm gonna travel a lot, get to know Germany, and Europe, you know, maybe even stay here after discharge. I've heard you can do that," I said.

Abruptly, Alan asked, "So here we are again. Have you asked yourself why the Air Force shipped us to Germany instead of Vietnam?"

Der Alten Scheune

Baden
Baden-Baden
1 KM

I didn't answer right away. "Well, yes and no. I guess one thought that crossed my mind was they sent me here because sending me to Vietnam might look like they were punishing me for writing to my Congressman. But I also wondered if it was normal rotation and they didn't need anybody from my old career field."

"How many troops did they need in your career field at San Ramon?" Alan asked.

"Well, now that you mention it, we *were* pretty overstaffed..." Slowly, through the residual, diaphanous haze of cannabis, it began to dawn what he was getting at. "So, how come you guys got stationed here?"

I looked at Tony: he was slowing down. I looked into the back: Tim was gazing out the window. Alan was looking right at me.

"Ever hear of the novel by Thomas Hardy, *Far from the Madding Crowd?*" he asked.

"Sure, I've heard of it. I *was* an English major. Can't say I've read it."

"Well, that's us. Far away, where we can't cause any trouble." Alan leaned forward, speaking quietly. "Henry had a bit of a – um – nervous breakdown at Sheppard. An Air Force doctor put him on Librium instead of making him go 4-F. Next thing he knew, he got orders for Kleinelachen."

"What about you?" I asked.

"Wichita Falls was a pressure cooker for everybody in crypto. Brass saw a Commie under every stone. A subversive plot behind every corner. Our loyalty was constantly scrutinized and everything I did, on-duty or off – well, there was just no trust at all. They were so paranoid they made me paranoid."

"All the time we were there, we never worked live. You won't believe this, but they had us working with a machine called ENIGMA that was built in 1943. We were supposed to be receiving and decrypting messages intercepted by an encryption machine that was in museums. So I decided to make a statement to the brass. I went to the library and found books and magazine articles from the '40s that told about great triumphs of the ENIGMA, and began reporting encrypted messages from World War II."

I laughed. "Did they figure it out?"

"Oh yeah, eventually. But it took them a while. I ended up having to drop some clues because they were so dense. Of course, the clues pointed right at me. I knew they would. I just didn't give a shit at that point. The really funny part was that if they tried to punish me — remember, this could have been a court-martial offense since it involved national security, so to speak — they would be incriminating themselves because they had bought it. So I was safe in that respect, but I was also burned — I lost my top-secret security clearance. That's why I got sent here — where I can't do any harm to 'national security.' The most classified message that goes through Kleinelachen is a telephone call. I basically have nothing to monitor. Which is fine with me. Henry Harold Henry and I have three years to put our brogans up on the desk and dig Europe."

My neck was stiff. I turned to look out the windshield.

"But here's the real question," said Alan. "Why did they send us here, to this peaceful, conquered country in Europe? Wouldn't it have made more sense to send us radicalized, angry, sick, anti-American types to Vietnam or Laos or Cambodia, where we would be pretty much assured we'd come home in a body bag?

"And if that were the case, then why do they send the poor, dumb, clueless, and illiterate clodhoppers to the front lines? Aren't these the guys who will come home from war and become the pillars of the community? "Does any part of this make sense to you?"

"It sure as hell doesn't make any sense to me," said Tony.

"Nope, me either," said Tim.

Ahead, the sign read

Baden
Baden-Baden

Chapter 11

Sedition
December, 1967

Now four of us in the barracks had our own stereo gear. Troops took turns playing records, except for me: I had nothing to listen to, so the week after Tony left, I took the courier to England to see him and buy some records. Tom gave me a weekend pass. That was the coolest thing about him being my supervisor: I didn't have to ask Buford for time off, which he would never approve. The uncoolest thing was I still hadn't seen one of my stories published, and whenever I asked him, he'd give me the line about Rome. One time it was "Rome wasn't built in a day." Another was "Rome wasn't conquered in a day," or "Rome didn't fall in a day." I wished I knew what he was talking about.

We touched down at Mildenhall. Tony picked me up in a Jeep and drove to the barracks. We trudged up two flights of stairs and down a long, seafoam green hallway with doors on either side, stopping at one. Tony put his key in the lock and winked at me. He pushed the door open. It was like our rooms at San Ramon: a bunk bed, desk, big easy chair, rock concert posters from the Fillmore and Avalon on the walls.

"Geez, man, you didn't tell me you had a suite! What's that on the table?" I asked, pointing at an odd globe.

"This is NCO quarters," he said, grinning. "I'm on the good side of the flight line crews. Give 'em rides to their planes. Take their uniforms to the dry cleaners. Stuff like that. One of the pilots, Captain Jennison, asked his NCOIC to fix me up with my own room. So I'd always be on call, you understand. And it's called a lava lamp. I'll show you what it does tonight."

"You're something else," I said, tossing my AWOL bag on the upper bunk.

"Well, as somebody once said, To the spoilers goes the victory. Ha! Ha! Ha!"

"Whatever that's supposed to mean."

Tony had to go back to work, so he dropped me at the main gate with instructions to take the public bus to Piccadilly Circus. It wasn't a circus, more like an intersection with a huge statue of a scantily clad archer with wings. I walked down Shaftesbury Avenue past a number of theaters and turned on Charing Cross Road. Kids and music and street activities were everywhere. Guys with long hair wore velvet bell-bottom pants, glistening silk shirts with puffed sleeves, rose-colored sunglasses. Girls wore mini-skirts, boots up to their knees, vests, paisley blouses. A clothing shop proclaimed "All The Latest Mods Styles" in its window. It was the Haight-Ashbury of London, but more upscale, stylish. I soon found a John Lennon hat, which I had coveted for some time. I stopped at a street cart for fish and chips wrapped in newspaper and learned the girls were called "birds." They were strikingly beautiful and I fell in love with every one of them.

I found a record shop on Charing Cross Road and bought a bunch of new albums: *Disraeli Gears* by Cream, the brand-new Beatles' *Magical Mystery Tour*, *Buffalo Springfield Again*, *Days of Future Passed* by the Moody Blues, *Procol Harum*, and the new Stones record, *Their Satanic Majesties Request*. Its strange cover reminded me of *Sgt. Pepper's*. I strolled down street after street, digging this foreign culture where people spoke my own language. I was no longer a GI. I was no longer an outsider; I was just another person enjoying the streets of London, England.

A stall outside a bookstore was filled with books that turned me on: Aldous Huxley, James Joyce, John Steinbeck, Heinlein, George Orwell, Anthony Burgess, Kerouac. There was a dog-eared used paperback copy of John Lennon's *A Spaniard in the Works*. I had *In His Own Write* from my mom, but this was new so I grabbed it. The cover of a novel caught my attention: a painting of a young man with psychedelically colored hair who looked like Bob Dylan. It was called *Demian* by Herman Hesse. I bought it, another called *The Hobbit* by someone named Tolkein, and an old used hardcover copy of William James' *Varieties of Religious Experience*.

Thirsty, I ducked into an Irish pub and ordered a beer. It was mid-afternoon and pretty crowded, so I asked a guy sitting alone if I could join him. He was scribbling on a typescript and waved his pencil at me in a friendly way. I sipped my beer; it was strong and cold and delicious. After a bit the guy put his pencil down, looked up at me and said, "So, you're an American, eh?"

He said he was editing his novel, based on his World War II experiences, which would soon be published. I asked its title, and he said it was *As Towns with Fire.*

We drank two pints of what he called "black and tan" and talked about writing. "Keep at it, lad," he said. "It's arduous work, but your story gets better the more you work upon it. Revise, rewrite, revise, rewrite your work."

He said he must be going. "What's your name, lad?" I told him, and he said he'd watch for it in print. I asked his, and he said "Tony."

"That's my best friend's name, too!" I said. We shook hands and said good-bye. As I rode the bus back to Mildenhall, I felt a new kind of mental stimulation, a new energy, an exuberance about my life. I tried to remember if, or when, I'd felt like this before. Maybe discussing philosophy in Professor Cohen's class at UC. Most definitely the first night of creative writing class at SRCC. The October night in the alten Scheune when we all talked late into the night.

• • •

Tony was in his room when I returned, listening to some strange piano music. "It's Liszt. Franz Liszt, you know, the German piano genius who lived in the 1800s. It's called *Années de Pèlerinage* — I think I said that right. It means years of pilgrimage. Liszt wrote music about his impressions of his travels to Switzerland, France, Germany — I don't remember all of them. I guess I could look at the record jacket, though. The thing that blows me away about this, especially when I'm high, is the way he tells me stories about the countryside in the music. I get off on this as good as I do listening to...um...like, 'East-West.' Hey, maybe we ought to put that on."

I pulled the bag of records out and handed them to Tony. "Well, I bought some new stuff. Maybe there's something here you'll get off on."

"Oh, wow, far out," he said as he flipped through them. "Hey, this Beatles record — it's an EP. Only four songs." We lit a joint and listened to it. "I like 'I Am The Walrus' best," he said, and so did I, so we listened to it again. Tony put on *Sgt. Pepper's*. "I swear, I never get tired of listening to this," he said. "It's all different songs by each of them, but they're all woven into this — this — trip, you know, how it all makes sense as a symphony, sort of."

145

Tony dropped the needle on "A Day In The Life." George strummed his guitar, then John began playing piano . "You ever listen to Beethoven?"

"Sure, of course," I said, "my mother is into classical music. Played cello in high school and college, too. I heard a lot of classical as a kid."

"Well, listen to a piano trio or one of his late string quartets. Then listen to "A Day In The Life." I tell you, man," he said, rocking back and forth, "that's some heavy stuff. Deep connections. A lot of that old classical music was written in a prescribed structure. Then along came Beethoven. He changed *everything*. The man had a major infinite improvisational mind-boggling mind."

We listened in silence to "A Day in the Life" all the way through. The piano chords died out and I heard noises and some gibberish that sounded like "Lucy look the other way" chanted over and over in a distorted chorus. "What's that? What's that?" I said.

"Haven't heard that before, have you?" said Tony. "It's on the English pressing. We never heard it on the American one we bought back home."

"Those guys," I said, smiling and shaking my head. "Hey, you want to hear the Rolling Stones' response to Sgt. Pepper's?"

"For sure, man!"

I got up to put on *Their Satanic Majesties Request*. Tony gazed at the album cover, then picked up the Sgt. Pepper's cover and held them side by side, looking at one and then the other. "Hey, let's smoke some of this first." He held up a little wad of aluminum foil. "It's hashish. It'll blow your mind."

It did.

Then the record began with a piano and squealing trumpets and the Stones' invitation to sing the song with them, to open our heads and let pictures come. So we did.

• • •

We took the bus back into London on Saturday. Tony got us tickets to see a play called "Oliver!" in the New Theater. I'd never been to a real live stage production before. I knew the story of Dickens' novel and was surprised at how much I liked the corny acting, especially the Artful Dodger, but my heart was touched when Nancy sang, "As Long As He Needs Me." We emerged in the late afternoon and walked back through the Soho district to a neighborhood where the streets were filled with Oriental and Indian faces. Tony guided me into an Indian restaurant where we were seated in a private room. He pulled out his hash and a little pipe and lit up.

"Hey, is this OK? I mean, in here…."

"Sure," Tony said. "It's where I buy it."

We toked up. A beautiful Indian girl came into the room. Tony introduced her as Amita. She took our order and brought us incredible spicy curry to assuage our munchies.

• • •

Monday came all too soon. From the air, Kleinelachen looked dingy and colorless. Maybe because it was. Buford raked me over the coals for not bringing the mail pouch from Ramstein, like I was supposed to think of that. The troops reported he'd been on a rampage all weekend, then pulled a surprise white-glove inspection earlier in the morning, terrorizing Tim and Ricky in particular. Now I joined his shitlist, and we were all grounded for petty things – the mail pouch, a dustball under a bunk, fatigues that weren't freshly pressed, a blanket that wasn't stretched tight enough to bounce a quarter off of.

I don't know why Buford chose us to pick on when he had so many choices. Irish got drunk every weekend, staggering around the barracks reciting Robert Burns or Dylan Thomas poetry at one o'clock in the morning. Ricky always played his stereo too loud and was a big beer drinker as well; he and Irish were now drinking partners. One difference was that Ricky liked to get into fistfights, and didn't seem to have much trouble finding Army troops at Ma's to brawl with. From what I heard – mostly from him, with his incessantly accenting his sentences with "fuck," "fucker," "you fucking asshole" and "FUCK! FUCK! FUCK!" – he won most of the time. The only thing that saved him from getting busted was he didn't fight on base.

Of course I knew Buford had it in for me. I'd been on the wrong side of him since the night I reported for duty.

Tim was another matter. He wasn't a very friendly guy. You might say he was an introvert, but it was more than that. It felt like he had a high standard by which he judged people and his opinions. Right from the first time I met him, I'd always felt like Tim was a challenge to figure out. Therefore, I figured it was pretty easy for a stupid clod like Buford to hate him.

There was another possibility. Maybe Buford sensed we were heads, which he would completely hate and use to get us dishonorably discharged and probably thrown in Leavenworth if he could. Of course, it was OK to be juicers like Irish and Ricky because intoxication was accepted by society. Whatever his reasons, there was no doubt in my mind that Buford was laying for us. Although it was probably futile, I resolved to keep out of the kind of trouble that would attract Buford's attention.

Tim did not share my sense of caution. In England he'd bought a copy of *Quotations of Chairman Mao*, also known as "The Little Red Book." He carried it in his rear fatigue pants pocket all the time and pulled it out whenever he had a chance to read from it, either to himself or anyone who'd listen. One day I was walking across the parade field when I saw Tim standing in front of half a dozen troops. He was holding his copy of "The Little Red Book" high in the air and reading to them:

> History shows that wars are divided into two kinds, just and unjust. All wars that are progressive are just, and all wars that impede progress are unjust. We Communists oppose all unjust wars that impede progress, but we do not oppose progressive, just wars. Not only do we Communists not oppose just wars, we actively participate in them. As for unjust wars, World War I is an instance in which both sides fought for imperialist interests; therefore the Communists of the whole world firmly opposed that war. The way to oppose a war of this kind is to do everything possible to prevent it before it breaks out and, once it breaks out, to oppose war with war, to oppose unjust war with just war, whenever possible.

"This is exactly the situation we Americans face in fighting the war in Vietnam," Tim said to his audience. "We chose to participate in an unjust war that the French started. It was unjust because their – and our – sole interest was plundering their natural resources. Once the French realized they couldn't take over the country, they left. Now we're in over our heads. Johnson has committed us to a war we have no chance of ever winning. We're dropping napalm on their villages and killing innocent Vietnamese. We're bombing the shit out of the Ho Chi Minh Trail, but the supplies get through anyway. We're flying American troops into the interior of North Vietnam to root out the Vietminh, and for what? So our brothers can get killed or disabled beyond belief by the Vietcong.

"What can we do? You and me? We can't rebel or demonstrate or become conscientious objectors, because we're U.S. Government Issue conscripts. The U.S. Government owns us. But we can write our senators and congressmen and tell them we think this war is wrong! This is an unjust war, and as long as there is a Mao they will fight us back because the Commies know it's an unjust war, too. They're opposing our unjust war with their just war. All they want is freedom for people to make their own choices. *Isn't that what America was supposed to be about?"* The American people are just like you and me, troops. They don't want this war. They hate watching soldiers get killed on TV news every night, just like you and me. But Johnson's committed us, and now he says we've got to stay and we've got to win. Win? *Win?"*

I was standing far enough away not to be part of this obviously illegal assembly, but close enough to hear what Tim was saying. He was an excellent speaker, and it was obvious he knew what he was talking about, even though I suppose you could disagree with his point of view. I have to confess that most of what I knew about the war going on halfway around the globe came from reading the *Stars and Stripes*, which was surely biased in the opposite political direction.

Then I saw Sgt. Buford walking rapidly toward the group with Air Policemen on either side in their white helmets and white gloves, rifles across their chests. They were approaching Tim from the rear. The troops in the audience saw them and realized what was about to happen. They started hustling away.

Tim looked over his shoulder. Buford didn't say anything, just kept marching closer until he and the APs were about six feet away. The troops had dispersed. Tim turned to look at Buford and the two of them just stood there, more or less staring each other down, Buford with his armed guard, Rosenkrantz at attention with his Little Red Book pressed against his breast. I was reminded of my namesake's novel, *The Scarlet Letter*, for some reason. Maybe Reverend Dimmesdale. I probably should have been thinking of the movie "Gunfight at the OK Corral" instead. I let the thought flee.

Tim won the staredown. Finally, the first shirt turned on his heel and left with the two armed APs. Yet to my mind Tim had waved a red flag in front of a bull. I mean, we *were* at war fighting the Communists. The Russians, also Communists, were backing the Vietminh. What could be more anti-American than supporting the Communists? Tim walked over to me, grinning.

"And I thought *I* had pissed him off when I wouldn't shave off my mustache," I said. "Do you realize you could have gotten an Article 15 for an illegal formation? Probably court martialed for inciting revolt? Preaching Communism? I don't know, Tim, you were advocating — what is it called — sedition, I think! Jesus, man!"

He stood there and grinned at me, then said, "But I am a Communist."

The loopy bastard.

A few days later he came storming into the barracks, cursing and hacking. He ripped off his parka and threw it against his locker.

"Goddam Buford," he said.

"What's up?" I asked.

"Pulled my pass again. Three days I had off. I was going to head up to London. SHIT!" he yelled and threw his hat against his locker.

"What for this time?"

"He pulled a spot personal inspection on me at the radar trailer. Said I needed a shave and a haircut. Brogans needed to be polished. Uniform needed to be pressed. The works. I was just at the barber three days ago. Oy vey, that prick!"

Tim had bad acne, and when it was acting up, like it was now, it was real hard for him to get a close shave. Anybody else would have let it slide, but not Buford. If he had it in for you, you knew it. Now Tim knew it, too. He grabbed his coat and hat off the floor, put them on, and stormed out the door. A big draft of cold air blew in and the steel door slammed shut.

I went back to my book; I was re-reading Allen Ginsberg's poem "Howl," which I'd bought the night Kathleen and I went to City Lights Bookstore. I loved the way he wrote the stanzas; a theme and then one, two, or three lines to explore it. I was at the part where he wrote

> *who studied Plotinus Poe St. John of the Cross telepathy and bop*
> *   kabbalah because the cosmos instinctively vibrated at their feet*
> *   in Kansas,*
> *who loned it through the streets of Idaho seeking visionary indian*
> *   angels who were visionary indian angels,*
> *who thought they were only mad when Baltimore gleamed in super-*
> *   natural ecstasy, who jumped in limousines with the Chinaman of*
> *   Oklahoma on the impulse of winter midnight street light small-*
> *   town rain...*

Amazing poem, as much for his Beat Generation as for my own. Line after line, it excited me as the images and experiences riffed out of Ginsberg's imagination. I sought comparable perceptions, riffs, of my own. What struck me about these few stanzas was how much they reminded me of my acid trip with Tony, still my first and only, surprisingly still illuminating my consciousness.

Then again, maybe not so surprisingly.

A few stanzas further on I thought of Tim as I read

> *who distributed Supercommunist pamphlets in Union Square weep-*
> *ing and undressing while the sirens of Los Alamos wailed them*
> *down, and wailed down Wall, and the Staten Island ferry also*
> *wailed,*

It wasn't long before Rosencrantz was back, this time with a huge leer on his face. "Got him! I got the arschloch!" he shrieked, a clenched fist waving wildly, turning into a boxer's punch in the air.

I looked up at him. "Arschloch?"

"Cocksucker. *Auf Deutsch.* I don't know Yiddish for it. Buford, Nate, *Buford.* I outfoxed him. I'm moving off-base. He won't be able to dick with me any more. I'll wake up in my off-base apartment, I'll go to work at the radar site, then I'll go home. Not to the barracks, but to my own place. I'll get a car and drive straight to the radar site. No more inspections, no more him laying for me when I walk across the base. Out of sight, out of mind! Ha-ha-ha!"

Tim was a madman, but I was happy for him. "So how'd you pull this off?"

"I just went to see our buddy Milo up at Admin," Tim said. "I told him Buford's out to get me. Us. I told him I wanted to file a grievance against him. Milo — he's pretty swift, you know? — he said, 'Cool it, Tim, don't get mad — get even!' I said sure, but how? He asked me if I knew that AFCS troops were eligible for separate rations *and* an off-base housing allowance. No, I said, you're putting me on! But it's a fact."

"This is incredible news! How come?" I asked.

"It's because we work shifts around the clock. We disrupt normal duty and quiet hours in the barracks, plus the mess hall may not be open when we go on or get off a shift. It's the same deal as if you were married. So I'm getting a room off-base in Zweiflüssehausen! I put in the paperwork with Milo and very soon I am going to be figmo for this barracks scene, man!"

"And nobody ever told us," I said, jealous as hell. "Wait! Does Buford have to approve this?"

"Nope. At least I don't think so." Suddenly in doubt, his face fell a little. "I mean, it's AFCS Command level. Oh, I expect Col. White will have to sign off on it, since it'll come down from Ramstein. And I have to maintain an area in the barracks even though I don't use it. You know, snug the sheets, dust the dresser. But it's all in the regs, man. It's all legal. It won't be long till I have that fat-assed hillbilly off my ass for good! You can do it too, Nate!"

Secretly, I wasn't so sure Tim could get away with it. I knew his family had money, and he could probably get some help to rent an apartment and buy a car. But I couldn't afford it, since I was still helping mom out. But more power to him; he'd figured out a way to get out from under Buford's thumb and I was totally envious of his newfound freedom.

. . .

Christmas was fast approaching, and with it came a wave of homesickness. I wanted to be in America, home even if it wasn't home any more. I imagined decorating the tree, smelling hot apple cider with a cinnamon stick, watching presents pile up under the tree, and my two stupid little brothers shaking their packages to try to guess what was inside. I could even hear the insipid Christmas music by Mitch Miller or Perry Como or the Ray Conniff Singers that my mother played over and over on the hi-fi.

It occurred to me that I should buy my mom and brothers some keen German Christmas gifts and get them in the mail, *macht schnell*. As I muddled through what to get them, I received a surprise package. It was from Jane, wrapped in brown paper and tied with coarse string. I was seized with embarrassment. I hadn't written her since I answered her first letter. *Oh wow, I better think up a present for her, too.* I hurried back to the barracks. It was a book. The dust cover was gray and the yellow title read, *The I Ching or Book of Changes.* I opened it and a letter fluttered to the floor. *Boy, good thing the postal clerks didn't open this, because Jane didn't pay first-class postage.* It read:

Corte Madera
December 10, 1967

Dear Nathaniel:

Christmas isn't very special in California because the landscape and the weather don't change. No snow, except if you can see the mountains, like

Mt. Whitney or the Sierra up near the Nevada state line, but down here in Marin it's just another bright sunny day. Maybe you're the reason last Christmas was special, because you spent it with me and my family. I wanted to give you a really special Christmas present and remembered how you were interested in Confucius and ancient Chinese philosophy, so I talked to this Buddhist monk customer who comes in Ouroboros all the time and he recommended this. It looks like something you can get into. I hope you'll come back and, like the monk in the store said, "throw me an I Ching."

Merry Christmas, Nathaniel Hawthorne Flowers.
I miss you.
I love you.
Jane

Chapter 12
Zeitgeist
January, 1968

January 3, 1968

Dear Nathaniel,

First of all, Happy Birthday. My, you are now 23 years old! It's hard to believe you've been in the Air Force for three years. I hope you celebrated your birthday in the manner of the young gentleman that I know you are, and that you didn't do anything you might regret later. I always worry about you because of New Year's Eve celebrations.

We all thank you for the Christmas presents. I love my Hummel figurine and hope you'll add to my collection over the next few years you're there. The boys loved their tin cars, the Volkswagen and the funny little tank wagon. They asked me to ask you if these are real German vehicles.

We're doing well here. Ernest and Frankie have made the adjustment to their new school, and I think they're studying harder, or at least getting more homework – one or both – because they're definitely spending more time on their schoolwork. I'm thrilled to be working in a library again, and also quite happy to be out of the retail clothing trade. What a mindless job that was! You might understand that working in a school makes me feel closer somehow to your dear father, whom I still miss so very much.

I'm going to end this before I grow maudlin. We send our love and best wishes for you in the New Year. I hope that you have many wonderful experiences in Europe over the next 2-1/2 years. Is it possible for you to take a leave and come home at some point in time?

Love,
Your Mother

• • •

"I don't know why, but Richie Havens singing 'Freedom' at Monterey Pop popped into my head this afternoon, and now I can't stop playing it," I said. Tony had flown in from Mildenhall and we had just arrived at Tim's new apartment in Zweiflüssehausen, a ten-minute walk from the base. Alan and Henry Harold Henry and Tony and Ricky were here. I couldn't figure out why Tim had invited Ricky, but everyone seemed to be having a good time.

"Well, freedom," said Tim, "that's something in short supply here in the military."

"Yeah, especially for you fuckin' Commies," said Ricky with a harsh laugh.

"Commie? Who's a Commie?" Tony asked. Silence. The mood in the room changed.

Tim held up a copy of *Pravda*. "I am."

Alan shook his head. He lit up a joint and started it around and started rolling another.

"That's just plain fuckin' weird," said Henry Harold Henry, staring at Tim taking a toke. He handed it to Ricky, who passed it to Henry without smoking. He got up, went into the kitchen and came back with a bottle of Zweiflüssebrau, the village beer. He sat back down on the bare wood floor and sucked loudly on the beer bottle, then let out a belch.

I looked around the room. A little refrigerator in the tiny kitchen. Next to it the bathroom door stood open. A mattress over in the corner. Two wall lamps provided dim light. Outside the bare windows it was dark night. Tim had been here a week and our first get-together was getting a little strange.

"Tim, you don't know a thing about Communism," said Alan. I stared at him; there was no expression on his face.

"Oh, is that right?" I looked at Tim; his face was turning red.

"If you did, you wouldn't be saying you are one," Alan said. "You say you're a Commie because it's your statement of rebellion against the military establishment. I dig that. But if you were a Communist, you wouldn't want to be a Communist, I guar-an-fucking-tee it."

"Oh? So what do you know? What makes you the expert to tell me what I know and don't know?"

Alan gave Tim a steely glare, then looked at the joint in his hand. He knocked the ash from it with his middle finger and said, "I grew up in Cambridge. You can bet your stupid ass I know. Ever heard of Bob Akullian? No, I didn't think so. He runs a Communist-socialist bookstore in Harvard Square."

Tim was silent, then he said, "You *think* you know. You know what *you* know. I know what *I* know. I don't feel like I need to explain anything to you. And just because you have silenced a man doesn't mean you've changed his thinking."

"Yeah, big deal, I know that quote too, but you got it wrong," said Alan.

"Why don't we listen to some of this new music I brought back from London?" I said. "How about *Their Satanic Majesties Request?*" The mood eased and Tim put on the record, while Ricky jumped up to fetch another beer. "Anybody else want one?" he said from the doorway, a big silly grin on his face. Nobody did. Tim went into the kitchen and whispered something to Ricky, who listened and shook his head. Tim put his lips close to Ricky's ear and whispered again, but this time he left his cheek touching Ricky's cheek. Ricky saw me looking at him. He pulled away from Tim and flushed, then nodded and they returned to the group.

"Tony and I listened to this in England," I said. "It's the Stones' reply to *Sgt. Pepper's*."

"Oh, far out. Yeah, look at the cover picture," said Henry Harold Henry. "They're definitely putting the Beatles down."

Tim leaned over to look. "Is that smoke or clouds?" he grinned.

The Stones launched into "Sing This All Together," and the mood mellowed. Now we were starting to groove together, and I started really digging on it. My buddies. It felt good, all of us together, like the song said, opening our heads to let pictures come. My thoughts floated from troop to troop, thinking about what each guy was like and why I liked him. This was the best ever, even better than the Haight. I felt a kind of mental frown when I looked at Ricky, but immediately dropped that dark thought.

Tony lit up his hash pipe as we rolled into "2000 Man" and started it around. We were all rockin' away, getting more and more stoned. My thoughts drifted into the music again; my kids don't understand me, it went. I tried to figure out how old I'd be in the year 2000. It was simple subtraction: 56. *Wow, that is so old.*

"2000 Man" ended and a soft electric keyboard tinkled behind the sounds of people coughing and talking, as if the Stones were sitting right here getting high with us. "Woooo," Tony said, exhaling a big cloud of smoke, "making fun of flower power. They cut so deep!" Then someone on the record said, "Where's that joint?" and a long, weird instrumental version of "Sing This All Together (See What Happens)" began. Everyone fell silent. It was a fine, long cut and I was riding a beautiful hash flume in it.

We flipped the record. Side two began with what sounded like a barker at a carnival. "Kind of interesting," said Alan, "how you can hear their English folk traditions in both albums, but each so different."

"Oh, right, the hurdy gurdy music," said Tim.

"And folk songs, and street bands, and Renaissance —" said Alan.

" — Yeah, like the Stones are poking fun at the corniness of the Beatles' Sgt. Pepper's band," said Henry, "a really *hard* put-down."

"She's a Rainbow" started up. "Yeah," said Henry Harold Henry, "listen to that! 'She comes in colors!' It's a razzberry to 'Lucy in the Sky with Diamonds!' But it's really good." The song played on, and the hash was hitting me so when "2000 Light Years From Home" began how it's so very lonely a hundred, a thousand, two thousand light years from home, I was gone, lost in outer space with the Stones and the music, way gone, almost like when I was that little speck of blue light flying through the universe the night I tripped with Tony.

The song ended and "On With The Show" began with the carnival barker again and Henry Harold Henry began chortling like he always does, shaking his head at how corny it was with the references to old "Stormy Weather" and "Moon River." Alan and Tim chuckled too and Alan said, "Boy, they are really ironic, aren't they?"

Ricky jumped up and cried "FUCK! What the fuck is this? WHAT THE FUCK are you guys talking about?"

"Sit down, be quiet, Ricky," said Tim, reaching up for him. "I have neighbors below."

But Ricky wouldn't sit down or be quiet either. "I don't know what you're talking about, all this stuff about the Stones and the Beatles and putting on and stuff. It's just music, you know? Why are you saying all this shit? What the fuck does any of this matter? It's just music! And you troops are just so full of bullshit, all this sing together and make pictures come bullshit! Is it because you're stoned? Because if that's it, fuck, man, get me the FUCK out of here! Fuck you fuckin' guys! This's too fucking weird for me!"

With a glaring glance at Tim he walked out, slammed the door behind him, and was gone.

Ricky's tirade made it really weird to be stoned. I remembered Tony talking about the girl who freaked out. Just like Ricky tonight. We sat, silenced. I was partly angry at Ricky for being such a dumbfuck and partly kind of feeling like we hadn't helped him get into the scene with the rest of us. I guess we'd expected he would just drop into our groove.

"Bummer," Alan blurted out. "But Ricky never belonged here. With us. In this group." He looked right at Tim. Wow, he'd just put to words what I'd been thinking, except he finished the thought.

"I apologize," said Tim. "It's my fault. There's some — well, shit — I need to get together. You were partly right about the politics thing, Alan. But really, the Party has something to offer. But there's this other thing...about myself...that I'm not sure about, and I go back and forth on it." He twisted uncomfortably. "I guess that's all I can say about it right now."

There was silence, then Alan said, "Commie or queer, either one will get you a dishonorable discharge faster than a speeding bullet."

My God, so that was it, a boy-boy thing was going on between Tim and Ricky. There was no tolerance of homosexuals in the military. If Tim, or Ricky for that matter, went to a shrink doctor or the chaplain — neither of which we had, of course — it was unlikely they'd get an understanding ear. In the military, any personal problem can be twisted into a violation of regulations. Maybe Tim liked to live dangerously: first a Commie, now a homo. But at the same time I wasn't sure he was really a homo. Maybe he was one of those guys who was just confused about the whole thing. Maybe he had a right to be confused, since getting laid was about as impossible as flying to the moon.

"I don't know about you troops, but I'm starting to come down," Henry Harold Henry said. Tony relit the hash pipe. Alan started rolling another joint. In moments, the room was filled with cannabis smoke once again.

"I'll put on some more music," said Tim.

"Hey, man, put on that new Moody Blues record," said Tony. "That'll put us back in a sweet place."

"Who's read *Stranger in a Strange Land?*" Tim asked. Everybody had. "What's it about?" It was our second meeting at his pad, *sans* Ricky. And, sadly, Tony. Tim looked around. "Well, I think it's about politics. Mike challenges the status quo and politicians can't stand being challenged. That's why you see so much oppression in the world. It's how Hitler gained power, and McCarthy when he said we – I mean the United States – had to purge the Communists."

"Nah, that's not it," said Alan. "I mean, yeah, it's about the outsider and how he makes the masses feel uncomfortable because he's got a different trip, sure, but Heinlein's basically retelling the Christ myth story."

"That's still about politics," said Henry Harold Henry. "The Roman rulers thought Jesus Christ was a threat. My dad once said two people can agree on something, but when there's three it's now about politics. Something like that."

"Sure," said Tim, "it's harder to get three to agree on something. It's often two against one, so it becomes political. Two against one. That's in the book, too, how there's politics going on even between the people who stand with Michael."

"I don't disagree with that," said Alan, "as a theory. But in *Stranger* it's far simpler. That's why I don't think Heinlein wanted it to become a book about politics and intrigue. He wanted to show how the greedy and powerful kill and squash ideas or views that are pure and true and gentle and right. The Romans kill Jesus because he's creating a new rebellious faction. Mike is Rousseau's natural man, and the wolves who try to get rid of him are modern man, and Heinlein wants us to see that the natural man is preferable but doomed to failure because he is too much of a threat to modern man."

I was trying to remember what my roommate Richard said about *Stranger* when we were at Keesler, but I was too stoned. "Boy, Alan, you sure know a lot of interesting stuff," I said. "This is pretty high-level philosophy, I think. Sounds like you took a college course or two...."

"I took *no* college, I did *not* go to college, and I resent that you think I learned this in college!"

"Well, ex-cuse me!" I said, laughing.

"Aw, Alan, ease up, man," said Henry, who usually seemed to be able to calm Alan down. "Nate didn't mean nothin' by it. It's just that you're such a fuckin' Einstein, it's natural to think you learned it all in college." And he chortled his chortle.

"Yeah, I know," said Alan. But you don't learn anything in college. Nothing. College professors — I love that word, to *profess* — *claim* — to know something. College professors are mediocre minds with a little tiny fucking bit of knowledge they learned second-hand from other professors and books. They stand in front of a classroom filled with students and *profess* to know everything under the sun when they don't know much more than students. And most of what they know is five to ten to twenty years old! Brothers, the whole higher education system is a joke!"

"Well, I don't doubt what you say is true," I said, thinking back to Chicago. The only course that stood out in my memory was philosophy; maybe college bored me. "But still, you can't get anywhere without a college education."

"Aha, and that's the great trick society plays on us, its youth," said Alan, waving his finger in the air. "Play by our rules, the adults tell us, or you don't get to play. You have gifts, but we intend to grind you up in our system and pop you out like little conformist sausages so you'll be just like us and won't cause anybody any trouble. You'll graduate college, get a job, wear a suit and drive a Buick or DeSoto and settle down in a little white house with a mortgage and a wife and have a couple kids that'll grow up to be just like YOU!" By now he was gesturing wildly. Spittle flew from his lips and his eyes burned in anger. "And if you don't want to play the conformity game, we throw you in the military and surely burn your brain and soul right out of you!"

Silence fell on the room again, but it felt like everybody was thinking about what Alan said. I was. "You remind me of a quote I especially liked when I was... in college...sorry, but anyway it was 'In the land of the blind, the one-eyed is king,' which also reminds me of Mike and the earth society."

"Ah, yes," said Tim, "that's actually from old folklore: *Blinden ist der Einäugige der König.*"

"Get outa here," said Henry Harold Henry.

"How did you know that?" I asked.

"Ah, college," said Tim, glancing at Alan. "A course in world mythology. The Cyclops. The Eye of God. The one-eyed Jack on the playing card. The pyramid on the dollar bill."

"All very fascinatin', I'm sure," said Henry Harold Henry. "But back to *Stranger*. I myself was grokkin' the grokkin'. You know, between boys and girls. Y'know, the sex!" Everybody laughed.

"Yeah," I said, "the people in the ninth circle. The ones who spread peace and love." I thought of Richard.

"More symbolism," said Alan. "Mike equals Jesus and the ninth circle equals the twelve disciples."

"Hey, that's what we ought to call ourselves," Tim said. "The ninth circle. We're all into peace and love, right? 'Where's that joint?'" There were more laughs. Alan handed him the rolling papers and bag of dope.

"Yeah, I don't know," I said. "I'm sorta not into names like that. I mean, we all had dumb names for each other in tech school, and I was glad to go back to plain old Flowers at San Ramon. Do we need a name for who we are? Let's just, you know, be in the now of being together."

"Right on, Nate," said Alan. "Then we don't have to have to label who or what we are."

"'Cause we already are," said Henry.

"It was just a thought," said Tim. "No name is good enough for me."

"I like it that we use our first names, too. Doesn't sound military," I said.

"Society always wants to put names to things," said Alan. "But you know, there is something culturally significant about our zeitgeist."

We all looked at Alan.

"Zeitgeist. That's not a name, right? It's a way of looking at things? A feeling about the times? OK? Here's what's going down: Our parents and their generation are scared of us. They don't want us doing our thing."

"Yeah! I saw that in San Francisco," I said. "If you smiled at a straight, he wouldn't smile back. If you flashed the Peace sign, he'd freak out and look the other way. And for sure don't hand him a flower!" I reached up and touched the bead necklace Jane had given me. It was still my secret talisman. I thought about Jane; I hadn't written to thank her for the *I Ching*. In fact, I hadn't even begun reading it.

"That's it, Nate," said Alan. "That's it exactly. And that is exactly what we don't want to happen. We don't want to scare the straights or freak them out. Our zeitgeist isn't just a fad. We want them to understand us, and realize we are the next generation of human beings!"

"Jeez, Alan," said Henry in mock awe, "That's such a far fuckin' out concept."

"There you go, sounding like college again. You know so much, but you haven't been?" I asked again.

After a long pause, Alan said, "Well, it's because my parents are both college professors. PhDs. Real hard-core tenured academics. *That's* how come I know so much about formal learning. I've lived in their world my whole life." I looked at him and nodded. "And that's why I hate it so much," he added.

"It's all cool, Alan," said Tim. "I went to college for a few years. Some of it was great, some not so great. It didn't kill me."

"Yeah, Tony, too. He went to UC Berkeley," I said. "He dropped out. I went for a year but I flunked out." My sense of shame and embarrassment seemed to have left me.

"Experience is overrated," said Tony.

"I salute you both for rejecting the system," said Alan, flipping me a salute with his left hand.

Tim said, "Actually, college is where I first learned about Marxism and Communism. Professor Davitskian. But you're right, Alan, I learned a lot more in the SDS meetings. From other people."

"What's SDS?" said Henry.

"Students for a Democratic Society."

"Oh. So that's Commies?"

"Forget about that and think about this," Alan said. "What was the best high you ever had, and I mean with whatever drug you used — alcohol, pot, mescaline, LSD, whatever. I don't know what all everyone here has gotten high on."

We pondered this for a minute, then everyone spoke up. The stories were different, of course, but everybody agreed that the first time was the best.

"Right on," said Alan. "So why is that? And think about it: if you go on smoking dope or dropping psychedelics, aren't you trying to recapture the feeling and experience you had with it the first time?"

We all nodded.

"So this is my point, troops," Alan said. "Isn't that really true of all the experiences you've every had? The first was the best. It was that experience we peaked on. That's what we need to do together, as a group. We need to make our times together, getting stoned, talking about ideas and books and life, we need to make every one of them a peak experience. Instead of remembering the first time as the best, we need to try to make each thing we do the best, and to take them higher and higher."

"Yeah, cool, so like how do we do that?" Henry Harold Henry asked.

"OK, we agree that we hate the military, right? We're against war, especially Vietnam. We gotta keep what's sacred alive while we're in the service. We gotta keep our heads and our souls to ourselves. Fucking Buford can't have them. He can have our bodies, and we'll do our duty, but when we're in our new zeitgeist it's all ours and the military can't get in. So we gotta stay pure, we gotta stay tight, people, never slack off. You know, we gotta keep troops like Ricky and Irish out of this. We can do things that are culturally significant."

Alan looked around the circle. "We gotta use getting high to create a higher consciousness."

"That's exactly what Timothy Leary said, when I heard him at Golden Gate Park," I said. "He says, 'tune in, turn on, drop out.'"

"Yeah, that's kind of the idea," said Alan. "Except we can't turn into acid heads. But we can learn to focus ourselves when we get high, go into a higher mind state, like monks and yogis do. Maybe we even could travel back and forth in time and space. Maybe have an out-of-body experience and see what happens once we die, without dying."

Alan was leaning forward now, really intensely into this. "We could be free, man, I mean *totally free* in our minds. And if we could learn to be free in our minds, well, maybe we could figure out how to be free in the world we have to live in, too."

"Ah, this sounds far out," I said. "I am definitely into this. But how do we do it?"

"Simple. We just do what we're doing. But we do it for a purpose, for raising our consciousness higher. Not just getting high to pass the time."

"Ha! Hahaha!" cried Henry Harold Henry.

"I think the music can be a way to higher consciousness," I said, wishing Tony was hearing this conversation.

"I agree," said Tim. "I was starting to feel that when we listened to *Days of Future Passed* last week."

"Ah, yes, the Moodies," said Henry, rocking back and forth. "Let's put it on again now."

We passed the pipe around with the hash Tony had left for us and started grooving into a deeper stone. Henry dropped the needle on The Moody Blues and the orchestra began, then the poem about the moon and the night and the colors and what is right and what's an illusion.

Days of future passed. What did that mean? Was it about memories? Was it about what was to become of us?

The Moodies sang of the smell of grass making you pass into a dream. It felt so deep and intense and peaceful to be listening to their music, tripping with them, and trying to pay attention to what they were saying to me.

Zeitgeist

I thought about zeitgeist. Zeitgeist, zeitgeist, the mighty light of ten thousand suns challenging infinity.

Zeitgeist.

What did Alan say it meant?

I knew what it meant.

It meant freedom.

Chapter 13
The Pieces Fit
February, 1968

The quiet of the night was broken by the sound of whispering cymbals. A piano stirred, then a horn blared in an interesting but dissonant melody. Still a two-striper, Henry Harold Henry had finally saved up enough money to buy his own stereo gear and was playing a jazz record in the barracks.

"Hey, Henry!" Irish yelled across the room, "What'cher playing?"

"*A Love Su-preme*," Henry yelled back. "John Coltrane. The Trane is my man, brother!"

Alan sat up on his bunk, crossed his legs and struck a listening pose. So did I, putting my book down and closing my eyes. Tim, who was waiting to start the midnight shift, lay on his back, his long legs hanging over the end of his bunk, hands folded across his chest as if he were praying. The music spun images in my mind.

"LITTLE DUECE COUPE YOU DON'T KNOW WHAT I GOT" filled the room. I looked up to see Ricky standing in front of his stereo, a look of angry glee on his face.

Henry Harold Henry got to his feet, turning toward Ricky. "Turn it off, Broward," he said without raising his voice. It was strange to hear him use Ricky's last name. Ricky didn't, and Henry moved down the aisle toward him. He reached out to Ricky's stereo and Ricky reached out to stop him. Henry gave Ricky a shove and he fell back on his bunk. Henry lifted the needle off the record and switched off Ricky's receiver. "You know the rules, jerkoff. One stereo at a time."

"Fuck you, asshole!" Ricky yelled at Henry as he walked back to his area. "Your music is puke! And so are you! Fuck all you fucking guys!"

Tim got up and walked over to sit beside Ricky. He put his arm across Ricky's shoulder and whispered something to him. They talked, and Ricky nodded and seemed to cool down. Tim got up and walked over to us and said, "Let's go over to Ma's for a beer, what do you say?" Everybody thought that was a good idea, so Alan, Tim, Ricky, Irish, Henry and I shrugged into our winter parkas and trudged through the thin scrabble of snow and ice to the gasthaus. As we walked, Tim said quietly to me, "It's the winter, you know." I looked at him. "He's never been out of Southern California in his whole life,. He's homesick for the beach. This's freaking him out."

Ricky and Irish started doing shots of Steinhäger and Zweiflüssebrau, laughing stupidly, getting quickly, uproariously drunk. The rest of us nursed our beers and laughed along with their goofy merriment until they stumbled out the door to the barracks.

"I really hate bein' around those fuckin' drunks," said Henry Harold Henry. We all nodded.

"There was a big thing about juicers versus stoners," I said, "in the Haight. Juicers were on a downer, and stoners were looking for enlightenment. Raising their consciousness."

"Of course," said Alan. "Alcohol's a depressant."

"All I'm saying is, let's try to stick to being stoners," I said. "You know, play along like we're regular troops, suck down a beer now and then, but be true to our pact to stay on a, you know, higher level." I put my fist down in the center of the table. Tim, Alan, and Henry put theirs on top of mine and we locked eyes.

"Oh, open, ye doors of perception," said Alan. We laughed.

"Hey, I wanted to tell you troops something," I said. "I got this book from Jane for Christmas. It's called the *I Ching*."

"You say that *ee jing*, not I Ching," said Alan.

"Oh. OK, thanks. So you know about it?"

"A little. Not much."

"Well, I dunno a thing about it and I want to hear all about it," said Henry Harold Henry. "Is it a mystery novel or what?"

"No, no, it's not a novel at all, or even a story. It's also called 'The Book of Changes' because it's like a way to understand stuff that's going on in your life, or to you, or around you."

"It's like a Ouija board," said Alan. "You ask it stuff and it gives you answers."

"Aw, a Ouija board is a Yiddish parlor game," said Tim. "My mother and her friends used to spend hours with that stupid thing."

"I don't know about that, but the *I Ching* is pretty different, I'm pretty sure," I said. "I just started to learn how to use it. The book says you're supposed to toss yarrow sticks to make it work. I don't even know what a yarrow stick is!" We laughed.

"So what did you do?" Tim asked.

"Well, you can also use three coins. I didn't want to use just any coins, so I found three Deutschemarks that were minted in 1944 – the year I was born. So I thought they would be special. I hold 'em for a long time to fill 'em up with my vibe."

"Cool," said Alan.

"Far out," said Henry.

"What do you ask?" said Tim.

"Something...that makes you think. It's kind of like a fortune teller, but more complicated than 'You will have a happy life' or newspaper astrology. See, it's based on these two forces, yin and yang, and they are lines in trigrams, and it takes two trigrams to make a hexagram–"

"Whoa, slow down," said Henry Harold Henry, and Tim asked me to explain more, so I told them everything I knew. "Then I hold the coins in my cupped hands and think real hard about my question and shake the coins, then let them fall. The combination of heads and tails make up a line, either solid or broken. There's more to it, but that's the basic idea. You create six lines and the order of the solid and broken lines identifies the hexagram. Then you read the *I Ching* to understand the meaning. Sometimes it's pretty obtuse!"

"What's obtuse?" asked Henry Harold Henry. *Oops, going through this twice.*

"Hard to understand. Subtle. Umm, the meaning is hidden."

"OK, far out."

"The first time I threw one I got the first hexagram in the book," I said. "It's six solid lines. Yang. That's masculine, by the way. Yin is feminine. It's called Ch'ien, The Creative. It's the best hexagram you can get. Really powerful. Time, space, the works."

We talked until Ma announced last call. Nobody wanted another beer, so we headed out the door. As we turned toward the gate, I could see headlights stabbing into the dark night. We hurried toward the barracks. A German ambulance was backed up with its engine running. Just as we got to the steel door it opened and two white-coated guys wheeled a cart out with a body covered with a white sheet. My heart jumped into my throat. The light shining from inside the barracks gave me a glimpse; it was Ricky. He looked passed out. There were bloodstains on the sheet, near his waist. We looked back and forth at each other. Then we saw a whole congregation of freaked-out troops watching from inside.

The medics slammed the ambulance doors and sprinted to the cab. The blue topknot light rotated and flashed as the ambulance pulled away. Its horn brayed like a donkey, even though there wasn't another vehicle in sight.

We rushed inside. Before we could even ask what had happened, troops were babbling all at once that Ricky had slashed his wrists. Everybody had a story about why it happened. Irish said he'd gone straight to his bunk when they got back without saying a word. Another troop said he'd laid down and started crying. Another said he'd heard Ricky was going to lose a stripe if he got another inspection demerit, and Friday inspection was tomorrow. Tim didn't add his two cents. After a while everybody wandered back to their areas. Cold as it was, Tim, Alan, Henry and I went out to the barn.

"This is my fault, my fault, completely and totally my fault," Tim said, once we climbed into the alten Scheune hayloft.

"You sound like a Catholic with all da mea culpa bullshit," said Henry.

"No, it's not your fault, Tim," I said. "Ricky's been heading for a major bummer for a long, long time. He was *so* angry. I never knew anybody so deep-down pissed off at everything and everybody."

"It's because I rejected him, we rejected him," Tim said, as if he hadn't heard a word I'd said.

"You said he was down because of the weather and being homesick," I said. "So he was already depressed, then all the booze he drank tonight pushed him over the edge. That's the whole story."

"Look, Tim, I don't know Ricky very well," said Alan, "but I'm pretty sure the guy was mentally unstable. The military is not the place for mentally unstable people. He was a Section 8 waiting to happen."

"You're right," said Henry Harold Henry. "Besides, the military brings out the worst in a guy — y'know, his weak spots. It kinda has to be like that. Think of the highest stress you can be under — somebody trying to kill you. We aren't under that stress here at lovely Kleinelachen, but still, it's our training. Some troops blow out in BMT. It just took Ricky longer."

"I agree, but there's more to it," Tim said. "I think Buford's been out to get Ricky. Break him." He exhaled and said, "And I think he finally did it."

"Yeah," Henry said, "I think you're right."

"Yeah, and you *all* better watch out," Alan said, pointing his finger like a gun around the circle, "'cause it's not like Ricky was the only one on his shit list."

• • •

For Nathaniel Hawthorne Flowers on Valentine's Day, 1968

Nate is living
enjoying
looking
smelling, alive
sensitive
living the light
He enjoys the flower

While I…

Nate lives the beauty
with Nature
in its course

While I…

Nate
lives to die,
But,
Nate lives
Nate lives
lives the life.

Nate IS
the artist
of beauty, of life

of the flower of Nature.
Beauty, sensation,
lovely Nate

Nate with still waters
That filter, live Nature

While I…

Nate – you
are beautiful
within to without.
Your eyes are
sensations,
perceptions,
that I see
of the Truth,
of Beauty,
Love,
Peace,
Nature.
May it crystallize
You
Forever.

While I…

I
Try
to Live
I
Am Not
Able to;
I missed
But
At times,

The Pieces Fit

Time
Stops
And I
Breathe
Perceptions
Sensations
Thoughts
Pictures
of Love
Truth
Beauty
of Myself
and Nature
of Living
of existing
of my Body
my beautiful self
of Life
Then
I am
alive also
and not
Gone away.

My Heart is Yours,
Jane

• • •

6069th AFCS Det.
APO New York 09131
14 February 1968

Dear Lady Jane,
    Happy Valentine's Day! I hope you're eating a big heart-shaped box-
ful of Whitman's chocolates as you read this letter. If you're not, then stop

173

reading and go get some before continuing! Ha! Ha! (I hope you don't mind me typing this, but it's hard for my thoughts to keep up with my pen. What thoughts? Ha! Ha!) OK, I am being stupid, so I'll just apologize for not writing sooner. I think of you often, and I really and truly look forward to every letter from you and have no excuse for not writing more often but you know, I'm writing all the time. I have to come up with an idea for a 500-700 word story about the base once a week. That's my job, write a story once a week. It does take some time and thought, because I keep hoping I'll get to see one of my stories in the *Stars and Stripes* pretty soon. It's been about six months now, and Sgt. Tremblay keeps saying "Take it easy, Flowers. Rome didn't burn in a day" or some absurd variation of that. I don't know what it means, or if there was ever a quotation such as this, or if he's just an idiot. I guess it means be patient. Maybe my writing is really bad. Maybe I should send you one of my stories so you can tell me what you think. Are you still taking classes? How is the bookstore? How's my MG? Say HI! to your mom and dad for me. I miss your front porch and our long talks. Send me a new story if you have written one. Oh, as I babble my way into infinity, I've been throwing *I Chings* and it is totally far out. I don't know what made you decide to send that book to me, and I have to confess I didn't get into it for a while, but it has changed my life, and the way I look at life, in all ways. Jane, it is full of ancient Chinese wisdom! Just what I need in this bleak land of emptiness and dreariness!

Well, I better get back to working on my story. This week it's about run-way maintenance in winter.

I'll try to write more often! Promise!

Always thinking of you,
Nate

P.S. Thanks for the Valentine's card and the cool poem you wrote for me!

• • •

I set the letter to Jane aside, spun a fresh sheet of paper into my typewriter, and started on my runway story. When I started writing in September, each story took hours and hours and my wastebasket filled with paper balls. Now, dozens of

174

stories later, I wrote better and with fewer false starts and revisions. The stories seemed boring, but writing them wasn't. *Was I becoming a better writer?*

As I wrote, I kept thinking about what I'd written to Jane about Tremblay and never having a word published. I wanted to talk to him about it, but didn't know how. He always rebuffed me with his stupid Rome aphorisms. It dawned on me: I could throw an *I Ching!* Now I was excited. I wrote furiously and finished my first draft; tomorrow I'd edit and revise, then type a new original and two carbons as usual, one for Buford to put in my file and one for myself.

It was late when I left Base Ops. The barracks was asleep, so I quietly got my book and coins and went back to my desk and gathered my thoughts. My hexagram was Lü, Treading (Conduct). The *I Ching* talked about a right way of conducting oneself, and that the weak can step on the tail of the strong without danger: It read, "one's purpose will be achieved if one behaves with decorum. Pleasant manners succeed even with irritable people." So, be true to myself and approach Tremblay honestly and respectfully. That was the ticket. I would call him in the morning.

• • •

"Sure thing, Flowers," he said when I called. "I'll be in the area all day. Stop by any time."

Tom was wearing his blues, but had his blouse off and shirtsleeves rolled up. An electric typewriter I hadn't noticed before sat on a steel table at a right angle to his desk.

"Flowers," he said, extending his hand. "You work out?"

"Ah, no, I don't," I replied. A big pause. "Do you?"

"Yeah," he said, lacing his big, thick fingers together and clumping his two hands on the stack of papers in front of him. "I get over to the gym once a day if I can. Good break from sittin' behind a desk readin'" – he thumped his fist – "these stories all day." I realized I was looking at maybe hundreds of news story manuscripts, and wondered how many were mine.

"Yeah, that's a great idea," I said. "I'll have to take that up. When we get a gym."

"You had lunch yet, Flowers?"

"Uh, OK, no, I haven't eaten anything since mess this morning. Most everybody calls me Nate."

175

"OK, right." He stood up and out we went to the NCO Club. Once we got settled with our sandwiches and coffee, Tom said, "So, how's it going? I mean down there at Kleinelachen."

"Ah, it's good, it's good, Tom," I replied. "At first I was sort of nervous that I'd run out of story ideas, but something new just sort of magically keeps turning up."

"You're a good reporter. I like your stuff," Tom said. "You keep at it. Keep meeting your deadlines — that's as important as the story itself. Line item in your performance review, you know."

"Yeah, well," I started, but I lost my nerve and took a bite of my turkey club sandwich to cover up.

"You want to know how come none of your articles have got published, right?"

"Yeah."

Tom leaned toward me. "You ever wondered why you got this assignment?"

"Well sure, but...."

He raised a hand to quiet me. "That was what we in the trade call a rhetorical question." He paused thoughtfully. "I often wondered if that term came about from the questions Rhett Butler asked Scarlett in *Gone With the Wind*."

I looked at him and wondered what the hell he was talking about. First Rome. Now this.

"Anyway, no matter. You were a radioman, right? Top secret clearance, right? You got sent to Germany, not Southeast Asia, right? Now you have a job with no security clearance, right? Am I right so far? Am I right?"

I nodded. He took a noisy slurp of coffee, and so did I.

"So, what happened in between these two MOSes?"

I started to open my mouth, but stopped. Was this another rhetorical question?

"I'll tell you what happened, Sergeant E-4 Nathaniel Hawthorne Flowers. What happened was *you*," he said, pointing an Uncle Sam-style finger at me, "wrote a letter to your *Congressman*."

He rocked back in his chair, arms crossed on his chest. I sat there dumbfounded. I hadn't realized how much he knew about me. Now I wasn't surprised.

"What's the mission at Kleinelachen? You got a hundred or so troops supporting a dozen or so running a radar set, right? And you got a hundred or so Army grunts supporting your support troops. So what do they need you there for? That's another rhetorical question: nuttin'. They need you like a hobby horse needs an asshole."

He brought his chair to the floor and took another slurp of coffee.

"So why am I there? Here?" I asked. I felt my world coming apart, like when my dad died, like when I flunked out of college, like when I tried to drive my Fury off the chalk cliffs. I wanted the pieces of my world to fit together and make sense. I was seized with the desire to throw the *I Ching*.

"You're there because the Air Force wants you there. Or you could say the Air Force doesn't want you anywhere else." The steely look in his eye seemed to soften.

What was this, some kind of vast conspiracy, like the potsage stamp in Pynchon's *The Crying of Lot 49*? I didn't believe things like this happened in real life. I had been taught to accept things at face value. I believed that you were assessed for your worth and ability to contribute, for your character, stuff like that, not that you were — I didn't even have the understanding to put words to it. I recalled the conversation we had driving to Baden-Baden. Nobody understood why we were at Kleinelachen.

"How come all your buddies at San Ramon got sent to Southeast Asia except you? The brass figured you might write your Congressman again, maybe say you were being punished. Couldn't kick you out for the same reason. So the only alternative was to ship you to Bumfuck, Germany, where you couldn't cause any trouble."

"But I get this great job as a *Stars and Stripes* journalist..."

Tom cut me off. "Busy work, nuttin' but busy work." He was smugly rocking on the back legs of his chair again.

"So, the reason I haven't had anything published..."

"Sorry, but you never will. The brass don't want to see your byline in the *S&S*. Specially since that front-page fiasco you wrote at San Ramon." He rocked forward and leaned across the table again. "Nate, we're an occupying force. Germany's a beautiful country. We got these people eatin' out of our hands. Enjoy the scenery, drink the fine German beer, kiss the frauleins. Have a good time, man! Travel around Europe. Just submit your stories, serve your hitch, don't make waves and the Air Force will leave you alone. Before you know it, you'll be a civilian again."

Existential ennui settled upon me. "I get it," I said. "So I guess it doesn't matter what I write, huh?" Tom shook his head, kind of apologetically. "I could be writing a novel, like Charles Dickens wrote his novels as a serial in the newspaper, and you wouldn't care, right?"

"Personally no, but remember, the idea is to keep your head down, am I right? However," he said, "you might want to enter the USAFE Short Story Contest. No harm in fiction. I think the deadline is 1 March. I got the flyer back in my office."

heyyyyy

Wild Blue Yonder

"Yeah, yeah, that might be good," I said.

We got up. Tom slapped my shoulder a few times, then gave me a curt nod with that big square jaw of his, as if everything was now OK.

Back in his office, he handed me the announcement for the short story contest. "Keep up the good fight, Flowers," he said.

"Thanks, Tom." As I left the building, I saw another flyer for the short story contest on the bulletin board. I yanked it down, balled it up and threw it into a trash can. No need to encourage competition.

• • •

I decided to visit the Ramstein base library before driving back. I wanted to see what they had on Eastern philosophy; as it turned out, not much. Lots of military history, including a set entitled *The History of the Decline and Fall of the Roman Empire* by Edward Gibbon. I flipped through a few volumes and found a mention of Rome burning for nine days in 64 A.D., but I still had no idea what Tremblay meant by it.

I wandered the aisles to the fiction section and soon came across Lewis Carroll's *Through the Looking Glass: or, Alice's Adventures in Wonderland*. I pulled it off the shelf, remembering how I'd read it as a kid compared to how I thought about it now, after hearing Jefferson Airplane's version. I thumbed it open; a sheet of paper fell to the floor. There was no date, no name, just a single paragraph that nearly filled the page:

I am Prometheus I am the Phoenix I am the sharpest sword of righteous thought forged in the fires of Blakean consciousness now mine mine alone alone that no man can rend asunder, given to me by the greatest force of life, of nature, of godhood, the god of gods of all gods it is my gift my salvation in the face of unrelenting fools and the faceless stupidity of the world this folly that is mankind wielding cruel and thoughtless power throughout the ages to oppress others in the unquenchable desire for money and power and all that is decadent and useless to the soul, pointless pursuits that people pursue but oh no this is not my fate this is not what I was put upon the earth for and yet I cannot call out and tell others for like the wise men like Socrates like the sainted martyrs of Christendom and how many countless other wise men from the past I would soon become the victim of those who would si-

178

The Pieces Fit

lence me, take my soul, take my mind, take the essence of my own truest self and sacrifice me to their mean and petty desires and then I would be dead of course without the opportunity to prove my worth the worth of my goals that I know to be the truest and purest and most useful of their kind, perhaps of all time but the meaning of my vision my message is will WILL that which was lost in the cacophony of worldnoise so I cannot know now how that is would could have been because I can only know the moment I am in and how the highest HIGHest expression my pale selfhood in this moment never as good as the first but better than the next and the next after that because remember what the dormouse said to feed my head so that my heart and soul and my pure free Nietzschean will forever prevail. No matter what.

Chapter 14
A Writer's Life
February, 1968

CALL FOR STORIES

Headquarters, United States Armed Forces Europe (USAFE) announces the fifth annual Short Story Contest. The contest is open to all members of the United States military service stationed in Europe or Great Britain. Closing date for submissions is 1 February, 1968. Winners will be announced 1 April, 1968, in the *Stars and Stripes*.

Rules and Regulations:

Stories will be an original work of fiction.
Stories will be typed and double-spaced.
Length of stories will not exceed 5,000 words.
Deadline for submission of story is 1 Feb, 1968.
One entry per person.
Put name and duty assignment at the top left corner of the first page.
Do not include rank.
Provide approximate word count.

Judging will be conducted by a board of five USAFE writers, editors, and USAFI teachers. Stories may be published in a special edition of the *Stars and Stripes* (to be determined).

Prizes will be:

1st Place: $50 U.S. Savings Bond and 3-day pass (subject to CO approval)
2nd Place: $25 U.S. Savings Bond and 2-day pass (subject to CO approval)
3rd Place: $25 U.S. Savings Bond and Zippo lighter with USAFE crest

Good Luck to All!

Nathaniel Hawthorne Flowers
6069th AFCS
APO New York 09131

THREE TO GET READY
Approx. 3,000 Words
Will Be In Submission to the USAFE Short Story Contest, 1968

The table was a dozen scenarios all being acted out at once. From where Chris sat, banging his foot against the heavy, rough-hewn table leg, the red-and-white-checkered tablecloth ran away from him, spreading into the cross-stroke of a capital T that the tables formed. In front of most of the people clay mugs with thick handles held the golden dregs from huge wooden casks of beer; others at the table sipped white wine from small crystalline goblets.

Soft, warm light came from small lamps, suspended on the walls, enclosed by open-ended rectangles of opaque glass. Their light made the pine walls glow; the knotholes seemed to assume a personality of their own in the warm, dimly lit room. People's faces melted, disappeared and reappeared as they moved between shadow and light. The two tall candles on the table tossed shimmering light in locks of hair moving to and fro, sparkled in brown, green, blue eyes, and winked back at them.

The people at the table seemed to pass in and out of Chris' consciousness; their voices he could no longer hear, only the soft lilt of a German folk song, sung by some Teutonic version of Charles Aznavour from the small stage at the other end of the gasthaus. Chris saw people lean forward to say something across the baskets of bread and rolls and the delicate plates of hors d'oeuvres with tiny, twin-pronged forks, over the elevated platters upon which rested half-consumed birthday cake, tall green wine bottles. Cheers went up with raised glasses, people smiling, laughing, but none of this reached Chris. Gradually, the length of table became a blur to his eyes. His foot quit its table-nudging, and he focused on the girl seated next to the celebrant of the birthday party. Like a telephoto lens mounted on a precision-made camera, seeking the one perfect scene in a vast forest, so did he seek her face from among the other, already non-existent, faces at the table.

He leaned back in his chair, hands in his lap, and his eyes went out of focus, smearing the walls, the lights, the people into a gauze-filtered Technicolor collage.

Three, thought Chris. Three witches met Macbeth. Thrice did we count before throwing the fraternity-initiated into the lake. Three acts has the play. Third time's the charm. Three times does the conductor tap his baton on the music stand before beginning the symphony. Three times have I seen this face in three days. Three times means not by accident. Three times means the Fates have something in store for me – for us. Three times means we are destined to meet.

ONE

Chris thought back to the afternoon three days ago. He and several friends had walked into the Flughafenstube, the little watering hole near their air base, nothing more on their minds than a few beers. The chill air, collected inside overnight, was just beginning to thaw; the sun flooded in through the open door and now-unshuttered windows, piercing the wheat-gold curtains, fragmenting in the cracked varnish on the elbow-worn tables, making every particle of dust reflect in unremitting, embarrassed exposure. The hausfrau was her usual, smiling, "Ja, Ja," self as she turned to get the beers. Chris pulled his hands out of his faded blue Levi's pockets, sat down, then turned on the bench to survey the room.

And there she sat, looking right at him. Right beside Smoky, who was looking out the open door as he drank his beer, oblivious to the meeting of their eyes. Chris could not drop his gaze; the girl bore such open directness in her eyes that the usual pangs of violation, of flirting with someone else's property, the feeling of having stolen even a moment of her attention, did not occur to Chris. Then her eyes flicked away from his for a hint of a second, but not to Smoky, then back to Chris, and then the moment was over.

The beers arrived and Chris turned to grab his bottle, but made sure he could still see the girl. Smoky – Staff Sergeant Will "Smoky" Smollach, United States Air Force, Base Supply. Lean, medium height, wiry brown hair that stuck out in an arrogant cowlick at the back of his head. Smoky, whose long face seemed both sagging yet taut in its deep creases and in the gatherings of a million miniscule wrinkles. Smoky, who was said to be engaged, apparently to this beautiful creature.

Her eyes were haunting, two pale, violet blue, newborn eight o'clock moons if there had been twin moons in the sky. Long lashes of the purest charcoal black, with the faintest hint of blue eye shadow that made the eyes tease and taunt. Her shoulder-length hair, coal black and free, bounced gently when she moved her head. Save a touch of the palest pink on her lips, she wore no makeup. Her skin was so pale and so soft-looking that Chris thought, *if she touches her cheek with her finger, she'll leave a bruise*. Her slender nose, the slightly flared nostrils, the delicacy of her nearly full lips, gave her a patrician air in which Chris felt almost inadequate before her.

More than once, more than twice she looked at him as he sat there, for all purposes engaged in conversation with the others. But his thoughts and his eyes were on the girl with Smoky. But Smoky seemed oblivious to her glances toward Chris. She wore a long-sleeved sweater over a prim blouse. Slim legs, crossed at the knee, appeared beneath the table. She was perfect: beautiful and perfect.

Gradually the initial infatuated sensations of the girl subsided and Chris was able to return to the conversation consciously. But his thoughts kept whisking back to her, then to his own girl back home, but the former thought dwarfed the latter. Two or three beers later Smoky and the girl left, but by then more guys were sitting around and Chris missed her as they walked out. He vaguely remembered getting back to the barracks a lot of beers later.

TWO

Late the next day, coming back along the narrow cobblestone street from the German village, Chris met with a trio of young boys playing in the street. The sun's rays were diffusing and spreading out through the clouds like pure red lightning bolts over the tops of nearby houses and through the late-summer trees. A soccer ball was skidding and bouncing across the pavement between two of the boys, perhaps eight or nine, while a long-haired six-year-old frantically ran around between the two in a hopeless attempt to get the ball. Suddenly, the ball flew high into the air, came down, bounced, and came straight for Chris. Surprised, unaware of its presence until it was upon him, he caught it by what seemed to him reflex action alone. The boys cheered and cried, "Hey! Heyheyhey! Hey! Hey!" to him, begging him to kick the ball.

Pleased, feeling more exuberant than he had felt in a long time, Christ joined in the game, exchanging simple German phrases with the boys, occasionally kicking a soft punt towards the little one, who would kick himself in a full arc, or sit on the ball, or miss altogether.

The church bell sang its song to six o'clock. Looking up and across the village, Chris could see a few birds winging home near the steeple and the Germanic purple-blue mist settling on the mountains of this Schwabish province for the evening. Bringing his gaze back to the boys and the game, poised for action once again, he saw a lone figure in a pale blue shift walking past the hedgerow on the opposite side of the street. Her hair was black, pulled into a ponytail. She turned and looked at him; he could just make out her face from where he stood. It was her, Smokey's girl. She smiled, openly smiled at him, and kept smiling as she walked by. Something inside him went soft and hard, dry and moist, a tightness in his chest that constricted his throat momentarily and made him throw his eyes to the ground. The boys sensed that something had happened and quietly moved down the street with their ball. Chris sat down on the curbstone and watched her walk away. After a long while, he got up and followed her route back to the base. He paused outside the Flughafenstube, knowing she was inside. With Smokey. Then continued on to the barracks.

THREE

"A toast, everybody!" It was one of the airmen to Chris' right, wine cup held aloft, looking at the head of the table. "I propose a toast to Smoky and Therese, and their happy marriage – whenever that happens!" Everyone laughed, cheered, drank. Chris felt obliged to raise his glass, even though his heart wasn't in it.

Tonight in the Flughafenstube again. Chris had been sitting downstairs, looking at the waitress he remembered he was in lust with, watching her black-stockinged legs swish beneath her German peasant dress, when one of the airmen he knew had came in and asked him to come join the party upstairs. Probably just another GI drunk party, he had thought; but he had gone and no, everyone was dressed up, a genuine party, and the few females there were, of course, had been lovely. But Therese – enchanting. She had been wearing a loosely-knit blouse that Chris could almost see through; imitation suede skirt with two wide belts running laterally across it, the two ends buckled together; mesh stockings, the haunting eyes. Her hair was gathered in a pony tail again, this time had been gathered at the nape of her neck and tied with a rust-red ribbon. Like the last time, she was radiant under the candlelight.

She had looked at him only once. Someone was forever attracting her attention. When left alone she would sit, hands in her lap, not looking at anything, just looking. Chris had wondered what she was thinking.

Smoky was getting quite drunk. He head lolled this way and that. A few people were leaving now; the day workers, the eight-to-fivers, the ten o'clock-to-bed set. The ones in the rut, the drag, the 20-year rut. Chris had brought his thoughts back. The chair next to Therese became vacant. Grasping his beer mug, Chris had made for it, sat down and immediately began talking to someone across the table who he knew vaguely from the orderly room staff. As the conversation gradually became more casual, he had glanced at Therese, drawing her into it. She had smiled a faint but patronizing smile; this was not stuff that would interest her.

"Say, listen," Chris had said, changing the subject, "Y'know where I'm going on my next leave? Holland. Amsterdam. The place is great. Everybody says so."

Therese had leaned forward now, eyes alight, mouth smiling, tongue just touching between white, evenly spaced teeth. "You are going to Amsterdam? *I* am from Amsterdam!"

Looking more surprised than he was, Chris had gazed into her face, scrutinizing her flawless, aquiline features, then, smiling, said, "No, I didn't, but I'd love to know *everything* about Amsterdam…."

More beer for Chris, more wine for Therese.

"There is so much to see, to do. Many bicycles, the canals, the tulips…."

Eyes now darting about Chris' face, then stopping to look into his eyes, then looking to see if others were looking, the tip of her tongue playing between her teeth, her lips, words flowing out soft and breathless, like melted Edam cheese, a smile lingering always at the corners of her mouth, the gentle movement of her lips as she softly spoke. Chris had moved his head nearer to hear her, Therese not minding that, him now smelling her perfume.

"…days, weeks to see everything…and Dutch beer, yes, so much better than German beer, of course!…."

More beer for Chris, more wine for Therese.

"…I think you're so fortunate, to have grown up here in Europe, to have seen so much. Most Americans don't even see all of their own country before they die, much less another country…."

He touches her arm, the smooth, soft skin of her arm, for emphasis. Therese now totally engaged with him. Smoky on the other side of her, totally unaware, waving a cigarette in the air, in mad conversation.

"…Americans know so little of life, so little of love, of living life…Europeans understand living and loving life…"

Too much beer for Chris, too much wine for Therese.

She smiles. He smiles, they smile a soft smile of two people who share a knowledge of a common feeling. Therese glances at Smoky, as does Chris, checking, then look at each other again. Thighs touch under the table, pressing, her soft thigh, soft like her face, her arm, be careful not to bruise it.

"Therese."

Hands longing to touch.

"Smoky works late tomorrow night…."

Her eyes smoldering, her face pale and wanton.

"Here, at eight?"

"No, not here. At the corner where I saw you last night. By the postbox."

Words slipping out from between moist lips, breathless signs, breathless in waiting anticipation.

"I have to go before – someone – gets suspicious."

"Chris – you know – you know how it is with me? Chris, Smoky goes to America in December…."

"We'll talk more tomorrow. See you at eight."

"Yes, Chris. At eight."

Chris got Smoky's attention, finally, paid the proper parting amenities. Outside, the night was clear; a light breeze, like a razor blade, seemed to cut through the hint of the sky clouding over. The October moon was suspended low on the horizon, barely visible over the village skyline. Much too beautiful a night to waste sitting around the barracks, thought Chris. Another gasthaus just up the strasse…. Walking, hands stuffed in pockets, Chris thought again of Therese. The vague shadow he had felt the day before, seeing her walking by as he was playing ball, her long glance at him; the tightness in his chest returned. He tried to shake it off, but still, it was there, undefined, unnurtured, unwanted. In association he felt dissociation. She was there but shouldn't be. Then she was there but, he felt, somehow, that she should be. There was a bittersweet happiness in what had happened tonight; the taste of the conquest, of stealing fruit from someone else's garden; but it remained aloof, out of reach.

187

Wild Blue Yonder

In front of the gasthaus a girl stood in a phone booth. Her blonde hair was cropped short; her ungirdled stomach sagged slightly in the dress she wore. Her face bore that mark of the lean war years, but Chris knew she couldn't be old enough to have known that sorrow. He drew closer.

Her pert little lips, thin but supple, spoke rapidly into the receiver. She saw Chris coming. She stopped speaking, cupped the mouthpiece, and opened the door.

"Entschuldigen Sie mich, do you have the time?"

The rest was easy. The girl ended her imaginary conversation and they went into the gasthaus. Chris knew all the overtures, the girl knew all the responses. The beer flowed until she wavered between sensuality and tipsiness; instead of a come-on or a line, Chris exuded a masculine tenacity, a man/woman/animal scent that permeated her body from lips to fingertips to loins. It was a communication that knew no boundaries, required no translation. Touch, look, suggest with smiles and unspoken words. Cigarettes shared, good American cigarettes; beer shared, good German beer: a national reciprocity, consummated by international, yet purely personal, copulation.

Chris left her small apartment very late. The razor's edge of night had dulled, the moon was high, the dawn-mist was gathering. The sun will melt it, thought Chris. He could not remember the girl's name. Being inside her was dim, shrouded in his memory. He considered blaming it on the beer, but could not deceive himself so. It had meant nothing, that was sure; yet the physical desire that had welled inside him early was, indeed, satisfied.

Therese, Therese. The uncomfortable feelings he had had about her now no longer existed. In a fell breath of relief he knew what it was that had twisted his soul, had struck the chord that vibrated either/or in his existence. He thought of Smoky, comfortable and drunk, knowing Therese was at his side and not worried. He thought of Therese and her last plea. For understanding? Or justification? He thought of the letters he got from his girl nearly every day, which would have been mundane but for the fact that there was a reason why they arrived with such consistency.

As he walked through the village, Chris passed a small stucco house. Surrounding it was a low stick fence. A huge sunflower bent its head over the fence, its small beam-like petals curled inwards. Some flowers can cover their hearts completely with their petals, thought Chris. This flower cannot. Its heart is too big. He recalled his older brother saying once that chickens would leap off the ground to peck seeds from sunflowers, and how he would shake the seeds out onto the ground for them. Chris stopped. Taking the flower by the stem, he shook it gently. The head swayed back and forth, but no seeds fell. He shook it harder. Still no seeds fell. Then the stem broke. Chris

188

looked at it for a moment, hanging, bent in half, its body broken. Then he broke the stem and held the blossom in one cupped hand. Some seeds fell out. Lifting the flower, in the moonlight he saw three seeds in his palm. He looked at them for a long moment, then one by one he poured them slowly onto the pavement. Putting the flower in his shirt pocket, he walked on toward the base.

Chapter 15
Change of Command
March – April, 1968

The Judgment
Enthusiasm. It furthers one to install helpers
And to see armies marching.

What the heck kind of hexagram was this? I asked the *I Ching* to give me counsel about the Tet offensive in Vietnam and the riots going on back home and if I should write a story about it. I threw my coins, totaled them, drew my lines, and got Yü, or Enthusiasm. The upper trigram was Chên, the arousing, thunder; the lower was K'un, the receptive, earth. I started reading; the lower trigram referred to obedience, while the upper was movement. The thunder moves, the earth obeys? I read on; no, it said movement meets with devotion to inspire enthusiasm. I kept reading; it spoke of music and ancient Chinese rulers and arrogance and having illusions. It was all over the place and no particular place. There was an interesting quote from Confucius:

> To know the seeds, that is divine indeed. In his association with those above him, the superior man does not flatter. In his association with those beneath him, he is not arrogant. For he knows the seeds.

I bowed my head and held the coins and tried to settle my mind. I was unable to understand what Yü meant. I would have to keep thinking – or not thinking – about it until it became clear.

My mother had written to tell me there was live coverage of the Vietnam War on TV. She said it was so bloody and violent she wouldn't let Ernest and Frankie watch.

I don't know if you know about this thing called Tet, but it's just awful. The general over there, Westmoreland, is on TV all the time saying the war is going in our favor and has described what we're doing as a war of attrition, which basically means we're trying to kill North Vietnamese soldiers faster than they can be replaced. Of course, this means he's sending more and more American soldiers to fight.

Seeing these battle scenes on the CBS Nightly News is almost more than I can bear. There are terrible scenes of our marines shooting their rifles and helicopters dropping bombs to protect a place called Khe Sahn. They are brave and determined, but when I look in their faces, I see little boys grimed in dirt and face paint. Someone, I think it was Winston Churchill (I should look it up; after all, I am a librarian) said that war is hell. It is. The TV news proves it over and over, every night. I pray that you will never have to see it first-hand.

I received similar news from Jane:

You wouldn't believe what's going on in San Francisco – riots, protests, sit-ins against the Vietnam War. I went to one – it felt outa sight to be part of a big group of people who are all protesting the war. It's wrong, you know, wrong wrong wrong to be dropping napalm and killing innocent women and children like that awful soldier Calley did. I'm sure you know all about this from your military newspaper. Speaking of which, how's it going with the stories you're writing? You haven't sent me one yet.

My courses are going great. I'll graduate with my Associate's degree this semester and I'm applying to UC Santa Cruz for September – the creative writing program, can you believe it? I think writing fiction is where it's at for me, and my teacher, Mrs. Alexander, is giving me praise and As for my stories, I can send you one. Or some? Maybe we can critique each other's stories!

Is there any way you can come see me? Please please? Or maybe I could come to Germany this summer? Or you could take some leave and I could meet you in Paris? Wouldn't that be romantic? Oh, Nathaniel, I just want to look at you and wrap my arms and legs around you and hold you tight tight tight forever and ever….

I love you <u>so much</u>. Be with me in your heart always,
Jane

I put the letter down, wondering who this Calley was. A photograph fell out of the envelope. It was Jane on Mt. Tamalpais, where we'd had our picnic. She wore khaki hiking shorts and a yellow halter top and a string of hippie beads with a peace symbol dangling between her breasts. Her golden reddish-blonde hair had grown down to her shoulders, and her blue eyes shone with love. I was sure someone took the picture of her especially for me, and it really made me miss her. She was a great girl, she really was. I felt a bulge growing in my pants. *I really should write her. Soon.* I wondered why it was so difficult.

• • •

"Anybody heard anything about Ricky?" Tim asked. We were in his apartment. He'd fixed it up with Marimekko curtains on the windows, purple light bulbs, some psychedelic posters from England and one from Germany that read "Krautrock." We sat on thin mattresses around candles in wine bottles. Alan was loading the hash pipe and Henry Harold Henry was doing one of his spinning twirling dances to some jazz thing with a guitar and sax.

"Nope," I said. *Huh.* If anybody should have heard from Ricky, I figured it would be Tim.

"Kinda funny," Henry Harold Henry said, gulping for breath, "how all his stuff disappeared after inspection. Poof! Gone."

"The military works in mysterious ways," said Alan. "Henry, what is that stupid shit you're playing?"

Henry held up an album cover with a great splash of bright orange and red color. "It's called 'Samba de una Nota so.' One note samba." Stan Getz and Charlie Byrd. *Jazz Samba*. It's a *classss-ic* jazz album."

"Yeah, classic my ass," said Alan. "It's corny."

"Yeah, well put this up yer ass," he said and flipped Alan the bird. He resumed dancing to the music while pretending to play the guitar.

"Very nice, your dancing the samba, but how about putting on something we can all dig?" Alan passed Henry the pipe.

Henry took a long toke, passed it to me, and bowed to Alan. "Whatevah your fockin' majesty commands is my mothahfockin' heart's de-si-yer." That set us howling with laughter. He sat down beside the record player and started picking out records. First he played, "The Wind Cries Mary" by Hendrix, then quickly played a cut from another record, then another, one song blending connecting in the beat or the instrument or the name or the subject, as one ended the next began, on and on, just amazing how Henry did this. The song was "Incense and Peppermints," which didn't sound like such a tasty concoction, by the Strawberry Alarm Clock. Henry Harold Henry stood and said, "My name is Henry Harold Henry and you're listening to Radio Kleinelachen. I hope you have enjoyed the show." He bowed again, a crinkly smile spreading across his face. We cheered and applauded.

"I talked to Tremblay last week," I said. "I told him about the letters from my mom and Jane, about the war protests and stuff."

Tim perked up.

"So, I told him I wanted to write a story from the Germany perspective, you know, like how the troops here see the war and what they think of the protests back home."

"And? What did he say?" Alan asked.

"Same old thing. I can write it, but he can't publish it."

"There's nothing about the protests back home in the *Stars and Stripes!*" said Tim. "I know more about it from *Pravda*."

"Oh, Jesus, here we go with the pinko *Pravda* propaganda again," said Alan.

"Man, cut him some slack," I said. "He has a right to his opinions, and you don't need to put him down every time he opens his mouth."

"Well excuse me, Candide," said Alan, and went to the bathroom. I started to say something, but didn't feel like getting things stirred up again.

"But aren't we winning?" I asked. "I mean, didn't we kick the Vietcong's ass at Tet?"

"No, we've already lost the war," said Tim. "From the American perspective, winning is driving the Russian-supported North Vietnamese out and giving the country back to the South Vietnamese people. LBJ and Westy think North and

South 'Nam would reunite to form a democratic government if the Communists left them alone."

"Right on. Doesn't everyone want to live in a free and democratic society?"

"Not right on, Nate, said Tim. "Some peoples prefer to be ruled by a strong leader like a king or a prime minister. Russia. Marx and Lenin. China. Mao Tse-Tung. Not everyone defines 'freedom' the same way as Americans. For example, take Che."

"Who is?"

"Che Guevara, a Marxist revolutionary from South America who believed that capitalism *and* socialism were evil and that freedom could only be attained through revolution and Marxist socialism. He was murdered by the military of Bolivia who were financed by the CIA and our military because he didn't support the American version of freedom. I have a Che Guevera T-shirt. I can't wear it, of course. I'd probably be court-martialed."

"He was killed by *our* government?" I asked, feeling like Candide again.

"Sure. Our government is always backing some dictator or revolutionary or government that wants to buy our idea of freedom. Of course, they usually take our money and support and then run their dictatorship anyway. Che was a Marxist, which translated into a threat to quote, democracy, unquote, in Bolivia. Don't you remember what Kennedy tried to do in Cuba? The Bay of Pigs in 1962?"

"Uh, yeah, I remember something about that," I said. I was a junior in high school, and was thinking more about cars and girls at the time. "So, Che's idea of freedom was revolution and anarchy? Is that the right word?"

"For sure. Whereas the American idea of freedom is a society that is peaceful and quiet and, well, placid. You know, like Harlan Ellison says, sucking on the glass teat."

"No, I don't know Harlan Ellison. Or what a glass teat is."

"He's a writer. He says the government wants people to just sit passively in front of their television sets to blind them to the political machinations going on. That's why Ellison calls TV the 'glass teat.'

"So, while society sucks the glass teat, they are pacified and oblivious," I summarized.

"That's exactly it," said Tim.

"Not my idea of the ideal society," I said.

"Mine neither."

"But I think that may be changing. I mean, my mom telling me about the war news on TV. How'd you know about him? Ellison?"

"I met him on a civil rights march in Selma, Alabama. He was going on to Los Angeles to write for the *L.A. Free Press*."

Alan came back in the room, zipping up. Henry dropped the needle on Dylan's "With God On Our Side," and we all sang every word like a chorus, sang it with passion as we thought about how much we hated war and hated the military and what our country was doing in Vietnam.

"I just don't get why the American government thinks it has to do this to Vietnam," I said. "I mean, look at all the troops – guys just like us – dying every day. For what?"

"For what?" said Alan. "Well, how about copper and manganese and coal and lead and oil and natural gas for a start?"

"Yup. It sure isn't about keeping the country safe from Communism," Tim said. "It's about greed and power and control. The French tried and failed. We thought we could do it. You ought to read Graham Greene's *The Quiet American*."

• • •

I was at work, secretly studying my Yü hexagram, which continued to elude my understanding, when the day's *S&S* hit my desk. The front page announced

GEN. WESTMORELAND TAKES TET
PROMOTED TO CHIEF OF STAFF

Not a week later I was sitting at my desk, looking out the window at the thick, misty, wet fog outside the Base Operations building. I grabbed my coffee cup and walked over to the urn supposedly reserved for flight crews. The voice of Ernie Hagan, one of the tower air traffic controllers, came over the PA system to announce that the courier would be landing at approximately 1030 hours. *Great! It furthers one to install helpers and to see armies marching.* Whoa! Wasn't that a line from that troublesome hexagram? I went out for the courier bag and looked at the *S&S* headline:

PRES. JOHNSON WILL NOT
RUN IN NOVEMBER

The Commander-in-Chief was reported as saying, "I shall not seek, nor will I accept the nomination of my party for another term as your President."

Westy gone, and now in November LBJ would be replaced, too. It would be interesting to see how the presidential campaigns went, since the American public had apparently turned against the war effort. Of course, I had no way of knowing anything more than my mother or Jane told me and what I read in the *S&S*; we had no American television, no American newspapers, and my German wasn't good enough to understand local TV or papers. I could ask Tim, but I could also count on him saying it was all propaganda. His propaganda vs. their propaganda. Still, I had to admit he seemed to get more accurate news about Vietnam than I did.

I told Milo I was going over to the 6069th to see if the commander had anything for the courier. Afterwards, I'd run over to the barracks and get my *I Ching* and re-read the Yü commentaries.

As I stepped inside Buford said, "Colonel White is retiring."

I looked at the calendar. It was 5 April. "This some kind of delayed April Fool's joke, Sergeant?"

"Nope. The commander has his twenty years in — more'n that, if ya wanna know — and he's retiring." He paused. "The commander don't like the way things are goin' in the military. Or the country. He's cuttin' his tour short. Wants to go home."

"When?"

"Soon's we have a replacement for him."

"Oh."

"You better sharpen your pencil, Flowers. We need you to write a story about the Colonel's retirement."

"We use typewriters these days, Sarge."

"You can write it with a fuckin' feather dip' in cat piss if you feel like it, Flowers, I don' give a shit." Buford yanked open a desk drawer with a screech of metal and pulled out a manila folder full of papers. He kicked the drawer closed with his brogan — no wonder it screeched — and tossed the folder across his desk at me. The papers spilled out. "Here's a bunch of background info on Col. White. Get busy."

197

"Sure, Sarge, right away." I scooped the papers back into the folder and turned to leave, then stopped and turned back. "Oh, the courier's here. Do you have anything to go out?"

"Don't you think I already know that?" Buford retorted. "Why don't you go git on it and fly the fuck out of my life, Flowers."

"Don't tempt me," I whispered under my breath as I pulled the door closed. I thought I heard Buford say "What?" Having forgotten about the *I Ching*, I headed back for Base Ops. With a warmed-up cup of coffee, I sat down and began reading the military life history of Lieutenant Colonel Theodore Xavier White. He was born and raised in Cleveland, Ohio, and enlisted in the Army at the age of 18 during World War II. After basic training he'd qualified for the Army Air Force and trained at Wright Field, named after the Wright brothers, who flew the first airplane there. After World War II, it was named Wright-Patterson Air Force Base.

Once he'd earned his wings, 2Lt White was sent to England and trained to be a navigator. He was assigned to a B-17 "Flying Fortress" bomber, and eventually flew a few missions as a co-pilot until his plane was shot down over Belgium after bombing Dresden in 1945. Medical records indicated that 1Lt White had both his legs broken and extensive internal injuries, but had been rescued, along with the gunner, and flown back to England. *Ah, this must be why he walks like he has a corncob up his butt.* After extensive rehabilitation, a promotion to Captain, and a Purple Heart, he was assigned to administrative duties. In 1947, Major White was sent to Ramstein AB to work in administration and oversight of the post-war occupation. As he told me when I first reported for duty, he'd never had an assignment outside of Europe. Wow, twenty years.

I wondered where he would go now, and what he would do if he didn't have a nearby Officer's Club where he could drink lunch. *Uncool, Nate, not nice,* I said to myself. But now I had a story to write for my weekly assignment, and as I thought more about it, I realized there was no way Tremblay could reject a story on a retiring commanding officer. I would soon be in print, whether he liked it or not!

• • •

The next morning, the courier landed and I left off my story on the CO to pick up the courier bag and newspapers. Today they were folded in half and tied. I slid the string off and read:

REV. MARTIN LUTHER KING ASSASSINATED

The story explained how the famous civil-rights leader had been standing on the balcony of his hotel room when James Earl Ray shot him in the head, two days earlier. The reporter quoted King from his speech saying he had been to the mountaintop. He'd seen the other side, the promised land. He was not concerned about living a long life anymore, had no worries, and feared no man. He knew he and his people would get there.

This blew me away. It was like he knew it was coming. The story concluded by saying King was the most influential figure in the long fight to get blacks treated as equals in the United States, but that he was also often accused of being an anti-war activist and suspected of being a Communist.

I caught the word *black*. Apparently, since I'd been in Mississippi, there had been a shift from using the term Negro to black. I had no idea.

Turning back to the article, I read that King was one of the leaders of the March on Washington in 1963. I remembered that almost as clearly as I remembered President Kennedy's being assassinated in Dallas a few months afterward. That was about the saddest day of my life, right up there beside the day my dad died. I knew I lost something that couldn't be replaced on both of those days.

And now as I sat at my desk, the piece of paper with the story of Col. White half-written sticking out of my typewriter, the newspaper in my hands, I felt incredibly sad like that all over again, bitterly sad about all the evil things that were going on in the world. Kennedy, King, my dad. They were leaders, men to look up to. Why did they have to die?

That night, Tim and I were in the alten Scheune smoking a joint and talking about the Martin Luther King assassination. "I really don't get it, Tim," I said, exhaling a big lungful of nearly smokeless air. I'd gotten a nice hit that would get me high quick. "You don't like somebody, so you just kill him? Jane told me about the riots at the Lincoln Memorial, of all places. You don't like it when citizens protest, so you send the cops and soldiers out to beat them? And this is a democracy?"

"Don't forget Malcolm X," Tim said, fully toked, holding it in, as he passed the joint back to me. "He got assassinated too, but you don't hear that much about him because he was a Moslem and a socialist."

"Yeah?" What was his trip? When did he get killed?"

"Man, Malcolm X was the father of the Black Power movement. But he was too far out, too radical. He was giving a speech and this Nation of Islam guy runs up to the stage and blows him away with a sawed-off shotgun. I think it was in '65. And don't forget about Che Guevara. These people scare the power-trippers. Hippies scare 'em. Anybody against the war scares 'em. And we're supposedly fighting dictators to make the world safe for democracy."

"Yeah, no shit," I said, "Like Jesus. He scared the Roman power-trippers." I was getting stoned, and the stone was making me feel even sadder than I already was.

"Yeah, you say 'no shit,' Nate, but you don't know. I was there, man, I saw it and felt it and lived it. Especially felt it, the fear and the hatred. There's all kinds of discrimination in the wonderful old U. S. of A. and it's not just blacks or Moslems or Jews. It's old people against young people, it's Dylan's masters of war against people who believe in peace and hate the way our country exploits the rest of the world for its own power and money trips. And you know what else is freaky? We sell other countries the guns and tanks and bombs and planes to make war against each other! That's the business of America, man! We're the warmongers, man. I was in SDS for almost four years. I studied, I learned. I stood on the lines. I marched. I burned my fuckin' draft card, for all the good that did."

"No shit," I said. I was really stoned and had to think really hard about what Tim had just said. "SDS. I remember you mentioned that. That's Students for a Democratic Society, right?"

"Yeah. Well, first I was a member of the Student Nonviolent Coordinating Committee, even before I went to college. We worked for civil rights, you know, desegregation and voter registration and stuff like that in the deep south. But I got totally radicalized by the hate we had to face when we marched from Selma to Montgomery. And I guess that's what got me interested in SDS. There were communists in it, you know, like cells, and I saw socialism as a way to make all people equal and free."

He paused, and I said, "How old are you, Tim?"

"I'll be 25 in July," he said. I'd thought he was a little older than me. "I guess I wanted to feel like my...not being...interested in girls, ah, I guess I felt like that was a human rights issue too, and I wanted to see if I could feel equal and free in my sexual...preferences."

"But you joined the Air Force knowing that homosexuals aren't supposed to...."

"Yeah, but remember, man, I'd burned my draft card, I'd been radicalized, I'd dropped out of college. Just like you. I'd been out of college for over a year and I was about to get drafted. If the Army had got me, they would have made mincemeat out of me. I took the high road, just like you, and enlisted. No draft card needed. So, once I was in, I felt I could keep the secret. And you know something? Now I'm not really sure if I'm queer or not. Ricky and me — we never, you know, did it. He's queer as a three-dollar bill, and I think he wanted to...go...further, but it, like, turned me off. I'm thinking it might just be some other way for me to feel like a radical." He untangled his long legs and stood up, pacing back and forth among the haystacks, rubbing the back of his head. "I don't know, I just don't know."

I reached in my pocket for my pack of cigarettes and dug out another joint. As I lit it, our eyes caught and we held an intense look until the match went out. I felt like we had found a new level of trust.

"Well, you know your secrets — all of them — are safe with me, Tim." *It is good to install helpers.*

"Thanks, Nate. I mean it. Thanks a lot." We gripped in a hippie handshake.

Chapter 16

Liederhalle
April, 1968

"Look, man, I'd like to eat some real German food that isn't a schnitzel sandwich," Alan said. "We've hardly been off-base. Want to go to Stuttgart for the day?"

One of the odd things about the Kleinelachen troops was that hardly anybody ever went off-base. I rarely saw a face I didn't know at Ma's; apparently most troops drank their watered-down Budweiser in the so-called NCO Club.

"Yeah, for sure, sounds great," I said. I liked the idea of spending some time with Alan.

We got off the trolley at the Hauptbahnhof in the center of Stuttgart. All around us were wooden carts filled with bright colorful flowers for sale. We wandered up and down the winding little *strasses* of old-fashioned gingerbread houses and shops filled with curious things. Ahead was the Altes Schloss, or old castle, apparently still pretty busted up from World War II bombing, right next to the Neues Schloss, which looked pretty old itself. The most beautiful girl I'd ever seen in my life approached. She had dark hair that matched her cape and green eyes that matched her beret, and she smiled a little smile at me as she passed by. I stopped, turned, and was about to call back to her when Alan yanked me onto a park bench under a tree, pulled out a joint and lit up.

"Hey, man, what are you – did you see that girl –"

"Forget her. German girls don't shave their armpits. Or their legs." So we got high and Stuttgart got more colorfully, intricately interesting. We walked through the castle grounds until we came upon another platz filled with more pretty *fräuleins* selling flowers.

"I wonder who that is," said Alan, pointing at a tall greenish statue.

"Guess we're supposed to know," I replied.

"Well, whoever he is, he looks very hip. Very cool."

"Yeah, the robes, the book in his hand, the flowers in his hair. Had to be a hippie."

A German civilian walked by. "Wer ist dieses?" I asked.

"Schiller!" he snapped. "Das grosse Friedrich Schiller!"

"Danke schoen, danke," I replied.

"The Great Schiller," said Alan. "Philosopher and writer. I remember something about him and Goethe being buddies."

"Oh, yeah, Goethe. *Sturm und Drang!* Wow, man!"

"And *Faust*," Alan said. "One of the great bad guys of literature."

"I wouldn't say he was a bad guy," I said. "Stupid. Greedy, maybe. I mean, like, nobody makes a pact with the devil."

"You don't think so, huh?" Alan snorted, but my stoned thoughts had drifted back to Yü. The earth: receptive, innocent, obedient. Above, the thunder – *sturm und drang* – a power so great it could twist your thinking. Enthusiasm should never be an egotistic emotion, the *I Ching* said. Exactly what happened to Faust. Interesting. Interesting.

Smoking the pot gave us the munchies. We went looking for a restaurant. On the corner of Torstrasse and Nesenbachstrasse we found the Gaststätte Tauberquelle, a rather plain-looking restaurant with whitewashed walls and rows of shuttered windows. A plaque read 1879.

Alan studied the menu in a glass cabinet beside the door with a stoner's attention to detail. My mouth was watering, so I said, "Look, man, it's been here for almost two hundred years, so the food must be OK." A jolly man greeted us in the local Baden-Württemberg dialect, which I found difficult to follow, and escorted us to a table. We started with two Dinkelackers, the best local brew. I slurped. Alan slurped. "I think Zweiflüssebrau is better," he said. I nodded.

The menu was entirely *auf Deutsch*. Alan ordered Putensteak mit Früchten, Käse überbacken Kroketten und Salat, a steak casserole baked with fruit and cheese, and a salad. I ordered a Rostbraten mit Bratkartoffeln oder Spätzle und Salat, a pork roast with potatoes and noodles.

"This is great chow," said Alan. "I dig getting out in the culture, don't you? Hey, try using your fork and knife like Europeans. They don't switch them back and forth, like Americans do." He demonstrated. It was so simple, so efficient.

"What I meant about the culture," Alan said, "you know, Germany — all Europe, I suppose — is, we should be getting the most out of being here."

"Yeah, man. Well, we are right now, aren't we?" I raised my glass of beer and we clinked and grinned at each other. For a moment I felt comfortable with Alan Gardner, maybe for the first time. "Hey, man, you know, I had an interesting thing happen a while back, when I was up at Ramstein. I never told anybody about this, but I was in the library, and I picked up their old copy of *Alice in Wonderland* they have, and a piece of paper fell out. Somebody had written the strangest story. It started out 'I am Prometheus' or something -"

"I wrote that," said Alan.

I practically fell off my chair.

"Henry Harold Henry and I were TDY at Ramstein for eighteen fuckin' days between Mildenhall and Kleinelachen. Uncle Sam never gave us a reason, just put us on day duty every day. We cleaned trash cans, pulled KP, mowed lawns, painted officers' quarters — every shit job there was. One day I got assigned to clean up the library. All I could think of was how much I hated giving up my freedom to the military so I could fight for some stranger's freedom. Isn't that about how it is?"

His face turned hard.

I nodded, said, "Yeah."

We solemnly clinked glasses and drank.

"I was totally pissed, especially after we'd gotten kicked out of Shepard and now this, not knowing what was gonna happen to us. The librarian was gone. I sat down at her typewriter and wrote that."

"Man, it blew me away. I said to myself, I really would like to meet the troop who wrote this. And you'd heard 'White Rabbit,' too. So it was you...."

"It's the first paragraph of a novel I have all figured out in my head. I hid it, figuring I'd go back for it, but...."

We finished our meal and continued wandering. We came across the Liederhalle Platz. It was a beautiful, modern building; banners announcing upcoming concerts hung from light poles.

"Look, Alan!" I said. "Ravi Shankar! I saw him at Monterey Pop, just before I came over here! It was outasight!"

"Well, no shit," said Alan. "Was there anybody you *didn't* see at Monterey Pop?"

"We have to go," I replied. "He is the coolest of the cool. The Beatles studied with him. You know 'Within You, Without You?' George Harrison? He learned to play the sitar from Ravi Shankar."

"No shit?" said Alan.

"No shit," I replied.

"Then of course we have to go see him."

"It's just a few weeks from now. C'mon, let's get tickets."

• • •

Buford had posted a new order on the barracks bulletin board:

Effective 15 April 1968, Lt. Col. Theodore X. White will be relieved of command of the 6069th Air Force Communications Squadron (AFCS) and 1Lt Salvatore M. Antonucci will assume command of the 6069th AFCS.

On 08 April 1968, 6069th personnel will fall out at 1200 hours in the Base Ops flight briefing room for transfer of command. Khakis mandotory.

Buford entered the room where pilots would normally be briefed prior to flying a mission and bellered, "Ten-HUT!" We jumped to our feet and saluted. Tim stamped his brogans twice.

Col. White entered. "At ease, as you were, at ease." He gripped the sides of the podium as if he needed support and began to speak. "My fellow airmen, I'm going to keep this brief. For twenty-six years I have worn the uniform of our country, serving in many capacities to keep the world free of the forces of evil – first Nazism, then Communism. The American forces liberated Europe from these threats, and I am proud to have served that cause."

The colonel was pale and his voice warbled as he spoke to his squadron – all thirteen of us.

"Today we fight Communism once again, this time in Southeast Asia. As in the past, it is a time when we, the freest people in the world, need to be united. But even within our own country, the greatest country in the world, we are divided, and a house divided against itself, whether that division is about purpose, truth, or the American way, cannot stand. That is especially true of you airmen, who have enlisted in the cause of keeping the peace and ensuring the freedom of all men, regardless of their country or race or color, for if they desire freedom it is our God-given duty to help them to have it. That is what we're doing in Vietnam, and you need to remember that you are sworn to protect, honor, and defend those people.

"I came to Germany twenty-one years ago to protect, honor, and defend the newly forged peace with Germany and to ensure the freedom of the peoples of Europe. That was America's commitment after World War II, and all Americans, both the civilians back home and the troops here in Europe, believed in that commitment. At that time, we were thought of as heroes, and by God, we were. We trounced the Nazis and brought Germany out of its dictatorship and back to a democratic state in harmony with its European neighbors. We have kept that commitment, and have made it ever stronger over the years.

"Over a hundred years ago, the United States were not united. North fought South in one of the bloodiest wars of all mankind. Now I see America as a nation divided once again, but this time it is civilian versus soldier, father against son, even brother against brother. Little do those who dissent realize that we fight for peace!"

The colonel smacked the podium, a grim look upon his face. The room was filled with total, absolute silence.

"You — you and I, all of us — must fight for peace. We must fight so that America's ideals will prevail to keep all people free in the grace of God. It is our legacy to future generations. We must not allow ourselves to doubt the wisdom of our leaders, and to obey the orders of our superiors. We cannot allow ourselves to lapse into suspicion of our great country's motives or to become prisoners of sinister ideas and forces.

"Yet sadly, this is exactly what I see happening to many of our troops in uniform. War, which is the personification of good versus evil, has become politicized. Its motives have been thrown into question. Under such circumstances, and given the fact that I have given my service and have succeeded in my mission here in Germany, I find I am no longer in a position to shape the destiny of either today's or tomorrow's armed forces. I do not believe I should command in a time when individual selfishness reigns over selflessness. I cannot conduct my command in the face of the contrariness of ideological forces that are totally and utterly unpatriotic and illogical.

"Therefore, it is my decision to step down as the Commanding Officer of the 6069th Squadron, Air Force Communications Service, and devote the time that remains to me to writing my memoirs. In a week's time, First Lieutenant Salvatore M. Antonucci will assume command of this unit.

"As I leave, I want you to know that I'm proud of you airmen and what you have accomplished here at Kleinelachen. It has been an honor to be your commander. I trust you will carry on your duties with the same earnestness for Lt. Antonucci. Some of you may go on to duty in the war zone. Some of you may reenlist and stay here in Germany. Others may want to complete their military obligation and go home. To all of you, regardless of your future, I thank you for your attention and say good-bye and God bless you, and God bless the United States of America."

Col. White snapped to attention and whipped off a salute. Buford snapped to attention and saluted, and we all jumped to our feet and saluted, too. He tottered out of the room and Buford followed, scowling over his shoulder at us. We stood looking at one another, baffled. It was a grand performance. I wasn't sure if I wanted to laugh or barf.

I took notes during the commander's farewell speech, which I used to wrap up my article for the *S&S*. I sent it up on the courier the next morning, feeling smug that I'd finally see a story in print. I stopped by HQ to give the CO a copy, but Buford said he wouldn't be in. *Oh, yeah, probably tea time.*

That night, we got one of those funny little spring snowstorms with just enough snow to turn the ground white. The next morning, as I went to get the courier bag at HQ, I saw an Army ambulance from Patch Barracks. Medics in white fatigues made dark footprints and twin tracks in the snow as they pushed the gurney. A human body was covered by a sheet. Buford was there, and I ran over. For once he was not angry. "It's Col. White," he said. "Died in his sleep. He done went to his maker all quiet and peaceful."

Poor old guy couldn't take it. Couldn't face life without the military.

I called Tom to tell him what had happened, and asked if he wanted me to add a final paragraph to my story on the commander.

"Sorry. Since Col. White's dead, the story's now an obituary," he replied. "I gotta turn it over to the obits editor in Frankfurt. Gotta kill your retirement story."

• • •

Ravi Shankar with his sitar, Ali Akbar Khan playing sarod, and Allah Rakha drumming on the tabla, were about to perform in the Mozart-Saal at the Stuttgart

Liederhalle

Liederhalle. The walls and stage and roof were all natural wood; ceiling lights shone down like tiny stars. There wasn't a bad seat in the house. Alan, Tim, Henry Harold Henry and I were so close I could see the golden ring on Ravi's big toe.

• • •

Tony couldn't come, but suggested I fly to London Town to score some good drugs for the concert. We returned to the same Indian restaurant, but this time were escorted to a private room where we sat cross-legged on a floor covered in large, multi-colored silk pillows around a gilded table. Sitar music played softly. An exotically beautiful Indian girl swayed into the room wearing diaphanous green and gold pajama pants and a tiny matching top that left her beautiful tummy bare. It was Amita! Tony stood and, to my surprise, they embraced.

Amita served us fruits and dates and sweet lassi tea. When she bent over, the silver necklace between her swelling breasts tinkled; she smelled like Arabian nights. She loaded a beautiful decorated pipe she called a chillum with hashish and we took hits, one at a time. That was followed by a meal of garlicky naan breads, spicy-hot lamb curry and shish kabobs. Afterwards, we drank spiced masala tea which I soon learned was brewed with marijuana. We had a few after-dinner hits on the chillum and fell into a langorous state, lolling about on the pillows with Amita until the inevitable kissing and touching commenced, first with Tony, then with me, but soon it was just the two of them and I passed out, delirious from the most sensuous night of my life. Amita's uncle, who owned the restaurant, possessed the finest hallucinogenic drugs. I left with a packet of little pink tablets of psilocybin with the word Sandoz stamped upon them.

• • •

The raga swooped through us as we became completely and beautifully stoned on the psilocybin. Minutes, hours, days, eons passed, then it was intermission. We went to the lobby to get something to drink.

"I saw him — all three of them — at Monterey Pop," I said. "Ravi and Ali Akbar Khan and Allah Rakha. Their ragas are like — psychedelic symphonies."

"Yeah, Nate, you already told us. At least three times," said Alan. "But still, I think it's groovy that they do it without drugs. They get a natural high just playing the ragas."

"I wonder how they do that," Tim said.

"I don't know, but I'd like to get to that place," Alan replied. "High without drugs. Not that I think drugs are bad," he added with a wry smile.

"No, drugs aren't bad," Henry said. "To each his own path to higher consciousness. I mean, I can't play a sitar." We laughed.

"Some drugs are definitely bad," I said. "Like, I would never shoot heroin."

"Not exactly what I would call consciousness-expanding," Henry added.

"For sure," Alan said. "It's not about the drug, it's about higher consciousness. You don't get that with just any drug. For sure not alcohol or pills or cocaine or heroin. I think we all agree on that. I mean, like Leary doesn't say 'tune in, turn on, drop out' about heroin."

The house lights blinked. We returned to our seats and the beautiful psilocybin high started coming on all over again. Ravi, Ali and Allah assumed the lotus position and as they began to play I could see they were communicating at a deep and intense and profound level with each other. I felt them offering an invitation to join their experience. The music flowed on and on and seemed to blend into the gentle wood of the walls, the stage, the floors, the seats. Everything was becoming one and the same; everything emanated from the music. Everything was everything, inseparable, lightcolorsoundsmell swirling in my consciousness until it, and I, left my body and became the blended sense of senses.

The concert ended. We sat perfectly still, still stoned, still totally blown away. This was beautiful, perfect. None of us wanted it to end. Even as the three musicians left the stage, it felt like the ragas were still playing inside me, around me. *Within you, without you*, as George would say.

An old wrinkled hand reached between Alan and me and touched his arm. It was a delicate hand with long painted nails, rings with large green and red and blue stones glistening on every finger, and a lace cuff at the wrist. Alan turned to look back, as did I.

"Young man – young men – I am most curious what you're doing here." The quavering voice came from an elderly woman sitting behind us. She was dressed in what appeared to be multi-colored gowns and scarves, silky layer upon silky layer. She held tiny opera glasses on a stick. She had a very strong aura of authority. A woman of similar age and dress stood beside her, looking on. We stood up and turned around.

"We...came...to hear Ravi Shankar," I said.

"Of course, of course you did!" the woman trilled back. "But of all the entertainment available to you in Stuttgart tonight, why Ravi Shankar?" She spoke with a British accent.

We looked back and forth at each other for a minute, then Henry said, "His music is spiritual. It takes us to places in our heads where we haven't been before."

"I saw him in California," I said. "Before I came here — and then I saw the sign a few weeks ago...and I knew my buddies would want to see him."

"It's just — really, like the *most* intense experience," said Alan. "Like Henry Harold Henry said — spiritual. You see, we're on a spiritual quest. Together."

"Are you now," the woman said, then she smiled a great huge beaming smile. "That is *most* interesting. I would be *most* grateful if you would join me for afternoon tea next week to discuss this further. This is my companion, Elspeth Maclainie." Elspeth handed each of us a small white card with a name and address printed in scrolly golden letters. It read

Dame Marion Edith Cornwall-Etherington
Fruchtkastenhaus bei Schillerplatz Stuttgart
642 860

"Please call to arrange a visit. Thank you, and good night, boys." The old ladies gave us a warm smile, nodded, and exited.

We looked at each other, wondering what had just happened.

• • •

We shared a taxi back to Zweiflüssehausen and crashed at Tim's. When I awoke, I could still feel the psilocybin buzzing inside me, like the acid trip with Tony but not quite as intense. When we got back to the base, there was a message on my bunk to report to the CO. I cleaned up and fell in at The Dungeon; 1Lt. Antonucci was sitting at the colonel's old desk. I pulled a sharp salute and said, "Sgt. Flowers reporting as ordered, sir." He snapped an equally crisp salute back at me and said, "At ease, Flowers."

I sat down on the colonel's college chair. It felt different. I didn't miss the colonel; I wondered if I should, or why I should. The same desk was no longer covered in deckels or coffee cups or even coffee rings. There was a short, tidy stack of papers on the right, and a shorter stack on the left – In and Out, I imagined. Antonucci's wooden name plaque was front and center. He leaned forward and clasped his hands.

"Flowers, I'm happy to be the bearer of good news today. You've won third place in the USAFE Short Story Contest. Congratulations!" Antonucci stuck out his hand and shook mine, hard, almost as if he were angry. A tight grin traced across his face. He quickly released his grip, picked up a sheet of paper and handed it to me. It was a letter of congratulations from General Beauregard.

"Wow, far – ah, thank you, sir, Lieutenant, sir," I said, relieved I wasn't in some kind of trouble.

"I read it, Flowers," Antonucci said, sitting back down and picking up some papers. My story. The light from the bare hanging bulb flashed on his gold lapel bar, right in my eye. I wondered why second lieutenants got gold bars but first lieutenants got silver. But the gold wasn't gold; it was brass. The silver wasn't silver, either; it was chrome. Oh well. "It's pretty good. Did you write this from, ah, personal experience?"

"Ah, nossir, I didn't, actually. Maybe from wishful thinking! Hahahahaha!"

Antonucci laughed with me. "Well, it's a good story. It has just the right – what should I call it, moral tension, would that be accurate?"

"Ah, yessir, moral tension, that's one way to describe it. I suppose I would have said *je ne sais quoi*. Hahahahaha!" He looked at me, puzzled, but didn't say anything. "So, sir, do you know who won first and second prize?"

"No, I don't. I'd check with your NCOIC."

"Right, sir." I paused. "Thank you, sir. I appreciate your – congratulations." I saluted and cut out for Base Ops and my phone. "Hi Tom," I said, "I just heard from my CO that I won third place in the short story contest."

"Right, right, right you are, Flowers. Congratulations."

"Ah, I was just wondering, *Tom*, who the other winners are."

"Well, let's see," he said; I could hear papers rustling in the background. "Yeah, here we go. First place – that's a Captain L. L. Hardy stationed in Berlin… attended the Iowa Writer's Workshop…story was called, "Missile Away," about how an ICBM nearly got launched by a false alert.

"Second place to a second looie, named, ha, Woo – oh, Portia Woo, actually, a WAC. Ph.D. in language studies from the University of Hawaii. Teaches languages at USAFI." He paused. "So, it looks like 2Lt Woo wrote a story called "The Last Petal," about a little Vietnamese girl whose parents are killed by the Vietcong and left to wander alone in the jungle until American soldiers rescue her. Seems you're keeping pretty good company here, troop."

"Yeah, cool. I'd love to read their stories sometime," I said drolly. "Tom, do you know how many stories were submitted?"

There was a long pause. "Well, according to this, there were only three."

Chapter 17
Children of the Future
May, 1968

Spring arrived right on Mayday, and a beautiful day it was when I woke up in Tim's apartment in Zweiflüssehausen. The night before, Tim, Henry Harold Henry and I had gone out for Walpurgisnacht. It was quite strange; farmers lit huge haystacks afire, and there was a great deal of drinking and revelry on the village streets, although we saw no witches. Henry and Tim had already left for duty, so I walked through the village watching women sweep and scrub the streets and sidewalks after the night's revelry.

I had a coffee and strolled by the stone fountain, the date 1079 carved on it, past the Zweiflüssebrauerei to the fork in the two rivers that gave the town its name. They burbled along, bright in the sunlight, the larger one driving a paddle-wheel behind the brewery. *Nature and mankind, working together*, I thought as I sat tossing pebbles into the water. Screwy stuff ran through my mind in a morning-after stoned stream: Did Col. White die for our sins, the sins of all who make war? My dad died not because of war or even because of the love of literature, so why do we die when we do and how does it feel to leave others behind and leaderless? Do I miss the Old Man's leadership? No, he was the nonexistent nonexistential leader but not like my dad who I still miss who was not a leader like that kind of leader but he led and guided with ideas, always with ideas made from words, much better than the refuse of war, the shrapnel of hatred and battle. Like in *The Quiet American*. What Fowler sees and will only see, will not participate in the war, the anguish of being the reporter, the observer, not allowed to feel, *not even to feel the love or loss*

215

of Phuong. No, no, Tim, you were wrong. Graham Greene's novel was not about why Americans or even the French were in Vietnam, it was about why any country thinks it ought to try to dominate and rule another and what a loser idea that is, even for us U. S. here in Germany. How do we presume we can change others to our way of thinking? Or do the people fake us out and keep living their own way because that's what they know, and is that Fowler's idea to just take no stand and let it all be hands-off like a scientist?

But I am no scientist.

• • •

I read somewhere — maybe it was in Hesse's *Demian* — that there are no coincidences, so when we found the home of Dame Marion Edith Cornwall-Etherington and her companion Elspeth Maclainie was around the corner from the statue of Schiller, I wasn't surprised. Theirs was a huge, four-story house of stone and thick timbers and plaster with a red-tiled roof. It stood in a private courtyard beside several other mansions that circled a statue of a naked boy peeing into a fountain.

"Ach, you vould be der joung yentlemen, come vor tea," said the butler, opening the door. He was wearing a coat with tails, a white shirt with a lace front, knee pants with white stockings and black patent leather slippers. He excused himself to announce our arrival.

"Woo-hooooo, far fuckin' out," exclaimed Henry Harold Henry as we looked around.

"Cool. Very, very cool," said Tim. "I really dig this old European culture. I'll bet this place is at least two or three hundred years old. Lucky for us that our brothers in arms didn't blow it to pieces in World War II."

"Well, they bombed the shit out of plenty of other stuff," said Henry.

"No cussing, Henry," said Alan.

The butler returned. "Kommen Sie mit mir bitte." We walked down a long hallway paneled in dark wood. Huge oil paintings of ancient men stared down at us. We reached a staircase about twelve feet wide. On either side stood suits of armor, shined to a mirror finish, each holding a spear. We climbed the stairs past tapestries and statues, strolled in an arc around the balustrades past many doorways until we arrived at tall double doors with elaborately carved panels. The butler said, "Mesdames, zee boyz are here."

We entered an amazing room. It was round, maybe fifty feet across with a domed ceiling about twenty feet high painted with blue skies, white fluffy clouds, and naked angels flying around shooting arrows. It was corny but beautiful. The walls were lined floor to ceiling with bookshelves on either side. Tall leaded windows faced the courtyard. Beneath them ran a red velvet bench, and above were stained glass murals depicting naked men and women cavorting in a forest. Happy guitar music filled the room.

A round, flowery rug covered most of the floor. In the center was an octagonal table upon which stood an extraordinary hookah about three feet tall, surrounded by tufted overstuffed pillows. Several overstuffed chairs. A divan from which Dame Marion rose. She wore a velvet robe and scarves that flowed behind her in the draft her rather large body created as she walked toward us.

"Thank you, Günther," she said. "My dears, it is *so* kind of you to come visit," she crooned. "Please say your names for Elspeth and me."

We introduced ourselves, and as we did Dame Marion held our hands in turn, saying our names and how good it was to meet us. She wore extravagant rings with large colored stones on every finger. A multitude of bracelets clinked on her arms. Strands of beads hung from her neck, and a string of pearls wound round and around her piled-up hair.

"Please call me Dame Marion," said Dame Marion. "What would you gentlemen like to drink? Elspeth?" She dangled an arm in Elspeth's direction, her forefinger extended. Elspeth, wearing a shimmering blouse and black pants with huge bell bottoms, moved to a silver cart covered with liquor bottles.

"Ah, nothing," I said. "We've sort of stopped drinking alcohol."

"Oh, splendid, splendid!" Dame Marion said, and Elspeth smiled as well, her first. "I say, you are indeed meeting my first impressions of you at the Mozart-Saal. But you do partake of hallucinogens, do you not?"

Alan looked at me and wiggled his eyebrows, then glanced at Henry, who was gawking at the hookah. Tim stood, silent and tall in a civilian version of parade rest. A slight smile crossed his lips, but he didn't say anything.

"Ah, well, far out," I said. "So, why did you want to invite us here?"

"Yes, of course!" she cried, laughing sweetly. "But let us sit down and share the pipe. Now, I know you said you don't use alcohol, but if you don't mind, Elspeth and I like to add a bit of brandy to the water in the hookah. Cools the smoke so it doesn't burn our old throats, isn't that so, Elspeth?"

"And it's just so, Marion," Elspeth replied. She took a bottle of Courvoisier and a pitcher of water from the serving cart and began filling the hookah. Dame Marion's accent was distinctly British; I wondered about Elspeth's.

"Excuse me," I said to her, "I'm trying to place your accent. Are you Irish?"

"Most assuredly not!" Elspeth snapped. "Oi'm from Edinburgh. Scotland!" She rolled the *burrrrrrah* beautifully.

"Beg your pardon," I said. "No offense."

"None taken," she replied, smiling kindly. Dame Marion had seated herself on the floor cross-legged and we did the same, then she signaled us to take one of the hoses. I gazed at the hookah; its glass vase was deep scarlet red with intricate designs of gold leaves, which I recognized were the marijuana plant. The base and stem were also gold. There were six hoses with ivory mouthpieces, each with a golden cap. At the top was a pure white bowl to hold hashish or marijuana.

"'Tis Turkish," Elspeth said, noticing my attention, "about four hundred years old. The smoking bowl is made of meerschaum." She dropped a chunk of hashish the size of one of Dame Marion's ring stones into it, plucked a foot-long matchstick from a nearby vase, scratched it to life and touched the flame to the hash. We all took a gentle toke and heard the gurgle as the smoke passed through the brandied water. A sweet, gentle smoke filled my lungs, nicer than I'd ever tasted. I held it down for a long time, feeling it curl through my head. My buddies were doing the same. Elspeth folded herself into the lotus position and held a tube as well. She and Dame Marion hit the hash as hard as we did. I was stoned in short order, but not a stone that made me want to go inside myself. *Au contraire.* I felt my awarenesses multiplying like circles rippling from a stone hitting water.

I looked around the table, feeling a deep connection with the group. A rich smile spread through my whole self to see us four American GIs sitting lotus around a table in a mansion in the middle of Stuttgart, Germany, getting stoned from a hookah full of hashish with two women old enough to be our grandmas. Laughter rose from my belly and spread, a laughter of oddity and joy mixed with grateful contentment. The others laughed too, like they knew my secret but no matter, it felt like home being here. I imagined my father standing in this magnificent library reading to us. I wondered if he would get stoned with us and I figured yes, he would, he would do this with us. But probably not my mother, she would not approve. All the while, strange guitar music played what was this song, I knew this song

"'Tis Django Reinhardt playing with his Hot Club of France Quintet," said Elspeth, "His rendition of Ravel's 'Bolero.'" I looked at her; had I spoken aloud? She smiled and nodded at me.

"I love jazz," said Henry Harold Henry. He looked at Dame Marion. "What is a Dame? Why are you a Dame?"

"Well, my dear boy — Henry, isn't it? — you see, I was a young girl during World War I — we called it the war to end all wars, but of course it was not — did not — and I had just married a handsome young officer in the British Expeditionary Army. Oh, the letters he wrote me!" and she was lost in her memories. "He was killed, of course, leading an attack at Aisne, in France. The attack was successful, and as he had died valorously he was made a Knight of the Order of the British Empire by King George the Fifth. Posthumously, of course. As the wife of a knight I was made a Dame."

"Wow," said Henry. "That's sad, but it's kind of far out, too. Did you get married again?"

"Sorrowfully, no," Dame Marion said. "I just never found a man to equal Sir Robert. Robin. But several years later — it was 1921, was it not, Elspeth? — I found my lifelong companion, who sits here beside me today." Elspeth reached over and squeezed Dame Marion's hand. They smiled fondly at each other. "She, too, had lost her lover, although he was not yet her husband, in the Great War. We met at a salon in Paris, where we emigrated after the war. We had our family inheritances and could live wherever we pleased. And I say, Paris was *such* a gay place in the 1920s!" Dame Marion waved her hands in the air like an orchestra conductor.

"Aye, and well into the '30s," Elspeth added.

"Yes, yes, my dear. Wine, Champagne, hashish, opium, outlandish carryings-on at parties with the poets, artists, musicians — oh, there were so many artists! That's where we met Django, after he burned his hand and developed that lovely style of playing the guitar. I daresay we knew the greatest hearts — and minds — of our generation! Elspeth, do you remember Kiki du Montparnasse? Chez Kiki!"

"Aye, all too well," Elspeth replied, a wide smile creasing her face. "But t'was Ezra Pound and Anaïs Nin who were my favorites. Why, they read at her salons, to be sure."

I couldn't help comparing my hippie days in San Francisco. "I always thought a salon was a beauty shop."

219

"That's true, Nathaniel," said Elspeth. "Yet in France a *salon* is a gathering where artists and intellectuals enlighten and entertain one another. You could say we're having a salon here this afternoon."

"Us too!" I exclaimed. "We meet like a salon – the four of us. Five. There's Tony, who's stationed in England." I looked at the others, who nodded agreement.

"And so it was, right up until war began all over again," continued Dame Marion, as if I hadn't interrupted. "Oh, that little monster Hitler!" She paused to regain her composure. "The Nazis marched into Belgium, then France. We left Paris for Switzerland, which of course was neutral. We took a suite at the hotel Eden Au Lac in Zurich, thinking we wouldn't be there long, but stayed for nine years. Charming place, quite near the opera. Then we came to Stuttgart."

"It was Thomas Mann who suggested we move to Germany," Elspeth said. "Don't you recall, dear?"

"Well, of course I do, Elspeth. He had just finished writing *Doctor Faustus*. Was it not he who guided us on our first excursion into Germany?" She looked around the table at us. "Tom loved Germany, of course, even though his conscience wouldn't allow him to live here any longer. I'm still convinced *The Magic Mountain* was his finest novel."

"Sure and true, many agree with you, dear. We have a signed first edition, just here," said Elspeth, pointing to the bookcase.

"What an irony, though; it was set in Switzerland, where he lived out his days," Dame Marion continued. "Lovely man, queer as a corkscrew, of course, but so profound of thought; I still have all his letters. Dear me, who could not love Germany, even with all its delusions of grandeur? The great minds – Mann, of course, and Wagner, Goethe, Nietzsche, Bach, Beethoven? The French, delightful as they are, are utterly incapable of deep thought! Montaigne, the last French thinker. Ha! *L'affaires de coeur*, that's all the French think about! Of course, the expatriate intellectuals had left Paris by the start of World War II. So we left as well."

"We'd grown...mature by this time," Elspeth said. I did a quick calculation in my head: they must have been in their 50s then. "We were past dancing on tables in the French bistros. The salons were no more. Thomas was right to say the country to live in was the one that had lost the most, since it would be the one to strive the hardest to rebuild itself. We felt as kindred spirits with this country." She rose to her feet. "Now we've been chatting you lads up unmercifully. May we offer you afternoon tea?"

We nodded and smiled gratefully; it was definitely munchies time. Elspeth walked to a thick golden rope and gave it a two tugs. Moments later the doors opened and a maid appeared carrying a large silver tray. "*Merci*, Isabelle," Elspeth said and poured dark green tea into cups so thin you could see through them. "Petits fours," she said, pointing at the pastries, "éclair, tart, glace, meringue, puff, macaroon, shortbread." I was so hungry it didn't matter what they were called. We set to them, trying to mind our manners.

Elspeth crossed to a handsome wooden cabinet, opened the doors and started a new record. A clarinet twittered, then set up a mournful wail as an orchestra came up in the background. It was an incredibly sweet sound.

"Oh, man, I know this song," said Alan. "It's — "

"'Rhapsody in Blue,' by George Gershwin," said Henry Harold Henry. "My old man used to play this record all the time, and I mean *all the time*. But this sounds different."

"'Tis the 1924 recording, by the Paul Whiteman Orchestra," said Elspeth. "T'was the premiere, in New York. 'Tis Gershwin himself playing the piano."

"I should mention, boys, that this is marijuana tea," said Dame Marion, raising her cup to her lips, her little pinkie stuck out straight.

I just busted out laughing. I could not believe this scene. The other troops joined in and soon the old ladies were laughing too, all of us laughing together, great, enormously fun laughter, a bunch of happy people having a salon and getting stoned at high tea.

Everyone settled quietly into the intense and complex Gershwin as the afternoon sun sank lower in the sky, illuminating the stained glass windows. All so dense in my mind. I was ripped from the tea and riffing on the images, ripped riffing deep down ripped on the tea tea ha! Ingesting better than smoking, riffing on tea. The old Kerouac beatnik term for marijuana, tea party, afternoon tea, riffed riffing on those lovely nude women in the stained glass, their glowing white pudgy bodies long golden hair with strong stout men, their long dark hair and flowing beards. Huge old dark trees, leaves covering pussies and penises. Little angels, cupids, flying around playing lutes and flutes enticing them to copulate, riff riffing how such high art could be so lewd but no it was not, just the beautiful stuff people do, they touch they play they make love and along come little babies to fill the world. All so simple, just go into the woods, back to nature, it's all right, all right—

I came back startled by the sound of a crash. I looked up to see that Elspeth had struck a large brass gong with a mallet, and was about to do so again.

221

"Now that she has your attention," said Tim, giving me a grin and a poke.

"I'm *so* stoned," I said.

Dame Marion swept into the room, wearing a chin-to-toe gold sequin gown and a blood-red cape thrown over her shoulders. Elspeth had changed into a maroon waistcoat and pantaloons with gold trim. Dame Marion took her place beside Elspeth and said, "We will now perform a missa entitled "Flos Regalis: Agnus Dei," written by the Englishman Walter Frye, circa 1475. A missa is composed of intertwining voices that perform a recurring set of duets, sung as part of a religious service."

Alan and Tim and Henry Harold Henry and I glanced back and forth in wonderment. The two women began to sing. They swooned, they dipped, they sang like angels to God up in the sky. It was short, too short, too hauntingly beautiful.

We clapped our hands and they bowed, then Elspeth walked over to the grand piano. "Elspeth will now play 'Nocturne in A-flat Major' by John Field, an Irishman who created the musical form in the early 1800s."

Elspeth played a brief, lovely piece that again held me in a spell. Again, we were driven to applaud, Dame Marion too. Elspeth rose and took a bow.

"More!" cried Henry. "Can you play another?" She did. We applauded until she rejoined us at the table. Dame Marion handed her a silver box with tiny pieces of colored stone set into its lid. She opened it and filled the hookah's bowl with green chunks.

"I *know* you will enjoy this," Dame Marion said with a wink. "These are dried peyote buttons, crushed with the leaves of the marijuana plant." I loved the way she pronounced *pee-yoi-tay* and *mar—ee—yuana*. "We save this for the *most* special occasions!"

Elspeth lit the pipe and once again we puffed on our hoses. "Not too much at first," she said. "Wait a few minutes until you can feel it, then have another puff." There was a little bite and the smoke had a distinct kind of thickness, but it didn't taste or smell bad. I waited; nothing happened, but then it felt like a great plains windstorm was rushing from the back to the front of my head. When it arrived at my temples and forehead, it had become a tornado and whipped my consciousness into a froth. Oh, wow. *Oh, wow.*

"Yeah, you got that right," said Tim. I guess I'd spoken aloud. Again.

"Yeah," said Alan, rolling his body in circles. "Oh, man, this is so far out."

The pressure grew and the intense windstorm became a tornado, my brains leaking out my ears, not a bad thing, just let it happen. Oh-oh, there goes time.

No past no future herenow. I'm dissolved into a bubble a puddle ka-thunk KA-THUNK ka-thunk KA-THUNK my heart beating. Spreading slowly the tornado windstorm breeze quietly wispily clouds gliding twisting turning disintegrating in the air, air in my lungs filled with coursing churning rivers rivulets streams waterfalling blood in my veins returning to my heart: ka-thunk KA-THUNK ka-thunk KA-THUNK. The kettle boiling it's hookah-hookah time, time for another toke: whisssssp shirring whoooo whooooosh a tumbleweed and there's a shadow a man a cowboy riding his horse in the frigid illumination of a moon the size of God. Clump-clop-clump-clop yip-yipiupyip as the coyote watches, the wild wise coyote, no a wolf: a spirit rising now the wolf hears the gong and turns its head

GONG GONG Elspeth whanging that huge brass cymbal again. I open my eyes see Dame Marion standing with the stained glass windows behind her, haloed in the setting sun. Elspeth lighting a ring of candles around her. Dame Marion wearing dozens, hundreds, of colored scarves flowing and shimmering around her in sunset rainbows beautiful so beautiful her hand reaching toward the sky

"Dame Marion will now perform the first dance from Igor Stravinsky's ballet, 'Le Sacre Du Printemps,' or 'The Rite of Spring,'" Elspeth announced. "This dance is called 'The Consecration of the Earth'." Dame Marion raised her hands above her head then brought them down as she knelt until they rested on the floor. Elspeth went to the phonograph. "This is the premiere recording, Paris 1929, Pierre Monteux conducting the Grand Orchestre Symphonique." The peyote had driven me inside where I loved to get high, but now all I wanted to do was watch the old gal dance.

It was the most beautiful and extraordinary dance I have ever seen. A single instrument began to play – I think it was the oboe – sweet and mournful at first. Dame Marion raised her hands in an arc and began to dance like a young ballerina, running and swirling and dipping and rushing here and there. Her movements were totally grooving with the music. I fell into it, left my body floating, an ethereal discorporate other self. She seemed carried on the silk scarves, tossed about by the movement of the air in her wake. I opened my eyes; she danced ever more frenetically as more instruments joined in and the music grew more intense, then my lids closed again. *Pee-yoi-tay* images swirled in my head. I'd heard this music before – it was from the cartoon movie *Fantasia!* I flashed on how as a kid I was so crazy about it that I watched it three times in a row. Tonight, the music was no longer a cartoon but an artistic ballet and the intensity of the music the movement flowed through my mind so strong too strong. I closed my eyes: now the cowboy horse wolf moon desert tumbleweed pulsed in and out of intense focus. I yanked my eyes open Dame Marion dancing in the candlelight behind a movie screen, pale transparent shadows, with my western projected on the front. I felt my eyes close fell in the falling sky and music

I returned to cheering for Dame Marion. Henry Harold Henry stuck two fingers in his mouth and let go an incredibly loud wolf whistle. By now it was dark and I was hungry again. As if she read my mind, Elspeth rose to pull the golden rope. Before long the French maid opened the doors and said, "Le dîner est servi, mesdames et monsieurs."

Twelve tall-backed chairs surrounded the dining room table and four crystal chandeliers as bright as stars hung above it. Dame Marion sat at the head of the table and we gathered near her. Dark red wine was poured into goblets and there were numerous toasts to her and Elspeth on their performances. They toasted us on being a good audience. We ate bratwurst, mashed potatoes, beans, carrots, sliced pork roast, spatzle, and a stuffed goose. Dinner concluded with strong, dark coffee, a chocolate torte and Courvoisier from a tall crystal decanter that must have held a gallon of brandy. Elspeth passed a tin of Astor cigarettes around the table. We toasted again and again: the Damen, the dinner, Isabelle and Günther, the artists, Paris, Stuttgart, our evening together.

Dame Marion said, "You boys may wonder why two old ladies invited you to our home as we did." We looked at her, then each other, and nodded. "Well, in truth, we admire the Adonis-like beauty of the young male of the species," she said, and they both started giggling. We more or less joined in.

"Boys," she continued, "we have been *patronnes des arts* since our arrival in Paris. We have encouraged, and often financially supported, some of the greatest *artistes* of the twentieth century. I shall not name names, for that is not my reason for speaking of this. But we did fund publication of Hermann Hesse's *Demian*, and ever since have been acolytes of the god Abraxas. Since we wear the mark of Cain that he describes, we have sought out others of a like ken. You boys are the first we have met in many a year."

I shot a glance at the others. We'd read the book and discussed it, of course, but apparently nobody was sure how to respond. I said, "For sure. We've read *Demian*. We saw the mark on you too, although not until today." Maybe it was true. We were in a realm pretty much outside our normal experiences which, now that I thought about it, was exactly what we sought.

"Oh, *boys*," Dame Marion sighed, clasping her hands together, her bracelets clinking, a wide smile creasing her old face. Elspeth gazed at us, perhaps skeptically. "I can't tell you how wonderful it is to know we have this *profound* rapport! Oh, my dears, it is as it was when we were young again, like you. Those were the days. We were free, free from war, free to create, free to be whoever we wished to be, whether harlot or harlequin! These were our ways, miracles everywhere. Where did they go? They were gone but now those days have returned to us, in you.

"Oh, my dear Elspeth," she said, swooning in her memories, pausing to sip her cognac. "You know, boys, I feel there is a strong parallel between our times in our 1920s and yours, today. So much unrest, all of society bursting at its seams! We must love these changes, embrace change, live for change! Without change we die inside!" Dame Marion swooned again.

Elspeth rose and lifted her glass. "I quite agree. Lads, we *are* the same generation, forty years apart," she said. "We were called the lost generation. You are the next generation of change."

"Yes!" Dame Marion said, clapping her hands together. "We shall call you — oh dear, let me see, what shall we call you? Elspeth, help me here — they are changing, they are creating the new order, they are filled with hope and optimism, they...they...are the children of the new generation! What do you think?"

"Perhaps," she replied. "Perhaps the new order."

"Aha, en Francais *les enfants du nouveau régime.*"

"How about children of the future," said Henry Harold Henry, startling everyone.

"Oh, my dear boy, that is utterly perfect!" cried Dame Marion, and both she and Elspeth began clapping. "*Les enfants du futur.* Or perhaps *auf Deutsch?*"

"*Zukünftige Kinder,*" said Elspeth. "No, that doesn't feel right."

"I kinda like it in plain old English," said Henry.

"Yeah, me too," said Tim.

And so it was, we had a name after all.

"So, my children of the future, if you have satiated yourselves, let us adjourn back to the library, for the eve is still young and more pleasures await."

Once more we gathered around the hookah. Alan dropped a chunk of our hash into the bowl and we smoked it and then we smoked some more grass and *pee-yoi- tay.* Just when we were totally completely stoned out of our heads, Elspeth put on some very heavy classical music, which she introduced as Tchaikovsky's Hamlet Overture-Fantasy. "'Tis truly a tone poem, for it's no overture to anythin'," she said. As it played, she handed out handwritten scripts for Shakespeare's *Hamlet.* "You shall be Horatio," she said, pointing at me, "and you, Alan, shall play Hamlet. Tim, you are Marcellus. Henry, you are Bernardo. The ghost shall be played by Dame Edith, and I shall direct." We did a little run-through, for we skipped a few scenes, then gave it a real performance. I know we hammed it up a bit, but we were so stoned that it seemed to come off just great. Then, before we knew it, Günther announced it was after 0200 hours and did we want to go home? He gently collected us and drove us in Dame Marion's black 1938 Mercedes-Benz saloon car to Tim's apartment, where we crashed, smiles on our faces, awaiting the dreams of sugarplum fairies.

Chapter 18

Socrates Island
July, 1968

Tim, Tony, Alan, Henry Harold Henry, our new friend, Aaron, and I stood on the deck of the ferry *Niña* as we left from the port of Piraeus, headed across the Aegean Sea to Crete. As we chugged out, the sea grew black and the sky filled with a gazillion stars, the universe revolving evolving spinning away in its quiet perfect mysticism. *How far we've come.* From Stuttgart. From America, a place I had trouble remembering. After a while we grabbed a row of deck chairs, wrapped up in blankets, passed a joint, then fell asleep.

• • •

Tony had come for a weekend in early June, partly to hear about our visit to the "grand dames," partly to mourn the assassination of Bobby Kennedy. "I can't believe it!" he cried, really upset. "Somebody – some – what? – is out to kill all the people who want peace and change and a better America." We spent all afternoon trying to figure out what was going on back home, then gave up and went to Ma's for something to eat.

When we got back to Tim's, Tony opened his rucksack and waved a record with a wild psychedelic cover all silver and gray. "Cream's new album, *Wheels of Fire*," he said. "It won't be in shops in England for a few weeks, but Amita's cousins got me an advance copy. It is *astounding*, troops! Double record set, one studio, the

227

other live at the Fillmore. Remember the Fillmore, Nate?" He dropped the needle on the first song.

"How could I not?" I said. He also brought two copies of a paperback novel called *The Magus* by John Fowles and the *Tao Te Ching*, "'specially for you, Nate, since you're into all that Oriental stuff." I grabbed it, thanked him, and began turning pages. It was a book of Chinese wisdom, kind of like proverbs or poems, a perfect companion to my *I Ching*. Its wisdom came quickly, without coin-tossing or endless studying. I was glad to have both.

We fought for turns reading *The Magus*. Nicholas, the English narrator, leaves London and his girlfriend to teach at a boys school on a Greek island. One night in the old barn Alan said, "You know something, troops? This is just what we should do. Take a 30-day leave and go to Italy or Spain or the French Riviera. Maybe even a Greek island." The idea of an island sounded wild and risky and dangerous and adventurous. *Outasight*. Everyone wanted to do it. The troops struggled with Buford to get leave approved, but in the end, we were owed it and couldn't be denied.

• • •

We met Aaron in Athens the first day at a cool little sidewalk café where we sat eating grape leaves stuffed with rice, lamb kabobs, wedges of feta cheese, tomatoes in olive oil, olives, cucumbers, salty little fish. He was very thin, wore jeans with paisley patches, rope sandals, a tie-dyed T-shirt under a sleeveless vest that looked cut from a Mexican rug. His hair hung down to his shoulders and was held back by a red bandana. He had a warm smile underneath a ragged, wispy mustache; a pirate's golden earring dangled from one ear. I envied his total freedom to be and dress however he wanted. He looked hungry so we invited him to join us.

"You dudes been here long?" he asked.

"We just got here," Tim said. "Why?"

"On holiday?" he asked.

"Yeah, you could say that," Alan replied. "How about you?"

"I'm from Oregon. Portland. I been here, ah, you know, a while. You know, out of the country. Coupla years. Uncle called my number so I split. Canada, UK, Europe. No way I was gonna kill for the War Machine."

"Right on," Tim said. "How do you like Greece?"

"Can't really say yet, dude. Heard there was some cool stuff going on, good folks to meet, you know?" He wiggled his eyebrows and grinned. "So I came down. You dudes, like, looking to get turned on to some good times?"

We nodded and he told us about an island off the coast of Crete where hippies from all over the world gathered. "It's pretty secret. You gotta know somebody who knows about Socrates Island." I couldn't believe we'd hit on an adventure the first day.

"That's the name?" Tony asked. "Socrates?" Aaron nodded. "Oh, wow, that is so far out! Troops, we gotta go!"

"You…dudes. Yer, like, GIs?"

We looked down, embarrassed, afraid we'd disqualified ourselves.

"Ah, it's cool, it's cool," Aaron said. "It's just…your haircuts."

"We're in the Air Force because we didn't want to get drafted into the Army," Tim said. "But that's it. We hate the military. And war. Hey, are you Jewish?"

"No, I'm an atheist," Aaron replied. "Are you?"

"I'm a Communist," said Tim.

Aaron's eyes widened. "Well, ah, far out, dude."

"But I'm Jewish, too," said Tim. "I just thought…Aaron is a Biblical name that Jews like a lot."

"Nope. My parents are Unitarian." He dove back into the food. Between bites, he asked if we could loan him the money to get over to Socrates Island. "I'll pay you back."

"How much is it gonna cost?" Henry Harold Henry asked.

"About a hundred and fifty, two hundred drachmas for the ferry to Crete. Five or six dollars each. Then a fishing boat to take us to Socrates. A dollar, maybe?"

Alan burst out laughing. "Our treat, man. When we get there it's your treat, if you get what I mean."

"Yeah, for sure, I'll make sure you dudes have" – he grinned – "a high time!"

• • •

We awoke to the rising sun; on the horizon was land, Crete, the port of Heraklion. A decrepit old fisherman in Khania took us to Socrates Island in his decrepit old boat for fifty drachmas. It was a slow, rough passage. After about two hours I saw a long thin piece of land. A small mountain peak, perhaps an old volcano, half-covered in whitewashed houses. Dark-colored rectangles – blue, red, yellow windows, shutters, and doors – stood out in the brilliant hot sun. A blue dome with a cross topped a church. We docked on a broad expanse of beach. As we jumped ashore, I gave the old man an extra ten-drachma coin.

Early afternoon, hot as hell, not a soul in sight. We crossed the beach; little thatched roofs covered tables around an outdoor bar. Behind it, a weathered wooden sign on a whitewashed building read HOTEL.

We eventually roused a fat sleepy little man, wiry gray hair bursting out of his head and a mustache to match. He wore a wrinkled striped fisherman's shirt and heavy wool knee pants and a colorful sash for a belt. He said "Hallo," all smiles, and something in Greek. We didn't even know how to say we didn't speak Greek in Greek.

"You speak Eenglish?" We nodded; American. "Hallo, boys. I Demos. Have nice sleepings rooms for you. Two beds. Nice. Ten drachmae one night." Thirty cents a day. "For each." We looked back and forth at one another. Demos apparently misunderstood our hesitation, said, "OK, for two."

"Dudes, I'm going to sleep on the beach," said Aaron. "I don't need no bed, but can I leave my backpack in your room?"

"You sure?" I asked.

"Yeah, it's cool. I like sleeping outside. We was always going camping back in Oregon. Except when it rained!"

We got one room with five bunks for 25 drachmae a night. Demos gave us a crumpled old cardboard OCCUPIED sign in English and Greek to hang on the door; there were no keys. Plastered walls about a foot and a half thick, so the room was cool. Bare wooden plank floor. Cheesy reproduction of Jesus on the wall, sink with a single light bulb over it, shower. I pulled the light chain; nothing. We tossed our rucksacks, went to the beach and pulled wooden deck chairs into the shade and settled in. I closed my eyes, listened to the waves skittering up the beach. Free for a whole month! It was beautiful, peaceful, but still really hot, even in the shade. I pulled out my Swiss Army officer's knife and cut the legs off my jeans. Lay back down thinking I should keep a journal or write letters to Jane. A moment later I was siesta-ing with the others.

• • •

Young guys our age, hippies and beach bums, sat around tables softly speaking in several languages. The sun was low. Aaron made long shadows wandering around the tables, hippie handshakes, talking, laughing, moving on. Skipped back across the sand to us.

"Dudes here from Holland, Belgium, France, England, Denmark, Canada — maybe a few Americans, not sure. And chicks, man." He got that look in his eye every guy recognizes.

"They're sleeping out in tents, huts further away down the beach and 'round the other side of the island. The natives live in the village up there." He pointed up the mountainside.

"What do the people do? How do they live?" Tim asked.

Aaron shrugged. "Dunno, dude. They just live, I guess. You get by. It's what you do. You know, we find our own ways."

"Ex-pats?" Tony asked.

"Some. Not many 'cause this place is a well kept secret. These dudes I talked to, they said it gets real interesting at night. C'mon, let's get a table and a drink."

In broken English the bartender pointed, said, "Retsina, is Greek wine; tsikudi, Greek gin; mastika, ouzo — is anisette, yes?, Metaxa, kir, Campari, crème de cacao, Pernod, Brandy Jerez. C'est far out, no?" He laughed and poured us retsina; it was strong and bitter. We copped a table. Nearby a guy stood at a stone cooking pit grilling something that smelled really good, making me hungry as hell.

"Yassas! Hallo!" the man said, laughing and stabbing and turning the food with a thin steel spike. "You have eat? This octopus, very good with retsina!" he said. "This dolphin? This langouste, shrimp? This calamari! Fresh lamb! Very good with retsina!" he said, pointing at my drink. "You know is white wine with pine resin! Here," he said, "you have plate!" New tastes exploded in my mouth, complemented by the retsina.

Somebody dunked the sun into the ocean down off the tip of the island and darkness crept toward us. A gas motor started up nearby; Christmas tree lights sparkled to life in the thatched roofs. Quaint, sing-songy folk music began playing from a tinny speaker at the bar. The bartender brought refills, marked our deckles. Aaron beckoned; Alan and I followed him to the table. Two guys, one wearing a floppy cowboy hat, sunglasses, Zapata mustache, ragged T-shirt, the other lean, curly black hair, rather large nose, big lips, unshaven face. They spoke English with a little accent. A rolled-up piece of latigo on the table near their drinks. "You want *kif?*" said Curly; opened it to reveal rows of joints. Cowboy jerked his thumb up and said, "You want some toke?" I looked at Aaron, grinning, nodding, *See, I told you I'd take care of you.*

"How much?" Alan said.

"You have American dollars?"

"Some."

"Two for one dollar. Twelve for five. American. We have matchbox, too, to roll your own."

"Good shit?" I asked.

"Have some toke, see for yourself," said the cowboy again. Lit up, passed it around.

It was a very good sweet stone mellow. They were from Belgium, but the pot was from *Coop'haan*. Looked around: Guys drinking, talking, laughing, smoking, everything easy. The ocean caught fire as the sun slid down and the translucent ghostly full moon rose up through the goldenred wispy clouds. Lights twinkled around the bar's thatched roof as the sweetsad Greek folk music wafted through my ears. "Is wonderful sound of lyra!" cried the bartender and turned it up. The jays kept going revealing new layers of stone My God, we eat drink smoke talk just be together sharing what we are who we are it's just natural, so natural this is our world so easy you are just in it, no need for yessir nosir shined shoes pressed uniforms protocols orders it just is, I already know how to do this Ialreadyknowhowtodothis, we love need want to be together, need this need to be together so we do it easy as pie, it's how we know our place in the universe know God Buddha Apollo Zeus Athena Poseidon ah those great Greek gods! and the nameless formless godliness inside me that makes me know there is a God yes we need God it's just that we've changed the ways to need know Him, I think....

Lights and music went off. The generator fell silent. The luminous dial on my chronometer read 10:00. Darkness, the darkest darkness I had ever not seen in my entire life. Soon I could see the entire sky full of stars, the Milky Way, the glowing tip of the last call joint we shared before heading back to our room. I unbuckled my chronometer and dropped it into my backpack.

• • •

First up in the morning, I fell out to the beach bar for strong Greek coffee fruits and a sweet bread Demos called *soorekki*. I ate, drank, opened my *Tao Te Ching* to lesson 48:

Socrates Island

Learning consists in daily accumulating;
The practice of Tao consists in daily diminishing.

Keep on diminishing and diminishing,
Until you reach the state of Non-Ado.
No-Ado, and yet nothing is left undone.

To win the world, one must renounce all.
If one still has private ends to serve,
One will never be able to win the world.

Read it two three four times. Wow, so heavy. I wanted to dig it, all of it, but I couldn't get there yet. Didn't want to give up and I *thoughtthoughtthought* until it came: *I need to change something find a different Way a new path to grok this* so I read the words again and again until exasperated I decided to go for a run down the beach, ran in my cutoffs and brogans until I reached the tip of the island where sand and rock met the crashing waves and as I struggled to catch my breath and caught the warmth of the sun in my face all nature was happy with me and my action my seeking and I knew what I had found was change, perhaps to better myself perhaps not, but change. I resolved to run every day for the freeing spirit I had found and to give up cigarettes to prove I was serious.

Jogging more slowly as the sun rose higher I met Alan and Tim at the bar. "Where have you been?" Tim asked. Saw God, I replied, our favorite old stoner line but Alan said God or Dog? and I answered there's no difference to the Tao it's all one. Henry Harold Henry and Tony joined us and we sat talking most of the morning.

"This island isn't the Real World," said Tim. "We're GIs, so we say the Real World is civilian life, but this isn't the same."

"The Real World is memory," said Tony. "It's what we lost when we joined the service."

"Yeah, it's in our heads," said Henry.

"Wow, do you think we can ever get it back? After we get discharged?" I asked.

"Hmmm. Maybe," said Alan. "The Real World is what you imagine it is. It's your perfect vision of the world, the Platonic ideal. It may only exist as an imaginary ideal."

"What's a Platonic ideal?" asked Henry.

"Plato, the Greek philosopher," I said. "He -"

"Oh, who gives a shit what Plato thought," said Alan.

"Well, you brought him up so what do *you* think?" Henry asked him.

"I think...wherever I am is the best place to be," said Alan.

"Yeah, so did Candide, and he ended up in the shits," Henry said.

"Well," said Tony, "that's true, but Pangloss wanted Candide to understand that it was the search, not the destination, that counted. That's how you learn."

Candide again. It seemed I was the only one who hadn't read it.

"Learning is overrated," said Alan. "We don't trust our true selves enough. We have to have a so-called expert give us the proof, the evidence, the belief."

"But that's *truth*," said Tim. "Without it, what do you have?" Tim asked. "A bunch of poorly informed thoughts and sensory impressions. I think different than you, I see and hear different things. Our differences aren't truths, they're perceptions."

"There is no *truth* and the world isn't what you perceive," Alan said. "It's more and it's less. All at once."

"You sound like Lao Tzu," I said. "The part I read today is about thinking and perceiving until there's nothing left to perceive or do and you get to a kind of good place, I can't remember exactly -"

"It's called *wu wei wu*," Alan said. "Doing-not-doing. To do without doing. It's essence, or what Tim calls truth. One of the great fundamental precepts of Taoism."

"Let it be and it will be its true self," I said.

"Yep. Like *Demian*," said Tim. "Boy, Alan, for somebody who didn't go to college, you sure sound like somebody who went to college."

"Ah, all this bullshit philosophizing is boring me," said Alan, standing. "What say we hike up the mountain and see what that village is like?"

• • •

We climbed a terraced stone walkway past an old woman dressed in black head to toe, picking oranges and lemons from trees, dropping them in clay pots hung on a donkey's back. Vegetables and grape vines grew all around us; sheep grazed in the distance. These people were self-sufficient. We climbed sweating through an open-air market where people traded food hides blankets rugs baskets

234

up to an outdoor restaurant with round metal tables shaded by Kourtaki umbrellas. Now we could see the whole island. A young boy brought five glasses of retsina then came back with plates heaped with *meze* finger food. A second round of wine and our conversation resumed.

"Who do we think we are anyway?" Alan asked. "Who said we could figure out how the universe works or what life is all about?" He picked up a small stone. "What if this is our entire universe, just a stone or a grain of sand on the beach of an even greater, more vast universe? I just mean, really, what do we *really* know? We're such arrogant assholes, thinking we're the only planet with life. There may be life forms that our senses can't even perceive!"

He was on a rant and we let him rave. Finished, we asked the boy for our check and he smiled and bowed and made a gesture that meant *it's nothing* but we left a bunch of drachmas on the table anyway.

Back at the beach we doffed our clothes and went for a swim in the Adriatic, so salty it buoyed us like beach balls. Collapsed on the sand for siesta *need to learn the Greek word for it* and when we awoke it was high tea time a la Socrates Island. An idyllic day with the promise of more to follow.

• • •

"Troop?" I said to the sound of sandsteps as I lay soaking the sun, reading musing dreaming riffing on these days and nights of island bliss filling me like pot smoke.

"Pardon?" was the reply. "Please, do not let me disturb your meditations. Like you, I seek the peacefulness of the beach and rest from the endless conversations."

I looked up at the cowboy Belgian who sold us the joints. "Sure," I said and laid back down.

"My name is Jens. Thank you for allowing me to share in this space and time with you."

I reached over to shake his hand. "Nathaniel. Nate."

We lay on the beach without speaking for a long time, then he offered a cigarette but I waved my hand *no*. "Tomorrow night," he said, "you and your *amis* —you call each other troop? – please come to our camp. We have a little party."

"Sure!" I said, way too enthusiastically.

• • •

"Anybody seen Aaron lately?" I asked. Nobody had. Aaron drifted in and out, which was fine; he was doing his thing and we were doing ours. Nevertheless, he deserved to know about the party.

The moon was full and bright, a beacon on the path through the woods. Firelight flickered ahead. We came into a small clearing surrounded by thatched lean-tos and tents. I saw Aaron, sitting in the circle around the bonfire. He grinned and gave each of us his familiar hippie handshake, eyes gleaming happily in the firelight. Maybe ten people; they shifted to make room for us. I was between a big guy with a full beard and bushy eyebrows and tiny eyes and a nice-looking girl in a skimpy brown tunic dress, her legs tucked up sideways. She had a pretty round tan face, big sweet brown eyes and full smiling sensual lips, her dark brown hair pulled into a bun, a feather sticking up from a beaded headband. A pale tiny girl with corkscrew blonde hair wearing baggy jeans and a tie-dyed blouse beside her. Big guy nudged me; a joint making its rounds. I took a nice long toke and passed it to the Indian princess.

Across the circle an older guy with a very intense face sat with another girl about the same age. A bota started around cool fresh water courtesy of the Indian princess beside me. "Wow," I said, "Thanks. Nice surprise."

She smiled. "Water is more precious than wine on Socrates Island. There are only a few cisterns, and they rely mostly on rain." She stuck out her hand. "My name is Susie."

"I'm Nate."

"Oh, so *you're* Nate," she said and pressed her hand on my arm. "This is my friend Emily." She looked up as the older man stood. "Let's listen to Gould."

"Soph-ro-syne," said Gould, very loudly, crisply, in an English accent. "The most precious ideal known to Western man, created in the city-state of Athens over *two thousand five hundred years ago!*" He paused; I held the thought as best I could. Smoking so much pot every day made it a little slippery.

"Soph-ro-syne," he said again, softly. "the joining of two words: *sophia*, or wisdom, with *syne*, beingness or doingness. Sophrosyne means to possess balance, proportion, moderation, and symmetry. It lives in the Greek man you meet today; have you noticed that he does not get drunk, like Americans? It is said that Alexander the Great failed to conquer the world because he lacked sophrosyne!"

At this, some people laughed softly. The bota arrived and the man drank.

"Have you been to Delphi? No? You should, for it is an alter worth worshiping before. Two of the most notable concepts underlying sophrosyne can be found there: 'Know thyself,' and 'Nothing in excess.' Think of their antonyms: to Greeks,

236

the gravest sin is hubris, or arrogance. Hubris leads a man to excess, whether power, money, women, war — and always comes to naught in Greek tragedy. That is a great lesson for all civilizations."

Gould continued speaking but my thoughts turned to my studies. *How does a man know the Tao?* Is this not a universal search for understanding oneself, life, the universe, God?

"...But perhaps the most amazing — and I do not use the word in a positive sense — thing is that today, in modern Western civilization, sophrosyne and its direct application to life have been all but forgotten. Here, the most central construct of Greek philosophy — the way to live a good life by acting in harmony with the gods and their simple teachings — has been burnt into dust beneath the feet of twentieth-century European existentialism and, by extension, American capitalism. Sartre tells modern man that he is *ens causa sui*; Ayn Rand espouses worship of selfishness and greed." His voice rose: "The hell with the spiritual. The hell with God!"

He sat down, apparently finished. Tony said, "This is very interesting. I've never heard of sophrosyne before. You describe four things, balance, proportion, symmetry, and — ?"

"Moderation," Gould replied.

"Right, moderation, and when I think of the classical period in Athens, it seems perfect. But would it work in today's civilization? I mean, our lives and times are so much more complex, and the world is not isolated city-states like then... *Time* magazine said God is dead...can we have sophrosyne today?"

"Point well taken," Gould replied. "Nietzsche's dangerous nihilism and abject atheism utterly poisoned the twentieth century. He would have had great trouble accepting sophrosyne. No wonder God is dead! We're morally and spiritually bankrupt today!" He raised his arms in supplication, swinging them back and forth around the circle. "But you know what? We — all of us sitting here — we could be the new Athenians. We've seen how men have poisoned Western culture in our time. We must once again embrace sophrosyne and return to the simple life. We must — get ourselves back to the garden!" His fist shot straight up into the air, and everyone cheered — I mean the entire circle.

I asked, "What's ensconsuey?"

He chuckled. "I'm sorry if I was unclear. *Ens — causa — sui*. You are your own creation. It's Latin for being the prime mover of your own self. You are your own God. There is none other besides you."

"Then God is a tautology?" I asked.

Gould gazed into the fire a long time, finally said, "Quite possibly."

A few more joints, talk, a hug and see-you-again from Susie before we walked back to the hotel. Tony said, "I found out Gould was a don at Oxford before he 'renounced the material world' to live here. Nicole, his girlfriend, was a grad student of his."

"I didn't like him, at all," Alan said. "He's a typical ivory-tower intellectual show-off."

"That's kind of overly critical, I think," I said. "He just wants to share his ideas. How can that be bad?"

"Aw, he can't get out of the classroom," Alan said. "He thinks he's Aristotle running the Lyceum."

Ah ha. Gould reminded Alan of his parents.

"Well, that's what he knows how to do," I said, remembering my father's living-room literature lectures.

"I never expected to meet such an interesting guy on a desert island," said Tim.

"I liked it when people started making music," said Henry Harold Henry.

What if what Gould said was true? I knew for sure there was a force of life in the universe greater than me and within me, too. I didn't fully get it yet but the Tao, not philosophy, was guiding me toward it. Professor Cohen was really, really wrong: I was no existentialist.

• • •

I developed a new routine: run on the beach in the morning, strong black Turkish coffee and bougatsa rolls filled with feta cheese, study the *Tao Te Ching*, throw an *I Ching*. Sometimes I'd join the troops to do stuff. I got to know guys at the beach bar. We talked about the Vietnam war, student riots in Paris, (not just America), dropping out, ex-pats, being a conscientious objector versus serving, like we did. Everyone was sick of *"l'autre régime"* – they called the world's scumbag politicians and their dirty politics parading as doing good for the world when in fact is was their own lust. Nils, an ex-pat from Denmark, said "Politicians crave power and businessmen desire money. They help each other in their gain, then make sure no one else can have either." I agreed with him. Gould portrayed classical Athens as the best of all possible worlds. Was the Real World of America the best or worst possible? Could Socrates Island be the best? Or was the best place wherever you were in the here and now? That's what the Tao would say.

Socrates Island

Gould didn't speak every time we went to The Lyceum. Tony, Alan and I usually sat together; Henry strolled, danced. Tim, usually found with a bronzed god in tight shorts and tight T-shirts, didn't always come back with us after Lyceum. Susie always sat next to me, and her roommate Emily, Minnesota Norwegian, psych major, sat on her other side with Tord, a tall blonde guy from Sweden. Emily was plain but Susie was farm-girl pretty, full breasts tugging against the leather birkin a village woman had made for her from goat hide which barely covered her pink bare butt. From Amery, Wisconsin, a junior at U Madison (sociology) on summer vacation, she and Emily had stumbled their way here much as we had.

Gould's topics were always interesting, at least to me: the Mona Lisa smile ("Oh God, how boring," said Alan), Darwinian evolution ("Plants make love, not war. Why are humans the only animal that kills its own? I ask you, is this the product of the higher development of intellect and consciousness?"), sex ("So far as we know, homo sapiens is the only species that engages in intercourse simply for pleasure"), world genocides ("White Europeans settling North America obliterated over four hundred native tribes, some which dated back over 15,000 years!").

Susie leaned over and whispered, "I'm supposedly one-sixty-fourth Kickapoo, on my mother's side," laughing softly, her lips almost touching my ear.

The constellations turned in the beautiful night sky.

• • •

As I walked up the beach after a morning swim Aaron came up, said, "Good night to visit the Lyceum."

"Yeah?"

"There'll be acid."

My heart leaped. "Oh, wow."

"Bring some money. This guy Teodoro just got back from *Coop'haan.*"

"I'll tell the troops." Tony was in, of course; Tim said hadn't dropped before and neither had Henry Harold Henry. Alan just nodded and didn't say anything.

• • •

Teodoro walked around the bonfire wearing a big smile, his beads and bells playing jingle-jangle, sugar cubes in one hand and money in the other, whispering "Two dollars, two dollars," like he was taking collection in church. Joints went around to ease into the trip as a flute and drum and guitar played. Tony and I sat together like in California so long ago and next to me Susie. She came on first, "Oh, *wooooow*," and kind of swooned, her ponytail head touching my shoulder as I began to feel mellow then psychedelically exotic and soon the LSD trance was upon the whole circle even those who hadn't dropped in this our shared community head trip blasting off into the great dynamic pulsating universe above the crackling fire, the music flowing over under around us as arms draped over each other's shoulders forming a complete ring rocking and moving like enchanted mystics. Susie began to hum softly to the flute and I hummed with her and other voices joined us and the hum turned into Om Om Om carried around the circle and up the fire into the crackling sky, long and soft and deep joining us like earthairfirewater in one harmony one spirit rising, and I was so happy, so happy to be tripping on this lovely acid in this timespace, electric rivers of happiness rippling through my thoughts out my arms and fingers tickled tickling tingling with the electric touch of our arms, how close we were! so close! my beloved friends in this electric river flowing round and round together in the circle circular whirlpool around the energyfire, Tony joyous beside me and then Alan, deep thoughtful Alan, quirky little loveable Henry beside him, Susie and I holding hands, Tord with Emily, Tim where was Tim, yes there beside Teddy and Gould and Nicole and the others, all my deepest friends, Troops in the Army of Being, heads up ten-hut! to the here and now that's what we have and here we go right Tony? he's all blissed out Susie looking at me soft full red lips gently parted so I smile why wouldn't I? she's so pretty so we kissed, kissedkissedkissed for about twenty-seven eons oh wow this girl takes my breath away, sucked right out in an electric French kiss quivering pulsepounding as I pant for air, for Susie, for her wet red lips forming a perfect smile a tiny O the Oh-Oh-Oh of our lips touching again, fingers too, wanting to touch everything, all entwined with her, inside out, and oh, to look, the looking into big brown deep eyes, lost in her Kickapoo princess eyes, revolving devolving inside her, feeling her my our heart beat, can we synchronize ta-dum tada-dum to the drum the strum playing on as we rise holding hands the guitar and flute and drum playing inside us in our cobra transcen-dance, glowing happy in the golden firelit musicnight that conjoins us in this conjoining perfection, ah just so, man woman yin yang make us one together in her joyful smiling face, our allness draws us together, our bodies so close now my hand slides to her barely birkin-covered rump as we dance into the acid union of body and spirit, the perfection of nature's unity reaching up coming down touching us in holiness as we give ourselves over completely to touch,

240

our vow to keep the vast cosmos together because it is us, ours, we are it, we are all together *oo-koo-ka-choob* all one ours to keep infinity going as far as it goes, its path our path I pull her close, toes knees thighs bellies, her soft breasts, our breath sighing together, she says "Nate, Nate," and I say "Jane, Jane." We stop moving, I look into her face, not Jane's face, a beautiful face dark eyes and soft sadness as I pull back "I'm...sorry...someone...I love...back home..." and Susie wraps her arms around my neck, hides her face, nods, nodding, I hear a little sobsnuffle, we hold on tight to just what we have, dancing silently into the long dark blackness of our Socrates Island night, swaying in the shimmering firelight, ours the most important drama in the entire expanding exploding cosmos that surrounds us.

• • •

Sun and morning on the beach blaring in my face. Beside me the Kickapoo princess. Crawl to my feet. The world looks funny. Still silent Susie sleeps. The ocean froths, seethes; clumps of clouds blot the sky. Gray. Sky, beach, water, trees, everything gray. Blink. No color. Anywhere. I felt like I was looking at me looking at the scene in front of me. Totally weird. I walked down the beach and saw myself walking away from myself, making backwards footprints in the sand. Susie grew smaller as I walked back. Not a good feeling; I couldn't tell what was real. I stopped, rubbed my eyes. The film now a grainy washed-out pastel.

"Susie? Susie." I knelt in front of her.

She opened her eyes, smiled. "Good morning, Nate," and reached up for a hug. I wanted her to hold me more than anything. I scooped her into my lap, wrapped my arms tightly around her. I felt so strange, maybe a little scared. "Susie, I think I'm still tripping. I feel like I'm in a black-and-white movie."

She held me like a mother would, gently kissing my face. "It's OK, babe, you'll be fine. Let's just sit here and be quiet for a few minutes, then I'll get us something to eat. Something in your stomach will help bring you down."

She wandered into the nearby trees and returned with some yellow fruit and flowers in her hair. "What's this? I asked.

"The islanders call it cydonia. It's the only name I know for it. It's a little tart, but delicious."

I took a bite; she was right. Soon I felt a little better. She held me and I let her. I got the psychedelic shakes. Susie felt them and wouldn't let me go. After a while she said, "Feeling good enough to walk?"

241

"I don't know. We could try it and see if the movie is still going." It was, just a bit, but the world was returning to color. "How about we go back to my hotel?"

As we walked Susie said, "Oh, Nate, I'm *sooo* happy we tripped together." She squeezed my hand. "I mean, I know what you said. About Jane. That's cool, I mean it's *really* cool you were true to your old lady, but you were *sooo* good to me last night. You were a beautiful tripping partner. I had such a beautiful night with you, beautiful Nate, beautiful Natey." She kissed my cheek.

The weather began turning weird, making me feel weird inside again. The sky got dark and angry; wind whipped up. It looked like rain, the first we'd had since we came to the island.

"Let's get going," I said, pointing at the sky. We moved quickly over the ridge and down the beach to the hotel. Warm torrential rain let loose before we made it, driven on powerful winds. In two seconds we were both totally soaked. The wind propelled us to a running pace and blew Susie's feather and flowers right out of her hair. Inside, I opened our door. The troops were still asleep. "C'mon," I whispered, "let's get dried off." We tiptoed into the bathroom, shed our wet clothes and tow-eled each other down. I gazed at her unassuming nakedness, a beauty I had never before seen, yet our intimacy had passed from sex and desire to a brother-sister fondness – another first for me. Shivering a little, we slipped under the sheet on my tiny single bed. She curled up and I spooned her, trying not to poke her with my rock-hard dick, but it made me obsess about sex so I turned over and she spooned me. *OK, so much for brother and sister.* We soon fell asleep and when we awoke the storm had passed, the acid had pretty much left my system, and the movies were over.

Susie stayed with me all day and all night, "Just to be sure you're OK," she said. I didn't mind. I introduced her around at the bar, where we sipped retsina and talked about growing up in the Midwest. Somebody offered us a joint, but for once I didn't feel like it. I told Susie all about Jane and as I did, Jane became more real to me. "I'll bet Jane likes getting high with you too," she said. That night I slept fitfully, imagining it was Jane who held me.

After breakfast, as we walked her back to her tent, Susie began jumping and dancing and swinging her arms, shouting, "'Time has come today! Young hearts can go their way!'" over and over. I wiggled my eyebrows. "Oh, you haven't heard 'Time Has Come Today' by the Chambers Brothers? Oh, Natey, you *must* hear it as soon as you get home." She started singing again, 'I might get burned up by the sun, but I've had my fun. Time has come today!'" and thrust her cheerleader arms into the air.

Chapter 19
Time Has Come Today
August, 1968

"Troops," Alan said, "we need to talk. About falling out." We were having the usual, coffee and bougatsa, at the outdoor bar.

"Argh! Is it time for that already?" I asked. I was on island time, had lost track of any real sense of time.

"Yeah," said Alan. "About whether to go or stay."

"Stay? Here? On Socrates?"

"Why not?" said Alan. "It wouldn't be hard."

"We'd be AWOL," I said.

"Nate," said Alan, "the military couldn't find us in a million years. Even if they wanted to," he added. I knew what he meant by that. Why had we been sent to Kleinelachen in the first place?

"Yeah, but what about going home?"

"Go home to *what*?" Alan snapped. "The United Snakes is a viper pit! You guys don't know this, but Henry Harold Henry and I heard from some of our buddies who've come back from Vietnam. Civilians hate us! They think we're the enemy! They believe everything they see on TV. This ex-troop was walking down the street and a straight spit on him. They only hate hippies more than GIs. Is that the *home* you want to go back to?"

I looked at the others. "What about you, Tony? Tim? What do you say?"

Tony squirmed. "I don't know, man. I mean, London's pretty groovy. Amita. I've got an ol' lady now…. I'd stay there, you know, after I get out. Nothing really to go back to the States for…."

"I really *really* want to go back. To California. I want to see Jane," I said. "I want to finish college. There's the GI Bill, you know. And even if stateside isn't great, I want to go back proud with an honorable discharge."

"Oh, troops, I don't believe my ears!" cried Alan. "You guys would give up your freedom for a little pussy? Where are your ideals? What about all those ideals we talked about? Is it just talk? I mean, shit, we've been living The Man's lie all these years and now it's just OK, cool, I'll just cop out, get a job, get married and have kids, wear a suit, buy cars and refrigerators and a house with a picket fence and...." He got up, paced, got red in the face. "I thought we were buddies! I don't even *know* you guys!"

"Alan, that's not the whole picture and you know it," I said. "What we've been doing – I thought we were learning how to go back into the Real World, so that –"

"I'm staying here," said Tim.

"On Socrates? No, you're not!" Alan yelled. "We all stay or we all go, don't you get it? If even one troop goes back they'd find out where the others are."

"I suppose you're right," said Tim.

"He is," said Tony. "They'd interrogate your ass until you told them where we were. Buford would come for us. And wreck this paradise for everybody."

"Well, I love this place but I wanna go back," said Henry Harold Henry. "I fuckin' miss my Miles Davis and Ornette Coleman and Monk and Sonny Rollins, all that jazz. I can't be happy without my jazz."

• • •

There was incredibly loud silence between us on the train back to Germany. We got into the Stuttgart Hauptbahnhof after dark on Wednesday, the last day of July, caught the Flughaven bus, hopped off at the Kleinelachen main gate and signed in at 2307 hours. We'd made it back from leave with 53 minutes to spare. Tony caught the courier to England the next morning.

"Hey, man, come up to see me soon," he said. "Lots to talk about. Eat some good Indian food."

"For sure," I said. "Maybe this weekend."

He climbed on the plane. I went to my desk and called Tom to say I was back.

"Am I getting a story from you this week, Sarge?"

"No, you're not, *Sarge*," I shot back. "By the way, did the paper ever print our short stories?"

"No. Not yet. Let me know what you'll be writing about next week. When you can."

• • •

1 August 1968

To: All Kleinelachen Air Force and Army Personal
Fr: SSGT Wilford H. Buford, 6069 AFCS

You will fall out Saturday 3 August at 1845 hours at Hangar A for the movie "the Green Berrets" with John Wayne at 1900 hours. Attendance is mandotory.

Milo, of all people, was standing at the hangar doors with a clipboard, checking us off as we entered. I stuck my thumbs in my ears, wiggled my fingers and blew him a raspberry. He cracked up.

The credits rolled and the movie began. John Wayne, a full bird colonel, came on-screen. It was really bad. Most of the actors were too old. Somebody guffawed, really loud, starting a bunch of troops snorting and laughing.

The funniest line was from a guy in a helicopter who said "This trip is gonna make LSD feel like aspirin!" Alan said, "I've had enough of this shit," got up and left. Henry Harold Henry followed, then Tim and Irish, who said something I couldn't make it out. I stayed. I had a story idea.

• • •

"The Green Berets"
Hollywood Tries to Take On the Vietnam War
      A first-run movie is now being shown to USAFE troops. "The Green Berets" stars John Wayne as a U.S. Army infantry colonel, also a Green Beret, who is sent to Vietnam to accomplish a mission no other officers have been able to: setting up a base of operations deep in Vietcong territory. It takes him about thirty minutes of movie time to get there, since he needs to meet with other top brass along the way, drinking, saluting, and paying the necessary deference to rank. Once he arrives, he quickly scans the compound and orders that the perimeter be wid-

ened and a few other perfectly practical and obvious things be done. Surely we didn't need a green beret colonel to make these decisions!

Curiously, the American green berets and the forces Col. Wayne commands are unable to secure the base until, at the very final moments of the battle, two Air Force jets strafe the compound and kill every last Vietcong with machine gun fire. Mission accomplished, Wayne and his green berets head off on another mission, to kidnap a NVA general, and at this point the movie really becomes sloppily sentimental

"So, Sergeant Flowers, did you enjoy the movie last night?"

I looked up from my typewriter. "Good morning, Lt. Antonucci, sir."

He sat on the corner of my desk with a cup of coffee he'd obviously drawn from the Base Ops coffee urn.

"It was OK," I said. "I'm writing a review for the *Stars and Stripes.*"

"A positive review, I trust?"

"What difference does it make? It'll never see print anyway. By the way, sir, do you know if my short story is going to get published?"

Antonucci grimaced, then sighed. "No, of course I don't, Flowers. Ask your NCOIC." He lowered his voice. "Have you ever heard of *redemption*?"

"Sure," I said. "It's like forgiveness. It's a big concept in Christianity."

"That's right. Flowers, I've been reviewing your files. You're quite a guy."

A shiver trickled down my spine. Surely Antonucci knew about my writing my Congressman, losing my Secret clearance, why I was sent here and given this absurd assignment. I was seized by the thought that Antonucci was a power freak who planned to use or manipulate me in some way.

"You're intelligent, observant, well liked by your fellow troops and your NCOIC – although perhaps not so popular with Sgt. Buford, but then who is?" He gave me a wink. "And you've been to college."

I was having trouble following his line of thought. *What's he setting me up for?*

"Thank you, sir," I replied, glancing at the copy in my typewriter.

Antonucci raised his coffee mug, took a sip and set it down on my desk, all very slowly. He looked me in the eye and said, "Have you ever thought about OCS?"

Officer's Candidate School? Was he nuts? Wear a uniform on campus, graduate with the degree they dictate, then turn in your stripes for second looie bars and serve another six years? "Uh, no sir," I said, "I haven't. Really thought about it."

"Well, you should, Flowers. You're wasting your time and the Air Force's, writing stories that will never be published. You have two more years in your enlistment. Two more years of service without dignity or purpose." He leaned forward again, speaking softly and gently: "I can help you, Flowers. I was OCS and I know how it works. I can write the recommendation, speak to the right people. I can redeem you in the eyes of the United States Air Force so you can make a *real* contribution to your country."

I slapped the desktop and said, "Sir, that's *exactly* what I've been thinking! The movie last night was like a message from God. He said, 'You're not serving your country, Flowers.' That movie made me realize that I want to be a Marine. I want to go to Vietnam! I want to fight! Kill! Destroy! Truly serve my country! Yes, sir!" I jumped to my feet and saluted Lt. Antonucci. Startled, he jumped up and saluted back. I stood there, holding the salute and fairly shouted, "The Few. The Proud. The Many. The United States Marines!" I snapped my hand down and so did Antonucci.

The whole room fell silent, even the typewriters. Milo stared at me from across the room, his jaw slack.

"Well, Flowers," said Antonucci, "I don't think I've ever encountered a situation where a man wanted to transfer from one branch of the service to another. I'll…look into it…." The look on his face changed. "I'm…glad we had this little talk this morning. About redemption. I'm sure we'll talk again about…this, won't we?"

"Oh, Yessir. Thank you, sir, thank you for bringing…this…to my attention, sir." He smiled a thin smile. I stared back.

Later, I stopped in at The Dungeon to drop off copies of the *S&S* and the courier pouch. Lt. Antonucci wasn't there. Buford gave me a vile look and said, "Gone hafta shave off that caterpillar if'n you wan' be a Marine, pussy."

"Watch your mouth, Buford, or I'll tell the lieutenant you're queer," I said. He turned beet red and swung his feet off his desk so fast he banged his leg against an open drawer. "Argggghhh! You — I'll git ya, Flowers!" he yelled. I slammed the door behind me.

That afternoon, Milo came to my desk carrying a thick binder. "Dude, we have to talk." We went into the briefing room and closed the door. "Dude, that talk about joining the Marines…." He let the sentence dangle. I wondered if Ricky had taught Milo to say dude. We looked at each other, then began to laugh. "I gotta tell ya, I think you had Antonucci going. He may still be wondering if you were serious. But anyway, when he talked about your having two more years to go, I got to thinking." He opened the regulations manual. "Listen to this:"

> An enlisted man wishing to transfer from one branch of the United States Armed Forces to another branch of the United States Armed Forces must have met all the requirements of his career field and terms of enlistment in order to meet the eligibility requirements of the service to which he intends to transfer. Under no circumstances will the enlisted man be required to extend a term of enlistment past the original and initial term of enlistment. The enlisted man must complete the original terms of enlistment, and at the time of termination may voluntarily apply for and enlist in the new branch for its specified term of service.

"I don't get it, Milo," I said.

"Nate, here's the point!" Milo said, pointing at the print. "'*Under no circumstances* will the enlisted man be required to extend a term of enlistment past the original and initial term of enlistment.' You were illegally re-upped for eighteen months in California! The reg says you're only obligated to serve out your four-year enlistment – then you're done, troop! I'll file a DoD Form 88. You'll have to be discharged in January."

My eyes swept around the meeting room: the tables where pilots would never sit, the podium from which flight crews would never be briefed that stood in front of the deep blue velvet curtain with the U.S. Air Force eagle symbol on it, the U.S. flag hanging limply on its pole nearby. I only had six months – less, actually – and then I was a free man. Six months, not twenty-four. I felt a huge grin spread across my face. I said, "Then can I join the Marines?"

• • •

I'd sent postcards to Jane and to my mother from Athens, the typical "here we are on leave, this place is beautiful," and so forth. My mother replied

> How nice that you've been able to travel in Europe. I've always hoped you could learn about other people and explore their cultures, but I'm curious how you were able to afford an entire month of travel to Switzerland and Italy and Greece on your Air Force pay?

Why was she trying to make me feel ashamed? Maybe I should be sending more money home, but I felt sending half my pay was plenty. Actually, it wasn't half my pay now; it was half my Airman Second Class pay, plus I was getting separate rations, but still. I wadded her letter into a tight ball and lobbed it into the trash can.

Jane's letter was sweet but tinged with disappointment that I hadn't used my leave to see her. She asked the usual questions — where we'd gone, what we'd done, what were the people like, but between the lines were unspoken thoughts. She didn't sign off "Love" but "Yours" instead. I had put distance between us, and she was right to imagine things. I wanted to tell her what really happened, but there were things I didn't want exposed to the military censors. Then it occurred to me: I'll write her and mail the letter from London!

• • •

I was sitting on the Indian tapestry carpet in Tony's penthouse-like quarters. We passed a joint back and forth. "Hey Tony," I said, "This rug. Does it fly?"

He laughed. "Yeah, sky pilot, it flies all right. Amita gave it to me. Just take another hit and it's off you go, into the wild blue yonder." He sang the last. "Tell me again when you get out?"

"Umm…early out date is 18 December. You…?"

"I have a almost year to go after you," said Tony, "November 22, 1969."

"Tim gets out next August. Alan and Henry Harold Henry get out next October. What're you gonna do?"

"I'm pretty sure I'll stay here in England," Tony said. "That's, you know, what Amita wants. I mean, she was born here. This is home, you know?"

"Alan's for sure gonna get a European discharge. I don't think he'll go back. Henry's dad says he'll help him open a radio and TV repair shop. He can put his Air Force training to use."

"Tim wants to finish college, right?" Tony asked.

"Yeah, me too. Jane got into UC Santa Cruz. Creative writing. I could dig that."

"Oh yeah, that's right, you've pledged yourself to Lady Jane," Tony chuckled and said, "This is for you."

It was the Stones' "Going Home," and as I listened, it really did make me think that maybe I'd rather be with Jane than go traveling around the world by myself.

We rocked along in stoned delight until Tony said, "Did you hear about the Democratic National Convention? It's in your hometown. All hell is busting loose." He said hippies and yippies were demonstrating and being viciously attacked by Chicago police. "I saw it on Amita's telly, BBC news. It was sickening, man. The pigs were beating on these kids so hard, man, and they were really getting off on it. Amita hid her face. I was so fucking ashamed of my country right then. Land of the free! Equal rights, freedom of speech! My ass! I really got nothin' to go back there for."

I made a mental note to ask Jane how she felt about the anti-war demonstrations and cops beating up kids. I found myself making mental notes to ask her about a lot of stuff lately. The Stones' "Lady Jane" started playing in my head. Time to start my letter to her so I could mail it before I left Monday.

• • •

We headed over to Amita's family restaurant and smoked some incredible black hashish.

"Oh, wow," Tony said.

"Oh, wowwow," I said. Two more tokes and I could hardly sit up. "Jeez, Tony, I'm think I'm goin' into a coma. Hehehehe."

The munchies attacked and we chowed down on some incredibly spicy lamb curry, na'an and wine. I told Amita about my Oriental philosophy studies. "You know about Vedanta?" she asked. I shook my head. "You will be interested. All thought of truth comes from Buddhism. China, India, Japan, all come from the same Bo tree." We talked until the restaurant closed at 0100 hours, then headed back to the base. Settling on Ali Baba's carpet again, Tony dropped a chunk of black hash into his brass pipe. "Thanks again to Amita," he said.

Once I was semi-conscious again I said, "We gotta listen to this new record I got today. Susie was singing and dancing to this song, 'Time Has Come Today.'" He looked at me with a smirk. "Nothing happened! Nothing!" making him laugh out loud. "She said over and over that I had to hear it." I dropped the needle on the cut.

The first sounds were the clip-clop of drumsticks, then somebody said "Cuckoo." We looked at one another and knew we were in for a trip. In my mind I saw my Kickapoo Princess, beautiful free spirit Susie, chanting "time has come today, time has come today." Eleven minutes later, the song had made us more stoned than when we started.

250

Tony leaned forward, bowing all the way to the floor. "I've seen God!" he exclaimed. "Yes, 'My soul's been psychedelicized!' What do you call something like this? Wow, man, I want to drop acid and listen to this."

Now I understood why the song meant so much to her.

"Young hearts can go their way," sang the Chambers Brothers. It was Susie's mantra. Now it was becoming ours, too.

"Nate. Nate?" Tony. I'd gotten lost inside my head again.

"Yeah?"

"Do you remember the ending of *The Magus*?"

"You mean what happened to Nicholas and Alison? In the park? I mean, it was kinda vague."

"Yeah. Do you think they got together?"

"I don't know. Maybe. They sure had a lot of stuff to work out. What do you think?"

"I'm not sure. It's hard, though, isn't it?"

"What?"

"Getting things to work out. With women. People. Life."

I didn't answer. There was no sound except the ticking clock: five minutes past three. "Man," I said, "the whole universe is watching us through the window, to see if we get it figured out." A few minutes later we were both sound asleep.

Chapter 20
Oktoberfest
September, 1968

On the courier flight back to Kleinelachen I read the pamphlet Amita gave me, "Principles and Purpose of Vedanta." I recalled Jane once mentioned Vedanta, that the Ouroboros Bookstore had Vedanta books. I re-read with more interest. The discussion of Karma struck a chord:

> All the good that comes to us is what we have earned through our own effort; and whatever evil there is, is a result of our own past mistakes. As, moreover, our present has been shaped by our past, so our future will be moulded by our present. This brings great hope and comfort, since what we ourselves make, we can also unmake.

My God! This is the answer I'd been seeking to the problem Dylan had raised: how to quit thoughtlessly repeating mistakes over and over. I read on; Vedanta says we have past lives and so we repeat mistakes from them until we figure them out, then we're freed. By consciously acknowledging that we make mistakes, we are able to truly correct them and thus move closer to God. The beautiful thing was to reach *Mukti*, or absolute freedom – that was the goal. I had to talk with Tony about this.

Reading about *Mukti* made me think of going to church as a kid. We'd say a prayer that absolved us of our sins, then we could sin again for another week. I didn't learn to stop sinning, because if I did I wouldn't need to come back for my weekly redemption. You just stayed a dumb, repeat sinner forever. What a scam job.

Something from the *Tao Te Ching* came to mind. When I got back to base, I found it:

> When all the world recognizes beauty as beauty,
> this in itself is ugliness.
> When all the world recognizes good as good, this in
> itself is evil.
>
> …Therefore, the Sage manages his affairs without ado,
> And spreads his teaching without talking.
>
> …And yet it is just because he does not dwell on it
> That nobody can ever take it away from him.

So it must come down to this: There is only good or bad in the way I think. If I do not presume to make a judgment about someone or something, I can't be drawn to respond one way or another. An eye for an eye is not the act of the sage. Neither is sinning and then saying a prayer for forgiveness redemption. Indeed, that kind of thinking keeps me from reincarnating to a higher level of spiritual consciousness.

• • •

"How's Tony?" Alan asked. We were getting high on Tony's hash in the alten Scheune.

"Great. We had a great time. He's got it made in the shade — big room all to himself in the NCO barracks, a foxy girlfriend, best dope in London."

"I like talking with him, too," said Alan. "He's really smart, but doesn't flaunt it. He's, like, integrated his learning into the way he is — you know? — he lives his knowledge. It's part of him."

"Yeah, I see what you mean," I said.

"I wish I could say the same," Tim said. "I mean, I read about politics and ideologies but I don't live them. They're just words on a page. Remember when we read *Demian*? I really lived that book."

"Kinda hard to be a Communist when you're wearin' the enemy's uniform, ain't it?" said Henry.

"No," said Tim, "because I'm really a spy. A double agent."

"Or maybe it's because it's all bullshit," said Alan.

"Man, don't start with that again," I said. "Maybe he just hasn't learned what he's supposed to learn from it yet."

"Listen, troops, I hate to change the subject," said Henry, "Actually I don't hate to change it at all, but anyways, Oktoberfest is in a week, and I think we ought to go."

I wondered why we wanted to go to a beer festival, but everybody shouted "Yeah! Right on!" and other stuff, and so it was decided.

•   •   •

My Dearest Darling Nathaniel,

Thank you for the longest and sweetest letter you've ever written to me. The island – what an adventure! (I'm so happy to know I was there with you – at least in your imagination!!!) You write so well, Natey. You *cannot believe* how happy I am for you! Oh, just to think I will see your handsome face in just a few months instead of years. But darling dearest Natey, I would have gladly waited the whole three years for you. All I think about is being together with you again. Imagine us going to college together! Walking to class holding hands, discussing our assignments, reading our writing to each other and then, when we're too tired to talk any more, getting under the covers and turning out the lights and…!!!!

You write about your Tao studies so well. I mean, I've read some of that at Ouroboros, but you seem to really get it. You make it apply to your life, but it's hard when I think about trusting the Way, as you say, and just going with the flow. We really didn't grow up that way, did we? Aren't we supposed to struggle and strive for the things we want? Oh, I can imagine talking about this for *hours and hours!*

I know you will be a great writer someday. And I hope you'll write to me again, soon!

All my love,
Jane

• • •

Irish overheard us talking about going to Oktoberfest and begged us to take him along. Tim's ancient Volkswagen had died and he'd replaced it with an Opel, which had room for six, so there didn't seem to be a reason to say no. Tony arrived, we got our three-day weekend pass, and headed south to München.

Irish quaffed bottle after bottle of beer on the way, but once we got to Oktoberfest he went wild, gulping huge liter steins at every beer tent and tossing down schnapps at the hard liquor stands. He pestered everybody with dumb jokes like "You know wha' happen to the Irishman who walk inna bar wid a canary on his shoulder?" but then couldn't remember the punch lines. Then it happened: A Bavarian beer maid walked by carrying three beer steins in each hand. Tim reached out, either for a beer or her breasts, and down the two of them went. Beer splashed everywhere. People scattered. Drenched in beer, the girl shrieked, trying to press down her billowing skirts and get back on her feet. Irish was lying very still, his face on the ground, maybe passed out.

Two politzei were there in seconds. They handcuffed him and started to lead him away. Alan followed them outside.

"They've arrested him for public intoxication, disorderly conduct, and assault," he said when he returned. "I asked if we could bail him out. Not a chance. He won't be arraigned until Monday or Tuesday."

"We have to be back tomorrow by 2200 hours," said Henry Harold Henry.

"It's his karma," I said. "But it was way cool of you to talk to the politzei, Alan."

"Had to be done," Alan replied. "We needed to know what's going to happen to him." He looked down and shook his head. "Dumb juicer fuck."

I glanced over at the beer girl. She was sitting with the people whose table she'd stumbled into. I went over and apologized to her for Irish, for us, the Air Force and the United States of America.

Three guys about our age walked over and sat down with their beer steins. I looked at them and they smiled, so I smiled back.

"Guten abend," one said. He wore longish curly brown hair with a Bob Dylan hat stuck on top. "You are Americans?"

I nodded. I said, "My name's Nate. This is Tony, Alan, Henry, Tim."

"Ich bin Herman, und zis is Thomas, und Dieter. The – uh, other boy – he vas mit you?"

256

"Yeah, *was* is right," said Henry Harold Henry, drawing his lips tight across his teeth.

"*Entschuldigen* — we are sorry for the misfortune. It is not — ah — the luck for the Irishman, *nicht wahr?*"

We laughed. "No, he's not a lucky Irishman tonight," said Alan.

With that we began a conversation that lasted until the closing time lights blinked. We put down a few liters of beer but none of us, not even the German kids, got drunk. The talk was far too interesting.

They were a lot like us, except they were students at Heidelberg University. We said we were GIs and told them we were ashamed of it, but they were unfazed. They treated us just like any other kids our age and asked us where we were from and lots of questions about America and why we were here in Germany.

"We're total misfits," said Tony. "We don't fit into America because we're hippies. We don't fit in the military because we hate war and challenge authority. We don't fit into European life because we're Americans. And we don't speak your language. If we don't know who we are, how can we tell you why we're here?" he ended with a sardonic laugh.

"I'll tell you what we're doing here," Tim said, "Keeping Germany democratic and peaceful and friendly with its neighbors. We're here to keep Russia out. We're here to protect your freedom, but ironically we have to give up our own freedom to do it. How do you feel about that?" I cringed. It was an incredibly provocative thing to say.

"*Danke*, we are grateful to you," said Thomas. He was lanky, with a long face and a scruff of beard around thin lips, pale blue eyes gazing out from under his long, curly hair. "You make possible civility and restoration of our society and traditions. If Hitler had conquered the world, we would be soldiers like you. If Russia had won War Zwei, we would be Communists. All of Germany would be like East Berlin. But because of you, we can study philosophy and history at university. Schönen Dank!"

"*Ja*, it's true, you have tamed the German temper," said Herman. "It needed this. I do not fully know this myself, but my father, my professors, tell me it is true."

"Boys," said Dieter, leaning over the top of his beer stein, "We are *Die Kinder der Zukunft.*" We stared at Dieter; he looked back, startled. He was a blue-eyed blonde who wore his hair short and shaved his face. He wore a white tunic and what the kids on Carnaby Street in London would call a Beatle jacket. "We reject

Nietzsche, Wagner, Hitler of course, and the ideals of Aryan supremacy," he continued. "We think of a Europa that is united, but still we have our own country's individual nature. And so with France and Italy and Spain and the others, each their own but all together. This is what we will seek. There are many who think like us at university. Many will join us to make this Europa possible."

"Um, did you say you called yourselves the *Zukünftige Kinder*? Children of the future?" Alan said.

They looked at each other and grinned. Thomas said, "*Ja, es ist die gleiche*, but *Die Kinder der Zukunft* is the better translation. *Ja*, we believe this to be true. It is what Dieter named us. It is the name of a record album by one of your countrymen, Mr. Steve Miller."

We burst into laughter and told them about the grandes dames.

"*Und so*," Dieter said, "You seek for the consciousness-expansion *auch*?"

"Do you mean are we...heads?" I asked.

"You, do you," Thomas put the tips of his thumb and finger to his lips and made an inhaling sound.

"For sure," said Tony. We nodded.

"Why?" asked Dieter.

"Why what?" said Tony.

"With the..." Thomas asked, making the sign again. "What are you looking for?"

"A way not to think about being in the fuckin' Air Force," said Henry. "Maybe a way not to end up like an ugly fuckin' uptight straight suit-and-tie American."

"Yeah, there's that," said Tim, "but for me, it helps me think about things in new ways. I don't want others to tell me what is truth."

"You have your own truth?" Herman asked.

"I'm workin' on it," Tim said.

"Well, we're all workin' on it best as we can, aren't we?" Tony said. "Maybe there isn't a single truth, you know?"

"Sure there is," said Alan. "Only Catholics go to heaven, there's only one God except for Moslims, Jews have the only true faith. Existentialism, capitalism, Communism, *übermensch*, the sun never sets on British soil, science. You're free to do your own thing as long as you don't hurt anybody. There's a few. Take your pick."

"Naw, naw, that's just raw unadulterated cynicism, Alan," Tony said.

I said, "I've found the simplest truth in my Chinese studies: Accept that what's going to happen is meant to happen. Free will is dust in the wind of fate, and fate is immutable...."

"Too passive, too easy," Alan retorted. "Just throw an *I Ching* and everything will turn out fine, huh?"

"Guys, cool it," said Henry Harold Henry. He looked at the German students. "Don't pay any attention to them. They go at it like this all the time." He grinned. "How about you guys?"

"*Ja*, we have found the truth," said Thomas. "It is to know that there is no truth."

Chapter 21
Touch and Go
October, 1968

When we got back from Munich, Dylan McKreven's bunk had been stripped and his locker and dresser drawers were empty. Totally gone, just like Ricky. Nobody said anything to us. We crawled into our bunks for some shuteye.

Monday, 14 October. Sixty-five days to go. I was at work; Milo came over to tell me Buford was looking for me.

"Yeah, for what?"

"I dunno. He just said you were to fall in as soon as you reported."

"Well, it'll wait 'til the courier lands."

I picked up the courier sack and walked over to The Dungeon.

"Where you been, Flowers?" snarled Buford.

"At my desk."

"Dinja get the message to report to me?"

"Here I am," staring him right in the eye.

He stared back. "I hate tha' fuckin' mustache, Flowers."

I threw my body into the position of Bob Dylan playing his guitar and started wailing, "'I'm gonna grow my hair down to my feet so strange, Till I look like a walking mountain range....'"

"Stop it! Shut up, you little asshole!"

"I'm not little. I'm five foot ten."

"By God! I'm gone have your ass for insubordination before you get off this base!" His face had gone bright red; I wished he'd have a heart attack. He raised his fist and shook it at me and screamed "Get outa here! Get outa here before I hurt you!"

"So, nothing for the courier, then?" I said and bolted out the door.

Back at my desk, Milo came over with two cups of coffee. "Hey, dude," he said, "you talk to Buford this morning?"

I snickered and launched into my Bob Dylan imitation again. He snickered back.

"Well, he was supposed to tell you to call Sgt. Tremblay. He has a new assignment for you, directly from USAFE. Buford was supposed to brief you. Here's a copy of the order that came down last night."

"Oh. I'll give Tom a call."

• • •

"Morning, Flowers," said Sgt. Tremblay. "Listen, I've got an assignment for you."

"So I hear, *Tom*," I said. "So give me the who-what-when-where-why."

"General Beauregard wants a story for the first anniversary of Kleinelachen going operational. He's going to spend a few days there, starting next Monday. You'll be attached to him during his stay, maybe come back up to Ramstein with him if he wants you to. It's a puff piece, Flowers."

I wondered why he took such pleasure in calling me Flowers. "You gonna publish it?"

"Well, of *course* we're going to publish it! He's the USAFE commander, for God's sake!" He lowered his voice: "Look, give the General a good show. Not just you, everybody. Single out some top-notch troops: your CO, of course, maybe the mechanic who maintains his plane, an ATC screen jockey. You know who. Go easy; he thought there were a few weirdos at the 20th birthday party last year."

"*He* thought *we* were weird?" I said. "*He* was the one dancing to Chuck Berry on the tables, drunk out of his skull."

"Forget that, Flowers, forget all about it. Look out for yourself. This is your chance to redeem yourself."

That word again.

"You handle this right, do what he asks, write a good story, you'll see your byline. But if it goes screwy and the General isn't pleased, I do the rewrite and get the byline. Got it?"

"Yeah, I hear it but I don't believe it."

"Believe it. Oh, one other thing. Take some pictures, eh?"

• • •

Four-star General Daniel Beauregard touched down in his T-38 for the first time at Kleinelachen Air Base at exactly 0900 hours, and taxied to a stop in front of Base Ops. All one hundred and twenty-two of us slightly chilled troops were standing at parade rest. I stood near Lt. Antonucci, my camera ready.

"Ten-HUT!" Two hundred forty-four heels clicked together. The General opened the cockpit and climbed down the ladder.

"Pre-SENT ARMS!"

He popped a salute, then threw an arm over Antonucci's shoulder like they were old buddies. "So, how's it going with your first command, Lieutenant? Let's head over to Base Ops. I need to get out of this flight suit. Gotta whiz like a race horse. Har!" A General's laugh.

I snapped photos.

The morning passed quickly as we inspected the base, as white-glove as I ever saw it, then it was time for lunch. The General, Antonucci, and two NCOICs went in, then Gen. Beauregard turned and invited me to join them. The food was great: thick steaks, fresh green beans, spaetzle seasoned with paprika, and pitchers of lemonade, definitely not from the Kleinelachen mess hall. The General called for a Scotch and water and got it. He talked nonstop about himself, his command, his travels.

"Hey," he said, "you boys hear the one about the married pilot and his bachelor navigator? They were best friends. Played golf, did all that buddy stuff. The captain was always bringing the lieutenant home for dinner with his gorgeous wife. Then one day he tells the navigator he's going on a 30-day TDY and to keep an eye on his wife, make sure everything's OK."

He paused, knocked back some more Scotch, grinned and continued.

"So the navigator does, and before you know it they're in the sack together. One afternoon, while they're screwing each other's brains out, the captain comes home on a three-day pass. Calls out his wife's name, but they're making too much racket. He goes up, flings open the bedroom door, and there they are, *in flagrante delicto.* "Martha! he cries out. "Not with a navigator!"

Polite chuckles. Warm boysenberry pie with ice cream. Another Scotch.

"General, sir, we thought you'd like to tour the radar facility," said Lt. Antonucci, "meet your controller staff." For some reason his face seemed red.

"Hell yes, of course I do, but first I want to see 'em do their stuff."

Antonucci raised an eyebrow. "Sir?"

"Gonna do some touch and gos, give 'em some practice with real aircraft. Hell, that courier's so damned slow Flowers here could probably bring it in. Speaking of you, Flowers, you're going up with me."

Sheer, ice-cold terror gripped my heart.

Beauregard leaned toward me. "That's an order, troop!" he said and laughed. "We'll talk while we're flying. C'mon, we'll have some fun."

I'd been ordered to have fun in a jet airplane with a pilot who just tossed down two Scotches?

I heard the General's voice through the helmet radio say, "The T-38 is a trainer, but in every respect it is truly a two-man fighter jet. You buckled in?" I yanked the straps again. I was terrified. Flying a jet airplane; had I really signed up for this? What was I thinking?

The General fired the engines. "Twin J-85 turbojets, with afterburners, Flowers. This baby can climb to 30,000 feet in less than a minute. Tops out at Mach I. I'll show you."

The jet shot down the runway like a bullet. He pulled back on the stick between his legs and up we went. Up. Up. More up as I heard and felt the engines roar behind me. I was beginning to feel the fear edge away when the jet went into an upside-down arc. My stomach fell into my lungs and I gulped for air. We were inverted for I don't know how long – eons – then the General completed the loop he'd begun and we shot out of it right-side up at an incredible speed.

"How'd you like that?"

"That was way cool, General Beauregard," I gasped.

"You call me Dan while we're airborne, you got that? What'll I call you? Nate?"

"Yes, sir – I mean Dan."

"OK, Nate, now watch this." We were going incredibly fast, but he pointed the nose up and the engines screamed. Dan started rocking the wings, making lunch slosh in my stomach. Suddenly I needed to take a dump, really bad. The next moment, all I wanted to do was forget I wanted to take a dump. Maybe it was just my body's way of trying to get out of this death-bullet.

I looked at the gauges, then over Dan's shoulder; they were identical. On the left was a bubble gauge, rocking back and forth as he tipped the wings. Beside it was the altimeter: 55,000 feet. I was glad I couldn't see the speedometer. We started slowing down, still pointing up, slowing, slowing, then the plane stopped! The engines were silent, then the plane fell like a stone. I was crawling in my seat. Every nerve and muscle and brain cell screamed.

"Called a high-speed stall, Nate," I heard in my earphones. "Pilot has to learn how to get out of one or lose the ship. Don't worry, though, this baby has rocket-propelled cockpit ejection in case the engines don't restart and we have to bail out. Don't even need to wear a 'chute, it's built right in."

The jet started to rotate, pinwheeling faster and faster as it fell. Clouds flew up past us at a terrifying speed. Just when I didn't think I could take another second, Dan re-started the engines and we flew on as if nothing had happened.

We took an aerial tour of Germany, Dan providing the narration. We flew up to Ramstein, ten minutes away by T-38, over the Nürburgring auto racing track, on to Heidelberg for a low-altitude swoop over the castle and university and an ancient bridge crossing a river. I wondered what Dieter, Thomas and Herman were doing. He tipped a wing and we headed southwest to the Black Forest, then east for a great view of Stuttgart (I thought I saw the statue of Schiller and the grandes dames' mansion), south at high speed down the Autobahn and its swift-moving traffic to München, then turned back north.

Once we were back in Kleinelachen air space, Dan established radio contact with our controllers and requested permission to shoot some touch-and-gos. We would come in on ATC precision radar, follow the glidepath and maintain the speed the controller gave us, then just as we were about to touch down, Dan would accelerate and up we'd go again. After we'd done a few, I told him it was pretty cool.

"'Preciate the compliment. Something every good pilot learns to do. Sometimes, just as you're coming in, a vicious crosswind sweeps across the runway. You feel you're losing control, that you're gonna flip, crash, and burn. Grab the stick, get the hell up and out while you can. That's why you practice touch-and-gos."

We touched down and stopped. I climbed down the ladder on queasy knees. General Dan followed. The CO and Buford were waiting. "How'd Flowers do?" Antonucci asked the General.

"Didn't crap his pants. Least so far as I could tell." He touched his nose, grinned and clapped me on the shoulder. "He's a good man."

• • •

The next morning, my story and the roll of film left on the courier. I was so excited I made an extra carbon copy to send to Jane. As I watched the plane take off, it occurred to me I could send her the story printed in *Stars and Stripes* itself.

Tom called to say my story would run the following Tuesday. I really couldn't believe it. But Tom said so. So maybe it would.

Tuesday came. I waited as the courier taxied to a stop and grabbed the bundle of papers and literally ran to my desk. Flipping through the pages, I didn't see the headline I sought. I went back through more slowly and came across the photograph of General Beauregard and Lt. Antonucci saluting each other on the runway, his T-38 in the background. It was on page seven. The caption under the photo read

USAFE CMDR Gen. Daniel Beauregard celebrates first anniversary of Kleinelachen AB with 1LT Salvatore M. Antonucci, CO, 6069th AFCS. *Staff photo.*

So much for redemption.

Chapter 22

FIGMO
November, 1968

After what happened to my *Stars and Stripes* story, I was pissed off. Really, really pissed off, for days. I consulted the *I Ching*. My hexagram was Sung, or Conflict:

The Judgment
Conflict. You are sincere
And are being obstructed.
A cautious halt brings good fortune.
Going through to the end brings misfortune.

My notes to myself:
OK, all I'd known was conflict ever since I got to this stinking little air base.
Yes, I tried to do my duty with sincerity, but was slapped in the face every time.
FIGMO. I have orders for rotation, which permits me to bring my activities to a cautious halt.

• • •

267

November 4, 1968

Dear Mom, Ernest and Frankie,

Guess what? I'm getting out early! Really I'm getting out on time; a troop I work with in Base Ops, Milo (he's from Terre Haute) found out it was illegal to extend me for eighteen months. Hooray! I just got my orders and will be home for Christmas. Would you like another Hummel figurine, Mom? Let me know. I'll try to find something for my thieving magpie brothers, too.

I really can't tell you how excited I am to be coming home, even though I hear a lot of bad things about what's going on back there. I've written 62 stories for the *Stars and Stripes* and not a single one was ever published! Can you believe that? I am just totally sick and tired of the military mind and the way I have been treated. I just want my honorable discharge and to go back to college.

Mom, can you write a letter to the Dean at Chicago – I can't remember his name – and ask if I can get back in?

Love,
Nate

• • •

November 16, 1968
Dear Darling Nathaniel,
Thank you for your wonderful letter. I'm so sorry about your story on the General. It was well written. I'm glad you sent me a copy. It was very good reporting. The best part was about your jet plane ride – WOW! I can't believe you got to ride in a *real* jet plane!
But to think they couldn't even give you credit for the photos! That's just plain mean.
You know I can't wait to see you and would love to spend Christmas with you in Chicago. But you've been away from your mom and brothers for so long. Why don't you go home for Christmas and then come celebrate your birthday with me? That feels like a great way to start the New Year off together. I really want to meet your family, but we can do that another time. Just come home to me as soon as you can!

All My Love (and I do mean <u>ALL</u>!),
Your Jane

• • •

"Milo, mere words cannot express my thanks for finding that reg. I mean, my God, you gave me back a year and a half of my life!" Milo, Tim and I were at Ma's. I raised my beer bottle and we clanked. "Tonight, you drink for free!"

"Well, thanks, dude, but really, I was just doing my job," he replied.

My promotion was screwed up by an admin troop like Milo who didn't do his job. Now Milo *had* done his job and un-screwed-up things. Yet if it weren't for that, none of this would have happened to me. If, if, I got lost in all the ifs.

"But I want to tell you, dude," Milo continued. "Watch your ass. You still have a month to go before you rotate, and Buford would like nothing better than to nail you for something – even a little tiny thing – and pull your orders."

"Yeah, I know it," I said.

"I thought that was all done with," said Tim, "after you did that story on the General. Didn't you say you're on Antonucci's good side?"

"Yeah, I did, but that fuckin' Buford doesn't have a good side," I replied. Milo nodded. "Did I tell you guys the joke the General told at lunch? About the pilot and his navigator?" I retold the joke. They grimaced at the punch line.

Milo said, "You know Antonucci flunked out of navigator school, right?"

I looked at him.

"Oh, yeah. *Nobody* flunks out of navigator school. It's an officer's worst disgrace."

• • •

Tony flew in for Thanksgiving weekend; we'd been invited to dinner at the grandes dames. Tony and Alan and Henry Harold Henry and I walked from the base through Zweiflüssehausen to Tim's apartment. Tony couldn't wait to open his rucksack. "Troops! You won't believe this! Look!" He held up what looked like a record album that was completely white.

"What's this?" said Henry. He looked closely and said, "Oh my God, it's a new Beatles record!"

"A two-record set, man!" cried Tony, jumping up and down like a kid. "And you won't guess what they're calling it in London."

We all stared at him silently, then Alan said, "*The White Album?*"

"Yes! Yes! The *White* Album! Isn't that perfect?" Ha!"

Tony pulled some hash from his rucksack and we lit up. Once we were going, Tim put on side one. The needle clunked, then the sound of a jet airplane's engines whining down flowed from the big speakers, followed by a strange strangled guitar note, drums, another guitar and the song took off, the lads singing about leaving Miami to fly back to the U.S.S.R. The irony struck; Alan cried, "Nathaniel Hawthorne Flowers, that's where you're going, back to the U.S.S.R.!" Everybody began rocking on imaginary instruments: Tony drummed, Alan and I played guitars, Henry thumped the bass, Tim joined in on the "Back in the U.S.S.R.!" chorus.

We settled down to listen. Tony introduced each song, played a side at a time. passed the photos of John, Paul, George and Ringo around.

"That was the greatest," said Henry Harold Henry as "Good Night" ended, "the best thing they'd ever done."

"Yeah, makes *Magical Mystery Tour* sound like a kiddie record," I said.

"'I dunno, 'Strawberry Fields Forever' was pretty good," Tim said.

"Yeah, 'cause it's Lennon," I said, "You know 'Revolution 9' is totally John's work."

"Brilliant. A collage made with sound. It reminds me a little of crazy 20th century classical music, like that ballet we heard at the grandes dames – Stravinsky?"

"Oh, far out, yes, far out," I said.

Henry said, "What's a collage?"

"You taking a bunch of colors and drawings and photos, images, just about anything, really, and paste them all together in a kind of abstract design on a piece of wood or canvas," said Tony. "Picasso made them."

"You're a regular font of knowledge, aren't you?" said Alan. The room grew silent, all eyes on Alan. He said, "You can really tell who wrote the songs."

"I noticed that on *Sgt. Pepper's* too," said Tony.

"But it's still the Beatles," said Henry Harold Henry. We were OK again.

"They're a lot like us – or we're like them," I said.

"How do you mean?" Tim asked.

"Well," I said, "each Beatle is different – like George is mystical and John is cynical, Paul is…"

"…the lightweight," said Alan.

"Yeah, I suppose, but Ringo is…"

"Ringo is Ringo," Alan said and everyone laughed. "But I interrupt. Your point is…."

"Just that they – uh, we – are all different, but they play together, they're a group, they – we -"

"We're mates," Tony finished my sentence, using the English word.

"Yeah," said Tim. "I really like the way we can each be different and let each other be different and still be *mates*."

"And we never even needed a name," said Alan. "Remember? No Ninth Circle? When we decided no nicknames?"

"We just are," I said. "We just are who, and what, we are."

• • •

The next afternoon we headed to Stuttgart in Tim's Opel. At the Schillerplatz we bought the old girls bouquets of flowers, a lapel flower for Günther and a corsage for Isabelle. We introduced Tony to the grandes dames. Dame Marion greeted us with kisses, Elspeth a handshake and quick smile.

"Well, Nathaniel," said Dame Marion as we set to smoking the hookah, "so you are going home to America soon."

I nodded. She toked. We toked. "Well, in each ending there is a new beginning," she said. "Of this you can be sure: you are all very special young men, and capable of great things. We shall miss you, Nathaniel." Her face grew sad, and so did Elspeth's. "We shall have a fine sendoff for you today, and a wonderful dinner to honor your Thanksgiving holiday. Elspeth, I don't believe we've ever celebrated this holiday, have we? Ever on, Nathaniel! Elspeth and I shall watch for word of your great achievements in the world press." She touched her handkerchief to the corner of her eye.

We played the Beatles' *White Album* for them. They loved it. Every so often, Dame Marion would trill out a comment like, "Oh, listen to that harmony!" or "Aren't they just terribly inventive?" Once Elspeth said, "Didn't that just sound like a theme in Elgar?"

We had another fabulous dinner, Dame Marion raising a glass of wine time after time, supposedly to the fabulous new life that awaited me. Pretty soon, I wasn't so sure I wanted to leave this one. "Here's to you all you boys!" she said. "You have given us so many hours of pleasure and good conversation. We were meant to meet at the Ravi Shankar concert, weren't we? Oh, that reminds me! Can you be our guests for the annual performance of Beethoven's Ninth Symphony?"

"Sure!" we said in unison. "When is it?" I asked.

271

"Always on his birthday, December 16." Two days before I was scheduled to leave.

I said, "Isn't there a poem or something by Schiller in the Ninth?"

Elspeth stared at me. "Ach, lad, you know that?"

"I just remembered it," I said. "My mother listened to classical music all the time. She probably told me."

After dinner we returned to the rotunda library, where Elspeth announced we would all be joining in a performance. "'Tis a scene from Shakespeare's *The Tempest*," she said. We looked at each other.

"What?" she said. Do you know the play?"

"Yes and no," said Tim. "We read it in high school." He looked at us. "Jeez, it just occurred to me that Fowles was retelling *The Tempest* story in *The Magus*."

"Remember we told you about going to Greece? Socrates Island?" Henry said. "Well, we read a novel before we went there called *The Magus*. This guy Nicholas goes to this Greek island to teach at a boy's school but he sticks his nose into this strange guy Conchis' business and gets caught up in this drama and trying to figure it all out, like, what's real and what's an illusion. He figures out this girl he's nuts over is an actress playing tricks on him, and Conchis is, like, directing the play. And so he's trying to figure it all out while having to deal with this really incredible girlfriend back in England who he broke up with and -"

"Aha," Elspeth interrupted, thankfully. "And you know the word 'magus' means magician. *The Tempest* took place on an island, where a magician named Prospero confused people with illusion and reality. He manipulates a lad named Ferdinand into falling in love with his daughter Miranda."

"No shhhhh…kidding," said Henry.

I said, "And now, here we are again. Returning to it. To play the roles ourselves, for the first time."

"You're quoting Tom Eliot, you rascal!" cried Dame Marion.

Elspeth assigned us roles from Act II, Scene I, and we began reading our parts aloud, growing ever more confident and playful as we went on. We were soon acting as well, posing or gesturing or making faces until our laughter made the production more or less fall apart. Even Elspeth, playing Ariel, was carried along by our clowning. Tired out by our efforts, we fell in around the hookah for refreshments.

"Boys, that was too grand!" said Dame Marion. "Such fun! But I want to tell you something quite important, something that will not only resonate to the core of your very beings, but will influence and shape you for the rest of your lives.

"Elspeth and I have spoken of this at length. We feel you represent the inconsolable generation. Other generations of young men have entered into military service and have worn their country's uniform in battle. This is something you will not, cannot, *must not* experience. On the other hand, you can never be the so-called 'flower children' of your generation because you have been soldiers and you know, existentially, that you are not free and can never be. Your sense of who you are will always be tainted by your lives as soldiers. You will always be nether-people, neither one nor the other, seeing freedom around you, perhaps partaking of it in small quantities, but never will you possess it in your soul.

"You will live lives of struggle against the fundamental angst that the military has burned into your hearts. And my heart, and I know Elspeth's heart as well, go out to you as you face your future. It will be so much different than ours, your sisters from your twin generation, as we fancy ourselves. The best you can hope for is to beget children who will overthrow society, for that must be done. Go forth into your future, oh children of the inconsolable generation, and know that you go with our hearts and minds and souls joined with your own."

• • •

We were quiet and sad driving back to the base into the late night. I cared for these two old ladies; they were our spiritual grandmothers. I said so, and the others murmured asset. Tim said, "Children of the inconsolable generation. She told us last time that we were the children of the future." When we got back to his apartment, Alan dug out *The Doors* and played "The End." I fell asleep on it, but it was OK because I already knew what happened.

Part IV
Home

Chapter 23

The December of My Dreams
December, 1968

It was the December of my dreams. The last December I'd spend in this man's Air Force. I couldn't even imagine what I'd be doing a December from now, but I knew I wouldn't be wearing a uniform.

My orders arrived with my departure date (still 18 December) and itinerary: fly the courier to Mildenhall (see Tony once more), leave the next day on a MAC transport for McGuire AFB, New Jersey, begin outprocessing (up to 48 hours), discharge 22 December (free man). All I had to do now was wait, the single most profound lesson a troop learns in the military.

Fourteen days. I packed my clothes, books, records, tapes, and stereo gear in a wooden crate the military provided, my name, rank and serial number stenciled on it. I would be spending the last few weeks without my music. *Well, I can always play it in my head.*

• • •

The 16th arrived and with it Tony on the courier. "Man, I didn't think I'd be able to make it," he said, a huge smile on his face. "I had to swap for a double shift with another troop, but I couldn't miss this. Beethoven's Ninth, live!" The five of us would attend the Beethoven concert after all.

We joined our two psychedelic grandmothers in the lobby of the Liederhalle. We hadn't had a chance to get high before the concert, but stepping into the

Beethoven-Saal — where else would Beethoven be performed? — was a trip itself. Like the Mozart-Saal, it was done in light-colored woods and everything was curves and sweeps — the overhead lighting, the seating, the stage, even the room itself.

"Wow," said Alan, this place is just — plain — beautiful."

So were the Stuttgarters: Men wore tuxedos and women beautiful full-length gowns and gobs of jewelry. And they smelled wonderful. Even the grandes dames were dressed to the hilt. Fortunately, they had secured a box for us, so few could see how shabby we looked in comparison.

We watched the musicians warm up, tuning their violins and cellos, tooting, tightening drum heads, getting their sheet music organized. Then, at exactly 2000 hours, a man in a tuxedo came on the stage and greeted us. He introduced the music and the conductor, impeccably dressed in a tuxedo with long coattails, carrying his white baton, walked on stage and bowed. The audience went completely nuts. He bowed five more times. To make them stop, he turned, faced the orchestra, tapped the music stand for silence, and raised his arms above his head.

From the first notes, I was in awe. The music completely filled the Saal. It was exquisite, passionate, a little confusing at first so I let it bypass my brain and go directly to my senses. I closed my eyes; Beethoven was making pictures for me at some subconscious level. Every so often I opened them to watch the conductor move his baton or the different instrument groups play their unique parts, but my vision would blur and pass beyond the stage to a transcendent place of the deepest, most abstract thoughts. Startling new sensory perceptions flowed in and spiraled deep; what they were I did not know. Or care. I lost track of time; the music became my time, my now, my Tao.

The music stopped. The musicians rested their instruments; sounds of the audience moving, fidgeting, coughing. I looked to my left at the grandes dames and we exchanged smiles of contentment. People wearing black robes entered the stage behind the orchestra. "It's the chorus," Tim whispered. "It's the fourth movement. You know, with the Schiller poem." *The fourth?* I'd listened to three movements already? He leaned toward Tony and pointed to the program.

The conductor tapped the music stand, raised his baton and brought it down with a furious stroke, igniting the orchestra into a frenzied tangle of music that sounded like a musical storm. *Sturm und Drang.* Beethoven introduced a theme, then another; it kept changing, but grew more gentle, more mellow, but the angsty stuff kept coming back, too. I closed my eyes, stilled my thoughts, just listened.

A vaguely familiar melody arose, very sweet, very peaceful as it emanated first from some oboes and violins and big basses. Repeated over and over, it was a soothing balm that conquered the earlier harshness. *Make love, not war.* Peace, not war. Peace. The theme swelled as the entire orchestra began to play and it was so powerful, so incredibly overwhelming, that I knew I was blessed to be sitting here. It was a high like none I'd ever known.

The music whipped into a frenzy and climbed to a crescendo. A man began to sing in a deep, rich voice, *auf Deutsch* of course. Schiller's poem; I wished I understood the lyrics. The female chorus joined in, and it was holy, heavier even than Procol Harum, maybe the most spiritual music I'd ever heard. I felt pressed into my seat by the powerful emotions churning inside me: they touched me so deeply I felt like a tree whose roots went from my inner self deep down into the earth, like into the heart of the cosmos, into the history of the universe and the origins of man, the act of creation, my penis like a root of that tree reaching to connect and to mate, a jittering spasm of sperm spurting out of me up into the sky and then I was that blue spark again, now plunging into the earth as flowers bloomed and the chorus sang in beauty and intensity of the glory of what I was and what I could be and I felt the tears running down my face, hot, hot tears, great chugs thumping inside my chest, my throat in a knot trying to force the emotions back down because I saw my father, my lovely, kind, intelligent father who created me in my mother's womb and named me Nathaniel Hawthorne Flowers after his favorite author and who in his unconscious wisdom had a vision of me becoming a writer too, my father, taken from me in the prime of his life, my life, my father who I missed so much, had not until this moment realized how much. The chorus sang on, and my chest heaved with all the pain and loss throbbing out of me, the anger and resentment I had never allowed myself to feel flowing out in the tears pouring from my eyes in rivers. Tim, good kind Tim, took my hand and held it, just to let me know I wasn't alone and I gripped his hand back and we sat transfixed until the last, liberating chords, knowing neither of us was alone.

• • •

Morning, and Tony left for the courier; I told him I'd see him the next day. Alan and Henry Harold Henry had left for air traffic controller duty. Tim was just getting up. "Hey," I said. "I'm leaving tomorrow on the morning courier."

"Yeah, I know," he said halfheartedly.

"You wanna do something tonight? Auld ang syne and all that shit?"

"Yeah, I dunno," he said. "Maybe."

"OK. I understand." I started to leave. "You know where to find me."

"Nate."

"Yeah?"

"I'm gonna miss you."

"I'm gonna miss you too, Tim."

"I figured out I'm not really a Communist. I just wanted to piss off the Air Force. Maybe get tossed out on a Section 9. But I changed my mind. After, you know, Ricky and Irish. I just want to get out with an honorable discharge."

"Good for you. You'll get it, and we'll get together again. I know we will."

"You *sure?*"

"Positive, man."

• • •

Tony and I got high one last time the night before I left, but I didn't feel as high as I did listening to Beethoven's Ninth and told him so. "Yeah, dude, we're seekers, you know, always on the lookout for the ultimate high. Trying to get back to the best one we've ever had. Sometimes we forget there's more than one path to consciousness – and they aren't all with drugs."

"Alan said something like that once, about trying to recapture the best trip and never being able to. And you knew this all along?" I asked. "How come you were always the first to get stoned?"

"Not all along," Tony said, flopping on his bunk, "I guess I'm lazy. Your Tao stuff, you know you can get high doing that, too. Kama Sutra. Zen. It all works, but you gotta study, meditate, work at it. Pot, psychedelics, they're just quick and easy ways to raise consciousness. And I'm lazy. Ha! Ha! Ha! Ha! Ha! Seriously, though, speaking of consciousness. You're on your way back to the Real World. Did you say good-bye to your brothers at Kleinelachen?"

Of course I had. Those guys meant a lot to me. Everything. They were my whole world for a year and a half, including Tom and Milo. "Everybody promised to keep in touch," I said. "Alan carried my duffel to Base Ops, even out to the plane. He threw his arm over my shoulder and whispered 'I love ya, Nate,' and handed me that Prometheus thing he'd written."

"Nice, really nice," said Tony. "These may have been the best days of our lives. I've heard it said that military service isn't worth a nickel but something you wouldn't trade for a million dollars — I think that's right. You're the first to leave. I'll be going back to Kleinelachen to see the troops and the grandes dames. Don't forget us, my friend."

"You know I won't," I replied. We went to Amita's for dinner and good-byes.

• • •

The transport ship touched down at McGuire and taxied to a large hangar. There were eighteen of us — eighteen on the 18th — and a bunch of wooden shipping crates. I looked around for mine, but it wasn't on board; probably already in Illinois. A staff sergeant wearing a flight line parka and pilot's sunglasses stood at the foot of the ramp with a clipboard. We filed out and gave him our names. I looked at the sky; solid gray, not a bit of dimension to it. Welcome home.

A small blue bus arrived and the NCO herded us on board. Still wearing the sunglasses, he said, "You're going to outprocessing."

"Well, no shit," said the troop next to me.

My outprocessing documents were in a sealed manila envelope Buford had given me, which I'd carried tucked tightly underneath my arm ever since I left Kleinelachen.

"You hold tight to this pouch, Flowers," Buford said. "This's your ticket out. Wouldn't want to see you fuck up now, would we?" He winked.

"Thanks, Sarge," I said, and stuck out my hand. We gripped; there was a struggle to see whose was strongest. A tie. "No hard feelings. Be well."

"You too, Flowers. I'll be out in a coupla years. You ever git ta' Arkansas, stop by mah donkey farm. Ah'll let ya kick my ass." Then he let out a laugh that sounded just like a donkey braying.

Now, as I stood before Airman Rivera at McGuire, I learned that Buford had indeed had the last laugh. "Sergeant Flowers, I don't see your DD214 Request for Discharge, or Standard Form 89 medical record in your papers. Did you get immunizations in Germany?" I gave him the startled glance of a deer caught in a car's headlights. He sifted through some papers on his desk and showed me the forms I was missing.

"Can we do those here?" I asked.

"Sure, that's not a problem, but what about your immunizations?"

"Airman Rivera," I said, "I wasn't on sick call once while I was in Germany. There wasn't even a medic on base. We had a First Aid kit at Base Ops."

"Well, there's nothing we can do about that. You gotta have the shots and stay on base during the incubation period until you check out OK."

"How long will that be?"

"Um, not really sure. A month?" I stared at him, aghast. "Maybe a few weeks?"

I leaned forward on his desk. "Rivera, my first shirt did this to me on purpose. He hated my guts, so he fucked me. I really want to get home for Christmas. Isn't there anything we can...?" my words drifted away as I realized the implications of Sgt. Buford's heinous act.

"Sorry, Flowers," he said. "You're not the first troop this has happened to. You can talk to the outprocessing OIC, but you know that regs is regs."

Regs is regs. I got two inoculations and four booster shots and was assigned to the transient barracks. They were identical to Lackland. We fell out at 0500 and marched in formation to the mess hall. At 0730, each troop got his day's duties: policing the grounds, unloading and loading stuff in hangars, peeling potatoes, waxing floors in offices, cleaning latrines, until 1630. Sometimes we'd get a wood stick with a nail in the end and walk in the cold for hours stabbing trash.

Evenings were free. Sometimes I'd go to the day room to watch TV, but nothing interested me so I laid in my bunk reading or maybe talking with another troop. I wrote to Jane and my mother. I wrote Susie and Tony and Alan/Henry and Tim. I started writing in a spiral notebook, some just random thoughts, ideas about one thing or another, some poems for Jane. I wrote my dad, told him how much the Beethoven symphony made me miss him. I mused on the changes in my consciousness: no smoking pot here.

Christmas at McGuire was the most miserable, lonely day of my life. I called Jane from a pay phone; when my three minutes ran out, she called me back and we talked for half an hour. We talked again on my birthday. I called my mother, to tell her I still didn't know when I was getting out.

I told Jane I was writing and she was thrilled. I wrote scenes, fragments, dribbles of this and drabbles of that:

A Beginning!
    Chris, just out of the Army – all he has is a rucksack and typewriter. Finds a single room in a rundown rooming house in San Francisco, every night up late writing – meets a girl downstairs –

The December of My Dreams

Chris had swung his legs over the stumpy wall that surrounded the Coit Tower monument and sat watching the scene below for many long moments. Off to the right was the Embarcadero, with the myriad ships and lights and docks and piers all playing a silent game of quiescence. It made him restless.

I recalled my last conversation with Tony and suddenly knew that using pot and psychedelics was a way for me to release an inner energy I was now expressing in writing. All along, my inner energy was creativity! How could I have missed this? I began a real short story and made notes for several others. I was a creator, creating, creative. I was a writer. Hadn't I won third place in the USAFE Short Story Contest?

I was finally cleared for discharge on 10 January, 1969. It was a Friday and, no surprise, my processing wouldn't be completed until Monday. The weekend passed. DD214 in hand, I went to the mandatory discharge briefing. A tech sergeant explained to a roomful of us troops that we weren't out yet. "You signed up for six years. You've served four. You can, and very well may, be called back to active duty at any time during the next two years. In fact, you may be surprised to hear this, but six out of ten of you will re-enlist within ninety days. That's a statistical fact." Amid snorts of derision, he grinned and said, "So you *will* keep your uniforms clean and pressed and ready for use." We went back to our barracks, changed into civvies, stacked our blankets and pillows on the ends of our beds, grabbed our duffels and kissed the United States Air Farce good-bye.

As I sat on the shuttle to the Newark bus terminal, I pulled off my dog tags and touched the beads Jane had given me. My anger at Buford, my resentments at the stupidity and bureaucracy of the military system, even my frustration at being detained for over three weeks, dissolved. I was free.

Chapter 24
No Place Like Home
January, 1969

I arrived at the same place I'd started almost exactly four years ago, the Chicago Loop bus terminal. It was still January, still cold, but a sunny, clear-sky kind of day. And just as she'd been there to see me off, my mother was there to pick me up. We hugged briefly. "Son. Nathaniel." she said, maybe a little choked up. "It's been three years! Still handsome as ever." She touched my mustache gently. "I think I like this," she said.

We climbed into the same car, now four years older and showing its age as it squeaked, creaked, grunted and moaned out of the city, south through densely inhabited suburbs to Hinsdale, the one my family called home.

"Nathaniel, I looked into your enrolling at Lincoln Community College, but it's too late – the winter semester started January 6th," my mother said. "I think the best thing for you to do is get a job as soon as possible so you can begin contributing to the family. You can save money living at home so when you go back to college next fall you may only have to work part time."

"*Begin* contributing?" I said. "What have I been doing for the past four years? You don't call that contributing?"

"Please, let's not get argumentative about this," my mother snapped. "Of *course* we appreciated your help. It's just that now, with your potential to be a real bread-winner, you can do so much more to help us. Ernest is sixteen and Francis Scott is only fourteen. They can't work. *You* are the man of the family now, Nathaniel."

The apartment complex looked dingier than before, if that was possible. She pulled into the carport and the engine rattled to a stop. I grabbed my duffel out of the back seat and said, "Has my stuff arrived?"

"The ugly wooden box? Yes, some time ago," she said. "I had the men put it in the boys' room." A new television in a massive dark wood cabinet dominated the small living room. *Talk about ugly.* The sofa facing it was the same. "You remember the sofa is your hide-a-bed? Perhaps we can move into a three-bedroom apartment once you've gotten a good job." She looked at me with eyes that begged me to accept the situation.

I could hear the thump-thump-thump of music coming from a closed door down the hall. Opening it, I found my brothers listening to "Children of the Future." "Nate!" shrieked Frankie, and flung himself at me. We had a big hug. Ernest stood there, holding the album cover, looking at me with extreme trepidation. In the corner stood my wooden crate, open and plundered.

"Ernie," I said slowly. "You didn't."

"Anybody hungry? How about some lunch?" my mother said, standing in the doorway with a big smile. The boys ran out of the room, temporarily evading my wrath.

· · ·

I spent the next few days trying to adjust to my so-called home. In some ways I preferred McGuire's transient barracks; at least I had my own area. I found my *I Ching* on my mother's bedside table, but the coins went missing until I looked in Ernie's desk drawer while he was at school. My Oktoberfest beer steins were now flower vases. Books, photographs, souvenirs, all had been appropriated and used to decorate the apartment. One day I caught Frankie wearing my dog tags.

I needed to get back in touch with my spiritual life, so I re-read lesson 44 in the *Tao Te Ching:*

As for your name and your body, which is the dearer?
As for your body and your wealth, which is the
more to be prized?
As for gain or loss, which is the more painful?

286

Thus, an excessive love for anything will cost you dear
in the end.
The storing up of too much goods will entail a heavy loss.

To know when you have enough is to be immune from disgrace.
To know when to stop is to be preserved from the perils.
Only thus can you endure long.

I'd sent money home. I saved and saved for my stereo gear. Every book and record of mine held special meaning and memories. Now my possessions were apparently community property. As I read and re-read the *Tao* verse, I realized what it was really saying was that a man isn't defined by his possessions, but by who he is and how he presents himself to the world. I threw one *I Ching* after another, seeking its guidance. I needed to be calm in the face of change. I needed to maintain my respect for my family; they could at least try to reciprocate. The book said a leader must preserve his reputation as a thinker as well as a warrior. *Okay, I'll work on that.*

Inside of a week I was going stir-crazy in the little apartment. I was alone all day with nowhere to go. I had to get out, so I called my Uncle Ned in Madison and asked if we could get together in Chicago. Two days later, I was on the commuter train heading into the Windy City. It was filled with businessmen on their way to work, holding plastic briefcases, reading the *Chicago Tribune*. They looked like soldiers, except the uniforms were dull-colored suits and white shirts and striped ties. I wore jeans, a sweatshirt and my fatigue jacket. One of them sat glaring at me and finally said, "Hey! Hey you, hippie boy! What gives you the right to wear that coat? That's for men who serve our country."

I stared at him, then said, "I just finished four years in the Air Force, mister. Would you say that gives me the right to wear my own fatigue jacket?" He frowned, shook out his newspaper and hid behind it.

A few hours later I was telling my Uncle Ned about the guy on the train as we ate steaming bowls of noodle soup in a little Japanese place. He looked older; his face was thinner, longer. He'd let his graying hair grow long and had muttonchops and a droopy mustache below his large round wire-framed glasses. "Damned if you go to war, damned if you refuse to go," he said, shaking his head sadly. "There isn't one good thing about war, Nathaniel. I don't know if anyone has told that story more poignantly than Remarque, in his novel *All Quiet on the Western Front*."

287

"I know that book," I said. "We – my buddies and I – read it. In Germany."

"I'm teaching it now in a new course of mine called 'The Philosophy of Conflict.'" He lifted his soupspoon in the same old sideways manner and slurped.

"It'll be good for students to read," I said. I started to ask him if he knew a student named Susie, but thought better of it. I tried holding my spoon like he did; it worked surprisingly well.

"Maybe everyone should read it. Perhaps even the man you encountered today."

"Yeah, I wonder if *he* ever served in the military," I snorted. "What do you think of Nixon? Is he going to stop the war?" I'd missed the election campaigning news, and everything that happened at the Democratic National Convention. Even in the short time I'd been back stateside, I was amazed at how little we ever learned from the *Stars and Stripes* about what was going on here.

"Nixon isn't a good man, Nathaniel. He doesn't mean it when he pokes his fingers in the air in a peace sign. The man has no soul, no conscience. He's an incredibly selfish, self-centered power-monger. He'll do what's expedient for the military-industrial complex and whatever makes him look good."

"Aren't they all sleazeballs?" I asked.

"Pretty much," said Uncle Ned, "But it seems much worse now, with the way dissent is quashed." He mentioned the assassinations of Martin Luther King and Bobby Kennedy and the violent police attacks on protesters at Wisconsin. "I don't hold out much hope for the war ending any time soon."

"Uncle Ned," I said, "What was Voltaire trying to say in *Candide?*"

He sat thoughtfully, spooning some soup. "Voltaire was striking out against optimism, especially the optimism of Leibniz, a contemporary German philosopher. Voltaire had become extremely cynical, you see. He was disillusioned – well, by war, man's greed, the hypocrisy of organized religion." He paused as if to say, *Not much has changed, has it?* "There was a great earthquake in Lisbon that killed many innocent people. Voltaire couldn't believe a benevolent God would allow such a thing to happen. So he wrote *Candide* about a foolish man who believes "*Ce meilleur des mondes possibles."*

"Which translated means...."

"Roughly, that this is the best of all possible worlds. Which, of course, Voltaire most emphatically did not believe."

"What do you believe, Uncle Ned?"

"Well, Nate, I would have to say that some days this seems like the best of all possible worlds. But when bad stuff happens, and it often does, I lose my faith." He chopsticked a bunch of udon noodles into his mouth. "Kind of like the weather, you know?"

"Spoken like a true philosopher," I replied.

"I'm not a philosopher, son," said Uncle Ned, looking sadly at me through his glasses, now speckled with tiny drops of soup. "I'm a *scholar* of philosophy. I study it to understand what others have thought and written about. But I have no philosophy of my own."

"Don't call me 'son.' You're not my dad."

He looked down. "I'm sorry."

"So what *do* you believe in?"

He didn't reply right away, then he raised his bowl and glugged the last of his soup. Patting his lips with the paper napkin, he looked at me and said, "I guess I'd have to say that I believe in me. In the sustained power of my thought to understand the world around me."

"Jesus, Uncle Ned," I said, probably too loudly, "you're more cynical than Voltaire!"

"That may be true, but I can assure you that it's all I can be absolutely certain about. As long as I live, who I am and what I know will have to sustain me."

I chopsticked a couple pieces of tofu, mulling over what was surely the absolute failure of Western philosophy to understand the meaning of life, which the Orientals had figured out a few millennia ago.

"Can you help me get back into Chicago?"

My uncle leaned back in his chair, resting his arm on the table. I could see the frayed cuff and worn leather elbow patch of his sport coat. "I don't know, Nathaniel. Adele – your mother – asked me to look into it before you came home. The Admissions office said you were to provide evidence that your scholarship had improved…well, I said, I could write a letter to the Dean…then your mother and David mentioned they thought your attending Lincoln Junior College in Hinsdale for a while was a good -"

"David? Who's David?"

"David is David Steele. Your mother didn't mention him? He's the school superintendent she's been seeing for quite a while now. I believe they're planning to get married…."

My mother has a boyfriend? Getting married? No, she hadn't mentioned it, and I wondered why. I looked out the steamed-up windows at the people passing by, grim-faced as they hustled to lunch or back to work, caught up in this ridiculous world. I wondered what kind of hexagram I'd get if I threw an *I Ching* right now. My thoughts drifted; my eyes went out of focus and the street scene blurred and I could see that this city was gone, gone, gone, a life that was not for me, far beneath me, nothing like what I wanted for my own life. "Forget it," I said. "I don't even want to go back there. Thanks for talking to me, Uncle Ned. Lunch is on me." I grabbed the check and headed for the cash register.

• • •

I hardly knew what to do with myself after Uncle Ned and I parted company. The sidewalks were cold and clotted with snowdrifts. The people looked unhappy. Beautiful young women in tall leather boots and sheepskin coats, their long hair flying in the Windy City wind, hurried by. Cars honked their horns incessantly, inconsiderately splashed slush. A man sold hot dogs from a cart. Steel boxes displayed newspapers with headlines of despair. Three young men, all pink baby faces and innocent eyes, who had surely never seen a day of military service, stood laughing and smoking cigarettes on a corner.

I looked around at the clutter and confusion. *Is this the Real World I longed for?* I'd been more at peace with myself in the Air Force. There was conformity, to be sure, but at least I still had my creativity and intellectual freedom. This society, this civilization that swarmed all around me, felt far too constricting. I remembered the discharge briefing NCO say some of us would be back in three months. Was this why? *No, no, no, not ever. I worked too hard to get out. I'm not going back.*

I walked and walked and talked to myself. I looked up at the street sign, which looked fairly new:

Dr Martin Luther King Jr Drive

I turned onto it and walked toward Washington Park. A guy passed me quickly, gave me the finger and shouted, "How many babies did *you* kill in Vietnam, asshole?" His fierce anger struck fear in my heart; no one had ever spoken to me like that. I thought about ducking into the park to hide, but it was too cold. I knew I could walk all the way across the park and be at the U of Chicago, warm up in the library or cafeteria, but I just couldn't do it. I turned onto Garfield and walked at a quick pace toward the Loop. People left me alone.

I came upon a bookstore and ducked inside to warm up. On a table was a stack of books with a sign, "Just Published." A new novel by Vonnegut! I opened it to the title page:

Slaughterhouse-Five
Or
THE CHILDREN'S
CRUSADE
A DUTY-DANCE WITH DEATH
By
Kurt Vonnegut, Jr.

A FOURTH-GENERATION GERMAN-AMERICAN
NOW LIVING IN EASY CIRCUMSTANCES
ON CAPE COD
[AND SMOKING TOO MUCH]
WHO, AS AN AMERICAN INFANTRY SCOUT
HORS DE COMBAT,
AS A PRISONER OF WAR,
WITNESSED THE FIRE-BOMBING
OF DRESDEN, GERMANY,
"THE FLORENCE OF THE ELBE,"
A LONG TIME AGO,
AND SURVIVED TO TELL THE TALE.
THIS IS A NOVEL
SOMEWHAT IN THE TELEGRAPHIC SCHIZOPHRENIC
MANNER OF TALES
OF THE PLANET TRALFAMADORE,
WHERE THE FLYING SAUCERS
COME FROM.
PEACE.

Us troops had read *Cat's Cradle*. Now Vonnegut had written a new novel we could surely get down with. I bought it and caught a bus to Union Station, thinking how we could resume our book discussions by mail, starting with this. I would read it as quickly as possible, write the troops, encourage them to read it and write back. I began at once. It was a wild, delirious, crazy book: Germany, Communists, so much like what I'd just left behind.

• • •

Slaughterhouse-Five wasn't long; I finished it that night after everyone went to bed. Billy Pilgrim struck me as something of a Candide, as I understood him; I really needed to read Voltaire's book. I went to work with my mother the next morning and wrote a letter to the troops on her office typewriter, the original to Tony and a carbon to Alan asking him to share it with Tim and Henry Harold Henry. As an afterthought, I sent a carbon to Jane. A week went by and every day I looked for a reply. At least from Tony. Another week and nothing. As Kilgore Trout would say, so it goes.

I did hear from Jane. Not only had I already gotten five letters from her in the first two weeks, but she wrote me back about *Slaughterhouse-Five* the same day. A night later, she called.

"How'd you get the phone number?" I asked.

"We have this really great phone service here in the States. It's called directory assistance."

"Ha, ha, ha. Jane. It's some kind of sweet to hear your voice."

"How's everything going? I mean, you know, with…everything."

"OK, I guess. My mom wants me to get a job and go back to community college next fall. I saw my Uncle Ned. He's a college prof, you know. He thought it was a good idea. He says Chicago probably isn't in the cards. Besides, I can't get my scholarship back."

"Oh. That's too bad. What would you do? For work, I mean?"

"My mom — she has a — she knows the superintendent of schools here. He said he'd give me a job in the audio-visual department. You know, because I have radio training. But I don't know…." As we talked I realized what a miserable idea it was, riding to work with my mom, pushing carts with tape recorders and projectors from classroom to classroom, smiling at her boyfriend David as we passed in the halls. "Hey, we shouldn't stay on long. It's expensive."

"It's OK. I told my folks I'd pay them back. Sometime." We laughed at that and talked another ten minutes, but never once did she ask me if — or when — I was coming to see her. Not once.

I didn't say anything either; it was as if we were observing radio silence. But the next day it hit me like the old safe falling from the skyscraper window. Wham. I was waiting for something, waiting like we always did in the service, but there was nothing here for me except the waiting. And I had no idea what I was waiting for. I didn't need to consult the *Tao Te Ching* or the *I Ching* to know that. I was the more or less grown-up guy come back from the military who'd once been the kid who used to live with these people in another time and another place. All that was gone. I started throwing out the waiting, the wants, the needs, the conflicts, the old detritus of the *you wills* and *you ought tos*, all those tired obligations I no longer believed in, clearing mental cobwebs from my mind until I saw a bright light beyond. A light that filled my heart with the purest, most unbearable happiness I had ever known. I knew what that light was. I knew it as well as I knew anything about myself. It was Jane.

I sat down with my mother later that night at the kitchen table. "Tell me about David," I said.

She looked at me, then said, "Did Ned tell you?" I nodded. "David's good to me, Nathaniel. The boys like him. He's outdoors-y, takes us places. We spent a weekend camping at the chalk cliffs out on the Mississippi. He sings and plays guitar. You should hear him sing 'Puff the Magic Dragon!'" Her face lit up.

"That's great, Mom. For you and the boys. A chance to be a family again." I toyed with the sugar shaker. "I gotta go, Mom. This won't work out for me. Gotta be moving on." I swallowed. "Gotta go find my own life."

She looked down at her hands clasped on the table. She still had her apron on from making dinner. "I know," she said, and a tear rolled down her cheek.

"I've been thinking. I was kinda selfish. I thought I was the only one who lost dad. I didn't really think about how it was hard on you, maybe because you were always so angry about it. Heck, for a long time I didn't even know how bad *I* felt about losing him. It took Beethoven to tell me." I reached out, covered her hands. "I'm sorry. I love you, mom," and she burst into sobs.

Saturday morning I packed my duffel bag with my civvies and uniforms and re-packed my wooden crate. My mother drove me to the commuter train. That night at Chicago's Union Station I boarded the California Zephyr. Two days later I got off in Emeryville, California, into the waiting arms of a beautiful blonde girl named Jane Chandler, her hair blowing wild and free, the bright California sunlight reflecting off the puddles of tears filling her blue eyes.

She said, "Hi, Nathaniel."

I said, "Hı, Jane." Our lips met in a clumsy kiss. We hugged each other like crazy and shook and shivered with joy and excitement and probably more than a little bit of longing. I was finally, truly, home.

Bob Dylan's Dream

While riding on a train goin' west,
I fell asleep for to take my rest.
I dreamed a dream that made me sad,
Concerning myself and the first few friends I had.

With half-damp eyes I stared to the room
Where my friends and I spent many an afternoon,
Where we together weathered many a storm,
Laughin' and singin' till the early hours of the morn.

By the old wooden stove where our hats was hung,
Our words were told, our songs were sung,
Where we longed for nothin' and were quite satisfied
Talkin' and a-jokin' about the world outside.

With haunted hearts through the heat and cold,
We never thought we could ever get old.
We thought we could sit forever in fun
But our chances really was a million to one.

As easy it was to tell black from white,
It was all that easy to tell wrong from right.
And our choices were few and the thought never hit
That the one road we traveled would ever shatter and split.

How many a year has passed and gone,
And many a gamble has been lost and won,
And many a road taken by many a friend,
And each one I've never seen again.

I wish, I wish, I wish in vain,
That we could sit simply in that room again.
Ten thousand dollars at the drop of a hat,
I'd give it all gladly if our lives could be like that.

10246361R00175

Made in the USA
Charleston, SC
19 November 2011